ABEN·5.99
(Rom)

DISCARDED

He rose, lifting and cradling her safely in his arms.

Alyce lay against Dare's broad chest in complete trust and within moments they were atop his mighty destrier. She couldn't have prevented herself from leaning into his welcome strength to save her soul from perdition. If the worst fears of others were justified and the nature of her savior what they whispered in secret, 'twas precisely the price she would pay. In that moment it seemed well worth the cost.

The deeper they rode into the forest, the deeper became the awareness stretching between them. From beneath her ear, Alyce could hear the pounding of Dare's heart.

Purposefully closing her mind to the conscience fair screaming warnings of a shame to come, she reveled in the remembered feel of his hard mouth on hers and ached for its return. A moan rose from her depths. The sound was more than Dare could withstand. He bent his head to take lifted and silently pleading lips in a succession of slow, brief, tormenting kisses.

But still it was not eno

D0206837

Books by Marylyle Rogers

Dark Whispers
The Dragon's Fire
Chanting The Dawn
Hidden Hearts
Proud Hearts
Wary Hearts

Published by POCKET BOOKS

Most Pocket Books are available at special quantity discounts for bulk purchases for sales promotions, premiums or fund raising. Special books or book excerpts can also be created to fit specific needs.

For details write the office of the Vice President of Special Markets, Pocket Books, 1230 Avenue of the Americas, New York, New York 10020.

DARK WHISPERS

MARYLYLE ROGERS

POCKET BOOKS

New York London Toronto Sydney Tokyo Singapore

This book is a work of fiction. Names, characters, places and incidents are either products of the author's imagination or are used fictitiously. Any resemblance to actual events or locales or persons, living or dead, is entirely coincidental.

An *Original* Publication of POCKET BOOKS

POCKET BOOKS, a division of Simon & Schuster Inc.
1230 Avenue of the Americas, New York, NY 10020

Copyright © 1992 by Marylyle Rogers

All rights reserved, including the right to reproduce
this book or portions thereof in any form whatsoever.
For information address Pocket Books, 1230 Avenue
of the Americas, New York, NY 10020

ISBN: 0-671-70952-6

First Pocket Books printing February 1992

POCKET and colophon are registered trademarks of
Simon & Schuster Inc.

Cover art by Elaine Duillo

Printed in the U.S.A.

To Gary, my knight . . .
Twenty years and still shining

Author's Note

When King John died in 1216, he left his nine-year-old heir, Henry, in the hands of a warrior who became known as the Good Knight, William Marshal, Earl of Pembroke and Striguil. Under the Marshal's leadership, the invading French were defeated and the English crown was saved for Henry. Yet Henry proved to be a weak man, easily influenced by others and never steadfast. No royal decision could be counted on to remain unchanged in the passing of time. After the Marshal's death, Henry constantly fell under the influence of one greedy man or another. Before long the French, who had failed to conquer England at the opening of Henry's reign, found an easier path to the same end—they seized control by controlling the king.

Hubert de Burgh stood at Henry's side and held sway over the young monarch from the Marshal's death until 1232. In that year Hubert's old foe and longtime opponent for the king's ear, Peter de Roches, Bishop of Winchester, arranged his fall from power by virtue of charges involving everything from treason to murder by the Black Arts. The bishop, less priest than soldier, was easily as greedy and even more ambitious than De Burgh. Moreover, the latter had leastways been English, with some respect for the good of Englishmen, while the bishop was from Poitiers and thought only of himself and those of his countrymen who came at his call. Among those who came to England was Peter de Rievaux, alternately termed the bishop's nephew or illegitimate son. De Rievaux was made treasurer of England, a fine plum for the avaricious man he was.

Under the bishop's influence, the conflict between royal and baronial power rose to new heights. The fickle Henry charged first one and then another of his lords with treason, holding their lands forfeit to the crown only to later reverse his decision. The Marshals, sons of the Good Knight who had saved Henry's kingdom for him, were easily the biggest threat to royal power (and thus to the powerful men behind the king) as they controlled massive stretches of land and were far wealthier than the king himself. No problems had arisen during William's, the elder son's, lifetime (during which Henry was a minor). But when Richard, the second son, took the title and lands, he became the leader of the baronial faction struggling to force the Frenchmen who held sway over the king from power and restore control of the king and the kingdom to Englishmen. While fighting for this goal, by treacherous advice he was trapped but declared he would rather die with honor than flee the fight and incur the reproach of cowardice. Standing with 15 faithful knights against 140, he was mortally wounded.

The bishop irretrievably fell from his position of influence after the English Archbishop of Canterbury (in 1234) publicly presented written proof to the king that the bishop had ordered the murder of Richard Marshal by arranging the treachery and commanding his death.

This, unfortunately, was not the end of French ascendancy over Henry. A mere two years later he wed a French princess. She and the many family members who accompanied her to England soon dominated the king. The barons' dissatisfaction continued to grow; and the largest baronial uprising to date, occurring between 1258 and 1266, did not end until young Prince Edward (I) took a personal hand in seeing it done.

During this era religion was an important influence in the peoples' lives, and to them the devil was as real as the certainty of a living God. Thus, too, superstition was an integral part of life, and for men to be charged with crimes committed by use of the Black Arts was not uncommon (Hubert de Burgh, for example).

Also, as marriage amongst the wellborn was not a matter of attachment between the two central parties but rather a matter of alliances between families and estates, marriages between children, even babies, were frequently arranged. Were a baby girl wed in the cradle, it was likely she would be raised in the groom's castle. But were the role reversed and the bride older than the groom, this was neither necessary nor always desired.

A wellborn woman's dowry was that which she brought to a marriage (usually land but sometimes other items of value) and which by virtue of the ceremony was transferred from her father or male guardian to her husband. Her dower would be that portion of her new husband's possessions which, by virtue of the marriage contract (the first prenuptial agreement) and publicly announced at church door, would be hers should he die before she did. Though not always true, her dower was often the same as what she'd given as dowry.

Prologue

Castle Wythe, 1202

The Demon is reborn." The chill disgust contained within those four curt words added another layer of cold to a dreary chamber poorly lit by the weak light of cloudy morn falling through shutters half-opened over one small window. 'Twas a disgust built of years, which its recipient, a healthy babe but minutes old, could nowise have earned.

Lying exhausted by the travail of birth, the mother recoiled as if physically struck by the words of her pale-complexioned and ever withdrawn husband. She pushed tangled soft brown strands from her eyes yet refused to lower them to the crying infant squirming at her side. Too well she understood the source of this pious man's strange denunciation of her dark-haired newborn, so utterly unlike himself and so nearly the replica of another.

"My wretched sire's mortal soul departed as this being drew his first breath. Aye, the Demon lives on—but this Rhodare's black wickedness will find defeat 'neath the virtuous light of my Gabriel."

With Cyril's decision to see the babe bear his detested father's name, Elinor would not argue, even were it possible for her to gainsay her husband and lord. Like the first, the babe would be christened Rhodare, and like the first, "Demon Dare" he would doubtless be called. No matter his innocence at birth, he was doomed to carry the burden of past wrongs.

Silver tears trickled through tangled threads of labor-mussed hair, but feeling the weight of her own guilt, Elinor could not, would not, look upon the newborn. Not in that moment as Cleva lifted the small bundle, and from thence onward as seldom as possible.

1

Behold the Virgin Wife." Though softly spoken, the low words sundered the warm peace of a hazy autumn dusk as effectively as an invisible blast of cold winter wind.

Frozen midstep by the deep voice laced with wry amusement, Alyce stared blindly down the green length of her daygown to the fertile ground beneath her feet. As she was caught unprepared amidst the herb garden in the shadows at castle back, this new presence stole awareness of the neat rows stretching all around, awareness even of her companion.

Only one thought survived the muddle of emotions and wild responses too suddenly revived to be tamed. Dare had returned. Though two seasons had passed since last they'd met, by potent memory alone she saw both the rare, slow smile breaking across his saturnine face and its echo in the cool mockery of blue ice eyes. Thankfully her fears had once more proven groundless. She had feared for Dare's safety. Oh, how she had feared—just as she did each time her father dispatched his favorite knight to fight in his stead at their king's side.

'Twas said the devil's own were impervious to battle's harm, that such was the notorious "Demon Dare's" shield

3

against the deadly weapons of his foes. Alyce wouldn't accept it as true. Surely Dare's powerful defenses were built of naught but his own remarkable skill—and great good fortune. Yet although her trust in his military prowess brought comfort, with his every departure to join King Henry's unending battles, this reliance upon even a small measure of fickle fortune bred in her a deeper trepidation. In each instance she feared that mayhap this time his extraordinary luck had been depleted and he'd find himself forced to surrender the ultimate price in recompense for its temporary loan.

For all that Dare's safe return released a wellspring of relief to bubble within Alyce, it was tempered by his warrior's skill in finding the weak link in an opponent's armor. In this instance, his verbal attack against her most vulnerable point. She needn't turn toward the darkly handsome knight to see him, intimidatingly tall and broad even to his fellow men but overwhelmingly so to a woman of her inconsequential size. Not that her pride would allow him to see her quail before him. Not now, not ever. His next words drove deeper the sharp tip of his barb.

"Mayhap 'tis no longer so?" As Dare had known it would, the implied insult to the purity of her honor brought Alyce sharply around to face him with sparks in clear green eyes and an angry pallor that made the light dusting of freckles across her cheeks suddenly bright. Although the flaming red hair of her childhood had settled into a deep chestnut ever hidden 'neath a modest headcloth, surely the temper which was its counterpart had not waned. Whenever they met, he found himself driven to crush the unnatural shell of control she strived to wrap about her unruly spirit and thus loose the fires in its core.

"You—" No! Alyce commanded tempestuous emotions back into safe, sane channels. Dare couldn't truly believe what he'd insinuated. Truly, he couldn't. Therefore, she mustn't let him ignite her shamefully hasty temper with such ease, mustn't betray all the earnest effort she'd expended to meet her father's expectations. Constantly admonished to control an unfeminine nature, she ever strived to be a dutiful daughter and obey. Moreover, she was proud

4

of her progress toward the goal. She *had* succeeded in restraining her headstrong ways for months (never mind that they numbered precisely the same as those since Dare's last appearance in Keniver). Even had she tried to accept her father's urgings to emulate her stepmother. Though 'twas an objective which could surely be better attained were the cloyingly sweet Sybillene merely submissive and not (to Alyce's mind) so disgustingly manipulative.

No, no, and no again! She'd fallen into wrongful criticism once more! Green eyes glared at the unyielding warrior returned. Must be Dare's disruptive influence that summoned disrespectful thoughts. Must be his fault! An action threatening to rob her of the chance to prove she'd learned to force willful emotions into the rightful mold of feminine reserve. Rob her, also, of the chance to prove she was a woman grown and not the tempestuous child who'd trailed the wickedly handsome boy and allowed herself to be so mercilessly teased. Still a habit with him.

A strangled growl from the throat of a third penetrated Alyce's heated concentration on her mocking foe. She glanced sideways to a younger man plainly filled with frustrated rage but equally as plainly incapable of standing strong against the dangerous knight. Enough was enough and too much! They'd an audience. Alyce clamped a waspish retort tight between set teeth. The presence of this other, who'd never before had reason to suspect her else than the soft and yielding image she sought to project, reinforced her determination not to lose her temper and thus forfeit her hard-won composure.

"How could I, or any other, be blamed for wondering," Dare continued in a deceptively quiet tone, delighted by Alyce's barely restrained and poorly hidden anger, "when you've a male companion so constantly at your side, he seems your shadow?" Warm blue eyes went cold as with slow deliberation they measured the length of the ineffective boy-man ever hovering close to the delicious maiden, wife for six years yet still unclaimed.

Alyce felt Walter shrinking from the warrior's aura of power despite the indignation painting a bright flush on his normally sallow face. Commiserating with the young man who was her friend, friend and no more, Alyce made a rash decision. Walter could not help the timid nature incapable of meeting Dare's forceful personality, and nowise could she permit Dare's constant pricking of her to extend to the far weaker man. Womanly restraint not withstanding, once they were alone, she would tell the arrogant knight just what an odious toad he was. Others might fear him, but she never had nor would! She refused to wonder at the repeated need for such vehemence in her declarations of bravery.

"Walter, take the produce we've selected to the cook." Without shifting the green flame of her gaze from her sardonic provocateur, she thrust a nearly full basket at the thin figure nearby, paying no heed to the several leeks which tumbled to the narrow pathway at their feet.

Casting a murderous glare of mute resentment toward Dare, Walter accepted the crudely woven cook's basket, stalked down a ribbon of use-smoothed dirt between well-tended rows, and disappeared into the ancient castle's tower.

"In truth a poor specimen," Dare murmured, staring after the departing figure while contempt turned the corners of his mouth downward. He rarely spoke with strangers, and as seldom as possible with those he knew. To his mind, 'twas dangerous to reveal inner thoughts and thus risk a potentially harmful invasion into the jealously guarded corridors of his soul.

Yet when blue eyes layered in frost by bleak thoughts turned toward the small female, the heat of her return glare melted a fair way into the thickness of Dare's icy armor. An unbidden smile lifted one corner of his mouth. All his wise precautions to hold others at bay were inadequate to stave off Alyce's innocent and likely unintended forays. Over the years he'd learned to strike first, keep her off-center and unaware of how easily she could overmaster his defenses. Asides, he enjoyed watching the sparks struck by goading this fiery vixen.

Aye, a vixen Alyce was, and were it his choice, he'd see her untamed like the wild fox whose pelt was near the same hue as her rarely glimpsed hair. Toward that goal he'd first see she left off the endless veils and barbettes that covered not only lush and richly glowing locks but even swathed the area below her chin and much of cheeks now anger-bright. That she was forever tucking invisible ringlets, seemingly escaped, beneath the barbette's tight frame proved these garments naught but a physical reflection of her inner struggle to crush an unruly nature.

Alyce opened her lips, intending to defend Walter and deliver the planned scathing denunciation of insolent words, but Dare moved a step nearer. At this proximity his eyes glittered down at her with such intensity, her words dissolved and every rational thought melted away.

"What sorry whim possessed you to settle for such an unworthy creature as lover?" A landless second son, unwelcome in his own noble home and utterly unworthy of any wellborn female, Dare had no right to comment upon his foster father's choice for Alyce's mate—but suffered under no like restraints against condemning her selection of constant companion.

The words pierced a fog of confusing responses, and once temper-blushed cheeks went pale. He *did* believe her capable of such faithlessness. Alyce was appalled.

As he saw in the damsel's shocked expression the truth that she was virginal still, a white grin of satisfaction swiftly flashed across Dare's dark face. Never had he honestly thought elsewise, yet he was pleased by this visual confirmation that it was so.

Although Dare's unexpected and direct assault squelched the fire fueling Alyce's intended attack upon him for impugning her virtue, she promptly defended herself with the single weapon in her possession. Surely the only one required.

"I am a wedded woman!" Squaring her shoulders and lifting her chin, with slow, distinctly spoken words Alyce proclaimed, "I will have no lover."

The mocking smile ever guaranteed to rouse Alyce's temper reappeared. "Doubtless your husband will be devastated to learn of your chastity vow—when he's a decade older and better able to understand the full import of his loss." Irrationally compelled, he punished them both for the invisible wall between them. Not one built by her choice or his, but one which could be neither moved nor breached.

He'd been present in the small and poorly furnished chapel the day Alyce was by proxy wed to one whose family then assumed the onerous duty of her dower lands, lands far from the baron's own but neighboring theirs. That had been the first and near only time Dare had wanted to challenge a decision made by his foster father. From Lord Halbert's view, it was wisely done. Nonetheless, only by exercising long-practiced restraint had Dare been able to stand mute and watch while the little spitfire was put forever beyond his reach. He'd burned with the injustice of the life he had been born doomed to live, the certainty that as a deeply disdained younger son, though son of an earl, he could never have claimed Alyce for his own.

Beneath Dare's sardonic and unswerving gaze Alyce bristled with renewed anger. Too upset to form words sufficiently coherent to verbally launch a counterattack, she advanced upon her tormentor—all masculine power, grace, and taunting self-assurance. His assault was unjustified! Her consent had not been sought before, a twelve-year-old, she had been wed. How could it be elsewise when no lord consulted his daughter before making arrangements that were not hers to choose? No, it had not been her choice to wed with a babe in his cradle, a babe unable to consummate the bond. Even now, although she was eighteen, the husband she'd yet to meet was but six. Still she had never, never taken a single action to dishonor the vow given. How could this bold knight think elsewise? How *dare* he believe her guilty of such faithlessness? Peach-bright lips parted to vigorously inform him of the wrong in his wicked accusation.

Sword-callused fingertips brushing across the softly opened portal sealed the repudiation unspoken in Alyce's throat. Her body went hot and cold all at once. The deliberate action overwhelmed her with dangerous sensations yet failed to give any hint of the warning to come after.

"You've too much fire to waste your youth on a cold,

chaste marriage with a child-husband." Even as he touched her mouth, then burrowed slightly beneath the barbette's edge to stroke the soft, warm curve of her cheek, Dare's smile faded and he cursed himself for a fool. In all the years they'd shared the same castle, seldom had there been physical contact betwixt them. Her response was pure delight, but the deed that had won it was a disastrous mistake which could only add painful memories of silken flesh and tender lips to dreams of what could never be.

Alyce found in Dare's words an oblique reassurance that he knew his wild claims were unfounded. Yet while they calmed her temper, his touch had kindled the flames of a very different fire. This was wrong and she should move away. She should but she couldn't. Fascinated by the moody boy now devastating man for as long as she could remember, she made a hitherto unsuspected discovery: With tenderness he could as effectively shatter the rigid wall of demure self-restraint her father had taught her to build as his baiting roused her temper. Drowning helplessly in pools of blue, once ice but now the searing shade found only at the tip of the hottest flame, Alyce couldn't breathe. She felt the invisible contact jolt like lightning all the way to toes curling inside thin leather slippers as if to hold tight to the firm earth beneath.

As he watched Alyce's hungry response to his merest touch, Dare's head tilted back with a purely masculine arrogance. Had this virgin wife any notion of the reason for her so very tempting response? Nay, she clearly had none, and with that silent admission he again silently condemned himself for permitting even this small pleasure. Her all too evident vulnerability was but a further sign of the never-acknowledged yet ever-tightening cord of awareness stretched between them. One whose source she hadn't the experience to recognize, but he assuredly did. Folly. This was folly. Still, 'twas a bond he could not break. (Nor, truth be known, did he wish to see it utterly sundered—merely safely restrained.)

While Dare seldom bothered with the rules governing others, where Alyce was concerned, it was a far different matter. Cynical self-contempt tilted one corner of his mouth upward. Early he'd learned that the thrill of wild danger associated with him attracted even the haughtiest of women. With little enough effort on his part, he could have near any female he desired, save for the one he wanted most. Alyce alone was unattainable, forbidden to him. He'd comforted himself that such was the secret of her potent allure. Surely if ever he took his pleasure of the delicious creature, the need would be sated and bother him no more. A hollow consolation, yet, fortunately, one unlikely to be tested.

All hint of mockery faded while the slow smile curling the dark knight's mouth held an enticement that worsened Alyce's breathless condition. Filled with the promise of forbidden delights and a lure to wicked temptations, 'twas a smile whose rarity deepened its seductive appeal. Of a sudden, green eyes widened. This then was *the* smile against which, be whispered words true, no female could remain indifferent. 'Twas a tale impossible for her to refute. Though never afore had she been subjected to its power, she found (to her shame as a woman wed) it was true of her. In belated self-defense, her gaze dropped. Yet even staring at the unmoving rows of green herbs flourishing between strips of brown earth, she felt the pull of his presence. No wonder women seemed always to swarm about him like bees to honey. Try to resist as she might (and she had), Alyce, too, had ever felt herself drawn to the strikingly attractive man. She deemed it a small miracle that she hadn't, before this moment, betrayed her guilty response to him who should be as a brother to her.

Dare had come with his older brother, Gabriel, to foster under her father's tutelage while she was yet a babe. She'd grown up knowing it rightful that she view both boys as her siblings, but long ago she'd privately admitted an inability to find with wild Dare the same easy camaraderie of kinship she shared with gentle Gabriel. Unable to longer deny the summons of a steady blue gaze, her face lifted toward the too long absent knight while the slight frown puckering her brow with puzzlement wordlessly pled for answers to unfamiliar needs.

Snaring green eyes, Dare watched them go wide and deepen as if to swallow him whole. Only guilt for having exercised his experience on the virtuous damsel and the knowledge that 'twould be cruel to further misuse her helpless response restrained a warrior's natural instinct to seize an unguarded prize. With any other woman he'd have no hesitation, but not with Alyce, never with Alyce. The mockery returning to his smile veered inward. His family had the right of it. He was rotten to the core, caring little for anything or anyone—save this small but fiery virgin. And, he silently justified his intent to speak further, 'twas his concern for her which made it only right he should warn her of the pitfalls inherent in her own passionate nature.

"One day, inevitably one day, you will be confronted by a need to share your fires with a man, elsewise you'll smolder inside until all your sweetness turns to bitter ashes." The deep words flowed like an enchanted river of honey, and rather than taking offense, Alyce felt herself drawn perilously near to a shimmering shore.

Having no doubt but that he spoke the truth, Dare readily conceded he'd near consign his soul to perdition if only it could be he who was permitted to initiate Alyce into the fiery mysteries and honeyed delights of intimacy. Consign his soul to perdition? The thought deepened the bitter curl of his lips. Most would say he had no soul with which to bargain. That black truth reinforced the certainty that she could never be his. A distasteful reality which wiped every trace of warmth from his face as in an utterly emotionless tone he cautioned, "Choose a lover carefully or too likely the flames will be doused before they truly blaze."

The abrupt chill of Dare's last words broke Alyce free of the net of enthrallment he'd so easily cast about her. Yet, all too sensitive to the continuing danger of his exciting nearness, she jerked back and stomped her foot, purposefully feigning a high temper to shield the frailness of her defenses. Delicate brows rising in disdain, she snapped, "Need a man? Like you?" Her voice dripped with apparent contempt for his arrogance in presuming to advise her on intimate matters, on a sin she would not commit no matter the temptation—not even the blue-eyed temptation facing her now.

Rapidly dwindling sunlight rippled over night black hair as Dare threw back his head to laugh with pure enjoyment. She was good for him. Whether for fear of his wicked reputation or proven record in battle, precious few would risk standing against him as did this dainty creature. Did she truly possess an innocence so pure she failed to know what response such a challenge demanded? Or did she speak it apurpose to secure her goal? Mattered little if 'twere the first or the latter. It was time the fire-vixen learned the folly of her ways.

Alyce was disgusted with Dare's continuing ability to find more enjoyment than sting in her display of temper, but in the next instant rational thought evaporated like rain amidst roaring flames. Swept full against a broad, muscular frame by bands of flame-forged iron, Alyce went disgustingly weak while Dare proved just what a wicked danger he could be. Helplessly melting into his powerful embrace, Alyce looked up into a potent, sensual smile returned and a gaze that lured with wordless promises of delights unknown.

The shocked awareness turning green eyes molten further weakened Dare's hold on the limits he'd intended to impose while merely frightening the naive female into wiser deeds. He bent his dark head to seek the peach nectar of her mouth—indescribably sweet and more precious for its scarcity.

Wild sensations throbbed within, stealing Alyce's breath, leaving not even enough for a sigh as his firm mouth brushed achingly across hers, once, twice, and once again, tempting her into yielding what was not a woman's to give any man save husband. Driven by an instinctive craving to be closer still, with a hungry sigh Alyce wrapped her arms about broad shoulders, twined her fingers into cool black strands, and tilted her face higher.

Curled toes lost their hold on solid earth as Dare's strong hands locked about the amazingly tiny waist lost 'neath a loose gown's abundant folds. He lifted her mouth to a level with his, crushing the forbidden maiden-wife even closer as he surrendered to her silent entreaty and parted her lips for the fiery excitement of the deeper kiss she so naively demanded.

"Alyce . . . Alyce . . ." Walter's distant calls broke through the garden-scented silence encompassing a wrongly matched pair within the haze of wicked delights.

Dare abruptly lowered Alyce and stepped back. With disturbingly unsteady hands he cupped slender shoulders and braced the wildly trembling beguilement she was with her creamy complexion passion-rosed and soft mouth slightly swollen from his kisses. Yet even with some small, sane distance between, blue-flame eyes threatened to consume the tasty morsel swaying toward a ravenous predator.

"Before you think to give yourself to a milksop like Walter, remember the sparks we set alight with even this innocent play." The pad of Dare's thumb brushed across softly bowed lips, and on an aching gasp they parted again. Alyce's spontaneous reaction won the return of Dare's intent, one-sided smile. He slowly shook his head, sending the shifting hues of sunset across dark hair. "Walter is nowise equal to your fires. Either you'd burn him to cinders or he'd smother your flame till nary a spark remained."

Off-balance and struggling through mists of passion as she was, the velvet caress of husky words lingered with a stunned Alyce while her devastating tormenter abruptly strode away. If Dare deemed this naught but "innocent play," then pray God she never be called to withstand a more serious assault on her virtue.

On a dark, moonless night ten days following his wrongful deeds in the garden, Dare tossed uneasily on his narrow pallet. Although the cramped bedchamber was shared between the castle's three knights, one was absent on the baron's behalf and another walked the ramparts performing his duty as night sentry, leaving Dare alone in its formless gloom. Memories of the flames he'd kindled in Alyce haunted him, deepening into slumbering fantasies of fiery delights long dormant now awakening at his call.

Dare's empty dreams turned to welcome reality as the

softness of a feminine form slid next to him. Sleep-drugged, he illogically accepted this as Alyce's longed-for surrender to passions raging far beyond rational restraints.

"Your fires are hot." His words were a low purr, giving texture to the darkness enveloping them. "And burn too fiercely to be wasted on a spouse of no use." Dare wrapped his arms about the forbidden body, urging it intimately nearer his own nude form.

The reverberating crack of a half-open door smashed wide to bounce against the stone wall behind jerked Dare to his senses. In the dim light of a firebrand left burning some distance down the corridor, he abruptly sat up to face the intrusion's source. Dare recognized the short, broad form filling the gaping doorway. His pale blue eyes narrowed against the inescapable condemnation embodied by the enraged baron as guilt roared through a sleep-fogged mind sharply called to full consciousness.

Halbert curled his fists to restrain a near-blinding urge to fall upon Dare, wrap mighty hands about the traitorous man's throat, and in fury crush life from him. He'd heard Dare's words and had no doubt but that they referred to a secret only his wife could have shared—the impotence of which only Sybillene knew. Though deeply shamed before this much younger and by all accounts virile man, Halbert could not claim the ultimate punishment of Dare alone even did his humiliated fury allow him to destroy a beloved foster son. Nay, to wrest such a price from Dare would require that he demand the same from Sybillene, the mother of his only son (and he a mere toddling). It was a deed he could not perform no matter the cost to his pride.

Even before the echo of wood splintering against stone faded into silence, Alyce rose from her narrow bed. After wrapping a bed fur tightly about herself, she rushed from her chamber, snatched the nearest firebrand from its supporting metal ring, and rapidly moved toward the origin of the ominous crash. Lifting the flames of the resin-soaked brand high overhead, she peered around her father's beefy shoulder and gasped.

The sight of Dare's bare chest alone was devastating of

itself, but the discovery of Sybillene's curvaceous form lying curled close against his side, covers pulled tight to her chin, was a crushing blow of another sort. Here was physical proof of why Dare found it so easy to believe she, a married woman, would take a lover. Plainly his own experience proved it a common enough event. Alyce had known before of his wicked reputation, but to here see its proof delivered a pain too sharp to easily survive. She felt physically ill and by sheer effort of will remained upright on legs that seemed stripped of bone.

To reinforce her perilously weak defenses, Alyce purposefully whipped her temper with the thought that he believed no better of her than of the plainly promiscuous Sybillene. Her building anger was fierce enough to match the leaping flames of the firebrand she held aloft. It might be common practice for him to forsake the rules governing their world, but not for her! No, never for her when, glancing sideways, she could see the price of such wickedness in the painful humiliation on her father's face.

Dare was stunned by Alyce's sudden appearance. With her in the doorway, hair flowing free and glowing as bright as flames a mere handsbreadth above, it was impossible for her to be in his bed. For the first time, blue eyes shifted from Halbert's furious glare. Twisting, he met Sybillene's sultry smile. Dare was easily as horrified as either Halbert or Alyce. He'd thought the baron's justifiable rage fired by his wrong in welcoming the man's married daughter to his bed—a wicked deed, yet not half so dastardly as to bed the man's young wife.

"You are rightly named the Demon." Halbert's snarl was cold as death. "And I call upon all the forces of heaven to damn you for the wickedness you've wrought this night."

The older man stepped forward, pulled his erring wife to her feet, and snatched the coverlet from the bed, leaving her bed partner bare. Watching Halbert roughly wrap the heavy cloth about Sybillene's abundant charms, Dare silently acknowledged the impossibility of his position. He had no plausible defense for his actions, sleep-befuddled though they'd been. What argument could he give? *I hadn't meant*

*to seduce your wife . . . merely your married yet still pure
daughter?*

Alyce pulled her wayward gaze from a broad torso where
the firebrand's golden fingers of light flickered across
bronzed muscle with its light arrow of curling black hair.
Stepping away, she opened the path of retreat for her father
and the bundle of his adulterous wife. Then, following their
lead, she turned her back on the scowling man and slipped
silently away, taking with her the only source of light.

Near the corridor's end a slender shadow sought to escape
advancing torchlight by ducking into the darkest reaches of
an unlit doorway. Facing the closed door, this unseen figure
prevented the gleam of a satisfied grin from exposing him to
those deeply affected by the scene so recently enacted. He'd
attained success in overcoming this initial obstacle on his
quest, and the prize at its end was in sight. A prize he would
seize by careful planning and steady, if slow, progress.

Still carrying the now-despised truth-revealing firebrand,
Alyce held her back straight until she'd entered and closed
the door to her own chamber. Once within, she allowed her
shoulders to sag beneath the heavy weight of unhappiness so
recently thrust upon them. Doubtless Dare would depart
with the dawn, be gone from Keniver and likely gone from
her life forever. The likelihood that she would never again
experience the power of his stunning smile or see the
taunting gleam lurking in the depths of ice blue eyes brought
an anguish far deeper than even the sharp sting in the
shocking sight of voluptuous Sybillene lying too plainly
passion-tousled in his bed.

Witless fool! She must hold tight to her hard-built control.
She'd no right to rue Dare's leave-taking. He was not now
nor ever could be hers, so best the dark knight and his sinful
temptations be away. Since the day they'd embraced in the
garden, she'd been troubled by vague dreams of him. Nay.
Alyce stoutly refused to permit this self-delusion. The
wicked Demon Dare had haunted her since long, long
before. He'd always been in her home. Always there and
always an enticement to wrongdoing.

Truth be known, 'twas his restraint and not her own

16

which had saved her virtue. Best he be gone, for were he to turn the full force of his charms upon her, she was surely lost. Neither that shameful confession nor her claim of righteous future intents lightened the bleak prospect of a life in which he had no part. Her distress intensified, a doubtless sinful reaction and one laid all too bare by the firebrand's bright glare. Abruptly dousing the offending torch in a water pitcher on the chest beside her bed, with the reassurance of an unshuttered window to quiet her fear of enclosed spaces, Alyce welcomed the unnatural darkness left in the wake of light suddenly gone to hide forlorn tears.

While Alyce blessed the gloom of night as shield for shameful tears, in his chamber Dare rose with a grace inbred to throw open a small window's shutters and greet the growing half-light of predawn. He was grateful for even this weak illumination to lend ease in donning the homespun garments worn always beneath the chain mail he soon would add. A demon, Halbert had named him. How could Dare deny the title his own father had cursed him with in the innocence of his cradle? Never before had he argued against the myriad wild rumors and half-true tales surrounding him. Too late now to begin, even did he wish it. Nay, he was in truth what his parent had proclaimed him born to become—a demon, and one plainly doomed to possess the solace of neither family nor home.

To the waiting satchel he carefully added his few valued belongings—a prized book, the silver spurs given by Gabriel upon winning his knighthood, and a faded crimson ribbon. The bag already held his several changes of homespun, one set of blue velvet garb equal to court occasions, and a minimum of other necessities. For near a decade he'd been a knight in Halbert Bohan's service, and by experience in his many forays on the baron's behalf, had learned to travel light.

Thrusting his dark head through the neck-slit of his chain mail hauberk and absently settling its great weight over broad shoulders, Dare grimaced into the unseeing chamber. His time in Keniver Castle was at an end. Years of practice in freezing painful emotions behind the fortress of ice he'd closed about his heart enabled him to suppress an aching sense of loss. Furthermore, by forcing his thoughts to practical matters, he ruthlessly fought to thwart the distressing prospect of forfeiting even occasional glimpses of the castle's fire-vixen.

Dare's expression grew grimmer as he picked up his sword belt from the simple chest where it lay. Leastwise he'd no reason to worry for his future. The fearsome reputation built by his strong sword arm and demonstrated military prowess would ease his way in securing a new post. Many times had great lords offered him positions of greater prestige and higher profit. He'd refused them all in loyalty to his foster father. Now he would seek out the one best-suited to his purpose. To Gilbert Marshal he would go. The Good Knight's third son had, years before, been fostered with him here at Keniver, and to this day remained his friend. Next he meant to cross the channel. Surely, were he to arrive with Gilbert's letter of introduction, an older Marshal brother, Richard, would take him into his French garrison.

A mirthless smile hardened Dare's lips even more. Aye, he would travel across the width of the cold, stormy channel and take up arms on foreign soil. Surely so vast a distance between himself and Alyce, the beautiful virgin wife, would sunder the thus far unbreakable bond forged long past betwixt them. Sane arguments had failed to keep her from Dare's thoughts and ever more torrid dreams—as witness tonight's and its dreadful result. Moreover, neither her empty marriage nor his impoverished state had proved sufficient to uproot her from his soul. How, then, asked the mocking voice of implacable realism within, could any stretch of earth or sea?

Irritated with his own cynical nature for leaving him unable to soothe a deep hurt with sensible delusions, Dare roughly closed the buckle on his sword belt, threw the packed satchel over his shoulder, and snatched up his helm. The decision to distance himself from all shreds of his past was one wisely made. Wise, Dare reaffirmed even as the cold smile on his lips firmed into a harsh line of self-derision. Wise but depressingly void of comfort.

Striding from the chamber and thence from the castle, he refused to look back at that which must be left and forgotten. Thus did he forgo a last glimpse of one watching from a window high in the tower, pale face framed by a cloud of hair turned to fire by the first rays of dawn peeking over the horizon.

2

The brisk early spring afternoon had scarce begun when crowds of people began pouring into the great hall of Castle Wythe. At first they came quietly in deference to their lord, seated at center of the high table, but soon their reserve melted into a muted roar wherein each tried to be heard over the words of many others.

From her seat at the table's far end, Alyce watched with great interest. Here were gathered several times over the number who dwelled on the whole of Keniver's lands. She had, late yestereve, arrived with her father and his wife, while young Hal had been left safe behind at Keniver with servants who coddled him near as much as his mother. 'Twas not that any specific threat haunted the road between Keniver and Wythe, but a dense forest lay there, and undeniable dangers could lurk in such shadows.

Due to their late arrival and the fact that they'd broken the morn's fast in the family solar, freeing the hall for servants to complete preparations for the event now beginning, this was Alyce's first opportunity to study the largest room in which she'd ever been. In addition to the massive beams required by all rooms of any size, two lines of round stone columns were necessary to hold the vast ceiling in place. Though no natural light penetrated thick stone at this level of the castle, oil-fed sconces spaced at intervals down parallel walls illuminated even the corners, while from above hung rings within rings bearing candles to see the room's center as brightly lit.

Curious about the lord of this great fiefdom, Alyce surreptitiously peered down the long, white-draped table past her father and Sybillene to Earl Cyril. Flanked by the cool grace of Lady Elinor on his right and golden Gabriel on his left, he waited with patience and pride to preside over the feast about to begin. Although until the past night she had never met the earl and his wife, it was plain that Cyril fair doted on his heir, while Lady Elinor seemed too cold to waste much emotion on anyone.

Alyce's gaze shifted to the line of trestle tables assembled below to bear an amazing burden of food. There rested one whole roast ox and several roast pigs, tightly bordered by a wide assortment of dishes containing both fish and fowl— fried, broiled, or baked in pasty pies. Not, however, a feast for the consumption of those wellborn or even those who dwelled and served within the castle itself. Rather it had been prepared as a gift to the people of Wythe's widespread demesne in honor of Gabriel's crusader's vow.

"'Tis unfortunate that the weather is so foul." Halbert's comment was soft and absently directed to the wife and daughter on either side.

Though Alyce neither stirred nor spoke, she heartily echoed his sentiment.

"On a finer day a public feast like this would've been held in the courtyard." Halbert continued his audible musing. "And Cyril could've toasted Gabriel's commitment from atop the stairway leading into the castle."

Alyce agreed. Had the skies not been so heavy and the ground not covered in either snow or mud, those who'd no part in the courtyard meal might more easily have withdrawn without offense, while those who were a part of it would surely have welcomed the greater freedom to enjoy its abundance lent by the absence of their masters.

Knowing she was expected to sit in demure silence for long hours while the masses devoured the bounty below, she sought to mentally prepare herself for the ordeal. Smoothing

21

the sides of her forest green barbette against cool cheeks, she wished for the company of another, even the company of Walter, whose constant attentions had begun to annoy. But on this occasion, when he'd truly be appreciated, he was not present. He'd departed at near the same time they had, but he had gone in the opposite direction to seek acceptance amongst those being educated at Winchester under the guidance of its bishop's supporters—the same bishop who would lead Gabriel on crusade. Though a life in the church might seem an avocation better-suited to a man such as Walter, one who'd neither physical strength nor skill at arms, Alyce wondered if Walter possessed the necessary selflessness. But then again, the bishop was renowned for his political power. Perhaps Walter thought to follow a similar path?

Earl Cyril rose to his feet, and Alyce politely gave to him her full attention.

Astride a massive steed halted amongst forest shadows at the crest of a gentle slope, a powerful figure gazed across the shallow valley covered by a recent layer of pristine white flakes. Pale blue eyes narrowed upon a mighty fortress laid square atop the next rise, corner towers soaring defiantly into cheerless gray skies.

Dare's vivid childhood memories of Castle Wythe were of a proud stronghold standing on high ground surrounded all about by fertile green fields. Neither the near score of years since last he'd beheld these impressive ramparts nor fields now snow-laden lessened his hereditary home's endless lure—despite the certain fact he would find little welcome within. His lips took on a cheerless downward curl.

Only for Gabriel's sake had he come. Two months had passed since the fateful scene in Keniver's tower. Time he'd spent with Gilbert, the friend from his youth. But for a beloved brother's fervent appeal that he come to wish him well on a "God-ordained quest," Dare would by now have been off to France. The hoped-for appointment to Richard Marshal's garrison had been cordially offered. 'Twas a welcome summons Dare was anxious to accept.

Exercising an infamous ability to block the weakness of

human emotion, Dare set aside his own preferences and urged his destrier into motion. With great haste he wanted to have done with his joyless and doubtless unappreciated task, have done so that for all time he might leave behind this physical symbol of painful rejection. He'd answered Gabriel's call yet had not journeyed to this place held ever-closed against him merely to bid the other good fortune on crusade. Nay, rather had he come to present the sensible, logical argument against his gentle brother's undertaking of so futile a cause.

Passing through the open and unguarded gate of the outer bailey wall, he eased Fiend into a canter. The lane beyond was oddly deserted at midday, though the multitude of muddy prints laid atop its once white surface proved how busy it had recently been. Ahead a small village crowded against the moat like an old and weary beast sprawled out to lap up life-giving liquid. Diverted from a fast-flowing river, unlike most, this moat's waters were clear and sweet and were a worthy barrier to threatening foes on three sides, while on the fourth the wide river itself provided the castle and its baileys with protection. Dare wasted no time in pondering the remarkable good fortune of the castle's inhabitants or the wisdom of architects who had planned it thus, not when he had grave matters with which to contend.

He suffered under no delusion that his mission would find success. There was little hope that he'd be able to dissuade an idealistic fool from fulfilling his lifelong goal—one whose seeds had been planted within a babe in his cradle and carefully nurtured. Still, only after delivering his almost assuredly fruitless argument would Dare feel free to depart for France.

Their father, as a youth trained by choice for the monastic life, had been obsessed by the dream of seeing the Holy Land held safe in Christian hands. Zeal thwarted by the death of older brothers and the original Demon Dare's insistence that he put off a monkish cowl to produce an heir for Wythe, he'd groomed his eldest son to perform the lost quest in his stead. Raised to view the task as the ultimate service to be rendered either God or man, Gabriel now had seized his first opportunity to perform the feat. He had committed himself to accompany the Bishop of Winchester (a man, though bishop, less holy than any Dare had ever met) on an ill-planned and, Dare strongly feared, doomed crusade.

The huge black stallion with his dark-cloaked rider crossed a lowered, unguarded drawbridge. That both this gateway and the first were abandoned made it clear every inhabitant of the demesne had been summoned to a gathering of paramount import. Very few—and none hereabouts —knew Dare well enough to recognize the growing tension in his brooding expression, as if shutters had been closed to block the light of day. Dare found concern in open and undefended approaches not only because from a defensive view such actions were foolish at best, but because they demonstrated how nearly too late he'd arrived. 'Twas plain that the purpose for the lord's possibly disastrous command for his people to desert their duties was to invite their presence at the celebration of what Earl Cyril would laud as a glorious event.

Leaving his steed in an empty courtyard where the trampling of many had reduced the snow to deep brown muck, Dare climbed broad wooden steps to the castle entrance one level aboveground. At the top he opened one of two massive doors and strode unobserved down the tunnel beyond. It passed through a stone wall so thick, two men could lie supine with feet resting upon the shoulders of the next without first or last touching either its beginning or end. At the tunnel's inner edge, bright light from massed torches and a myriad of candles flowed out above the dark throng of people filling the vast great hall with a sea of humanity.

Behind the outermost wave Dare stood in silence. Though his well-above-average height allowed him a clear view, his intense blue gaze was relentlessly claimed by the men he'd come to see—brother and father. Thus he'd no attention to spare for either the others gathered about the high table resting atop a raised dais at the hall's far end or the abundance of foodstuffs piled on a single line of tables below. An unnatural hush settled over the crowded many awaiting the time they'd be loosed upon such bounty. The next moment three horns were blown from a gallery high in one near corner, heralding the words of the earl rising to his feet.

"Lift your drinks in honor of my son, my heir." Silver goblet held aloft to gleam in constantly shifting flamelight, a thin, white-haired man gazed with undisguised love and pride at his golden heir. The honored man, tall and willow-slender, stood up, but with eyes humbly lowered beneath such praise. "He takes up the crusader's cross to go forth and do honorable battle on behalf of our pope and Christians everywhere."

While rose tumultous cheers of such volume as to shake massive beams overhead, a black tide of dread rose within Dare. His anxiety was for a brother lacking the training and, of more import, the ability to approach the task of battle with the cold dispassion which hard experience had taught Dare was necessary to attain victory—and survive. Though older than he, Gabriel was untested by deadly conflict. Never had Gabriel been forced to face the choice between surrendering his own mortality and the taking of another's life. Dare much doubted his gentle brother capable of the latter deed. Wanting to save him from the need to make so soul-scarring a choice, Dare pushed his way through the throng and moved around overladen tables to stand directly below the castle's lord.

"What you celebrate here is no more and no less than Gabriel's martyrdom on the altar of your selfish dreams." With freezing condemnation, ice blue eyes bored into the aging man responsible already for too much pain.

"No!" Cyril's rage burst out with sanctimonious fire. Although at first he was shocked by this apparition from his past, watery gray eyes narrowed on the image of his own father until it resolved itself into the figure of a different but equally unwelcome presence. "Gabriel was called to God's cause, and God will protect his path."

"Protect him?" Battle-tested and proven, Dare stood unflinching beneath the man's disdain. "As were the hundreds, nay, thousands who already have died alone and in agony on hot sands—far from either home or loving hearts?"

"Dare." Gabriel quickly stepped from the dais to insert the shield of his body between the two protagonists. "Thank you for answering my summons and for coming to see me before I depart—no matter your feelings on the matter."

The dark knight's unexpected appearance had drawn a silent gasp from the far end of the high table. Alyce had thought never to see Dare again, and assuredly not here in the home where, to her certain knowledge, he'd not entered in the score and more of years since being sent to foster at Keniver. Her initial flash of warm pleasure was soon snuffed out by the chill of his father's scorn for a repudiated son purposefully excluded.

"*He* is not welcome here." Cyril's spurning words were as dead and cold as the grave while his near colorless eyes seemed to look through the despised intruder.

"If Dare departs, then I also go." Too aware that it was he who'd unwittingly drawn Dare to meet this inevitable confrontation, for the first time in his life Gabriel faced his sire in open opposition. Then, flanked by two he loved more than all other mortals, with the conciliatory heart of a peacemaker he softened his stance to quietly plead. "'Twas I who begged Dare to come, and I who now welcome his presence. For my sake, Father, for the sake of the journey I soon embark upon, I pray you will honor my invitation."

Thick white brows knitted into a frowning line. Yet Cyril could deny his beloved son nothing and reluctantly nodded.

"Now, brother, let me take you to the chamber we must share, as the castle is full of guests arrived to wish me good fortune. Asides"— an affectionate smile accompanied gently teasing words—"you are doubtless in need of a bath." Mist gray eyes meaningfully measured the length of the travel-grimed knight fully armed amidst a gathering of celebrants in festive garb.

At mention of the bath by custom provided new arrivals of any import and personally supervised by the castle's lady, Dare's gaze shifted to the woman sitting silently in his father's shadow. His mother's face turned deliberately away—a further rejection, one expected but painful still. 'Twas clear he was not deemed worthy of such an honor. A self-derisive smile curled his mouth but did nothing to warm blue eyes until his attention turned to Gabriel. Then, for a moment at least, they softened with affection.

The crowd was irritated not only by the interruption of a rare opportunity to feast and drink at their earl's expense but by this threatened removal of the one in whose honor the banquet was held. Moreover, as they'd been whipped to a froth of support by their earl's urgings to pay homage to the one who'd be their champion on a glorious, God-inspired crusade, their oppressive condemnation threatened to overwhelm Dare on all sides. Despite an unchanged half smile, his face looked to be carved of a pure granite layered in frost.

How else but that these men of Wythe expect such wickedness from one damned at birth by the father they believed a pious man. In mirthless silence Dare acknowledged how little he wanted to be here and how willingly he'd have offered to withdraw. Yet he would never turn coward before any man nor shirk any challenge. It required a courage beyond physical strength to remain and face the disapproving crowd, but courage he had aplenty. He'd not depart until at least one further attempt had been made to speak sense to one needful of it. A deed he prayed could soon be accomplished, thus freeing him to leave this cheerless place where his presence was but grudgingly allowed. Nodding for his peacekeeping brother to lead the way, Dare followed while ignoring the disapproving glares of many and the mistrustful glances of more than a few.

Unfortunately, even after he reached the bedchamber of a size and opulence to match the earl's and thus worthy of the castle heir, Dare's hoped-for quiet time to speak with Gabriel alone was doomed by a plethora of castle-serfs hovering near. The first to arrive were not those expected.

A rotund man, wheezing under the effort of climbing steep, winding stairs, hauled in a large, straw-filled pallet and laid it alongside the high, heavily draped bed occupying the room's center. In his wake came two females who scurried about arranging linens, covers, and pillows while casting curious sidelong glances at the son of their lord who'd been both born and exiled before their own births. The younger was painfully timid, while the bold gaze of the older left little doubt that she found the dark and reputedly dangerous man exciting despite the lack of encouragement in ice blue eyes.

Having long lived without such pampering, Dare felt only irritation for the intrusion of this unsought assistance in accommodating all the needs they seemed to believe inherent in his unanticipated stay. Only after these three made themselves busy did others follow bearing a huge tub formed of wooden slats tightly iron-bound and looking like the bottom half of an oversize barrel. Thence came a rapid procession of many more to fill it with steaming water. Once 'twas done, Dare glared at the three interlopers first to arrive and the only ones who yet remained. The hefty man lost no moment in escaping, while the younger female's haste-stiff fingers lengthened her chore. The older girl no longer made any pretense of work and merely posed her voluptuous form to its best advantage.

Gabriel turned his back on the maid to face Dare and speak in feigned concern. "I will leave you to the private delights—" during a pregnant pause, golden brows wiggled suggestively above laughing eyes "—of your bath."

Dare near gnashed his teeth with frustration for the presence of people he wanted gone while departed the one he wanted to stay.

Nodding a bright head just once toward the dark man fairly growling with vexation, Gabriel grinned as he turned to leave. "Methinks you could well do with the mellowing of some such solace."

Gabriel's murmured recommendation did draw a low growl from Dare. Unfortunately even that menacing sound failed to evict unwanted company. Dare was in no mood to be manipulated by his well-meaning brother, and far less by the brazen female gazing at him as if he were some rich fruit ripe to be consumed. Impatient with the younger maid's slow pace, he implacably waved the two from his chamber. Thus he was left to bathe in solitude before the water lost all heat.

He stripped off his weighty hauberk, a task better performed with the help of a squire. But as he had none, he'd grown used to accomplishing the deed alone and without wasted time or thought. A good thing that, as he was preoccupied with such unforeseen impediments to the hasty completion of his objective as constant interruptions and the annoying presence of others.

Sinking into water already beginning to cool, he frowned. Leastways, he comforted himself, tepid liquid offered no temptation to linger—nor did it yield the ease for tension-stiff and travel-wearied muscles which he'd hoped to enjoy. Another wrong to place at the feet of those supplying unsought aid. With the small square of cloth and lump of lye soap provided, he scrubbed the grit of the journey from his flesh.

Finished, he gazed blindly into a dark corner while thoughts ever-controlled evaded their constraints to wander through corridors of his mind for years closed and barred. Would that he could as easily wash away the stain of disapproval, nay, hate that had been poured over him in this castle on the day of his birth. If not that miracle, then gladly would he settle for the words to explain its source. What black secret lay in the depths of this structure and in shadows of the past which required such a price from him? Was he truly Satan's son?

Water splashed in a wide arc as Dare abruptly stood and snatched the folds of a sizable cloth waiting atop the stool drawn close. Whatever villainy lingered here, 'twas a place plainly dangerous to his long-ingrained control. No matter the past or future, he simply was what he was. Dare stepped from the tub and, uncaring of the chill of smooth wooden planks beneath bare feet, briskly toweled dry.

From the high table Halbert watched while the masses, like ravenous beasts, fell upon the feast prepared for them. But rather than the scene below—rapidly descending into mayhem—he saw the scene wherein his foster son had been reviled by the father who should surely have loved him. Halbert always had and still did—even with the apparent proof of an inbred wickedness displayed by Dare on his last night in Keniver Castle. Possessing only one precious son (and, as unpleasant facts remained unchanged, not like to have another), Halbert found Cyril's attitude beyond comprehension. The earl's inflexible refusal to allow Dare home in all these years had forewarned this harsh attitude, but yet Halbert found it impossible to believe what he'd seen, and more difficult to understand.

Halbert had passed the long weeks and months since Dare's banishment from Keniver reviewing every detail of the wretched confrontation that had ended so horribly. That Dare had fallen to his beauteous wife's charms was proof more of an all too human nature than that of a demon. He could not, in honor, forgive Dare—but he could understand. Never again could the younger man be a trusted friend, yet it pained him to see the "boy" he'd loved as a true son so purposefully rejected by the parents who owed him much more. What pained him most of all was the memory of how he had used the same demon curse to cast Dare from Keniver.

Staring into the dregs of his goblet with regrets equally as bitter, Halbert acknowledged that whatever Dare's wrong, it couldn't have happened without Sybillene's willing compliance. She was nowise the perfect woman and wife he'd selected with such care to be the antithesis of his first spouse. Although it was true that Gladys—Alyce's flame-haired, headstrong mother—and Sybillene were in no way alike, the second had clearly been the poorest choice of the two.

Gladys leastways had been loving and faithful. Her sole wrong had been more his than hers. Try as he might, he'd been unable to quell Gladys's strong will and had felt his failure made of him a lesser man. Thus, when the daughter who took Gladys's life with her birth was seen to possess similar fiery hair, he'd been determined to prevent the newborn from developing the same unfeminine traits as she grew. In part to meet that goal, he had chosen sweet, submissive Sybillene to wife, and hold before Alyce as the epitome of womanhood. Only see how foolish he had been again and again.

Rousing himself from somber thoughts, he glanced to his left, where Alyce sat squirming in discomfort. As fervently as his daughter sought to conform with the mold of meek femininity he'd attempted to force upon her (and he knew that for his sake, she did), 'twas obvious she found the chore most difficult. Particularly when it demanded she sit for hours in the demure and silent manner expected of wellborn women on such public occasions as this. Aye, with Alyce as with her mother, he'd failed to completely master her spirit. Could he bear the blow to his oversensitive pride it would mean, he'd tell her it no longer mattered. He could not, but he would provide what limited relief he could.

"Does your head pain you?" He bent sideways to whisper the inquiry near Alyce's ear.

Startled by her father's unexpected—and unnecessary—concern, green eyes flew up to meet an odd smile.

"Mayhap," Halbert continued, "you ought to retire to the cool quiet of your chamber and seek to relieve it afore our feast begins this evening."

A loud crash resounding from just below drew Halbert's attention to the morass of people consuming the feast provided. One too sotted with ale had stumbled full across the bare bones of an ox, knocking the trestle table askew and landing himself, the ox's remains, and a multitude of platters and bowls upon the floor, where they lay atop rushes growing ever filthier. The man's predicament earned from his fellows a roar of laughter and a wry smile from Halbert.

While her father was distracted, Alyce's thick lashes blinked away her amazement for this excuse she hadn't dared to seek. She'd painted a wan smile on her lips by the time he returned his attention to her. Meekly nodding her assent to his suggestion, and exercising the self-control she'd spent years learning, Alyce restrained the desire for haste urged upon her by the prospect of escape. To move too quickly would rouse suspicion and bring unwanted attention. Just as she gained her feet, her father spoke again.

"If you should meet Cleva, the guard captain's wife, ask her aid. She has potions and cures of amazing powers."

The sparkle in her father's eyes kindled a glow of suspicion within Alyce. She hesitated. 'Twas if they shared a secret—one whose meaning was hidden even from her. She fought down an urge to question him on the matter with the certainty that now was not the time to stand about like some awkward land bird waiting to become the focus of not only the whole of those at the high table but the many filling the hall below. Moreover, what sense was there in questioning the source of a welcome gift which could still be snatched from her hands?

Wasting no further moment, she stepped down and hurried toward the stairway. Once she was safe within the shielding dimness at its base, not even the mystery behind this blessing unexpectedly given could prevent her from a renewed appreciation of wide, winding steps built into the considerable depth of stone walls. Compared to Keniver's narrow wooden stairs, exposed to the eyes of everyone in the hall below, these were remarkable. They were, however, more than a trifle gloomy what with no source of illumination save weak flickers from wide-spaced oil-fed sconces and rare gleams falling through arrow slits on each landing. Open to daylight—when daylight there was—they were wide at the outset but narrowed to long, thin openings designed to lend freedom of movement to defending archers while presenting minimal opportunity for successful attack.

Alyce began the climb, passing from one sconce's bright circle of golden light through a darkness lent ominous forms by the faint gleams of constantly wavering flames behind and ahead. Then, with relief, she moved on into another arc of light. For all her strong will, Alyce was shamefully uneasy amongst shifting shadows. Before leaving this bright area to negotiate the darkness between it and the next, she distracted herself with a pointed consideration of the most unique thing about Castle Wythe's stairways. Their make and lighting were points of interest, but what truly set them apart were their divided locations. Those ascending from the great hall to the family chambers above began directly inside the entrance tunnel. At one far end of the soot-blackened fireplace wall lay the start of those descending to kitchens and guardroom on the ground level and then down another flight further to the dungeons at bottom.

Once Alyce reached the higher level, her destination was near. Indeed, it was the first door on the right side of the long corridor splitting the square of this level in twain. Opening the sturdy oak door, she was pleased to find the candle still burning where she'd left it atop the small chest beside a narrow bed. As she'd forgotten, in her haste to depart the hall, to secure another already lit, the fact that it hadn't guttered out was a welcome reprieve.

This cozy chamber was much like her room at home. She only wished she could be as comfortable here. It was not that Keniver provided finer furnishings. It didn't. Simply was it that here the thick stone of two walls and the stout wood of the others allowed the entry of no natural light. At Keniver she'd the good fortune of a tiny window high in the wall and missed it more than she'd admit aloud. She'd never attempted to fool herself into thinking that she was else in the total darkness of enclosed spaces than a craven pigeonheart. Moving shadows and small places whose walls always seemed to shrink ever more tightly around her, these were her fears—the only ones she would confess even in private, and then only because she couldn't do elsewise.

After lighting a new candle with the old and settling its unlit end into the malleable wax of the first, she sank to the bed, at last allowing thoughts of the guest uninvited to overmaster earlier restraints. While in the great hall, enduring time that dragged as if manacled to leaden weights, she had struggled to bar Dare from her mind. This she had done for the sake of an illogical but very real fear that guilt for deeds both done and dreamt would glow like a beacon if allowed to linger in her thoughts—and result in a daughter disgracing her father.

Now those disturbing memories flowed over her like a river in flood. Memories of Dare teasing the child she'd been, but, too, always there to lend aid did she need it. Memories of the forbidden delights waiting within his tempting embrace. Memories of another in his bed. The fierce scowl earned by the last was in the next instant smoothed away. The natural healing powers of the mind had long since found a balm to temper the pain. Sybillene was banished from the view, leaving only a sight which added new dimensions to remembered fires. In truth, the image of Dare's bare torso had slipped into dreams wherein it was she who lay crushed to its heat, scorched by the same flames which awaited the wicked once their time in mortal realms had passed. 'Struth, a mortal sin, yet too welcome and too exciting to reject with ease. Alyce dropped full back upon the bed, impervious to its lumps while floating in the smoky mists rising from twined memories of what had been and fantasies of what could never be.

Of a sudden at corridor's end a door closed with a loud crash. Alyce instantly sat up. The candle, lit surely but a short time past, had near burned to its end. The time to gather for the feast planned for castle inhabitants must have drawn nigh. Best she make haste and join them directly.

Rising, Alyce grimaced at the creases her unthinking action had laid in a pale green overgown. She ran her palms across rich silk, ruing her error in ill using cloth so subject to wrinkles. There was no help for it. There was no time to change, even were her wardrobe of such a size as to allow it. Abandoning the futile effort, Alyce quickly tucked errant strands of fire-washed brown back under the forest green barbette framing her face. She then arranged its matching veil in neat folds before hurrying from the chamber.

3

Dare refused to lend even the appearance of support to Gabriel's quest by donning for the night's private feast the blue velvet of his best raiment, and instead chose a short undertunic of black and a knee-length overtunic of scarlet wool. These were among the several additions to his wardrobe that Gilbert Marshal had insisted he should have. In this moment he appreciated his friend's persistent goading, elsewise he'd have been forced to wear either the resplendent velvet or don homespun, certain to be viewed an insult. With the red garment he wore black hose whose thick wool clung to muscular calves, and the short leather boots with which Gilbert had gifted him on his departure. They were of a leather so soft and thin, they'd be useless for outside wear, and this, he thought with a smile in warm memory of a friend, might well be his only opportunity to put them to use. As he settled a wide leather belt about his narrow hips, a soft yet unrelenting tap sounded on the chamber door.

"Enter." Dare's single word was not invitation but cold command. Gabriel would enter his own room without knocking. Therefore, it was not him, and Dare had little patience to spare for any other. A muscle in his cheek clenched with an involuntary rejection as the door swung

35

open, revealing the too aggressive maid he had already sent away once this day. Apparently impervious to "subtle" rebuffs, she swayed into the room with a suggestive roll to well-rounded hips emphasized by a long, crude belt riding low over their curves, with ends trailing down the center.

"They bade me tell you the lord and his guests are gathering in the great hall." Pale brown eyes drifted over him from head to toe as she clarified the message. "For the day's last meal." By the sensuous smile accompanying an appreciative gaze, it was apparent she still found him as attractive as she had earlier while her companion did the work of preparing a bed whose pleasures, plainly, she was willing to share with him.

"If you have need of more than was provided, tell Tess—that's me—and I'll see that 'tis given you." Gleaming with unspoken promises, her knowing eyes offered an open invitation.

Dare was unimpressed. Some men might find it flattering to be so openly sought, as in his adolescence had he, but by experience he'd become a huntsman who preferred the thrill of the chase. He no longer had a taste for prey so easily won. Certainly not when there were important matters awaiting his attention. The last feeble light of dreary day fell through an unshuttered window to caress thick black hair with gentle beams as Dare wryly nodded before striding past Tess without another glance, intent on descending to the level below.

From the shadows of its entrance, Dare quietly took stock of those gathered in a hall still brightly lit but much less crowded. As always, those at the high table were seated down one long side facing the three rows of trestle tables assembled at right angles from the dais to accommodate the castle's lesser inhabitants. This, then, was the smaller celebration intended solely for castle residents and their lord's guests.

Only as Dare took the seat assigned him at Gabriel's side did he see what had gone unnoticed in the confusion and discord of his arrival. The latter group included visitors he'd thought never to meet again. Seated at the dais's far end was Halbert Bohan—Cyril's fellow noble, neighbor, and the one to whom he'd sent his sons to foster. Although as distant from him as two at the same table could be, Dare was cynically amused by the sight of the frowning baron holding his wife near shackled to his side. Although, not surprisingly, the older man pointedly refused to look his way, seemed he did see and rightly read the sultry gaze his wife held fixed on one he must believe yet a threat. Dare's eyes glittered with humorless amusement. Jealousy blinded Halbert to the only real danger his former knight represented. Aye, the baron could naught but be utterly unaware that the full impact of Dare's wicked desires centered upon Alyce, the daughter sitting at her father's side with eyes demurely downcast while earnestly striving to be the epitome of submissive femininity.

Alyce felt the tingling brush of intense blue eyes, and it was not so much a desire to meet her father's expectations which held her immobile as renewed alarm that she might betray the response his nearness provoked, a response leaving her caught between pleasure and shame. Her hands were shaking so badly, she daren't lift to her lips any morsel of food or sip of liquid for fear she'd inelegantly drop food into her lap or spill wine across the table's pristine white cloth. 'Twould embarrass her father were his daughter proven so inept before their host—and it would mortify her to demonstrate to Dare how vulnerable his mere presence left her.

To forestall such a miserable spectacle, she sat unmoving and stiff with the tension required to maintain a calm demeanor. Inside, meanwhile, her emotions struggled between a longing to be alone with Dare and guilt for a wedded woman's desire to win private moments with any man not her husband. To prevent their betraying tremble from being seen were she to fall to an instinctive smoothing of the green barbette's edges, she tightly interlaced her fingers. She'd grave apprehensions that, if Dare did not soon look away, the easily frayed nerves inevitably accompanying such a willful nature as hers would snap and end in an embarrassing scene.

The only hope for disaster averted lay in the unlikely miracle of a change in Dare's steadily cast lures. She was disgustingly helpless against the dangerous fascination he wielded so effortlessly. Admitting her lack of adequate defense did nothing to improve it. She could do naught but pray that someone would speak to him and shift his unwavering attention from her.

Her prayers were not blessed with the answer she sought. Throughout the seemingly endless meal, while many extravagantly prepared dishes were first served by pages on bended knee and then as graciously removed, no words were addressed to Dare. He gave the rude lack no notice—no surprise as she knew very well what masterful control he had of his emotions. She, to the reverse, became so incensed on his behalf that simply to shatter the gathering's cool facade, she near purposefully caused a far worse scene than the one previously feared. How could his own family treat Dare so shabbily? He had done nothing to justify this cold reception. 'Twas the first time he'd been within Wythe's walls since the day he, as a young boy, had been sent away to foster. And whatever he had done since, he had committed no crime before his exile. *This* crime was theirs!

Although her father had visited Wythe on any number of occasions in the past, neither the earl or his countess had ever come to Keniver, and until their arrival here the previous night, Alyce had never met Dare's parents. Having seen their reaction to him earlier in the day, Alyce recognized an unspeakable truth. They chose to avoid any place where they might be in company with their youngest son. It shocked Alyce and kindled her temper. Oh, she had—as everyone had—heard the tale of Earl Cyril's curse upon Dare. But she'd always thought that Lady Elinor, leastways, must host a mother's love for her son and that only a woman's subservient position in life prevented her from proclaiming him both blameless and beloved to the world. Now, if not by the icy core sensed at their first meeting, then by the memory of Lady Elinor's elegant but emotionless face turning coldly away from Dare even as Gabriel had welcomed him, Alyce deemed it obvious that the woman gave him nothing because she had nothing to give. Poor Dare. Alyce's tender heart bled for him.

She'd wits sharp enough to know the source of his

parents' attitude lay deeper than a mere reaction to his urging of Gabriel to renounce his crusader's pledge. That Dare had not been welcome in his ancestral home in all these years proved its source lay deep in the past's formless shadows. So deep, perhaps, no one could search it out and cast upon it the truth-revealing light of day? Hideous thought and one which, rather than easing her irritation with the hopelessness of the unchangeable nature of his parents' actions, fanned the fire of her anger.

To prevent the immediate taking of assuredly foolish actions, she clenched her hands so tightly that her nails laid half-moon imprints in soft palms. Someday, she silently swore, someday she'd find a way to bless Dare's path with the healing beams blocked by his father's curse upon an innocent babe. Though after this surprising meeting, she might never see Dare again, she would take this as her quest, and one sworn to as honorably as had Gabriel his crusader's oath.

Lost in a jumble of strong emotions, she peeked at Dare beneath lowered lashes. A mistake she should've anticipated. Potent blue instantly caught and held her gaze while breath caught in her throat on a tiny gasp. Afraid to reveal her intense feelings, through sheer effort of will she broke the bond, but not before Dare had glimpsed the fiery spirit alive and sparkling in the green depths of again demurely lowered eyes. He was inordinately pleased.

When removed were the platters emptied of nuts in spices, raisins, apples, and deep yellow cheese that had been the meal's final course, the lords and their knights withdrew to positions about the massive fireplace occupying most of the wall behind the dais. As men jostled amongst themselves to find positions of comfort, Dare unobtrusively maneuvered his brother into the cooler shadows on one side of the blazing hearth. With his back to others, even the damsel so recently the focus of his full attention, he sought privacy for words meant to be heard by Gabriel alone. A plan, unbeknownst to him, doomed by Cyril's watchful eye.

"Gabriel—" Dare began his plea for sanity, for sensible considerations unclouded by either religious fervor or paternal influence. "I pray you to pause and ponder the unavoidable perils inherent to the pursuit of an objective laudable yet unrealistic."

Though of like height, Dare was far broader of form and enough more of both physical and mental power that, rather than instantly refuting all arguments, Gabriel tilted his blond head and wordlessly listened. Asides, he loved this dark and reputedly dangerous brother. He would do this small thing to please him, although he would not break his crusader's pledge even for Dare. With an affectionate smile, he nodded a fair-haired head for his brother to continue.

Dare restrained a momentary flash of satisfaction, too aware of how short-lived it could well be, and carefully went on with his plea.

"'Struth, I am the younger of we two, yet I have years of hard experience in battle to back the warning I feel compelled to deliver. Pray heed my words."

"I allowed love for my son and heir to sway good judgment. For his sake I accepted your company, and this is how you repay my hospitality?" Bushy white brows lowered like a cloud over once pale gray eyes gone hard with fury and glaring at the offender's broad back as if intent on visually delivering a mortal blow.

Love for his son? As if he had naught but one. Dare flinched beneath his father's bitter words, but the motion was so slight and so brief that a moment later, none could say of a certainty it had happened.

"Yet what else should be expected from a demon—" Cyril's icy contempt shattered against Dare's stiffly held spine "—but that he ever seek to sever and put asunder God's design!"

Aware that the vast hall had gone deathly silent, Dare turned to meet the denunciation with narrowed blue eyes, proudly lifted chin, and a humorless half smile.

"I seek only to prolong my brother's life—to prolong the life of your heir." He spoke not to defend himself but to further his argument through the only channel left open to him.

"Hah!" Cyril scoffed at the claim. "You think only of yourself, of your worldly sphere, while my sweet Gabriel devotes himself to a greater cause."

As Dare slowly shook his head, the uneven ends of black hair trimmed by an inept companion-in-arms brushed wide shoulders. "Were I thinking only of myself, would I not applaud the end your holy crusade will likely beget? Would I not be pleased by the prospect of Gabriel's death, with its assurance of his inheritance and the whole of your wealth passing to me?" Though his sire was plainly unable to hear reason in any word he spoke, still Dare sought to drive the point home in Gabriel's heart.

Between gritted teeth Cyril spat out a venomous command. "Begone from *my* lands, from the inheritance of *my* son."

"Aye." Azure eyes hardened to ice proved that the affirmation of the single word included nothing of retreat. Rather the mocking gaze slowly measured the smaller, older man until, unequal to mastering Dare's wordless but unfaltering defense, Cyril fell back.

"Even knowing the certain animosity awaiting me, I delayed my own planned journey to venture here." Dare continued at last, and in a tone so flat, it revealed naught but the slightest taste of a bitterness tightly bottled inside. "I came for the sole purpose of begging my brother to carefully consider the folly of his plan, to calmly ponder the senselessness of one so ill prepared going out to meet the burning death stalking desert sands."

Blue eyes flickered briefly toward the subject of his words. Gabriel had moved to stand immobile at their father's side, and in his rueful grimace Dare recognized an unaltered determination. Looking back to his white-haired protagonist, Dare brought a quick end to this final plea. "That task I have done. My conscience is clear. Thus I will resume my interrupted journey and depart from Wythe with all possible haste. Depart from England, too."

"An end guaranteed to provide pleasure to both your mother and I." As utterly uncaring of his wife's pain and pallor as he had been for the past two decades and more, Cyril held himself firmly upright, determined to regain face before gaping onlookers. "A pleasure, I doubt not, to your foster family as well. Aye, your flight from home and country provides a just exile." He took cruel pleasure in making the Demon's most recent wicked deed known to all. "Exile is the penalty deserved by one so lacking in honor that he uncaringly deserted a worthy post and turned his back on a generous foster father merely to satisfy his greed with the riches and position offered by a more important and wealthier lord."

Dark brows arched, Dare briefly glanced toward an alarmingly white-faced Halbert, whose arm had clamped so tightly about Sybillene that she winced. Plainly, Dare wryly acknowledged, the baron feared he'd attempt to correct his father's mistaken understanding. Thereby threatening exposure of the shaming truth behind the lie of Halbert's explanation for why his knight had departed from Keniver in haste. An apprehension unneedful. Dare conceded his wrong, even if not the one Halbert believed. Willingly would he accept the fabricated excuse. To do elsewise was to force the proud baron into a humiliating confession. Dare had no wish for the man he loved as the only father he'd ever really known to suffer such a price for another's deeds—though it would be more payment for Sybillene's guilt than his own. With a bleak smile but warm eyes, Dare met Halbert's gaze before turning away.

Silence reigned in the huge hall as Dare swiftly, boldly strode down the path laid open through its width as curious onlookers hastily pressed back on either side. All attention centered on the leave-taking of this reviled son, and no sound broke the ominous hush until after the sight of the dark knight and even the sound of his booted feet climbing stone steps had faded. Only then did a swell of whispered conjecture rise higher and higher. The flow of speculation, embellished with repeated gossip of deeds surely proving truth lay at the core of the Demon's wicked reputation, was titillating enough to divert the crowd's attention from another form, small and slender, slipping up the same stairway.

Gaining the top of the steps, Alyce moved to stand motionless in a doorway left ajar. Aching with compassion, she watched the man too strong to bend, even when it seemed he must and likely should. Elsewise surely someday he might shatter as did even mighty beams when asked to bear a weight too great. Dare's back was to her, and while mentally seeking the means to ease his pain, she stepped soundlessly into the chamber, carefully closed the door, and slipped an iron rod through its hasp to prevent the easy entry of any other.

Intently channeling his attention to deflect the hurt in the rejection his father had renewed yet again, Dare fiercely concentrated on the paltry task of retrieving the few belongings he'd unpacked, and failed to sense Alyce's presence. Done with the small chore, he stripped off first the scarlet overtunic and then almost immediately the black one beneath, ruffling black hair. With none of his usual regard for good care, he turned and bent to stuff the garments into the satchel atop the bed from which he next jerked a homespun shirt.

Alyce silently gaped at the impressive view of his bare chest. Aye, she'd seen it before. Yet the pleasures bred by that brief but well-remembered glimpse were as nothing to those roused by this devastating display of powerful muscles. They rippled under the wedge of dark hair arrowing from broad chest down over a flat, firm belly to where hose fastened about narrow hips.

Not trusting her own legs for adequate support, Alyce leaned back against hands outspread on the rough planks of the door behind. Either she speak now or retreat with all possible haste from the enticing wrong too near. Choose now, her panicked conscience chastised, before he takes it to mind to strip off more of his clothing. Aye, he was a serious threat—not by any wickedness he'd done but by her own wrongful desires. Her initial urge to reach out and hold him in comfort for the anguish green crystal eyes saw clearly beneath his cold facade had long since been overwhelmed by a much stronger urge to step into his embrace for a far different purpose. To negate them both, she purposefully took the offensive.

"So once again you will flee?" It was her hope that this unjustified taunt would pierce his shield of mockery, open it wide enough to ease pressures building within. Yet as dust brown cloth was heedlessly crushed between mighty hands instantly curled into fists, and the powerful muscles of arms and bare chest tightened, she feared her attack too blatant on a man already near the end of his control.

Despite the shock of Alyce's presence, Dare glared down at fingers turned white by the strength of his grip on rough material. This further criticism, criticism by the one whose opinion mattered more than any other's, came near to breaking the bonds of a black temper seldom loosed. Not until he'd regained enough of his hold on the reins of self-discipline did he risk looking up at the fire-vixen who aught know better than to challenge him. Eyes narrowed so completely only a hint of blue could be seen between thick black lashes slowly studied his foolishly goading assailant—a mere two steps distant.

"Flee?" Dare's ice-layered word was an inflexible denial rather than honest question. "I am *not* fleeing! Merely do I relieve my loving family of the bane my presence is upon their celebrations—leave them to joyfully greet the prospect of one 'called to God's cause.'" The frigid curl of his mouth did nothing to lighten a black expression. "Nearer to a eulogy commemorating Gabriel's martyrdom to our sire's obsessive zeal."

In his pain, now too strong to be hidden even to those less sensitive to him than she, Alyce saw that not only had she failed to ease, but had increased Dare's woe. Without foreintent Alyce surrendered to her initial urge to offer physical comfort. Closing her mind against insistent warnings of what other hazards awaited there, she glided forward the slight distance required to wrap slender arms about the powerful man and reach up to gently stroke thick, dark strands as would a mother her bruised child.

Dare was startled by the action of one his opponent only moments before and went utterly motionless. Knocked off kilter by the sudden shift of focus, sane thinking had no chance to temper an immediate response to this forbidden dream come to life. His arms instantly went about the exquisite maiden-wife who leaned lush curves against him apparently without thought of either the temptation she offered or the driving hunger she roused. He desperately wanted to crush her soft body nearer and feed on the aching sweetness of her mouth.

Yet for all that he held Alyce more tightly still, Dare silently commanded himself to damp down flames that set his blood to steaming for this woman who quite literally belonged to another. By her delicious response to their innocent play in Keniver's garden he had recognized a great danger—dishonor for an adulterous wife and a sin sufficiently heinous as to stain even a demon's name. Aye, such remarkable responsiveness boded terrible consequences were he to take advantage of the chaste but vulnerable wife. With that truth acknowledged, he'd vowed that, even were they to meet again, he'd exercise his famous emotional control to prevent it. But now he, a warrior proud of his reputation for being hard and unyielding, feared himself unequal to the fight to withstand a tender foe's effortlessly wielded weapons. He felt himself weakening to the gentle and likely unintended assault of this small, enticing woman.

The moment strong arms closed about her, Alyce knew the error in her deed. Yet instead of pulling away from the devastating man, she welcomed this fierce excitement and with a revealing sigh melted into the cradle of his embrace. Too soon Dare would be gone, and never again would she be allowed to delight in his company, much less stand within the circle of his arms. 'Twas an opportunity too precious to be lightly tossed aside. Casting away all thought of wrong, she recklessly dove headlong into the hungry blaze only he could ignite. Her hands slid down through a night-black mane until her fingers curled in unbidden excitement over broad shoulders. Deeply aware of restrained power in the iron thews under cool satin skin, she rose on tiptoes to offer her mouth.

Rather than accept the gift freely given, with his lips Dare laid a searing trail down the elegant arch of a throat bared by her uptilted chin. So dazed by the wild sparks erupting 'neath his unexpected caress was Alyce that she failed to realize what Dare was about as he efficiently dispensed with both veil and barbette. Richly hued hair, though loosely bound in braids coiled at nape, was thus offered up to flickering candlelight which instantly burned across its bright surface like tongues of flame. Burrowing his fingers into the fire, Dare held her a breath away and lifted his dark head to gaze down into the oval of a sweetly flushed face framed by a fiery riot of curls too short to be restrained. He took terrible pleasure in the unshielded hunger in the passion-hazed depths of green eyes, and when an aching moan escaped from her in a desperate, wordless plea for pleasures withheld, it summoned from him the slow, sensual, and dangerously potent smile Alyce remembered full well.

Alyce's lashes fell in surrender. She struggled to be nearer still. As she yearned toward the kiss she sensed approaching, her thoughts overbrimmed with the memory of their last embrace, searing, exciting, and a wicked wrong she could not repent—not then and not now when again it hovered near.

Drinking in the spring-fresh scent of her, Dare bent to savor the peach wine of her mouth in a succession of slow, brief, tormenting kisses. Alyce bit off a sharp little cry as pleasure cut the ground from under her feet. Heedless to the fading voice of good conscience near-defeated, Dare answered her call by deepening their kiss to a hungry feast. While the last shred of reality slipped unmourned from Alyce's weakened grasp, Dare urged her back until she once more rested against the closed door. Pinning her there with hands planted firmly on either side of her shoulders, he lowered his powerful body into devastatingly intimate contact with hers and gave her the unrestrained ardor of his devouring mouth. Alyce moaned. Shivering uncontrollably, she was thankful for the sturdy oaken planks behind as every lingering fragment of strength deserted her.

"Dare? Are you there, Dare?" Gabriel's soft call came from what could only be a whisper beyond the barred door. "I would speak with you, brother, before you depart. Pray let me in."

The sound sundered the spell, and for several aching moments it froze them in place, although a dark head had lifted abruptly. Eyes smoky with desire and lips throbbing from drugging contact with his, Alyce gazed up at Dare, too lost in a sensual mist to immediately comprehend.

At last, breathing roughly and with near a feverish glitter in blue eyes, Dare gritted out an answer.

"I need a time alone, brother." The words were far harsher than normal. Caught in their passion, they'd clearly missed the sound of Gabriel's attempt to enter his own chamber. The unpleasant prospect of Gabriel discovering Alyce here—alone—with him while the hunger he'd roused was transparent in the helpless longing radiating from her taut body acted like a dousing of ice water. It washed over him and completely flooded away every lingering trace of warmth. He could not, would not, permit Alyce to be shamed by their wrong—one his weakness had allowed—not before anyone, and least of all her loving older and overly pious foster brother.

"I give you my oath I will seek you out before I depart, but go now and permit me this private time."

Even as green eyes struggled to focus on the source of this pleasure distressingly ended, Alyce realized his action was one undertaken to preserve her virtuous name.

While footsteps receded down the corridor, a penetrating azure gaze dropped to the too-tempting vision so near—lips rosed by his kisses and eyes drowsy with a deeper hunger than she'd ever known. But rather than triumph, the sight of his conquest swamped him with a guilt so sharp, it ate into his soul. Soul? As his sire would gladly announce to the world, a soul was a thing no demon possessed. One corner of his mouth lifted involuntarily.

"I am truly the demon my father proclaims me to be. I have been since the moment of my birth, and here I would have proven it yet again. I'd have taken your chastity but for my angelic brother's doubtless heaven-inspired intervention."

To clear it of passion's haze, Alyce shook her head while kindling her temper to refute his bold claim.

Dare's smile took on an honest if cynical amusement at sight of the angry flames beginning to burn in emerald depths. Nonetheless, he put his hand across her lips to forestall the argument clearly forming. He'd already sought to protect her from his brother's discovery of their wrong; he meant also to protect her from himself. Clearly, when exercised alone, his own vows of self-restraint were insufficient. But were the strength of her temper joined to his efforts to brace the wall that must never again be breached . . .

"Aye, here in Gabriel's chamber I would've found pleasure in claiming all your sweet innocence, would've robbed your child-husband of his rights and been gone to another land."

Alyce twisted her head, freeing her mouth from the muffle of his hold to flare back at him. "I wouldn't have let you!"

Dare's mocking laugh was so low, it seemed more a distant rumble. "You protested neither kiss nor caress. I've never needed to compel a woman's response. Yours least of all." He chose the words deliberately to grate upon her pride and add that further layer of defense between them. "Nor would I need coerce you into a fuller feast than we've tasted till now. That, too, you would give freely—were I to forfeit what honor I possess and accept your surrender."

Though disgusted with herself by virtue of the truth in his claim, Alyce couldn't deny it so. Moreover, he wouldn't have been fooled by any attempt she made. She had no doubt he'd experience enough to recognize when a woman had come to the point of yielding whatever he sought.

"Thus, sweeting," Dare ruefully continued, gently brushing a lingering caress over her blush-warmed cheek and down the delicate skin of her long, elegant throat to laces still primly tied at its base, "best you stay as far away from me as you can. Elsewise, no matter the pure intents of either you or I, nothing can prevent us from seeking the fulfillment we both desire."

His expression lost even the false warmth of his cynical smile with the silent acknowledgment of how needless was the warning when within days the width of the sea would separate them, imprisoning them in two different lands.

Whereas she was most oft forced to restrain herself from speaking too hastily, Alyce now found an unaccustomed lack of either words or will to say them. She continued leaning against the door, drawing deep breaths to aid in her battle to tame wildly fluctuating emotions: passion, temper, guilt—and a renewed loneliness looming just beyond the door. To stave off its dismal hold and win one innocent memory more to wield against its assault, she watched as

Dare moved to first pull on the discarded homespun shirt and then, with deceptive ease, don his hauberk's heavy shirt of joined metal links.

She could neither refute his claim of how simple it would be for him to seduce her nor defend her apparently flimsy virtue. Thus she remained mute even when he again took her shoulders in his hands to gently move her aside before snatching up his carelessly packed satchel and departing without a backward glance.

After their garden embrace, she had been right in knowing herself too weak to withstand any more serious assault Dare might make on her virtue, and she *was* fortunate that Gabriel had interrupted their sinful deeds. Why, then, whispered a mocking voice within, could she not deem it a blessing and squelch a traitorous wish to return to that frustrating moment and order Gabriel to begone, leaving them to pleasure in their wickedness?

Alyce was truly horrified by her own assuredly evil thoughts and refused to think further on the pain in this second farewell, pain which would doubtless haunt her during the dark hours of night. She concentrated with fine determination on smoothing her hair and firmly donning the modest restraints of both barbette and veil before peering carefully out a door opened but a crack. With relief, she found the corridor empty and quickly slipped from the chamber. She hurried to the stairwell and descended, unaware of the two men silently waiting in gloom behind the curtain of an alcove built into the width of the stone wall at the corridor's far end.

One, listening for her footsteps to fade, knew her identity; the other thought the female likely to be the ever-obliging serf-girl, Tess. Once the sound of Alyce's descent to re-join the self-involved crowd below fell silent, the pair picked up the threads of their interrupted conversation.

"I thank you for your concern, Dare, but I go with the bishop not for our father's sake alone. I go to fulfill my own close-held dreams." Gabriel steadily met a skeptical blue gaze. "Please understand that even be I doomed to the failure you predict, I am happy to be a small part of the greatest cause in all Christendom."

Though Dare still found it impossible to believe his brother unswayed by their sire's obsession, he restrained his grimace of concern in order to offer leastways a form of the good wishes so earnestly sought. "I will pray for your health."

"Pray rather for our success—'tis much more important than a single man's life."

Dare heard more than a faint echo of their father in the words, and a bleak smile crossed his face, but he nodded. "I will pray, too, that you find the goal you seek in your quest—though we cannot be sure God will hear a demon's prayers."

Gabriel clapped a warm hand over Dare's shoulder and lightly shook him. "You are no more a demon than I."

"Are you so certain?" Dare asked without expression to reveal whether the question was made in earnest or in jest.

"Aye," Gabriel instantly responded with a brilliant smile. "I would swear it on the True Cross."

Dare grinned, too. There could be no more absolute confirmation than that. "Aye, well, go safely on your desert quest, and return to Wythe all of a piece."

The smile faded from Gabriel's open face as he realized how very long it was like to be before he again saw his brother. "After the scene our father subjected you to," he quietly began, "I know you feel you can never return to Wythe—so long as he lives. But once I am its earl, I will welcome you home."

At Gabriel's earnest promise, a rare honest smile warmed Dare's face. He refused to verbally respond, choosing not to hurt his brother by voicing his determination to breach Wythe's boundaries nevermore.

4

Early March of 1233

I would go were it possible, but . . ." From his well-padded chair, Halbert grimaced meaningfully at the thickly bandaged leg resting atop a sturdy stool. "And as Cyril sent his sons to me for fostering, 'twould be an insult were I to send my message on so personal a matter with less than one he knows I value." His gaze rested gently on the one patiently waiting. "Thus, 'tis only right I charge my daughter to go on my behalf and personally place this missive in the earl's hands alone."

Under the emotional control earned and honed by long practice, steady green eyes revealed nothing of the turmoil inside as Alyce calmly nodded. Castle Wythe . . . a destination that would never be her choice. For all that Keniver bordered Wythe lands, as well as Pembroke, in her score and four years she had visited there only that single time. And it had ended in one of the most desolate experiences of her life. She dreaded a return to the castle where memories years old but far from forgot would doubtless leap to life and remind her of all that could never be hers, remind her of an oath made but never fulfilled. Furthermore, the circumstances requiring this journey increased the grimness of its prospect, proving as it did that Wythe Castle still languished in the depths of an unending grief.

You are a wicked, selfish female! Alyce's well-trained conscience lashed out, and guilt rose on a bleak gray tide of remorse for self-centered thoughts. Here she stood thinking of naught but herself while her father was in pain and the people of Wythe suffered under a far greater loss than any she had been called to bear. Thank the Merciful Lord, it was true that she'd never been called to endure the death of one beloved. Not that she didn't mourn for gentle Gabriel herself. She assuredly did, but it could never be as deep as the sorrow of a parent. With that thought, another followed as surely as night the day . . . and as black. Another wrongful thought it was, but still she wondered how much of Earl Cyril's distress was grief and how much guilt when the loss could have been avoided had he paid heed to Dare's warning.

"As you will, Father." Alyce reached out to accept the folded and sealed parchment from Halbert's hand. Her father had long since ceased urging her to be like any other woman, ceased lecturing her on the need to restrain an unruly nature. An end likely earned as such remonstrances were no longer necessary. She'd learned the lessons full well and had no need to remind herself of the overriding importance in being both a dutiful daughter and the submissive creature all females were born to be—leastways insofar as other eyes could see. Between overdeveloped conscience and rebellious nature, wars were wont to erupt and viciously prick beneath a cool demeanor.

Lifting the dull gray wool of her gown, Alyce gracefully turned toward the solar's outgoing door. Successful though Alyce had become in presenting a demure facade to the world, she constantly failed in quieting the voice of the fiery spirit inside. Face toward the unseeing doorway, she grimaced, unable to still the voice demanding to know what wretched imp of fate had leaped from forest shadows to spook her father's horse. 'Twas that foul deed which had abruptly sent the man to the frozen ground, ripped a gash in his leg, and now forced her to undertake this unwelcome mission. A mission with a destination where doubtless she'd be no more welcome than the message she carried, no more welcome than Dare had been when, near six years gone by, both had stepped within its impressive ramparts.

The same irrepressible spirit complaining about the circumstances making her trip necessary boldly suggested that this would be a fine chance to escape Walter's endless company, leastways for a pleasant if brief time. The man had long since returned from his training with the Bishop of Winchester. It had come as no great surprise to Alyce, who had thought Walter utterly unsuited for a life of self-denial in the first instance. Her father, as a soldier above all else and having no training to either read or write, had welcomed Walter. As a trusted family member and now skilled scribe, he'd given his wife's brother the position as Castle Keniver's clerk. Thus her father was happy. Walter was happy. Alyce rather less so. He was her friend, loyal and considerate to a fault. He was also the veritable shadow Dare had once named him, and after years of freedom from his constant hovering, she found his friendship more a weight to bear than a gift to treasure. That was an awful thing to say, her conscience instantly rebuked. In the same moment her wicked spirit shot back—mayhap, but a truth which 'twould be a lie to deny, and surely to lie would be the greater sin.

Alyce purposefully turned her thoughts from the subject of Walter with intent to mentally add to that somewhat uncommendable incentive another more praiseworthy. This visit would be her best and perhaps only opportunity to make progress toward fulfilling the oath she'd given when last at Wythe. Green eyes narrowed with new resolve as she moved purposefully forward to prepare for the task ahead.

It seemed to Dare that the parchment flattened against the rough planks of a crude table had a life of its own, rippling as firelight danced across its slightly crinkled surface. Impervious to the winter chill clutching the whole of this ancient stone keep high in the Welsh mountains, he stared at his first communication from the lady of Castle Wythe in the score and more of years since he'd initially been exiled from its noble walls, cast off like so much unwanted refuse. After William Marshal's death, Dare had returned to Britain with Richard. Here Richard had been invested as Earl of Pembroke in his older brother's stead. That a similar event had befallen Dare, leaving him heir to a neighboring earldom, had in no way lessened his commitment to Richard.

The bitter parody of a smile curled Dare's lips. He'd no reason to trust the sender of this appeal, no reason to care if its claim of near ruin was truth. By law the Wythe heir he might now be, but one rejected long before his right to inherit had become fact. Furthermore, for the wound of Gabriel's loss the uncomfortable truth that he was the only surviving son provided more salt to increase pain than healing balm of possession.

Richard Marshal straightened to his full height, having leaned over his seated knight's broad shoulder to read the missive from above. "Seems your sire has retreated too far from the secular world to give good care to your inheritance." Richard had used two justifications for his possibly selfish acceptance of Dare's continuing aid in the fight against the Welsh threat of Llewelyn. First, Dare not only had no desire to go home but rather had a positive distaste for the prospect; second, Llewelyn was as much a threat to Wythe as to Pembroke. But now . . .

"What reason has he to see Wythe well kept when his beloved son is no longer its heir?" Dare's words were as cold and flat as untrammeled stretches of snow-covered fields, while hiding beneath lay deeply buried pain struck anew. Blue-ice eyes stared at the unwelcome summons without seeing the words. His certainty of the crusade's ignominious failure had proven true. But his concern over Gabriel's ineffective military might had been shown more a jest, a bitter and painful jest. No infidel sword had Gabriel met. Nay, 'twas the crusaders' pestilence which claimed so many that had struck Gabriel down even before the legion reached the embarkation port of Tyre. Dare permitted few things to matter enough to see him hurt, yet the needless end, half a decade past, of that gentle, idealistic fool had accomplished that and more.

A perceptive man, Richard recognized the distress behind Dare's apparent disinterest. What awful burdens fathers could lay upon their sons. Earl Cyril of Wythe, from an unnatural hatred, had cast the darkest of shadows over Dare's path while Richard's own father, from love, had done much the same. Deeming Richard a sickly child and frail adolescent, he'd protected his second son by refusing to see him at risk and had disallowed his participation in the pursuit of martial skills his peers enjoyed so well. Richard had not been trained to arms until after his arrival in France. Richard took great pride in having then proven himself so skilled, he'd earned command over the king of France's army, and only a year past had faced down the English king with the threat of force. Proof, he felt, it was best to meet and master filial impediments. He had; Dare could.

"Still, you must go and attempt to right your father's wrong." Richard would much regret the loss to his army of this warrior of uncommon strength, valor, and loyalty—the loss most of all of a friend. Personal wishes aside, it was time for Dare to establish his rights. Though he had not earlier urged Dare to claim his position as inheritor of Wythe, here was proof that the heir's personal intervention was urgently needed.

Firelight gleamed on raven-dark hair as Dare slowly shook his head. "I will never be welcome there, no matter these words of desperation."

"Your mother has called for your return." Richard was not easily waylaid. Despite wild rumors and cold cynicism of his manner, Dare was as much a man of honor as was he himself. And no man of honor would turn aside from his responsibilities, from those dependent upon him as now dependent upon Dare were Wythe and all who dwelled upon it.

"She begs for your aid, and"—a mild note of reproof mingled with calmly stated facts as Richard circled round the table to face the seated man—"as her plea is for the lands which will inevitably be yours, you must go."

Mother? Not by the smallest flicker was emotion betrayed on Dare's impassive face. The term roused in him only the memory of a cold back ever turned to the boy he'd been, a vague shadow in the background of his visit to plea for Gabriel's reconsideration of the ill-fated quest.

Winning no response from Dare, Richard continued and his tone hardened to drive home one point important above all others. "'Tis your inheritance." Suddenly Richard bent to slap hands palm flat on the table and rested atop them a scant distance from an unflinching Dare. "The land is you! You can no more turn your back on it than you were able to halt love for a brother." He'd no need to mention the silent tears, as unnatural as rain abruptly spouting from granite, which he'd seen Dare shed over Gabriel's death.

The fervency in the earl's voice and unwavering gaze stripped away Dare's carefully constructed shield to lay bare a long-denied reality. One which could not be changed by the pain of a brother's death, the hate of a father, or even the fear of the people of Wythe. He *was* the heir, and Wythe *would* be his—nothing and no one, save the king, could change that truth.

A white grin flashed across Richard's weather-darkened face. He was pleased that this dark knight was beginning to accept the destiny awaiting him.

Dare responded with a smile full of self-mockery. Richard had instinctively hit upon a nerve buried in the hidden depths of his soul. In the whole of his life, Dare had truly belonged nowhere and to no one. Far more than for either meaningless wealth or position, he longed to possess a home, *his* ancestral home. 'Twas a secret desire never wholly admitted to himself, and one he'd never knowingly have revealed to another.

Richard broke the silence. "Go quickly, and take Thomas with you." In answer to the wordless question of raised black brows, he shrugged. "He'd be useless to me with you gone. I fear, distracted by his concern for you, he'd do something foolish or, worse, dangerous to himself and us all. Always he worries for you—like a mother hen for her chick."

Dare's smile warmed to an honest amusement at the thought of Sir Thomas Orlegh's short, compact body as anything so harmless. In truth, it was powerful and possessed of a speed and ferocity of action which had surprised many an opponent, with dangerous results.

"Ah." Richard saw Dare's skepticism. "Have you never seen a hen whose brood was threatened? Vicious!" He shook his head in mock terror. "Vicious!"

Dare laughed outright, a rare, deep rumble. Although he couldn't see Thomas as a mother hen, he and that knight shared a friendship stronger than any Dare had found with another. They had since the day they'd met. Before becoming a knight in the garrison at Pembroke and, as part of its guard, accompanying young Richard to the French lands his father had intended his second son to inherit, Thomas had fostered at Wythe under Earl Rhodare.

With a more avid interest than he'd ever admit, Dare had listened to the man's many stories about the prosperous and agreeable place Wythe had been. He'd listened even more intently to tales of the esteem and even love in which its people had held the just and honorable Earl of Wythe first termed Demon. The image of Sir Thomas Orlegh's round face and ever pleasant expression warmed Dare. He welcomed the prospect of the knight's companionship on the bleak journey that lay ahead.

"Enough!" Though quietly said, the command in Lady Elinor's single word cracked through the crisp air of a cloudy day. "To some small measure I can excuse your impertinent prying as an inadvertent discourtesy possibly born of concern for a foster brother. And—" she paused while her elegant jawline tightened, apparently with the effort of will needed to hide a growing distaste "—mayhap some portion of the blame lies with the sad lack of motherly influence upon your upbringing, but . . ."

The chill civility of the polite reprimand brought its target to a halt, unmindful of the steep drop from the near-lying edge of Castle Wythe's high rampart walkway. That the noblewoman who spoke was the very image of everything Alyce's father had for years sought to see her become made the brittle rebuke all the more effective. Alyce waited unmoving for Lady Elinor to pause and turn her way. How could Dare's own mother possibly endorse (leastwise by her silence) Earl Cyril's wicked treatment of their son? It was a question she'd asked herself many, many times, but this was the first time she'd had the opportunity to speak of the matter with Lady Elinor. And she *had* been tactful, restraining the demand for explanation fair burning unspoke on her tongue while gently questioning her hostess's attitude toward Dare. Only this far had she gotten on her vowed quest to lift the veil of Cyril's curse and free Dare's name from its assuredly unjust stain.

"'Tis a private matter." Although Lady Elinor's deep brown eyes narrowed, her expression was utterly devoid of emotion as she turned toward the impertinent visitor to conclude her lecture. "And one on which you've no right to concern yourself."

Alyce saw in her companion's mien the proof of from whom Dare had either inherited or learned the ability to freeze emotion. His mother was ice clear through. Bending her modestly covered head, Alyce glared at the dangerous layer of rocks littering the narrow strip of walkway beneath her feet. The woman's uncaring attitude earned a reverse response from Alyce, whose muffled but fiery spirit burned brighter in Dare's support.

"To ensure you take my meaning, I will state it more plainly." Lady Elinor's voice was implacable. "The relationship between we and Dare is one so personal that, I am certain, none of us would appreciate your meddling. Thus, I warn you not to interfere in matters you can't possibly understand."

Alyce's temper broke its bonds and flared in defense of the rejected child, now wronged heir. "'Struth. How a mother could allow her own son to be so wickedly abused, I don't understand and hope I never shall."

Lady Elinor stood impervious to the heated attack, her expression so cold, even the fiery blast of Alyce's temper had no visible effect. After several long, silent moments during which Alyce suffered a growing embarrassment for the ill-bred attack on her hostess, Lady Elinor inclined her head in the briefest of acknowledgments. She then calmly turned and resumed a steady pace, leading the way in crossing toward the next corner tower. Although Alyce did not regret her defense of Dare, she had no choice but to follow behind like a disciplined mongrel.

Slowly walking the ramparts of Castle Wythe, neither woman recognized the day's piercing cold for more than the chill within or noticed two horsemen lingering in the gloom of the distant forest edge.

The sight meeting the eyes of a man returning for only the second time in his adult life was familiar. And yet it seemed strangely like a pale shadow of the original. Castle walls were somehow shorter as if crumbling under the weight of heavily overcast skies. Riding nearer, Dare saw that, having long gone unrepaired, they were in truth crumbling. He winced at the plain fact that the once mighty fortress had fallen into such sad disrepair, likely a single concerted attack would bring it down. Moreover, though the bleak winter landscape provided only uncertain proof of infertile ground, its rows were not furrows but ruts hardened in unplowed ground, thus showing no sign of having been earnestly cultivated in many seasons.

This time, as the last, the outer bailey gate was unguarded, though clearly not to facilitate a celebration. Riding betwixt inner and outer walls, they found the village near empty. Earlier filled with content and well-cared-for townspeople, its inhabitants now had more the look of scarecrows, ghosts with hollow, lifeless eyes and gaunt bodies.

Riding beside his tight-lipped friend, Thomas, too, was appalled by the ghastly state into which this host of so many warm memories had descended. The lights of laughter seldom long absent from his eyes went utterly dark with dread that he'd find an equal disillusionment in a most specific vision inside. He and Dare had talked often of Wythe, but there were some memories he held private, some hopes he could barely admit and never share.

The dark heir to this abused fiefdom led his equally somber companion through an unbarred portal in the inner bailey wall. They cantered across a deserted courtyard to halt at the foot of the broad wooden steps leading into the main tower. Leather creaked as Dare dismounted. He handed his destrier's reins to an elderly serf who'd suddenly materialized, and silently acknowledged the recognition causing the man's wariness.

"Aye." A slight smile crossed Dare's face as he mockingly confirmed what must be the man's worst fear. "The Demon returns."

Ever a measure of Thomas's feelings—from merriment to fury—bushy tufts of gold and silver lowered over fiercely glaring eyes in wordless punishment of the craven serf. Dismounting, he, too, dropped his steed's reins into the man's hand. Dare aught reprove the insolent worm for his ill welcome of the fiefdom's heir, not jest with him.

Ignoring the disapproving frown his friend shot at his back, Dare strode up the stairs.

Alyce's silent gasp went unnoticed by either the men below or the woman standing rigidly at her side. God was punishing her! Only twice had she come to this castle. Only twice in her life . . . just as Dare had returned to his ancestral home but two times since childhood. Had to be more than a mere coincidence that their rare visits occurred simultaneously. Though the pleasure refusing to be tamed within would persist in naming it a sweet boon of fate, 'twas assuredly a punishment. The brief joy of his presence would inevitably be followed by endless days of desolate gloom intensified. And what if the devil should join the assault and throw full in her path the blue-eyed temptation which experience had proven was impossible for her to resist? What greater guilt would follow?

To drive wild conjectures away, Alyce shook her head so emphatically, the motion near loosed the constraints of veil and barbette. She whirled about and hastened to the corner tower without thought of the companion left behind. Rushing down the spiral stairway, for once impervious to the nameless terrors in its darkness, she breathlessly reached the foot of the steps at almost the same moment Dare strode from the long entrance tunnel. As he entered a great hall poorly lit by two malodorous resin torches and an ill-tended fire in the massive fireplace, Alyce solemnly watched. In the six years since last they'd met, he had become harder, more intimidating—and even more devastatingly handsome.

Unaware of either the woman stepping back into the shadows of the stairwell arch or the one more sedately descending to join her, Dare passed them by. He moved slowly into a hall darker, colder than he remembered, and so vast that the aging man seated at center of the empty high table on its far side appeared to have shrunk to the size of a frail child. Untidy white strands of thinning hair, tangled on narrow shoulders, did not stir as Dare approached. His father either had not heard the sound or did not care that someone drew near.

"Father." Dare began speaking firmly to draw the plainly disoriented man's attention. "I would speak privately with you."

"Nay!" An abnormal flush suffused papery white cheeks as a startled Cyril half rose and then fell heavily back into his high-backed chair. "You're dead, dead for years, dead, dead, dead and burning in hell." Arms wrapped tight about his narrow chest, the wizened frame rocked from side to side while faded eyes gleaming with unnatural lights seared over Dare.

Dare recognized the source of the man's error. Even his own father thought him truly the reincarnation of the first Demon. "Your sire is dead, but not your son."

Cyril turned his head sideways and leaned closer, examining the speaker from the corners of narrowed eyes. "Son? You are not my son. My son is dead."

"Gabriel is dead, but I live." Standing calm before this parody of the cruel but clever man he remembered too well, Dare spoke softly. "Your younger son lives."

"Not so, not so." Cyril resumed his rocking. "My son is dead and I won't let you inherit what was his. Let it rot, I will. Let it rot." His unfocused gaze fell to the floor as he repeated the words over and over like a litany of doom.

"Sire." Plainly Gabriel's death had unhinged his father's mind, and he must patiently seek a path through the labyrinth of the man's confusion to win the goal he sought. "No matter your distaste for me, think of the people of Wythe, all those others you rob by robbing me."

Cyril suddenly leaped to his feet, filled with the strength of his fury. "Why should I have care if the Demon's worldly sphere falls to nothing? It *is* nothing and you've no right to interfere—not yet, not until its earl is dead." He looked wildly around at the growing group of curious people drawn uninvited to the hall. As unkempt as their abode, they surreptitiously watched while their lord roared at his dark and silent foe. "I am the living earl, and until I am dead, the Demon cannot claim his mortal realm."

Dare froze in self-defense against the hate in the vitriolic words. His chin lifted and eyes narrowed to prevent the betraying revelation of any small hint of emotion.

In one moment Cyril swelled with triumph. In the next he clutched his chest. As if pierced by the invisible sword of Dare's ice blue eyes, he fell across the table, knocking a metal goblet down to bounce across the floor below and scattering the remnants of a half-eaten meal.

Dare instantly leaped up on the dais, rolled his father over, and laid fingers against a withered throat in a search for signs of life—however weak. There were none. Dare glanced at a woman who'd moved to the fallen man's side as quickly as he. Face deathly pale, his mother stood in a silence seemingly fraught with accusations while behind her gathered all who'd been audience to the scene. When his full attention shifted to the crowd, as if of one mind, they cringed from his obviously too powerful gaze. This craven retreat left but a single slight figure to face him unafraid.

Alyce's only thought was for Dare and how he must feel—mayhap not pain of loss but doubtless shock and needless guilt. Green eyes melted to a warm and gentle mist, and the compassion pouring from them amazed Dare so completely, he didn't think to question her presence. Rather, to this open faith freely given, he responded with a somber smile of gratitude.

While attention centered upon the Demon, Thomas stepped forward to lightly touch Lady Elinor's shoulder. She glanced behind and up into the eyes of a long absent friend. In her shock for the event just past, she made no demurral when the stalwart man wrapped a strong arm about her shoulders, providing a physical support much needed as the stability of her knees threatened to give way.

After a long and oppressive silence, Dare moved into the breach and took command of the disorganized demesne and its confused people. He efficiently dispatched first a messenger to carry the news to Henry's court and then, setting aside the castle's ancient chaplain, another to summon a churchman of sufficient rank to oversee his father's burial with the respect due a noble of his status.

Standing in the background feeling utterly useless, Alyce watched as Dare next turned to firmly remind Wythe's servants that life must go onward for the living and they'd be best served by a resumption of normal daily tasks. Admiring his calm assumption of Wythe's control, she observed all of his actions while Dare's friend, with Lady Elinor at his side, carried the dead earl's frail body to its bed. But more she saw as well—serfs casting sidelong glances of fear upon Dare and surreptitiously signing the cross as he passed.

Alyce's indignation over their unpleasant actions grew apace and she glared at the last to cross himself. The subject of her disapproval, a youngster midway between child and man, flushed but mutinously set his chin. His reaction increased Alyce's ire. She refused to look away from the culprit and lost sight of Dare until a broad, mail-clad chest suddenly appeared a mere handsbreadth from her nose. Discovering herself unexpectedly confronted with the man she'd watched near without pause since he'd entered the hall, Alyce drew a deep breath while wildly summoning the courage to look up. No matter the events just passed, when he stood so near, her heart pounded and her thoughts filled with the dangerously potent memory of intimacies once shared. Warning herself to keep her composure and meet this shockingly near focus of too many wicked dreams as coolly as a well-bred woman aught face any man, green eyes half-shuttered by thick lashes ascended shining metal links outlining the strength of his chest and strong column of his throat to— Green eyes abruptly widened. Mentally prepared to meet the power of his warm attractions, she was unpleasantly startled by Dare's complete lack of emotion. A lack not merely in his usual impassive expression but in remarkable eyes containing neither ice nor flame, and closed against her.

"I've ordered the men of your escort to make preparations for your return journey to Keniver."

Dare had seen Alyce's green fire eyes punishing the foolish boy. With the certainty that she'd put herself at risk and increased the difficulty of his already overwhelming task, he'd instantly stamped down the pleasure her wordless defense of him had wrought. Her temper would do nothing to endear either her or him to the people who believed him capable of killing his own father. Until he'd established firm control over the people and lands of his inheritance, no one could be assured of safety within the boundaries of Wythe, and he wanted Alyce away before any harm befell her.

Alyce blinked rapidly. Initially she heard less the meaning of the words than the tone in which they'd been said. Never before had Dare spoken so coldly to her. To others but never to her. Had he, beneath his impenetrable stone facade, been wounded more deeply by the death of an unloving sire than she'd thought likely? Whatever its source, she didn't want to leave him here and almost alone to meet the fear and even hostility of so many.

"But I could remain and help with—" Her voice was quiet and full of honest concern.

"Nay, you could not." Dare interrupted, mouth turning down.

Alyce felt frozen in place by the force of his apparent disgust. In truth, disgust it was, but for himself. Dare meant to protect Alyce from the danger in this volatile situation on unsettled lands and among fear-filled people. Protect her from the people, aye, but more to protect her from another and too likely greater danger—himself. In the midst of such cold condemnation he greatly feared the warmth of her compassion would melt through his shield of honor and weaken him to the temptation of a deed he'd sworn he would not do. He feared he would succumb to Alyce's unintended lures and claim the sweet solace he had spent too many years longing to possess.

In blue-ice eyes barely visible between thick black lashes

Alyce saw how useless was her plea to remain. She'd worried that the devil would put Dare's temptation to sweet, sinful pleasures in her path and had turned her will toward refusing its call, leaving her woefully ill prepared to meet his rejection. Yet what matter whether temptation or rejection? Its end was the same—an anguish that would surely ache all the days of her life.

5

If silence doesn't overtake that wretched woman soon, I'll . . . I'll . . .

Alyce clenched her teeth, striving to prevent the eruption of dangerously building irritation while resolutely averting the green fire of her gaze from a sobbing Sybillene. Saints' Tears! They'd all been under incredible strain these two days since her father had been charged with treason and hauled away to be imprisoned in the king's tower. But only Sybillene could or would use the ghastly deed as excuse to win attention for herself. Even young Hal, while his mother skillfully played the unjustly injured wife, bravely held his sturdy ten-year-old frame upright.

Sitting atop one packed and closed wicker trunk resting at the edge of the piled many waiting near the castle's outgoing door, Alyce gripped its edges so tightly, their pattern threatened to be permanently imprinted on her palms. She refused to so much as glance toward the deliberately staged, heartrending sight of fair femininity weakly leaning against a slender brother. Aye, she inwardly sniffed, let it be ineffectual Walter who consoled the calculating woman. In the next moment she not only decided 'twas more than what such a false display deserved but that by insulting Walter's abilities, she'd been as odious as Sybillene. Glaring at an inoffensive slipper, she ignored not only her piteously weeping stepmother but the small, self-important knight standing with his back to the door while outlining their imminent journey to join King Henry's ever-migrating court.

"We should, barring unexpected weather delays, within a fortnight meet with the king's court at Wulfstan." Sir Lester's uncomfortable gaze shifted between the wailing wife and defiant daughter of the traitorous baron. It took all his proudly held fortitude to keep from quailing at the prospect of dragging these two blatantly warring females (and the elder's dependents) on the mud-mired journey ahead. Pray God 'twould take no longer to reach the fiefdom of the noble who next, by royal command, would be "privileged" to entertain both the king and the whole of his entourage. Privileged? The cruel twist this thought placed on his mouth went unseen by ladies preoccupied with ill thoughts of their own. Such good fortune, he knew of a certainty, had near beggared more than one host thus blessed.

A fortnight, hah! As she clamped her lips together to restrain a cheerless smile, Alyce's intent stare shifted to the hall's rush-strewn floor. Clearly Sir Lester had caught no glimpse of her "poor, weak" stepmother's true demanding nature. But he would learn. To travel so far north with one as determinedly helpless as Sybillene would take far longer. By the speed with which her father had been arrested and control taken of lands then held forfeit to the crown, these royal minions had proven that they could move with great haste when commanded. Yet during the next step of their task, that of seeing the baron's dependents not only evicted but taken into the king's ward, they'd find what a delay-filled burden the former lady of Keniver could be.

Fine brows scowled above green eyes. Doubtless for the bestowal of a long-term income derived from Keniver, King Henry thought to win immediate payment in the gold much needed to replenish royal coffers. Gold given, some noble would be granted Keniver's income in further exchange for his vow to accept the responsibility of the disgraced baron's family members—until a more permanent resolution could be arranged.

"By what right do you take these people into the king's custody?"

The sound of the low voice pierced Alyce's gloomy vision of the future and set her heart to thumping erratically. Months had passed since last she'd heard its unmistakable cadences, months since she'd been politely but firmly sent from Wythe and returned here to her family home—home no more.

Sir Lester's mouth dropped open. He whirled toward a heavy oak door opened wide. In its frame, silhouetted against the murky light of bleak day beyond, stood a tall, intimidating form. The unnoticed arrival of a stranger was startling, but even more so was the audacity of any man either so brave or so foolish as to question a royal decree. Lester wore their monarch's colors and crest. Thus he was certain the intruder must know he represented the crown and his actions performed by royal command. Yet before he could sputter an answer, the dark newcomer stepped farther into a hall poorly lit by the faltering flames of its open central hearth.

"Lady Alyce is a woman wed and by rights should be safely delivered into the care of her husband's family." Dare was amused by the flustered royal deputy plainly horrified at the mere notion of a bold challenge to their sovereign's privilege to command what he would. Accustomed to doing, leastways being credited with doing, the unthinkable, and too familiar with the fallibility of nobles and even of kings, Dare had on occasion enjoyed shocking men incapable of taking like risks, men like this pompous little puppet who danced at King Henry's demand.

Complete and unwavering attention fully claimed by the one unexpectedly come to intercede for them, Alyce had none to spare for the short, broad, and barrel-chested knight taking Dare's place in blocking the light falling through an open door. Caught by the miracle of the devastating earl's arrival and, like sun-parched earth beneath life-restoring rain, soaking in the gift of his presence, she failed to comprehend the first exchange. But when he spoke her name, Alyce's attention focused on the words, and it was she who immediately responded.

"I am told my husband's family made no reply to the news of either my father's arrest or that I was to be taken into the king's ward." Thinking only of the underlying thread of contemptuous amusement in Sir Lester's announcement of this fact, her words were stoically delivered. Their choice plainly revealed the distance they wished to place between themselves and a traitor. When Dare's penetrating eyes shifted to settle upon her like a hawk sighting prey, she felt pierced by guilt for a wrong committed, and blushed. She had criticized her parents by marriage, and through them her husband. 'Twas, she'd been warned by her father many a time, an insult no man would forgive and a wrong no woman dare commit.

Her attention dropped to the taupe daygown sensibly selected to withstand the rigors of travel. She grew further depressed by an awareness of looking less than her best. But what matter in that? The man had, it seemed, come to save them from their greedy king's hold, yet he'd immediately sought to be rid of her—again.

Dare gave a grim smile to the top of Alyce's bent head, swathed as ever in a voluminous veil. By the glimpse of bright rose blessing her creamy cheeks and her quickly averted gaze, it seemed certain the rejection he'd delivered at Wythe had been all too effective, and she emotionally retreated from him now for fear of another.

Sir Lester had initially been cowed by the interfering stranger's aura of danger. However, during the moments of unnatural silence following Lady Alyce's speech (a quiet wherein even the traitor's wife ceased her crying), he recovered a sufficient measure of his dignity to attempt regaining control over the confrontation. Loudly clearing his throat, he purposely drew the intruder's attention. Then, chin lifted so high it threatened to break his neck, he strove to look down his nose at the much taller man again facing him. Ignoring the discomfort in his unnatural stance, he embarked upon a sneering rebuttal to the man's assault on royal authority. "Once its lord was charged with treason, all Keniver lands and possessions fell forfeit to the crown."

Studying his absurdly self-important foe, from the sparse hair barely covering a shining pate to toes protected by fine boots less suited to travel than attempts to impress, Dare wondered if the man truly was controlled by King Henry. 'Twas more likely that Sir Lester, though perhaps not admitted to himself, acted by the will of the man all England knew controlled the king—the Bishop of Winchester. Even discounting the bishop's part in Gabriel's death, Dare had no liking for the Frenchman who'd seen to it that all English advisors to the crown were replaced by his own countrymen. If his hand were at the root of the whole, it would reveal leastways one purpose behind assuredly false charges against Halbert Bohan for the villainy it was. The bishop's illegitimate son was ever greedy for additional properties to join the vast list already in his possession by way of an indulgent father.

Blue eyes peered steadily down until the smaller man shifted uneasily. Sir Lester mentally struggled to pull about himself the threatened cloth of a courage flimsier than he'd ever suspected and reinforced his self-confidence with an ill-considered disdain for the other. *He* was the king's man, Sir Lester reassured himself. *He* was in charge, not this unknown and obviously none too clever intruder.

"Therefore"—with a patronizing air designed to put the intruder firmly in his subordinate place, the king's knight deigned to explain what should surely be clear, even to a half-wit—"those who belong to the disgraced baron pass into the king's charge just as do all widows, heirs, and heiresses."

"By these words do you mean to tell us that Baron Halbert is dead?" Dare's eyes instantly narrowed to glittering weapons.

The question brought a fresh bout of sobs from Sybillene while Sir Lester's rash and belittling assessment of the man faltered.

"Nay!" Stumbling over the words, Lester hastened to

clarify his meaning. "Nay, he is a prisoner. A prisoner and very much alive."

The cold smile Dare gave the other was a blow in itself, and when he spoke, though the words were calm and reasonable, his voice was dangerously quiet. "So long as Halbert lives, his wife is no widow and not in the king's ward. Likewise, if Keniver is forfeit, then Halbert's children are not now nor ever likely to be heirs to anything. Thus, by right of the Great Charter, the king can have no lawful claim upon them."

Despite a vexation roused by the man's irrefutable logic, Sir Lester recognized the folly of continuing to argue a lost point. Only could he reinforce the one unalterable fact.

"They must all leave Keniver lands." An air of triumph saturated the stern statement.

"Aye." Dare's humorless smile deepened while an errant breeze slipped past Thomas's bulk in the open door to tease a calf-length cloak until it rippled like black wings.

Though he was annoyed, Lester's uneasiness was much increased by his intimidating opponent's calm agreement and, worse, amusement.

Dare suffered no remorse for unsettling the pompous knight's assumption of superiority. "And so they will. I mean to escort them to Castle Wythe, where there is room enough and more."

The king's deputy looked about to argue the right in his plan, but Dare lifted a gauntleted hand, forcing silence.

"There the ladies will be under the care of my mother, the Dowager Countess of Wythe." Seeing the shorter man silently gulp with the sudden realization that he'd all but openly insulted an earl, Dare found an unfamiliar difficulty in restraining a grin. "'Tis, as you must admit, a far more appropriate destination for these wellborn ladies than our bachelor king's court."

Alyce was no less shocked by Dare's plan than the king's knight, and again painfully clutched the edges of the wicker chest. By way of itinerant peddlers and the ever healthy gossip vine twining across the border between Keniver and Wythe, she knew of Dare's earnestly waged battle, one at least as fierce as any combat he had earlier survived. His back was turned to her, leaving her free to openly study its powerful breadth and steady her anxieties with visual reassurance of a strength equal to any threat. He was pure muscle and threatening grace backed by a sharp mind and force of will surely capable of overcoming all challenges. Leastwise she had and would continue to pray 'twas so.

Yet his current conflict involved a far more insidious foe, and against it she feared his undoubted physical strength would be of little value. To win this war he must, despite his wicked reputation, prove himself worthy to hold the loyalty and allegiance of Wythe's people. Moreover, he must overcome formidable odds and restore to his fiefdom the prosperity its previous earl had near destroyed. Tucking invisible escaping curls back under her barbette's restraints, Alyce dropped her gaze to the floor and blindly frowned at unmoving rushes once more. All the difficulties Dare faced contributed to her amazement that he was willing to assume the added burden of they who were now branded with the shameful wrong charged to their lord. She uneasily feared their presence in his castle would be a hindrance on the path toward the goals he sought.

Unaware of worries building in the woman behind, Dare shrugged and finished defining his intentions to the plainly defeated man standing mute before him. "Then, as time permits, I'll see Alyce safely delivered into the bosom of her husband's family."

"Surely you won't submit to the will of this man?" The whisper slipped into Alyce's ear like slow-acting poison. "A man near proven to be responsible for your father's plight."

Deeply intent upon her own qualms over the proposed journey, Alyce failed to immediately comprehend Walter's quiet, persuasive words.

Dare heard them with the clarity of a great bell tolling doom. He turned from Sir Lester, glanced briefly at Alyce, who seemed surprised as she looked up at the slender figure bending near, then the full force of his intimidating attention assaulted the source of this unforeseen attack. Walter suggested that upon him lay the blame for the ill which had befallen Halbert. What justification did he have? 'Twas a serious accusation, which demanded explanation. Particularly so when for weeks Dare had half expected to be charged with treason himself. Indeed, he'd expected it since the day not long past when Richard of Pembroke had been named traitor for leading a good many English barons in a quest to see the king's French advisors put aside and Englishmen restored to such positions of power. Dare had not been a part of Richard's band, but only because Wythe demanded his full attention. Nonetheless, for his friendship with Richard alone, doubtless the bishop would relish first the seizing of his inheritance and then either his reduction to mere knight or the greater pleasure of seeing him dead.

Walter had regrouped after a terrible blow to his plans, but a desperate need to win this bout bolstered his never strong courage, and defiantly straightening his inconsequential figure, he made a bold claim.

"I am the one best-suited to accompany Alyce to her husband's lands. Or, if not there, then surely 'twould be better were she to retire to her own lands, the lands of her dowry."

Walter's interference in this matter not of his concern, atop the dangerous accusation he'd made, threatened to sunder the tight bonds restraining Dare's black temper. His hands curled into fists and he took a step forward.

"'Tis not Alyce's choice nor yet Walter's." The announcement calmly delivered by an abruptly composed Sybillene distracted them all and brought Dare's imminent attack to a sudden halt.

"I am Alyce's stepmother, the mother of the Keniver heir, and Walter's older sister." Sybillene's usual coy softness had hardened into an implacable resolve. "Therefore, the choice is mine, and by my choice the Earl of Wythe's offer of hospitality will gladly be accepted."

A veil of submissive femininity again descended over Sybillene's perfect features while weak firelight earned renewed vigor in gleaming over polished gold braids neatly coiled. Leaving her young son in the shadows behind, she glided forward to lay a possessive hand on an arm still tightly flexed and smile up into pale blue eyes with a flirtatious batting of lashes.

At sight of the beauty near clinging to the handsome earl, the initial surprise on Lester's face turned to a knowing leer. But these bold deeds taken by a fragile and grieving wife suddenly transformed into seductive siren roused deeper suspicions in Alyce. Although Sybillene's provocative advances to the darkly attractive noble could be no surprise to her who had seen the woman in his bed, the lady of Keniver's uncharacteristic action in overruling her brother opened the door to all manner of dark thoughts.

Had the whole situation been prearranged to give her father's wife into Dare's hands? Alyce had refused to believe the evidence seeming to prove Dare responsible for Keniver's troubles. Now she pinched soft peach lips tight in mute resistance to silent whispers of unwelcome doubts stealthily slipping into her mind. Had her faith been misplaced? Had Dare and Sybillene plotted her father's imprisonment to make this move to Wythe possible? Dare wouldn't have come for her sake. He'd proven that by rejecting her company when last they'd been together. Moreover, he'd already sought to see the king's man deliver her to the parents of her husband. Failing in that, he'd sworn to see the deed done himself. Apparently he'd perform any feat for the sake of being rid of her.

Walter recognized leastways the doubts at the core of Alyce's confusion and was pleased. He'd lost this skirmish, yet with the help of powerful friends, there could be no question but that he'd win the war—so long as he kept his secrets to the last.

Dare, too, saw the confused muddle of suspicion and fading hope clouding green eyes and felt trapped by the inability to give the troubled girl an explanation she'd accept as truth. Alyce was unlikely to believe how happily he'd consign Sybillene to the royal minion's care. King Henry was welcome to the self-centered female. Dare had not come for her but for the sole purpose of saving sweet Alyce from the clutches of the fickle and untrustworthy king. Dare was too aware of Henry as the son of a royal father notorious for his lecherous demands on not serf or commoner alone but on women wellborn, even the wives and daughters of his barons.

Only to accomplish the goal of Alyce's safety was Dare willing to offer shelter to Sybillene, a woman already shown dangerous by the deed which had seen him cast out from Keniver. Aye, shelter he'd provide for the vain woman, but no more, certainly neither his interest nor companionship. However, 'twas plain in Alyce's poorly hidden anxiety that she would be skeptical of any claim he made for an aversion to Sybillene. A humorless half smile curled his mouth. Considering the compromising situation in which she'd seen them caught, how could it be elsewise?

The whole tangled web of truths and untruths woven together in the past to form the tight-knit mesh of his reputation mired his efforts at Wythe. As he had in dealing with its complications there, he again cursed his failure to earlier protest his innocence of those wrongs he had not committed.

Glancing from the distressed woman struggling to hide a wounded spirit to the mutinous brother of another, Dare silently accepted a further unhappy truth—he was left to be host to Walter as well. He calmed his irritation with a wry question. What danger was there in this ineffectual half man? Taking the man into his home would give him the opportunity to secure an explanation for the reasoning behind his accusation. As for Sybillene's unwelcome advances, surely with his experience he could deal with one woman easily enough.

Dare looked back to the tender fire-vixen whose heat seemed so well banked, it neared extinction, and longed to ignite the flames once again. But only with anger as he had since she was a child, and never again the forbidden blaze of passion. If handling the difficulties Sybillene and her brother presented were all he must pay to win a few last days, even weeks, in Alyce's company, then 'twas worth the price. The far greater difficulty would be in restraining his unholy instinct to claim that which was not his. To protect Alyce from that danger, he'd thought to see her immediately surrendered to her child-husband and put irretrievably beyond his reach.

6

W e'll make camp here." Dare signaled his followers to halt in a small glade closely ringed by deep forest shadows. Unwelcome to remain the night within Keniver's boundaries once he'd won the struggle for control of its dependents, they'd been forced to depart at an hour he'd never have chosen. They'd set out so late in the day that either they stop for the night midway to Castle Wythe or travel through the dark hours to arrive in early morn. These were his only alternatives, yet 'twas a choice that was no choice as the latter was clearly an impossible feat when burdened with the dragging weight of one weak man, two women, a child, and all their baggage.

To descend from her uncomfortable seat, Alyce accepted the aid of the guardsmen she'd ridden pillion behind. She held tight to the arm of the man who remained ahorse while, with greater strength than she'd have expected in a form so slight, he lowered her once more to firm ground. Thankful to again be standing safe below, she looked up with a grateful smile for the shy young man who seemed near her own age. He returned it with a child-sweet smile of his own and nodded a head covered in bright red curls, even on cheeks and chin, but did not speak.

"Arlen." Irrationally annoyed by the much younger

man's transparent admiration for Alyce, Dare interrupted their silent exchange. "See to our horses."

Arlen instantly swung toward his lord, nibbling his lips and flustered by not knowing what wrong he'd done to cause a dark scowl.

Dare felt shamed by the unspoken criticism to which he'd subjected this too sensitive but ever efficient son of his guard captain. Dare sent Arlen an apologetic smile. Then while the boy (and despite the beard, he seemed this to Dare) set about the commanded task, he turned toward his other men and continued delegating the chores necessary to see the camp readied. Once specific tasks had been named, he concluded with perhaps the most important.

"While Thomas builds the fire, the rest of you must needs find and store up sufficient fodder to see its hunger appeased throughout the night."

While Arlen moved to do his lord's will, Alyce made a show of gazing all about in an effort to hide the surreptitious stretching which might elsewise be deemed a complaint. Hours spent riding sideways on the rear of a horse—no easy feat in itself—had left her muscles aching and cramped. The last weak light of cloudy day filtered through branches of trees towering on every side, so massive they near twined above and across this small opening in the dense woodland. From branches above she looked down to a soft carpet of thick grasses cheered by an occasional flower, clumped ferns, and on one edge, a dense thicket of thorn bushes. Inevitably Alyce's attention was drawn by the man who held for her a fascination too strong, almost as if directed by wizardry or . . .

Helpless to look away, she watched as he moved. A stray breeze lifted his cloak, swirling it out from broad shoulders —like black wings. The wings of a fallen angel? The priests said that Lucifer had been the most beautiful of all in the heavenly host. Dare plainly fulfilled that description. But even as that image formed, another part of her mind instantly decried the condemning comparison and rose to defend the too oft wrongly maligned man. He was no demon, not truly. Merely was he a cruelly rejected child grown into tormented man, one who chose to hold vulnerable emotions safe behind the impenetrable armor of his reputation.

Of a sudden the powerful figure too long the focus of her thoughts looked toward her. Under pale eyes gleaming even in the colorless light of dusk, every sane thought fled. Breath caught in her throat as he approached, pulling hands free of heavy gauntlets.

"Dare." Sybillene's petulant voice sliced through the awareness stretching between the pair she meant to see more than physically separated. "I am weary and await your aid in arranging some suitable place to rest." Whatever the earl had intended to do for her stepdaughter, he had more rightly do for her. 'Twas only polite as she was the lady of highest rank.

Cynicism washed over Dare's handsome face as he turned to do the demanding woman's bidding with an overdone courtesy based in a contempt lost on the recipient too self-centered to recognize it.

The interruption gave Alyce an opportunity to clamp down on the wrongful response he roused from her with precious little trouble and regain some small measure of control. That Dare had instantly moved to answer Sybillene's call both deepened her suspicions and stirred to life the banked coals of her anger—an end he'd often sought.

She turned a cold shoulder on them and glared with an unwarranted intensity at a cart filled to overflowing with baskets, trunks, and tightly wrapped cloth. Leastwise Sybillene's impersonation of a weeping and helpless woman had been used to some good purpose. She had wheedled much from the grasping hold of the king's representative, who by royal command had claimed *all* things contained within the boundaries of Keniver. In giving her stepmother her due, Alyce acknowledged a depressing certainty. Had she been alone in arguing with the greedy knight, too likely her temper would've been lost and then they'd have been fortunate to depart with even a serf's cast-off rags upon their backs. Sybillene had won more, a great deal more. That most items amongst Sybillene's "loot" were her own possessions mattered little to Alyce. She had been permitted to take away the one small wicker trunk more than able to contain the items she most prized.

When Dare led Sybillene into her view while he retrieved a fine bed fur from the cart to spread for the woman's comfort, Alyce glanced into the growing gloom of dusk where figures robbed of color moved like shadows to gather needed firewood. Want her presence or not, Dare had rescued her from the king who had brought grief to her father and all in his family. A fact for which she owed him gratitude. To mitigate that debt in small measure, she joined the worthy search.

Buried in a wealth of ferns growing near the base of a towering oak, Alyce found a branch fallen years past. She lifted one end to drag her well-seasoned but heavy prize to where the earl's knight and friend knelt, urging to life the first flames of a central fire.

A merry grin flashed on Thomas's face as he rose to greet the young woman frowning with determined effort. "Thank you, my lady, for this fine donation to my cause." With the words, he swept a gallant bow.

Alyce passed the awkward "donation" over to one not so very much taller than she before answering his infectious smile with one of her own and sinking into a graceful curtsy. "And I thank you, gentle knight, for relieving me of its burden."

Thomas roared with ready laughter even as he put one stout-booted foot on the branch, reached down, and jerked the far end up to snap the thick limb in twain as easily as if it had been of no greater strength than a sheaf of straw.

Shaking her head in admiration for the feat, Alyce turned to re-join the search. She bumped squarely into another whose arms were heavy-laden. Only by a miracle of fate did the load of wood tumbling from Arlen's arms fail to crush her endangered toes.

"S-s-sorry. I-I-I'm s-s-sorry!" The words seemed to have been strangled from his throat, and he blushed so bright, it glowed even in the color-stealing half-light of dusk.

"Nay, it's I who should've been more careful." Alyce

instantly reassured the guardsman behind whom she'd ridden even as she bent to help in retrieving his scattered "donation" to Sir Thomas's cause.

Arlen was horrified that the fine lady felt her toil necessary to see his clumsiness undone and abruptly stooped to forestall the need. Instead his head came into sharp contact with hers, and he couldn't force a further apology from the tight muscles of his throat.

"I say, lad, what are you about?" Sir Thomas pulled both Alyce and Arlen to their feet before kicking the errant logs toward the fire's edge.

"I—I—I—" Arlen gritted his teeth in frustration.

Sir Thomas mildly shook his head and patted the younger man's shoulder comfortingly. "Never mind an answer, though I should think slow practice would lessen your difficulty in speaking."

If possible, Arlen's flush went brighter and he awkwardly whirled to rush back into the forest's shielding gloom, ostensibly in further search of firewood.

Lost in thought, Alyce peered after the fleeing guardsman. So it was only his stutter, obviously a great embarrassment to him, that had prevented him from speaking to her even once on their long afternoon journey. She'd worried that he, and with him others of Wythe, resented their earl's rescue of the dishonored Baron of Keniver's dependents. Arlen was a nice fellow, and if she could, she'd help lessen his difficulties.

Heedless of the blond beauty clinging to him as tenaciously as an ivy vine, Dare gazed at the cart piled high. To him Sybillene's baggage represented more a disaster than a victory. These spoils of her triumph included far more than he'd thought possible to remove from a Keniver held forfeit to the crown—and they required a great deal more of both labor and equipment to transport than he'd been prepared to handle. Though he'd brought an empty cart to the former baron's home, on the return journey he'd expected it to carry not only belongings but people.

The king's inflexible claim of all horseflesh, Dare had anticipated. Steeds were too valuable for it to be elsewise. Thus, he'd known the impossibility of seeing his "guests" mounted on horses once but no longer theirs and had planned to meet the need. His plan had been obliterated by this endless pile of belongings retained (a deed Sybillene had yet to cease crowing about with annoying jubilance). This physical proof of her successful negotiations had forced him to see Walter, Hal, and the two women riding pillion behind members of his guard. An unfortunate fact creating a further reason why they'd been forced to halt for the night short of Castle Wythe. Horses should be well cared for and never required to travel so long and so far with double burdens.

At first pleased by Dare's apparent interest in the spoils of her great coup against Sir Lester, too soon Sybillene detected a hint of distaste marring the earl's handsome face. 'Twas an insult to her dignity! She huffily released his arm and marched stiffly away. Her turned back and the withdrawal of her flattering attentions, she felt certain, was sufficient to punish any man.

Alyce was busy in again searching through thick grass and beneath overspreading bushes and fern fronds. Moreover, well entertained by several friendly guardsmen who appeared to find her path the best ground for a successful hunt, she did not see when the other woman stalked away from both the earl and the bed fur he'd laid out at her behest.

Dare's dark brows knit in puzzlement as his attention shifted to his guardsmen. They seemed in amazing good humor for people who'd journeyed long and far in a single day. It was surprising until he found the source of their enjoyment—Alyce. Of his guests, only she bent earnestly to the task of lending aid. It irritated him when her rescue had been his sole objective, and she the one he would happily have seen served by others. Then, as he watched, serious young Hal moved to lend Alyce his help with the chore. Seemed Halbert's quiet, stalwart son—in spite of the selfish mother who in Dare's memory of long-ago Keniver days had seemed ever hovering over the toddling he'd then been— was too honorable to let the burden of providing gratitude be carried by a woman alone. Dare was impressed by his display of a right character.

Meanwhile Sybillene and her brother stood close to still

weak flames, thoughtlessly blocking their heat from any others who might approach and impeding a disgusted Thomas's task. When Dare noticed their inconsiderate action, he was further irritated with the pair. And yet . . . A grim smile lifted one corner of his mouth. Their relative seclusion offered a fine opportunity for him to seek answers to questions raised by Walter's earlier accusations against him; answers he meant to have—now.

The brother and sister holding chilled hands outstretched toward warming flames were so involved in seeking their own comfort that they failed to sense danger approaching from behind.

"On your behalf, leastwise in part, I challenged royal authority, putting I and mine at risk. By right of that risk accepted, Walter, I demand of you an explanation for your statement laying the blame for Halbert's troubles upon me."

Walter swung around so sharply that only by unmerited good fortune did the edge of his cloak swirl through open flames swiftly enough to escape unscathed.

"How is it that you feel justified in denouncing me as the one responsible for the wicked wrong done Keniver's baron?" Dare's piercing blue gaze seemed to pin a gape-mouthed Walter to some invisible wall while, immovable as granite and far more threatening, he waited for the other to speak.

"How is it that you are blamed?" Sybillene's too oft cloyingly honeyed voice turned to acid as she stepped between her brother and the earl. "How else but that you be blamed when the letters Halbert sent you were intercepted? Letters all too plainly responding to requests from you and the Earl of Pembroke."

Lashes fell over sapphire eyes, hiding their calculating gleam as Sybillene rethought the direction of her defense. When they lifted, her gaze was a gently beckoning mist. She glided forward and with softly clinging fingers clasped hands that had curled into fists.

"Don't you see? The plot Richard and you conceived to rally the barons against our fickle king and his wretched French advisors, though mayhap laudable, has been revealed as treason." Sybillene moved her hands to slowly rub their palms up and down Dare's mighty forearms in apparent comfort for the disappointment that surely lay behind his icy countenance. "Halbert's response to your request for aid in plotting the deed proves it true."

Dare's smile had a sword's deadly sharp edge. Plainly it was only a matter of time before he, too, would be charged. Though he'd expected it to be so, this proof of its nearness was bitter and soured the words he spoke.

"Neither I nor Richard have ever requested help of any kind from Halbert. Why would we feel in need of another's aid in forming military strategies when already we've proven ourselves more than capable of devising our own?"

Dare watched the baron's wife delicately shrug, disgusted by her obvious lack of sincere regret for Halbert's plight. The only fear she'd expressed thus far dwelled on the danger her husband's arrest posed to her own comfort.

Although the basis for the charges against Halbert were ridiculous, accustomed to being credited with all manner of wild deeds himself, Dare was not truly surprised by the ploy used to incriminate his foster father. The Bishop of Winchester had earlier employed such false documentations to condemn and expel Hubert de Burgh from power in order that he might take the man's place. His scheme had proven a success. The bishop was now the force behind their weak king.

This was but the first move in a chess game with power as its prize. The bishop meant to see all potential threats to his influence removed from the board—Halbert but the first move to claim others of more import. Had there been spare time enough (and he'd had none) to ponder the matter, he would have foreseen the whole. Though named traitor, Richard was possessed of military might, vast wealth, and the great Pembroke lands. Thus, the Marshal's second son was far too strong to be easily eliminated. Doubtless the bishop saw in Dare a more vulnerable target and one which, once removed, would weaken the Earl of Pembroke as well. Dare's eyes went to ice. Forewarned, he would stand forearmed.

Alyce, having carefully placed an armload of broken branches atop a growing stack of others, had remained quietly in the shadows on the outer ring of light and saw Dare's impassive response to the explanation of an accusation. That lack of expression was not telling of itself but, by the cold glittering from between thick lashes, she recognized how deeply the news had affected him. With guilt or hurt? She wished she knew for certain. Although wanting desperately to believe him innocent, the evidence was strong—both in the seized letters and her memory of his dishonorable taking of her father's wife. Too well she recalled Sybillene's welcome of his arrival at Keniver naught but a few hours past. A welcome which in critical retrospect seemed more studied than natural. But then near every action the woman took was that, and surely no proof that Dare had conspired with her.

When unexpectedly Dare turned from the pair without further word, Alyce stood unmoving a scant two paces distant. His glance slid over her but away with so little interest that she felt assaulted. It seemed nothing (not even these dire accusations) and no one (least of all her) could penetrate his close-held armor against emotion.

Once the fires had attained sufficient heat and the pile of wood an adequate height, the company gathered in a loose ring about its flickering light to share equal portions of dark rye bread, salt-preserved meat, raisins, freshly harvested apples, and chunks of strong cheese. Only the earl stood aloof, eating his share just beyond revealing tentacles of flamelight while privately laying strategies to meet the coming threat.

"You are Richard of Pembroke's friend?" The question, diffidently asked, drew a pale gaze down to the speaker below.

Dare was startled by the boy brave enough to approach when plainly he'd sought solitude, but rewarded Hal's courage with a smile of welcome. "I am honored to have been named thus by him."

"And he, like my father, was named traitor to the king?" Hal's serious face showed the importance of the answers to his questions.

"Aye," Dare responded immediately, seeing the direction Hal was headed. "He was."

"But he is free?" Wide brown eyes met blue unwavering while childish lips were tightly pursed to prevent a betraying tremble.

"Richard remains free by virtue of a power beyond his unquestioned physical strength and courage. He has command of a large and fiercely trained army who stand between him and any who wishes him harm." Dare hoped these words would reassure the boy clearly struggling with troubling and very personal questions about how the father he'd believed a great warrior had been so easily seized, and if it meant his sire was guilty of a dishonorable wrong.

Dare laid a reassuring hand on the boy's shoulder as he continued. "Not even our king will lightly risk an open confrontation, for Richard also wields a dangerous measure of influence with many other barons. If not by the strength of his army alone, their combined might could well see our sovereign defeated—a shame King Henry is unlikely to tempt."

Hal gave the dark earl a solemn smile, nodded, and moved back into the fire's circle of light with renewed pride in the tilt of his chin.

In the growing silence of weariness at the end of the meal, Alyce had watched the exchange between powerful man and reserved child. She had seen desperate bravado carry Hal to the earl he'd surely heard termed the Demon, and, too, she had seen the gentleness with which he'd been received. Though always she'd idolized Dare, by this action tonight her admiration grew a hundredfold.

With the meal done and night fully descended to leave all beyond the ring of firelight in absolute blackness, there was naught left to be done but the finding of comfortable positions for sleeping. Guardsmen, presumably under orders from their lord, prepared cushions of fallen leaves, dried grasses, and uprooted ferns for the women's beds. Without thought of thanking those who'd arranged for her a resting place, Sybillene lost no moment in wrapping herself in not only her cloak but the bed fur Dare had laid out. She then settled for the night.

Alyce removed both veil and barbette but left her hair in neat plaits to preserve some semblance of modesty. Though she felt no need for more warmth than that provided by her woolen and fur-lined cloak, she could not so easily slip into dreams. Anxious for distraction from questions without answers, questions posed by concern for her father, for the people of Keniver—for her own uncertain future—she lay with back to the fire's comforting light and gazed into the anonymous depths of the forest beyond. With her cheek pillowed on palm-joined hands, her eyes slowly adjusted to the limited light and discovered the unmoving silhouette of the man leaning against a sturdy oak trunk. Though merely a deeper shadow against the blackness of moonless night, to her, Dare's form was unmistakable. Plainly he had his worries. She had worries, too.

In addition to her fears for Keniver's lord and people, she feared this joining of Wythe's demesne for the sake of the harm it might do Dare's cause. And even more, now she had time to think on it further, she was apprehensive about the unsavory position she had all-unknowingly put herself into months gone by. She would be a guest, likely unwanted and for some considerable time, of Lady Elinor. Having already been impertinent enough to criticize the woman's treatment of her son, Alyce wondered how she could restrain an unabated indignation over that abuse to live in harmony, or leastwise peace, within the woman's sphere.

Lost in these musings, Alyce had failed to notice as Dare disappeared from view. When she realized he'd gone, she visually searched the glade's perimeters without success. At length she decided it likely that he'd sought a resting place on the fire's far side, where, through flame, she could not see. She turned restlessly for what seemed an endless age. What point in striving for a sleep that would not come? Dare had demonstrated the best remedy for such difficulties. He'd sought the cool quiet of the night. There a chill breeze might blow the cobwebs of troubled thoughts from her mind. If such was the best cure, then best she seek it out before the night and all hope of rest was gone.

Alyce quietly rose from her makeshift bed and slipped into the shadows. Strangely, she had no fear of darkness so long as there were no walls to box her inside. Oh, she was not fool enough to risk aimless wanderings in the night's open spaces, but the prospect of moving into a gloom just beyond the circle of firelight held no terror. Thus, with the memory of Dare's example, rather than remaining in sight of the camp, she moved to the oak trunk's far side and leaned back against its impressive breadth to gaze blindly out into the impenetrable shades of night.

"With unrestrained plaits falling to your waist, you look like the tiny spitfire I remember ever struggling against me."

The husky words sank into the deep velvet night like stones into a pool. Alyce prevented herself from turning toward the dangerously attractive speaker, even when he lifted one weighty braid to smooth his thumb over its silken texture, but she could not restrain the smile brought by pleasant memories. Aye, she had argued with him on every possible occasion. It had been the only method at hand to win his attention—a goal hers as long as she could remember, and despite her father's consistent lectures on the wrong in her unruly spirit.

Dare saw the smile. Heartened by this proof of warm memories shared, he gently tugged until she turned her face to meet a softly indulgent gaze. "I detest your accursed headcloths and barbettes." The tenderness of his voice deflected the meaning of softly spoken words and lulled Alyce into meeting his smoldering blue eyes full on. However, the words he added ignited the dry tinder of a too long stifled spirit. "You may think them adequate defense against me, may think your flimsy facade of coolness enough to control the fiery spirit within, yet they are not. In truth, only do they increase my desire to set them aside."

"'Tis not a facade!" Alyce strenuously denied. "'Tis who and what I've become!" Though with Sybillene and Lady Elinor as examples of her father's notion of feminine perfection, she had come to question his judgment, she could not simply throw years of learning aside.

A white grin flashed across Dare's dark face. Her temper alone disproved her claim. Moreover, it rewarded him with the ever-sought response—a burst of white-hot fire.

Alyce gritted her teeth and only by strong effort of will prevented herself from falling to a childish urge to stomp her feet. Again, under Dare's bad influence, she'd fallen and become more of a toddling than a woman. In the next instant, as he moved to stand directly in front and loom threateningly near, her ever truthful conscience denied leastwise the last. Her temper she had lost, but not as a child, decidedly not that when at his mere nearness she felt herself fair melting in a way no child would.

Having Alyce so close and receptive was more temptation than even Dare's powerful will could withstand. Slowly he lowered his mouth to hers and with the experience of too many conquests gently, repeatedly brushed the smooth contours of her lips. They opened on a sigh, giving access for a renewal of the deep and passionate kisses whose pleasures he'd taught her years past.

Wrapped in the welcome gloom of night, Alyce sank into a mindless haze of desire, flowing into waiting arms like water downhill. Dare welcomed her, refusing rational thoughts of his oath not to tempt her into actions they were both sure to regret. He'd no excuse for this wrong save admission of a demonic influence. And if it were that, then be damned to the price of his soul, he had none.

"Alyce . . ." The whisper was laced with panic. "Alyce, where are you?"

Blue eyes flashed with dangerous lights as a dark head lifted and turned toward the crashing sound of another's approach. Many times Dare had wanted to retaliate against the interfering Walter, but never more than now.

Beneath a strong grip gone cruelly tight, Alyce returned to reality with a guilty gasp. Yet again she'd lost all good sense and near surrendered to the delicious sins offered by a man she felt more confused about than ever before. He'd warned her away, even sent her from him. But now—

"Alyce!" The word was no longer a whisper but a desperate plea for answer.

"Quiet, Walter." Alyce slipped from arms miraculously loosed at the sound of her voice. "Pray do not wake the whole of our companions."

As she stepped from behind the trunk's wide shield, Walter gave a tremulous sigh of relief.

"Saints be praised! I feared you hauled off by wolves or lured into danger by some wicked villain."

Alyce softly laughed at the mere suggestion of such deeds, and a gratified Walter failed to recognize the thread of irony running through her amusement. In truth, as Eve had been by the serpent, she *had* been lured into wickedness, and by a tantalizing demon offering forbidden delights.

While Alyce formally laid her small fingers atop Walter's proffered forearm, allowing him to lead her back to her waiting couch, Dare watched unnoticed from the shadows. Bitterness curled temper-thinned lips downward while guilt threatened to overwhelm him. Guilt? Only Alyce could rouse that emotion in him. Yet 'twas unquestionably merited, for once again he had truly attempted to seduce the last woman he wanted to dishonor. In spite of many reports to the contrary, he had never seduced either a pure wife or virtuous innocent, but tonight with Alyce, who was both, he would have committed that sin. He must, he would, put himself on short tether and never allow himself to be alone with her again. Only under such constraints could he risk permitting himself even the pleasure of her mere presence in his home.

7

"Y er grandfather 'ud never ha' done such a disgraceful deed, ner father neither." The frailty of the form issuing hostile words did nothing to lessen the vigor of their battering attack upon the leader of a mounted group emerging from beneath the fierce pointed teeth of the upraised portcullis guarding Wythe's outer bailey gate.

Dare reined to a halt just inside, and the heatless sunlight of a rare clear autumn day flashed over black hair as he nodded in acknowledgment of this elderly man who plainly felt accumulated years entitled him to reprimand his earl.

Once more Alyce rode behind Arlen; and when he brought the steed they shared to a stop a short distance from his earl's side, she tensely watched a muscle clench and unclench in Dare's cheek. Though unable to identify the reason for it, Alyce prayed Dare heard, as she did, the petulant disappointment in the depths of the aged man's reproach. She'd heard much the same tone in the too oft endless complaints of others of like years, and told herself his grumbling represented no serious grievance.

"By only one day has the lord's court been delayed." Dare held his voice to a mild tone and restrained his frustration with this demonstration of how little it took to strain the thin bond of trust he'd spent months striving to build between himself and his people. On a moment's further thought, he reminded himself that in the end this verbal assault, like chaff from wheat, sifted out to a more basic and less-disheartening truth. By making the first protest over real or imagined slights, Howell, the demesne's tanner and a man overproud of his free status, attempted to reaffirm his position as leader of the common folk. Likely Howell would find fault in anything he did. Dare could but go onward without permitting him the power to deflect a chosen course.

"I take most seriously my right and duty in this matter." Dare spoke only the truth. Every noble jealously guarded his right to make judgments on his own domain. He not least of all. "And tomorrow I will listen to my people's disputes and complaints."

Howell shuffled uneasily beneath a penetrating blue gaze. But—still unappeased—as he turned away and began moving off toward a home separate from the village and of finer construction than abodes there, he muttered. "Yer shouldn't ha' put strangers afore duty to yer own."

Dare went utterly motionless; even the tight muscle in his clenched jaw stopped pulsing. He'd no need to defend an action undertaken on behalf not of strangers but of his foster family, more his family than those living here who'd rejected his blood entitlement to home and recognition.

Though the scowling earl sat unmoving atop an equally immobile steed battle-trained to obey its master's slightest command, Alyce sensed emotion flowing out from Dare in great, towering waves, and beyond her control, her heart flew to him.

Feeling the whisper-soft brush of eyes gone to green mist, Dare slowly turned his head to meet their gentle solace. While his men, even Thomas, would hesitate to approach when his mood was so clearly foul and even less to extend a comfort he might resent as pity, here lay an open compassion given without fear. The same compassion whose weakening influence he'd feared so strongly that he'd once sent her from this place to which they now returned. A slow smile accompanied the narrowing of blue eyes to a fiery intensity.

Beneath the potent gaze, Alyce gave a silent gasp and nervously glanced away. She ought know better than to offer comfort, which would assuredly be returned by either rejection or an even more dangerous acceptance. Purposefully she gave her full attention to an examination of the scenery, using it to divert her attention from the man all too capable of recalling her gaze to his. Though her perusal had begun in a stubborn test of wills, she was soon captivated by the many differences between this view and the scene when last she'd visited. Gently rolling fields bore either the stubble left by a recent harvest or crops ripe and waiting to fall beneath strong-wielded scythes.

As pleased by this demonstration of the fine progress Dare had made in restoring Wythe as by her triumph over his lure, an unusual success, Alyce failed to see a cynical curve replace the predatory smile on his lips as he urged his destrier back into motion. He'd found the most effective strategy for keeping Alyce safely at arm's length—frightening her with the intensity of the feelings she roused in him. And doing so without the physical closeness certain to endanger his good intents.

While they rode on toward the next gate and castle beyond, Alyce realized how truly weary she was. Their journey had consumed the season-shortened daylight hours. Only the briefest of pauses had been allowed to rest horses overburdened and permit their human masters to share a small repast of limited variety, naught but the same salt venison, fruit, cheese, and dark rye bread of yestereve. Sensitive now to Arlen's reason for not speaking the day past, she'd intermittently, absently, talked of such matters as needed no answer save his occasional shy smile.

Like a jester's crimson ball, the sun seemed to lie atop the western horizon when Dare led his small party to the foot of a broad flight of stairs leading up to the castle's double iron-bound doors. He knew his companions must feel as did he—stiff from hours ahorse, covered in travel-grit, and hungry.

Lady Elinor awaited her son and their guests in the great hall and graciously came forward to meet the new arrivals at the arched opening of both entrance tunnel and ascending stairway. Exercising the politeness of long practice, she bade them welcome before summoning castle-serfs to carry their belongings and lead them to assigned bedchambers.

"Once there," she suggested with aloof courtesy, "I pray you will make haste to prepare for the evening meal as it has been postponed pending your arrival."

The first servant led Sybillene and her son up the steps. Another motioned her brother to follow, while the full half score of other husky serfs detailed to perform these chores bent to the task of shouldering the former lady of Keniver's many belongings. Likely a wise choice, Alyce wryly acknowledged. The long journey had turned her stepmother particularly irritable. Alyce knew she could wait with more grace. Toward that end, she patiently stood and gazed expectantly up spiraling steps for the first sign of a returning servant to lead her above while carrying her single wicker trunk.

"I am much disturbed by whatever sorry whim sent you haring off in such mad haste, leaving only the barest scrap of an explanation for me who was called upon to excuse your actions to the many." Elinor spoke quietly, ignoring the younger woman standing, back turned, several paces away. Despite the girl's insolent criticism during her last visit, as this rebuke for Dare's ill-done deed could be of no rightful interest to her, Elinor simply deemed Alyce's possible reaction too immaterial to be considered. "'Twas very wrong of you to be gone at a moment of such import to the people. And, I fear, will much hinder your purpose."

Lady Elinor's assumption of Alyce's disinterest was in error. The older woman's whispered reprimand came clear to Alyce's ears, and her spine straightened as if the barb had been aimed at her. Still, along with rising ire, she felt guilty for even unintentionally overhearing a conversation she was assuredly not meant to share. Expecting Dare to defend himself against the unjustified assault, she strove to restrain her indignation. But after a quick sidelong glance revealed Dare's face gone blank and thick lashes lowered in mute acceptance, Alyce's unruly temper flared. 'Twas beastly and utterly unfounded! First a being she adjudged a mere serf had dared reproach his lord. Now Dare's own mother condemned his loyal action.

"Had Dare waited a moment longer, 'twould have been too late to rescue his foster kinsfolk!" Green fire flashed as Alyce whirled to face a shocked Elinor. "Only did he demonstrate the kind of blood-owed allegiance his mother has never shown her son."

Ice blue eyes widened for an instant. Once again Alyce, by her defense of him, had allowed the untamed vixen still dwelling within to escape. He'd never doubted its presence but hadn't expected her to so wildly defy the rigid demands of polite behavior. More than pleased by her show of spirit, he would've congratulated or leastwise thanked her for this confidence in him, but already her cheeks were rosy with embarrassment and he hesitated to cause a deepening of her discomfort.

What a blithering simpleton I become whenever that man is near! Though she could not regret nor would she recant her defense of Dare, Alyce could feel her face burning with shame for the attack upon her hostess. A hostess, moreover, who had graciously welcomed them to her home, though she'd likely prefer to dispatch them to a fiery end (certainly the visitor earlier proven a discourteous creature). Now, just see with what wickedly rude response Elinor's politeness had been returned. Proved, Alyce mournfully acknowledged, what a wretched, ill-mannered female she was and how unworthy was she to be housed in Dare's fine castle-home. Better he consign her to the dungeons wherein musty damp and darkness might be expected to smother her fires into extinction.

Horribly anxious to be gone, without waiting for someone to lead the way, Alyce turned and blindly started up the steps at a rapid pace. Happily for her, Arlen had been sent by his father, the guard captain, to ask their lord for directions regarding the morrow's plans, and he had been witness to all, from Lady Elinor's assignment of rooms to Alyce's defense of the earl. Overcoming his astonishment at the whole exchange, he hastened forward to snatch up the wicker chest he knew to be Alyce's by virtue of having seen her search through it that morn. He then rushed to catch up and next pass Alyce on the steps to direct her path.

Dare shifted his attention from the rapidly disappearing figures to the older woman still at his side and caught a fleeting glimpse of admiration cross the smooth lines of the beautiful face little touched by age. The next moment he wondered if this surely false impression had been merely a trick of flames flickering in an oil-fed sconce burning just within the deeply shadowed archway.

Abovestairs, on the castle's highest level, Arlen led the way to the same small chamber Alyce occupied on her previous visit. Holding the trunk balanced on his shoulder with one arm, he pushed the door open with the other and stood back for the lady visitor to enter.

Alyce hesitated. It was dark inside. Yet beneath her guide's expectant gaze she stepped into the room, berating herself for a craven fool. Overwrought by the scene just past, she paused again. Then, compelled to accept the shaming truth of an inability to deal calmly with this additional strain, she threw aside any hope for an image of languid femininity and rushed to secure a candle from the daily replenished pile ever atop the bedside chest. With a half-apologetic smile she slipped back past the red-haired man startled by her desperate haste and into the corridor. There she joined its wick to the flame of a torch burning midway betwixt one end of the hallway and another.

Armed with the insubstantial candle and lent bravery by its faintly glimmering light, she reentered the chamber. Arlen followed with his burden, stumbled to his knees, and dropped the wicker chest. When its never sturdy clasp snapped open, Alyce's belongings scattered in a wide arc over the broad planks of a bare wood floor.

The action's shock released Alyce's too taut tension in inappropriate gales of laughter. She laughed so hard, tears sprouted and hid the sight of a young man's shoulders curling as if his embarrassment might reduce him to nothing as effectively as would salt on the pitiful slug he felt he'd become.

"Ah, Arlen," she gasped at last, wiping moisture from her

eyes with the fine linen cuff of a forest green camise and dropping to her knees beside him. "We make a pretty pair—me afrighted by unlit chambers that close too tight, and you ever finding invisible impediments."

Aye, a pair they were. He, for all his score and more of years, seemed not to have left behind an adolescent's awkward movements and lack of confidence. Just as she had yet to gain control over childish fears and tempers.

Eyes narrowed half in suspicion, half in hope studied the beautiful lady visitor. Arlen had expected to be derided for this further proof of his clumsiness. There was another woman (one of far less standing) who took pleasure in ridiculing him for such blunders. He should be accustomed to it—but was not and thought it unlikely he ever would be.

"I-I-I'm s-s—"

"Nay, Arlen." Alyce laid her free hand atop a fist clenched in frustration. "I am sorry. Had I not gone rushing back and forth in your path to see myself secure with candle lit, likely you wouldn't have fallen."

Illumination from that same candle still in Alyce's hand glowed on bright hair as Arlen stubbornly shook his head, determined not to let the lady carry his blame.

"Whatever the reason behind—" Alyce interrupted before he could speak. "'Tis a done deed and of no matter now." She tilted her head to the side and softly asked, "Would you, gentle friend, help me rise? I fear our long ride has left my legs too sore to be of much use."

Proud to be termed friend by this lovely and forgiving lady, Arlen scrambled to his feet and proffered his arm as gallantly as had ever any honorable knight in a minstrel's song. She laid small fingers atop his forearm and gave him a smile so sweet, he blushed in pleasure. From her unhesitating aid in the past night's search for firewood to her loyal defense of the earl who'd come to her rescue, Lady Alyce had shown herself to be the very image of what a lady aught be. And although he could never be more than the dirt beneath Lady Alyce's feet, Arlen was ever more deeply smitten by her—a feeling most unlike the torment to which that other woman constantly subjected him.

Amazed by the undemanding adoration brimming in the young man's eyes, Alyce blushed, too, yet felt strangely healed by knowing that despite her disgraceful behavior, someone admired her still.

"Thank you, Arlen, for bringing my trunk and showing the way. Likely without your help I'd have wandered into places I don't belong." She gave him a rueful smile which he acknowledged by shyly dipping a bright head before turning to leave her in privacy.

Alyce felt disoriented by the day's tangled emotions and events, and when all too soon came a summons to the meal her hostess had mentioned, she sent a message pleading deep weariness and a wish to be excused. Alyce was certain Lady Elinor would greet her absence with pleasure.

Left in peace, Alyce turned her attention to putting her trunk and its contents to rights until a knock sounded on the thick oak door. She opened it to an earnest young page who quietly introduced himself as James. He had come to deliver a platter bearing small but more than adequate portions from each of the variety of dishes served to those at table in the hall below. Once James had withdrawn, Alyce retired for the night, but only after blocking her door ajar. Ajar—yet so slightly, no one would notice—it eased her fear of the very real possibility that her candle might burn out and leave her to awake in complete darkness. Thus reassured, her night passed in a heavy sleep earned by the exhaustion of travel and a previous night of restless worry.

Wishing, uselessly, that she might fade from the view of others gathered at the high table, Alyce allowed her attention to wander no further from her barely touched morning repast than the pristine white cloth within a handsbreadth of either side. With the dawning sun, memories of her discourtesy of the past day had returned. Now that discomfort was compounded by pricks of a jealousy she was loath to admit. It was toward the goal of restraining the latter's increasing pangs that she strived so earnestly to ignore Sybillene, who, as lady of second import, was seated on Dare's left and flirting outrageously.

Surely ignoring the woman should be a simple task. Alyce

scolded herself for the urge to peek down the table. So long as she kept her gaze trained downward, it should be impossible to see beyond Sir Thomas, Lady Elinor, and Dare to Sybillene, four people distant. But . . . Even though she resolutely focused narrowed green eyes on the thick-crusted bread held tight in her hand, Alyce could sense each stroke of the woman's fingers on Dare's strong forearm, feel the warmth of the too sweet smiles with which she gifted him.

"Your mother has told me how honorably you've set about the task of restoring your demesne to its former prosperity." From the corner of her eyes Sybillene glanced coyly at the handsome earl and again lightly rubbed slender fingers over the masculine hand resting in dark contrast atop the white-cloth-covered table. "And I admire your prompt-ness in righting wrongs done."

Alyce was startled into looking at the speaker, and then from her stepmother to their noble hostess. She caught a flicker of distaste in brown eyes quickly shielded by lowered lashes. Distaste for Dare's attempts on Wythe's behalf or for Sybillene's misrepresentation of facts given which Lady Elinor had likely not meant as praise? The source of their hostess's expression, Alyce decided, must have been distaste for the actions undertaken by Dare. Seemed certain Lady Elinor and Sybillene would get along well together. As proof, only consider how oft her father had pointed to each as the epitome of feminine refinement?

Taking a deep breath to waylay both renewed shame and a rising resentment for Sybillene's hold on Dare, Alyce deter-minedly looked from the high table's occupants and out toward the people seated at three lines of trestle tables below. Her brows arched at an unexpected sight—the reflection of her own jealousy burning in the bold gaze of a tall, well-endowed female serf glaring at the possessive hand laid atop Dare's. Like a rabbit held in thrall by a poisonous snake, Alyce couldn't look away until this female, tossing a heavy tangle of dark hair shamelessly left free as no well-bred woman would, turned a cold shoulder to the dais. What right to Dare's attention had this voluptuous female? Peach-soft lips curled in a fair imitation of Dare's mocking smile. What right indeed? The question was no more than an unpleasant jest to one who knew full well how irresistible was the snare of his charms.

Simple meal soon done, the trestle tables below the dais were disassembled and stacked against long parallel walls to make room for the convening of the lord's court. The people, quiet and respectful, began arriving in small groups even before the high table's white cloth had been carefully removed. The hall was full by the time the table had been cleared of all but parchment and inkwell, utensils of a scribe but wielded by the earl himself to record each judgment.

With no useful task to busy her time, Alyce lingered in the back. She had never observed her father's manorial court. Wellborn women, her father had told her, had no reason for attending such an event. What interest could it hold for those to whom, as chattel, no law applied? Alyce had never told him she knew that what he said was not quite correct. Women had rights, too. Not many but a few.

Now she watched, intrigued, as Sir Ulger, the guard captain, stepped into the open space below the dais. She only vaguely recalled having seen, during her earlier visit, this stalwart knight with a face as surely lined by hours of outdoor labor as by age, and an unnaturally high forehead backed by a thick gray mane. He summoned each petitioner to meet the earl's justice, and justice Alyce was impressed to find it was. In the first half morn she watched Dare mete out judgments on such diverse complaints as a debt owed but denied, a disputed field boundary, and an unpaid fine demanded. He handled each with an evenhanded fairness but implacable command Alyce found worthy of admiration.

After judgment on the current complaint had been rendered, Sir Ulger moved forward again but with an unusual hesitation in his step. He was not pleased by this need to interrupt the much-anticipated people's day of justice, yet the news he'd just been given could not be delayed. "In the night there was a fire near the outer wall."

"Where?" The single clipped word revealed nothing while Dare's fingers went white with their dangerously tight grip upon a fragile goose quill.

"The tanner's." Ulger need say no more. This threat to the earl's hard-won acceptance by the people of Wythe was clear.

No visible flicker of response touched Dare, but Alyce recognized a peril unspoken by the collective gasp of the hall's gathered many.

Behind an impassive facade, Dare was horrified. First by the untimely end to the disgruntled man who the day past had foolishly attempted to rebuke his lord. And second by the certainty that this incident would lead many to wonder if their earl was responsible, if he'd wreaked this form of retribution upon Howell.

Unnoticed amongst a crowded hall focused on the exchange between guard captain and their lord, another man soundlessly limped forward to stand at Ulger's back. Chafing under the lengthening silence and shifting restlessly, Darwyn lost patience with this too tactful and annoyingly uninformative report. He broke in to deliver what he deemed the more important facts.

"Howell's dead—a wicked deed plainly done apurpose as 'twas not that deed alone." Now that Darwyn knew himself the center of all attention, his meager form puffed with self-importance as in a loud but ominous whisper he added, "The sign of the devil been scratched in the ashes both in front and in back—doubtless so as it could be neither missed nor mistook."

Unkempt tangles of dirt brown hair brushed his shoulders as he solemnly nodded. Next, to glean even the slightest trace of any effect his disclosures had earned, he closely examined first his earl and then wide-eyed common folk. Darwyn was pleased, and a particularly nasty smile twisted his thin lips. As he was born with a misshapen foot which left him unable to stand physically strong, his nature had grown warped as well and he reveled in such opportunities to manipulate, even to command the emotions of others.

Ulger's gray hair seemed to bristle with anger like a cat arching its back. He turned on his unsought companion and snarled, "Were you there? Is that how you can claim such knowledge?"

Horrified by this unexpected turn near charging him with the deed, Darwyn wildly shook his head.

"Then begone with you." The guard captain waved the man furiously away.

Cowering beneath the fierce command, Darwyn slunk off to the fireplace wall's far end and into the descending stairwell's shadows but paused on the first step to glare venomously behind at the earl's broad back. So focused was Darwyn on the subject of his sullen anger that he'd no thought to spare for the equally intent gaze bent upon him by the adult male guest come from Keniver also hovering unnoticed on the crowd's outer fringes.

Facing the new difficulties roused by this ominous event, Dare was content to permit Ulger's dealing with the insignificant meddler. He concentrated on the new trouble, new yet surely rooted in the past. Upon his father's sudden death, he'd heard the echo of dark whispers accusing him of dabbling in the Black Arts. Accused, worse yet, of wielding such powers to put aside the only impediment between himself and the inheritance of an earldom. In all the long years of being termed a demon and credited with every manner of wild deed, never had it been suggested that he'd serious dealings with the powers of darkness. These dire suspicions had hurt the more as they arose amongst people he'd begun to think of as his own.

He'd near left Wythe and its inhabitants to face a deteriorating future alone. Ulger had pled with him, on the people's behalf, saying that they feared only because they didn't know him, while Thomas had urged him to stay and prove himself to the people who had admired, indeed, had been proud of their first Demon Dare. He'd given serious consideration to the arguments of both men, yet in the end it was the memory of Richard Marshal's claim that he and the land were one which had driven Dare to remain. For the half year gone by he'd toiled to win his people's allegiance, and a mere sennight past he'd have sworn to good headway achieved. Now this single action, by a foe unknown, had thrust him back to the point of outset—if not further. But he had not lost the war. Dare's mouth firmed into an uncompromising line while his eyes narrowed to glittering shards of blue ice. His faceless enemy would find him an opponent not so easily thwarted.

With a grim smile Dare rose from his seat. "I will return to see our business concluded after the midday meal." From the massed people he heard a distinct grumble roll to join murmured apprehensions for the delay's cause. "But I invite you to remain and share in my bounty until I return."

At the prospect of consuming their earl's foodstuffs and not their own, the grumbling stopped, though nothing could halt the whispers of his past and possibly present ill deeds. Most had brought food, expecting to be here the full day. Yet Dare had little doubt that the entire group would eat of the castle's provisions and drink of its brew. Only could he hope they'd not have time enough to become too sotted for completion of the afternoon's business with some semblance of sobriety and without the brawls which so oft accompanied plentiful ale.

When Dare stepped down from the dais, with an equally determined air Thomas immediately joined the man who every day reminded him more of the grandfather whose image he was—not merely in face and form but in sharp mind and honorable heart. He admired the younger man all the more for a resolve unscathed by bitter circumstances. Dare's grandfather would have been proud.

"Let's away." Ulger approached from behind Dare and proved himself equally anxious to find the wretch behind this wrong.

Heartened by the freely given loyalty of his two most steadfast supporters, Dare motioned them to follow him from the great hall.

As the sound of heavily booted footsteps, unmuted by rushes covering oak flooring, echoed into silence, Alyce realized she'd been holding her breath and slowly let it out. She'd feared, one way or another, that the rescue and arrival of Keniver's dependents would result in further difficulties for Dare. Plainly she'd thought aright. Hah, a thing so obvious 'twas like saying that stumbling into roaring flames might cause pain. Alyce instinctively smoothed the sides of her barbette against cheeks gone cold with tension. The truth was clear. The tanner's indignation with his lord over the time and attention devoted to a foster family had been used for ill. By this apparent proof of dealings with the devil, someone sought to rouse renewed suspicions of black powers and sunder the fragile threads of the earl's newly established relationship with his people. Seemed to Alyce too likely to succeed. Images of fire and demonic signs would assuredly awaken the deepest fears of every Wythe inhabitant. That acknowledged fact reinforced her need to learn the truth behind the curse and prove to all that Dare was not demon but human—an all too mortal man and prey to the same hurts, physical and emotional, as any other member of humankind.

Alyce abruptly became aware of her surroundings, standing amidst people breaking into clots to speak in undertones of the wicked deed. She couldn't stay where she stood out like a single weed amongst neatly arranged flowers. Nor, after what she'd learned the previous night, did she want to retire to the small, dark chamber where walls seemed to close about her despite a candle's light. As people had begun surreptitiously peeking her way, she once again smoothed her barbette's edges and acknowledged a need for some task to keep hands busy.

With as much grace as she could command under the curious eyes of so many, Alyce turned and moved into the stairwell's distressingly shifting shadows. She would find Lady Elinor and offer herself to serve in any useful matter. Peeking into the family solar through a door slightly ajar, she found the one she sought and two more. Sybillene sat within the hearth's ring of warmth, near to dozing, while Lady Elinor quietly talked to a plump woman standing close. Alyce remembered seeing the cheerful-looking woman seated beside Sir Ulger at the head of the hall's center row of lower tables. With her gentle, amiable air, there was nothing intimidating about the woman. Nay, she was not intimidating, but she was interesting to look upon. Curious green eyes studied dark hair streaked by wide bands of white and worn in coiled plaits at the nape of a broad neck. Revealed by the wide mesh of a restraining crespin, the pattern thus woven was unique.

Alyce mentally shook herself free of distractions. This was no time to hesitate but rather time to seize what bravado she could muster and face the woman to whom she'd so oft been rude. Before she could turn into craven pigeon at the prospect of closely approaching Lady Elinor for the first time since her most recent discourtesy, Alyce pushed the heavy door wider and stepped inside.

"Pray, allow me to assist in the doing of whatever tasks await." When her hostess's fine, dark brows rose doubtfully, Alyce rushed to claim talents which, it was clear (perhaps with justification), were suspected lacking in one proven uncourteous and thus likely ill trained in a wellborn woman's proper duties. "For years I've shared in such chores at Keniver Castle." Alyce could truthfully have asserted experience in performing the major share of a castle mistress's duties. But she restrained honest words too sure to be heard as further insult, though in this instance insult of her stepmother rather than hostess.

Elinor's gaze rested on the woman earlier audacious defender of Dare, yet she was aware of Sybillene slipping silently away to avoid any expectation that she might also lend her aid to repay the gift of her keep. After a long pause which further strained Alyce's nerves, she nodded.

"Your aid would be appreciated in overseeing the weekly inventory of linens. I was preparing to do it myself when Cleva came and informed me that we are of a sudden called upon to serve the horde below a meal." Her tone revealed a hint of exasperation. "Thus, I must instead speak with those preparing what I fear will be an inadequate repast." Elinor rose as she spoke and modestly shook out the hem of her long gray overgown. "Cleva, I pray you to show Lady Alyce where the linens are stored."

With a cheerful smile and quick nod of her interestingly patterned head, Cleva looked to Alyce.

"Come, I'll show you where Orva and Maudie are waiting to begin. The linens are stored very near in an alcove at the stairwell's opening." Turning her comfortable girth toward the door, she motioned Alyce to follow.

"You are Sir Ulger's wife?" Alyce tentatively asked the

woman moving with more speed than her girth would suggest likely.

Cleva stopped so abruptly, Alyce came perilously near to bumping into her. "Aye, I am that, and Arlen's mother as well. And he do think you are the finest woman in all the world—Arlen, that is, not Ulger." She grinned but wrinkled her nose in acknowledgment of poorly chosen words. "I mean only that it must be thus as Ulger don't know you, while 'twas Arlen with whom you rode to arrive here."

"Arlen is a fine man and gave me aid when my too hasty tongue had me trapped on the edge of a peat bog." Alyce could see the curiosity glowing in Cleva's eyes, and to waylay questions for her meaning—which she had rather not answer—quickly continued. "When first I visited here with my father years past, he told me you had marvelous cures and potions to ease any ill. Is it so?"

Cleva was plainly flattered that her reputation as a healer had spread so widely. She grinned and nodded.

"I wondered . . ." Alyce hesitantly began. "I wondered if you'd permit me to help in their preparations. Even applications. I've an interest in medicinal arts and would be grateful if you would share with me some small portion of your knowledge." Alyce's conscience chided her for an untruth spoken, but she mentally argued an honest interest in the subject even if it was not her primary purpose in seeking Cleva's company.

"Whenever you have time unbespoken," Cleva instantly responded, "I'd be honored to share what small gifts in the healing arts I possess, and there's ever work to be done— curing, crushing, decocting, on and on."

Though Alyce had feared she'd forced an unwanted apprentice upon the woman, Cleva met her gaze so steadily, she was soon convinced the offer had been spoken in earnest. Without hesitation, Alyce nodded a pleased acceptance.

By midafternoon Alyce's stomach was making embarrassing noises in protest of the missed noontide meal, a choice she'd made to avoid the crowded hall. She lifted a stack of neat cloth squares from a stool brought into the alcove for that purpose and rose on tiptoe to place them atop the highest shelf. 'Twas amazing how tiring it was to direct two less than efficient girls in going carefully through the castle's mountainous store of bed, table, and bath linens. When she'd first met the pair, she'd thought them of a similar young age. But upon closer viewing Alyce had discovered that only the one who giggled almost constantly was less than a score in years, while the other, Maudie, was so timid, she merely seemed younger than she truly was.

Her back and legs ached unmercifully. Praise the saints, they were almost finished with checking for good care and amounts adequate to meet needs. (She uselessly wished for a more reliable notion of what was or was not adequate for a castle this size.) Alyce had been somewhat embarrassed by an inability to adequately direct without personally demonstrating each step in the process, thus tiring herself beyond all just cause.

Cleva appeared just as the last folded square of linen was returned to its shelf. She cheerfully smiled at the obvious relief on the lady visitor's face.

"Thought you might appreciate a few morsels of food to see you through to the next meal."

Alyce's answering smile was wide. "I admit I've begun to rue my decision to forgo the last." Yet even had Cleva not brought so welcome a proposal, she would've responded as readily to the open friendliness of this outgoing woman.

"There's many a tasty treat awaiting in the kitchen; come with me." Cleva instantly turned to lead the way.

Alyce glanced toward the two who had worked with her during the last few hours and quickly spoke to the retreating back.

"Cleva, my two assistants stayed with me and labored through the meal." Alyce paused meaningfully. "Doubtless they also would appreciate a sample of these promised morsels."

Cleva glanced back, surprised that a lady-born would consider any serf's discomfort. She grinned as warmly as bright summer sun. "Aye, there's enough and more for us all."

Orva giggled and without hesitation moved to join Lady Alyce while Maudie hesitantly followed a short distance behind.

Descending to the great hall, they skirted about its outer wall, passing between stacked trestle tables and people still crowded to watch as their dark lord delivered impartial judgments on the matters laid before him. Alyce caught only a brief glimpse of Dare as those gathered stood shoulder to shoulder and several deep. Frustrated by her unsuccessful attempts to see more, Alyce turned her attention to the soot-blackened fireplace wall they'd nearly reached. There a sizable woman presided over the sturdy young serf lifting a huge caldron into place. Most foods were prepared in the kitchens below, but it was here where stews and other such dishes eaten in vast quantities were prepared, and large animals were roasted.

Upon reaching one corner of the firewall, they began descending to a portion of the level below which, with bake ovens, spits, pans, and large cooking pots almost never at rest, was seldom dark or cold. Even in the deepest hours of night a shift of workers labored over fires to turn meats and stir bubbling concoctions.

Alyce was awed by the size of the castle's kitchen and the well-ordered actions of its small army of toiling people. She followed Cleva to the table pushed into a corner relatively quiet, if one discounted the constant clang of pans and sizzling of meats. While Alyce took a seat, motioning the hesitant girls to sit on either side, Cleva fetched a hand-sized pasty pie for each. Alyce watched in further amazement as the older woman lifted aside an unnoticed length of homespun, then reached far into a short, narrow opening to bring out a pitcher of milk.

"Put you anything deep enough into stone," she explained with a wry smile, "and stay cold it will."

The two who had helped Alyce with castle linens fair gulped down their pies at a single bite. Maudie was plainly uneasy in such close company with a lady of much higher station and quickly slipped away. Giggling Orva would happily have lingered in Alyce's presence for as long as could be arranged, if only to have something to boast of to her friends. But when Maudie withdrew, she had perforce to do the same.

As the two departed, Alyce gave them each a warm smile and soft word of thanks. Still, even before they were gone, Alyce's thoughts had returned to a subject seldom far from the surface and brought nearer yet by this morn's fearful revelation. She had not forgotten her vow to find and wield a truth-revealing light which would scatter the condemning shadows hovering over Dare. It was useless to seek further answers of Lady Elinor. That was clear. But by winning Cleva's promise to train her in herbal cures, Alyce believed she'd found an alternate source. She was certain others must possess the answers she sought, others here at the time of Dare's birth, others like Cleva. Thinking she'd time to plan a method to broach the subject before her "training" began, Alyce was unprepared to utilize this gift of an immediate opportunity to begin and paused, wondering how best to proceed. She'd a great fear of offending Cleva by asking pointed questions, as she had in her headlong attack on the topic with Dare's mother.

"Did cook assault your pie with an overabundance of salt?" Cleva asked the young woman whose fine brows were knit in a tight frown. "Or mayhap fierce white pepper?"

Embarrassment lent Alyce's creamy cheeks a red glow as she gave her head a brief shake. "I pray your pardon. Foolishly lost in thought, I dwelled upon a matter best ignored." Hardly that! Yet Alyce couldn't confess the bald truth of her ponderings.

Cleva's ready smile flashed again. She had a rough idea of the girl's concern. By nature observant, not to say nosy, and despite varying degrees of success in their efforts to shield honest emotion, she'd noted several actions. First, the earl's attention oft shifting to this young beauty; and second, Lady Alyce's irritation with the interest shown the handsome man by both Tess and the imprisoned baron's wife.

Cleva thought it might be a fine thing were Dare to have the wholehearted support of another woman in the castle, asides herself. Aye, a fine thing—but only were Dare able to accept the lady's attentions and his own responses in the manner sung of by minstrels. Their songs told tales of fine knights loving unattainable damsels from afar. (She'd earlier given her unsought blessing to Arlen's infatuation with the same damsel. Seemed for him a wise choice. One that would turn her son's thoughts from that other, utterly unworthy female.) It must be the same for Dare, elsewise awful deeds could follow and further muddy his already mired path.

In the second case, she prayed Lady Alyce understood the difficulty of matters at hand and still offered unstinting support. Cleva deemed it best that she probe to discover if this wellborn female was adequately apprised of the tangled dangers inherent in recent events.

"'Twere a wicked deed." Cleva went solemn with the words, and fire-glow rippled over the light and dark of her hair as she slowly shook her head.

"Wicked deed?" Alyce knew precisely to what Cleva referred—could be nothing but the deadly fire reported that morn. Yet she thought this a possible opening to topics she wanted to discuss.

"Aye, don't bode well for our lord, it don't." Again Cleva sorrowfully shook her head. "Though he has labored to bring the people to him, this proof of a devil bond, well, this . . ." The words trailed off into a despairing sigh.

"Dare had no devil bond! 'Twas his wicked father who named him demon." In his defense Alyce's temper flared free. An action thus proven not only the result of Dare's presence but one loosed merely by being within his domain. "How else but that a child so wrongly burdened struggle to win what should rightly be his? But an honorable desire to hold his hereditary lands is no reason to suggest he killed either Earl Cyril or the tanner. There is no true wickedness in him—none!"

Cleva fairly beamed with approval. Here was proof of what Arlen had told her of the lady's defense of their earl, proof that she knew the rumored wrongs and disbelieved them. Having earned this desired response, she hastened to reassure the fiery woman.

"With all you've said, I agree. I knew the earl from a babe.

Indeed, much of his first six years were spent with me and Ulger. And when he was gone I grieved his absence until the miracle of our Arlen's birth filled the void."

Alyce pressed her hands tightly to her cheeks, symbolically pushing unneedful ire back under firm bonds. Come to consider the matter, Arlen's birth must have been a miracle for Cleva, who it seemed certain would've been near an age where the bearing of a child was impossible.

"I pray your pardon." Alyce's voice was soft with regret for impulsive words. "Not for what I said, but the manner in which I spoke."

"No need, milady. I feel the injustice as strongly as do you. But I would add that although the old earl bears by far the greatest portion of blame for Dare's ill treatment, his mother is not innocent. Moreover, her actions are the more wicked still as 'twas born not of a wrong in him but a guilt in her."

Feeling herself moving nearer at last to attaining her vow's goal, Alyce tilted her head and studied a face suddenly closed for clues to the meaning behind her words. Seeing Cleva's gaze shift and widen, Alyce glanced sideways—and met a coldly furious glare. Lady Elinor stood not more than two paces distant.

8

Permit my baby to participate in your 'games,' I will—if you grant me a wish." Seeking a first indication of his response to her bargain, sapphire eyes peeked coyly at the devastatingly handsome man at whose side Sybillene sat. The earl's return for the noontide meal, a break in his usual habit, had filled the huge hall with the dull roar of the many guardsmen ever accompanying him, but she had no interest in any other.

Beneath Dare's charming smile, he was irritated beyond measure. How like the great schemer to manipulate every issue that came within her reach to further her own goals. Her "baby" . . . Aye, young Hal was that. 'Twas source of the problem he now sought to correct. While most boys his age had years earlier begun knightly training, Sybillene had kept Hal by her side. She was raising him as ill equipped to deal with the real life his future would assuredly mete out as Gabriel had been to face mortal combat. Dare felt honor-bound by right of the foster bond betwixt them to not merely see Halbert freed, but the man's son properly trained to become Keniver's strong and honorable heir rather than a replica of the milk-livered Walter.

Fortunately, such a program was already under way.

Among the nobles Dare had come to know during his days with Richard (and even before with Halbert) were several who'd had no hesitation in sending their sons to the new earl and proven warrior for fostering. A training system had been put into motion within weeks of his becoming Wythe's earl. Even had one of Dare's own vassels sent the two sons whom, during Earl Cyril's deteriorating days, he'd chosen to train himself. The older, Fanhurst, was now Dare's squire. A good-hearted adolescent was he, but by the indulgence of a father, inclined to be slothful, tardy, and far less than competent at any needful task. The younger, James, proved yet again how different two brothers could be. Shorter and slighter of build than his peers, he was near too serious in his earnest endeavors to prove himself the equal of any.

Blue eyes warmed as a pleasing thought struck Dare. James would be a good mentor for Hal—lending James confidence and Hal a gentle guide into challenges the other boys would already have mastered. But first he must bargain for Hal's allowed participation.

"I am not such a fool as to agree to any unnamed forfeit." Dare's lips had shifted into their more common mocking tilt, but he restrained an urge to jerk his hand free of the possessive hold she'd lowered upon it. He greatly regretted having yielded to the temptation of returning for the midday repast. It was not his custom to do so. Yet feeling heavily weighted by the certainty of progress lost and new dangers looming, he'd surrendered to the need for comfort promised by a glimpse of Alyce.

"'Tis naught but a wee, small thing." Sybillene lightly stroked the back of his hand, fascinated with its strength. "I would only have you ride beside and show me some little portion of your wonderful demesne."

Only that. Dare's smile never flickered, but behind it his teeth gritted. On any normal day the demands of his fiefdom would leave little time to waste on such unproductive pursuits, but after the ominous events of the previous day, he'd no time at all! At the scene of the fire he'd found only a small and possibly insignificant clue as to the identity of the deed's perpetrator—a footprint. Admittedly only a part of one and near overtrod by the villager who'd gone to fetch the tanner and discovered the home's charred remains. Only that single mark, and yet unique. Clearly it had been left by a fine dress boot such as those his friend Gilbert had given him, but made for a shorter, narrower foot. Few men could either afford or would be willing to risk so fine an article in mud and ashes—assuredly none of the peasants—and that limited the field of possibilities considerably. Nonetheless, he'd ordered an inquiry involving every person who dwelt within Castle Wythe's outer bailey—the gate guards would've allowed no stranger to enter without reporting the event to him. It was his hope that one under questioning might remember some little detail, some mention of an individual seen moving toward Howell's home, anything at all.

"And will you take me?" Sybillene tapped sharply against the hand she'd earlier caressed. She was not in the habit of being ignored when gifting a man with her attentions. "In exchange for Hal's knightly training?"

Dare's response was less than Sybillene sought. Rather than looking toward her, he glanced beyond to the boy seated on her left. The harshness of an irritated frown marred her earlier sweetly smiling face.

Examining the flirtatious woman's son, Dare acknowledged 'twas a miracle this youngster of dust-colored hair, coddled too long, possessed any strength of character at all. But in the few days since he'd brought Hal from Keniver, the boy had acquitted himself well. His sturdy form, clear and unwavering hazel eyes, and habit of answering any question, responding to any difficulty, without hesitation gave hope for better things. A fact which made it all the more important that Dare bow to Sybillene's wiles—in this small matter but no step further.

"I will do as you ask after Thomas has taken Hal to be introduced to his companions in training. Yet be aware that I can afford time for no more than a brief outing." He was anxious to resume his search for the cowardly knave who slunk through sinister shadows to strike with fire rather than stand in the pure light of day to challenge him face to face.

At the table's far end, another woman closely listened to the exchange between dark earl and golden beauty—by appearance a fine pair. A depressing but undeniable fact.

So Dare would go with Sybillene. Alyce intently studied the fine texture of the wheaten bread in her hand. He would submit to her wiles, and apparently most willingly. And a good thing that—if it won the prize. Her conscience mocked her for a liar. *Nay, truly,* Alyce strongly told herself. *I am happy that Dare will see Hal receive the training he should've been given afore.* 'Twas a hollow reassurance, yet this she could claim with a semblance of honesty. She was fond of her young half-brother, although Sybillene had seldom allowed the boy to wander far enough from her side that Alyce could truly claim to know him. But having seen him courageously approach Dare during their journey's night in the forest, she was proud and pleased to know Hal had more in him of his father than his mother.

Many and many a time she had considered going to the father they shared to speak of the unfairness in keeping a boy restrained from the pursuits of his peers. Yet her father doted on the boy, and she knew he couldn't bear to part with Hal in the usual way of sending him to be fostered in another lord's home. Asides, how could she, whom he had spent years attempting to train into a woman's submissive role, go to him with a concern over Sybillene's treatment of her son? How when it was Sybillene he'd told her to emulate? Just as he'd told her that Lady Elinor was the epitome of feminine refinement; Lady Elinor, the woman *she had* rebuked for her treatment of a son.

Alyce smoothed chilled fingers down her cheeks before dropping both nervous hands to the lap of her pale blue gown. She had accomplished nothing for either Hal or Dare and felt defeat glow like a black cloud on the horizon. As Thomas rose to his feet, her attention shifted to him, but her gaze couldn't help but slip to the woman beyond still fawning over the rough homespun molding Dare's strong arm. An unexpectedly fierce bolt of jealously flashed like lightning through the cloud.

As his friend stood and motioned the clearly excited boy to accompany him from the hall, Dare rose. He proffered his forearm to Sybillene. With the action he caught a glimpse of an interesting view. His disgust with this necessary jaunt in Sybillene's company had, of a sudden, been mitigated. In the flash of fire from emerald green eyes lay proof that Alyce cared enough to be jealous of time given another woman. 'Twas adequate reward for enduring a few hours within the selfish beauty's toils.

Glaring at Dare, who paused to don the hauberk left at the outgoing archway before again offering an arm to his companion, Alyce felt her vexation grow. This fierce concentration on the pair prevented her from noting the like emotion again emanating from the dark-haired female at a table below. Tess felt that enough was enough and too much. She would put an end to the competition from a "fine lady" who, as a married woman, had no right to seek the earl's company. Once before, Tess had near succeeded in attaining her goal. Tonight she would let nothing bar her path to that long held objective.

Almost alone at the table with Alyce, Walter narrowed his near colorless eyes in unvoiced resolve. He was seated at one end of the table, while Alyce occupied a seat at the other. Leaning forward, he looked around the Lady of Wythe, rightly holding a position midway between, and caught Alyce's attention.

"Come, walk with me."

Although she'd be glad of distraction from the bitterly unpleasant memory of Sybillene clinging far too tightly to Dare, Alyce had rather not go with Walter. Their transfer from Keniver to Wythe had given her a measure of distance from him, and she'd no desire to freely step back into the circle of his too-concentrated attentions. Her conscience instantly leaped to his defense. Walter was her friend and she ought not treat him shabbily. And yet . . . the mental argument continued. She'd promised to lend Cleva aid in preparing her herbal cures when time allowed. More important still, atop earlier discourtesies to their hostess, she'd not willingly add another by failing to render full assistance in any needful matter. She cast a worried look to the lady of Wythe.

Lady Elinor met the sidelong glance with a tight smile and

brief suggestion. "I recommend the orchard on the village's far end. 'Tis brightly hued and cheery at this time of year." With this, she, too, stepped down from the dais, leaving Alyce with no excuse that would not bruise Walter's feelings. Were she to claim an overriding need to lend aid to a peasant, be she guard captain's wife or scullery serf, he would of a certainty deem it a slight.

Walter lost no time in moving to stand behind Alyce. "It would seem a perfect destination as I've matters to discuss with you. Matters best talked of in privacy." He took hold of her narrow chair's tall back to ease her rising whether she willed it or no.

Alyce had done her best to evade Walter's hovering presence since the day of their arrival and had, until this moment, succeeded leastwise in avoiding time alone in his company. Now, however, the snare had been too well laid, and trapped she was.

"A brief walk." Alyce nodded with a less than honest smile. "But soon I must return." Lost in her own dilemma, she failed to recognize that this limiting of time surrendered nearly paralleled Dare's response to Sybillene's demand. "For the hospitality we've been given, I owe our hostess the fruits of my time and labors."

"A brief walk then, and after 'tis over, you must allow me to join my energies to yours in accomplishing whatever task needs doing." Walter's sincerity made it difficult for Alyce to openly reject another offer she had far rather refuse.

As he had won his objective, Walter's thin smile gleamed with triumph. He had surmounted this obstacle, and confidence in attaining the prize waiting at the end added an unusual measure of firmness to the actions he next took. First dispatching a servant to fetch Lady Alyce's cloak, Walter then solicitously handed her down from the high table and offered his arm in safely navigating through the throng of serfs filling the busy hall to quickly disassemble trestle tables.

Knowing Walter quite well enough to sense an ulterior motive behind this seemingly innocent invitation, from 'neath the cover of thick lashes Alyce peeked at the friend parading her across the chamber like a trophy won by valor in battle. Something was not right. Yet she'd no notion what Walter could possibly hope to gain during a walk within heavily fortified walls.

Alyce smoothed her free hand down one cheek. Had she gone witless? Thinking as if her friend were an enemy from whom she needed the protection of walls? How absurd! He could be annoyingly persistent in his attentions, but he could be of no danger to her or anyone else. And if he sought some goal from this "discussion," surely it was merely her safety. He plainly and possibly justly (though not in the manner he thought) believed Dare a danger to her. Likely he hoped to convince her to win free of the earl's hold.

Even as she nimbly sidestepped a falling trestle she pondered that strong likelihood and grew certain that such was Walter's purpose. Before they'd set out from Keniver, he had stated his case with unmistakable clarity and must now mean to do so again. What he thought she could do was the question when her stepmother, his own sister, had equally as clearly quashed his scheme for her "escape."

Once Alyce's warm, fur-lined cloak had been placed about her shoulders, they exited the castle with its assuredly curious crowd. Walter held his peace through the shadows of the entrance tunnel and down broad, empty steps leading to a courtyard left deserted by men with important pursuits to see complete. Only after they'd passed under the inner gate's two portcullises and set off across the wide drawbridge did he begin to speak—in an undertone intended to prevent even unseen listeners from hearing his words.

"You who were rightly trained by a father of honor must surely see the wrong, the threat to your good name, in remaining at Wythe. You cannot remain here in the hands of the same man who first deeply wronged your sire by wickedly seducing his wife, then caused him to forfeit both honor and home before, worst of all, being imprisoned."

Alyce inaudibly sighed. Her suspicions of Walter's motive had been correct. No surprise there. No comfort either. Hearing too much truth in his claim, she let her green eyes gaze upward to study a sky so heavily overcast, it seemed to drag as dishearteningly near as the discouragement hovering close. Despite tantalizing hints uncovered, she'd thus far failed in her quest on Dare's behalf, and now it seemed she'd failed her father as well. Although expecting some such purpose to Walter's "discussion," she hadn't been prepared for the hurtful truths behind his reasoning. Though she'd yet to accept Dare's guilt in the last of Walter's indictments, with her own eyes she'd seen proof of the first, and by virtue of that undeniable wrong alone, the rest of Walter's argument held a crushing power. By remaining willingly at Wythe, she dishonored not only herself but her father, too. Yet her heart trembled at the bleak prospect of leaving.

"I have nowhere to go." Desperate to justify staying where she'd no wish to leave, she offered the single objection that came quickly to hand, though she felt like a drowning woman wildly grasping at flimsy and inadequate ropes of straw. "My husband's family plainly wishes no open bond between they and a family tainted by the charge of treason. Likely they've no choice as of a certainty they'd find it difficult to overcome the stain spread to them by no fault of their own. I can't, won't, be responsible of an awful disrepute befalling people who've done me no wrong."

"Mayhap so, but—" though he admired her loyalty, Walter almost gleefully produced a rebuttal he knew she couldn't refute—"you can retreat to the lands of your own dowry, lands doubly yours by virtue of having been, upon marriage, named to you for dower. As a woman wedded, they belong to you no matter the charge laid against your sire. None can rightfully deny you their haven—neither your spouse's family nor even the earl."

"You made that same argument at Keniver, and there your sister, my stepmother, refused to permit me that option." As they skirted the village's outer edge, Alyce met Walter's growing satisfaction with firm resolve to disallow the thrusting upon her of a scheme too surely doomed.

"Nay. Already have I spoken to Sybillene on the subject, and she agrees with me. You risk what lingers of your fair reputation by remaining in the Demon's hold." Walter felt no regret for the green flare of pain in Alyce's eyes when he named the earl a demon. Best he see she not forget what a dangerous man Dare was.

Despite her best attempts to prevent it, Alyce's shoulders slumped. So Sybillene thought she ought depart from Wythe. Did she indeed. Her faint smile, so brittle it looked as if it might shatter, was a remarkable if faded reflection of the cynicism too oft upon Dare's lips. Doubtless the other woman was pleased by this opportunity to clear the field of any who might, for even a moment, distract Dare's attention from herself.

Alyce's gaze dropped to the ruts in a path they'd yet to leave though they'd already passed several neat rows of autumn-shaded trees—a sight too cheerful to bear. Walter had the right of it. 'Twas her honor which would suffer, and not hers alone, but that of her child-husband. Yet never had she wanted anything less. Save, mayhap, the unappreciated marriage bond her father had arranged.

Through narrowed eyes Walter saw her struggle between what was right and what she wished. Fearing her fiery temperament might see the latter win, he glibly used that very spirit to ensure she would do as he desired.

"Surely you can't mean to so easily surrender your good name?" Walter sounded appropriately scandalized, convinced 'twould rouse her temper.

Straightening with a pride unjustly attacked, Alyce looked direct into Walter's eyes. "Nay, assuredly I will not." In the quiet of her own thoughts she was not so certain of an honest zeal to back the claim, but how could she say elsewise?

"Then let's retreat to the hall and await the earl doubtless soon returning with my sister." Walter offered his forearm once again, and Alyce forced herself to unhesitatingly lay her small fingers atop. Without either having devoted a moment's interest to their supposed objective's brilliant display of bright hues, they turned to retread the path by which they'd arrived.

Their journey to the courtyard seemed to pass in a disgustingly brief time, and yet Alyce was so distracted, she barely noted the way. In truth, without Walter to physically lead her aright, she'd have paused to reflect on the matter weighing too heavily upon her. She was trapped! Trapped into doing a thing she'd no wish to do. She didn't want to leave Wythe, desperately didn't want to leave Dare. The conscience seldom silent for long rebuked her self-centered desires. If only for her father's sake, she must leave. Yet 'twas not merely for him that she must act. It was also her duty to uphold marital vows and preserve her husband's honor. Made no difference whether given to a babe or an old and doddering fool, 'twas her responsibility to keep those vows, and remaining within the "demon's" hold put them at risk—a risk even greater than Walter foresaw.

"Already they have returned."

Walter's low words broke Alyce's unseeing preoccupation with the sturdy planks of the lowered drawbridge beneath their feet. Glancing up, she saw two horses being led away from the bottom of the entrance stairway. She'd several moments to study them—one in particular, a huge black beast—before they disappeared into the stable built against the bailey wall. Fiend, Dare's destrier, was unmistakable.

Speak immediately when you see him, Alyce commanded herself once they'd reached those same steps. It must be done thusly, elsewise under Dare's potent presence she might fall weak to her own desires. With each upward step toward the heavy double doors, she bolstered her determination with brave admonitions to remember all the wise arguments her conscience had raised to enforce the need for this action. By the time Alyce reached doors slowly swung wide, she'd proudly convinced herself of a courage adequate to meet the challenge. Still she knew better than to risk the faltering of her false bravado in the tunnel's tightly enclosed gloom and closed her eyes, trusting Walter's care to see her safely through its darkness.

Even lowered lashes could not blind Alyce to a sudden flare of light as they entered the hall. Her heart beat out a rapid cadence of trepidation. Apprehension for an inability to do the deed? Or fear of unwanted success in winning free? After all, Dare had once attempted to see the king's knight deliver her into her husband's company. Failing that, he'd sworn to see it done himself. Mayhap he would have no care whether she remained or departed from Wythe. That possibility further weakened her resolve to speak an intent *not* truly wished. When anxiety-weighted eyelids rose, she found her courage further endangered by the power of a scowling blue gaze naught but a scant three paces distant.

Dare despised the frail "thing" at his sweet fire-vixen's side and would gladly have banished the weaker man from his home—from the earth itself. But by the very fact of Walter's weakness, 'twas impossible. Never, so long as he'd known Walter, had the man taken responsibility for himself. Always had he been dependent upon another. First resting upon his sister's tender mercies (as he was two years her junior, she had coddled him as a child in much the same manner as she now coddled young Hal), and then upon her husband's sturdy support. Now, with his brother-in-law imprisoned, Walter had nowhere but Wythe to go, no strength to rely upon but Sybillene. Dare would willingly have seen the wretched man a cast-out dependent upon what alms he could beg from strangers. But . . . plainly Alyce viewed Walter as a friend, and Dare would not risk injuring her by refusing aid to someone of import to her, however unfortunate he viewed their friendship.

Not daring to wait a moment longer, Alyce rushed to speak. "On the morrow I depart for Wrexdale." Fearing hasty words lacked force of will, she coldly added, "The lands of my dowry are where I belong and where I may preserve the purity of my virtue and honor."

One corner of Dare's lips lifted with wry humor. How like Alyce to make such a claim. Most men would say that honor was a thing no woman possessed—by her actions she might taint the honor of father or husband, but as chattel, she held none in her own right. Dare was not "most men," and this was not an issue he would debate with Alyce, for if ever any female had the courage and strength to hold it dear, it was she.

Alyce saw his mocking smile and resented his amusement at her expense. In her gaze green flames leaped to life to do battle with one of blue frost. "Aye, Wrexdale is where I belong and there I will reside until such time as either my father or husband is able to claim rightful dominion over me."

Dare recognized the thrown gauntlet in her reference to a rightful claim of dominion. He went still and cold, as if gone to pure ice while all remnants of amusement froze 'neath the depth of his proud anger.

"That you *will not* do!" Each clipped word fell from tight lips like icicles into the waters of a frigid moat.

"Oh, Dare, don't you think 'twould be best?" Sybillene, standing too long unnoticed at his side, passed a soothing hand down the taut muscles of an arm ending in clenched fist. The next instant she fell back from the fearful glare of distaste he cast at her, as if she were some loathsome rodent daring to cross his path.

While Dare's attention centered upon Sybillene, he missed the ripple of relief crossing Alyce's face. She smoothed a hand down a deep blue barbette before lowering tightly twined fingers to lie demurely against the soft and intricately embroidered girdle tied about her small waist. Dare was not so anxious to see her gone as she'd feared he might be—although whether due to a resentment of her challenge to his control or an honest wish to see her remain in his domain, she did not know. Nor was she willing to look deeper for an answer to the question when his command meant having the unappealing plan forestalled.

Dare returned the full weight of his attention to the rebellious female daring to question his right to claim even this little of her companionship, and in a flat, unbending voice he laid out irrefutable facts prohibiting her stated intention. "As a woman, a *virginal* woman unaccompanied by husband, father, or guardian to ensure your safety and the *virtue* you claim, you can neither journey to nor remain at Wrexdale—not alone."

Forgetting both her relief of moments past and the not-unjustified anger her verbal assault had likely roused in him, Alyce was infuriated by Dare's cold emphasis of "virginal" and "virtue" as if to question their truth when applied to her. Her sense of insult overrode all else, and a fiery temper burst free of its bonds. So untamed were the flames that their blaze overwhelmed even the ability to find words fierce enough to speak her disdain. Driven by frustration, she stomped a dainty foot so fervently, the leather-slippered weapon resounded against wood planking despite the thick layer of rushes between. The sound seemed to unnaturally reverberate ever more loudly in her ears. Abruptly swamped with embarrassment for the childish action, Alyce bit her lip while a tide of color spread up her elegant throat and thence across soft cheeks to rouge even the once pale cream of her forehead.

At the sight, Sybillene recovered both her composure and her hopes. If Alyce was not to begone from Castle Wythe, in her view, the next best option was this invisible but assuredly solid wall of anger dropped betwixt the earl and her stepdaughter.

Alyce abruptly spun about and, like an advancing firestorm, marched toward the arched entrance to exit tunnel and ascending stairwell. She need not, would not, remain to be further insulted! Green lightning flashed from beneath thunderously glowering brows. Glancing to the side, she caught sight of Arlen standing motionless, as if struck to stone, in the tunnel's shadows. When his expression of utter amazement for her bold battle with his demon lord gave way to awed admiration, it imbued her with a near uncontrollable urge to erupt in hysterical laughter. Clenching her lips tightly together to restrain the witless reaction, she surrendered the last shreds of her dignity and lifted the hem of her gown to make a dash for the upward steps. Even the shrinking walls of her tiny chamber would be better than remaining here below.

The lord's bed was amazingly comfortable! She could, and hopefully would, become accustomed to such pleasures. Tess nestled deeper into the feather mattress and with covetous eyes looked about the large chamber. 'Twas richly furnished with not only this high bed, draped with thick brocaded cloth, but intricately carved chests and even a Saracen carpet to warm the feet as one arose. Herein lay the goal hers since that night years gone by when in this very room she'd first seen Wythe's disdained second son. 'Twas a goal she had pursued with a fervency worthy of any great knight on some fanciful quest. She'd once come to this chamber at *his* invitation. However, they'd gotten precious few steps beyond the closed door and had shared naught but a single passionate kiss when some fool arrived to summon Earl Dare to receive an unexpected messenger from the Earl of Pembroke. That disappointing scene had taken place a mere sennight before came news of charges against Keniver's baron and the earl's immediate departure to "rescue" his foster family.

Try as hard as she might, she'd been unable to recapture the fascinating man's attention from the clutches of that wretched blond wife of another. Driven to a deed the other—as a wellborn and rightfully modest lady—surely could nowise commit, Tess had come and put herself into his bed! Experience (though not in the manner most believed) had taught the power of a voluptuous form, a power hers to wield over men who thought their gender made them all-powerful while in truth it made them weak.

Sitting up, Tess twitched the drape which opened toward the door into a perfect frame for the view she intended to meet incredible penetrating blue eyes when the door first opened. Reclining upon piled pillows, pulling a few dark curls forward to lie in shining contrast atop vast expanses of fair flesh, she struck a sultry pose and waited.

Dare's heavy tread coming down the corridor was unmistakable. Both worried and vexed by Alyce's claimed wish to flee from him, Dare had taken little note of the diversions provided this night in the hall by a troupe of traveling entertainers—two minstrels, a juggler, and far more rare, a fairly amusing jester. Alyce had departed the hall even before the troupe had begun their antics. Though she had attended the evening meal, unlike Walter, who'd absented himself under some foolish pretext, she'd spent its entire length glaring at untouched food. It worried him. He had refused to bend to her will. How could she possibly have expected else of him? No matter, the greater fear grew from how well he knew the fires of rebellion dwelling within her. Would she flout his command and attempt to do what she'd said? Pondering bleak thoughts, he pushed open the door to his chamber and took two steps inside before glancing up.

Tess's smile deepened triumphantly as blue eyes widened in surprise—surely a pleasant surprise. In the next instant she shrank back from the ice glittering beneath deeply scowling black brows.

"What sorry whim brings you to my bed—uninvited?" Did she think his one brief and quickly regretted attempt to ease with her what could never be shared with the other lent a permanent welcome to the pleasures of his bed? Fool! *He* had been the fool, and from that exercise in futility with the more than overtly seductive Tess, he'd learned himself doomed to desire only the one woman he could never have. That night's single gleam of good fortune was the interruption which had prevented an embarrassing revelation of his inability to complete the deed begun.

"I—I—" Tess initially stuttered in confusion but soon took firm hold of her surely logical excuse for coming. "Since the night a messenger intruded, we've not had an opportunity to resume our play." She flirtatiously peeked at him sidelong—to no avail.

"I simply thought to save you the difficulty of summoning me while so constantly surrounded by guests. I know the rules governing a gallant knight and honorable lord might not permit a public request." Shifting to rest on one elbow and clearly display her full bounty to its most erotic advantage, she watched for the weakening to pleasure she expected would soften a harsh glare. Instead, blue eyes narrowed with distaste while his cold half smile mocked her "thoughtful" action.

"You should believe leastwise some small measure of my reputation. I have shattered more rules than you are likely to ever know exist. And if I desired your so abundant charms, nothing and no one would prevent me from making my wishes clear." Contempt coated the words with ice. Unbeknownst to Tess, as much for himself as for her.

"But never would I accept a thing of so little value it needs must be thrust upon me unsought." Dare strode forward to jerk the covers from her nude form with one hand and scoop up the pile of her discarded clothing with the other. "Begone!" he roared, tossing the garments at the cringing woman.

Tess was stunned by his unexpected movements and shattering rejection. Nonetheless, she made haste to abandon the bed, pulling a formless gown over her head as she scurried from the chamber.

Watching her depart, Dare acknowledged an unjustified harshness he ought not to have allowed. But her unwanted surprise had been that one disagreeable event too many which had broken control already strained by time wasted with Sybillene and battered by Alyce's announced intent to leave. With a decided snap he closed the door behind a retreating back left bare by untightened laces.

A loud sound plucked Alyce from light and restless slumber. Oppressive darkness settled on her chest while an irrational sensation of walls closing in set her heart to pounding. Struggling against panic, she sat up to seek the reassurance in a narrow band of illumination falling through the door left ajar. Her eyes widened when a shadowy figure paused just beyond.

Quietly Alyce rose and moved forward to peek through the opening. The dark-haired servant so proprietorial of Dare stood close enough that Alyce could easily reach out and touch the woman did she wish it so. Her back was turned toward the door—her bare back—while with amazing dexterity she reached behind to pull laces tight and close the gap. What excuse could a serf have for being on this level at so late an hour of the night? Peach-soft lips curled in self-contempt. What excuse indeed. Had she not just admitted how possessive of Dare the woman was? Seemed she had an excellent rationale to support that sentiment. Certainly more excuse than Alyce had for her own jealousy—an emotion which had never bitten so hard as at this very moment.

Alyce remained unmoving until the other had threaded slender fingers through dark, tousled waves of hair and achieved some semblance of grooming before gliding from view. Feeling caught by an utterly unexpected blow, Alyce fell back to her bed. She dropped upon it so hard that under the rough treatment, widely woven cloth strips supporting a straw-filled mattress sagged and came dangerously near to snapping. Upon first seeing the woman's reaction to Sybillene's hold on Dare, she had assumed they were lovers. It was far from uncommon for wellborn men to seek physical ease with women of lower station, and she should certainly not be surprised by Dare's liaison with this sensual female. Yet these facts did nothing to lessen Alyce's distress, and the path to slumber's longed-for oblivion eluded her until the gray light of predawn had stolen purpose from the corridor's torch.

LADY MIDNIGHT

you are, with herbal salves, strewing rue and other
purgatives, preparing. He'll live. I know. He has said
how he... No. He is not your husband to be. I know...
stepmother... their presence in this... place... tis
numb her in... frozen... and take comfort... nights...
again... wish...

9

A persistent knocking forced Alyce from long-delayed
sleep, and unwillingly she rose on one elbow. Brushing hair
tangled by a restless night from green eyes, she struggled to
focus on the face peeking through the opening provided by a
door pushed further ajar.

"I am Tess, and Lady Elinor bade me come to aid you this
morn." The unwelcome intruder stepped boldly into the
small, dark chamber. "Says I am to be your personal servant
for all the days of your visit, same as Maudie will do for your
stepmother." While she spoke, Tess moved round to place
her lit candle atop the remains of the last to burn out.

Alyce's mouth fell open. What wicked imp of fate had
sent this particular woman to her? Had Lady Elinor somehow known what a blow Tess's attentions would be and
arranged it to punish her for the rebukes she'd spoken?
Surely not! Or mayhap so. Whichever made no difference
when in the end it was simply a reality.

"I don't want—" Alyce began despite the fact that the
woman had already moved to the bed's other side, cleared
the wicker trunk's top, and begun rooting through the few
neatly folded garments it contained. "That is, I'm accustomed to doing for myself."

On her knees and bent over the trunk, Tess straightened to

128

rest on her heels. "My lady commanded me to do for you, and do for you I *must.*" Determination glowed in the pale brown eyes meeting a green gaze directly.

Disoriented by lack of sufficient rest and this unexpected development, Alyce failed to muster a rational argument against the proposed relationship. Whatever she might say to deny the command would assuredly be reported to the one who had given it, and just as assuredly be received by Lady Elinor as a further insult. Alyce's shoulders slumped. For today, leastways, she would submit to Tess's ministrations. But afore the next dawn, she was determined to find some worthy excuse to end the unwanted service.

"This'll be a fine choice for a day so gray. Add some cheer, it will." Tess held up a crimson wool gown that glowed in gay contrast against her own dreary homespun dress. "Moreover, 'tis warm."

It was her favorite dress, and Alyce accepted the choice for the confidence it would lend to meet Tess's presence with an appearance of tranquility—once it had been donned. There the greater problem lay. She was more than a wee bit reluctant to leave the bed and its sheltering coverlet. Though all people slept unclothed, the prospect of rising before Dare's lover to bare her adequate but less plentiful bounty was too difficult to endure. Alyce suddenly reached out, snatched the gown from Tess's hold, and pulled it over her head. Having thus averted a threatened embarrassment, she stepped from the bed partially garbed while at the same time roughly tugging front lacings closed. She had never before worn this or any other gown without a camise beneath. But with its raglan sleeves narrowing to fit snug at wrist and of a length that they gently ruched, providing covering near to her thumb, she felt confident that 'twas modest—so long as the front were tightly joined and fastened securely at throat. Later, when alone, she would remedy the lack.

Tess was startled, but shrugging infinitesimally at the daft and incomprehensible habits of those wellborn, she turned and lifted the bone-backed brush earlier set aside to allow the trunk's opening.

"If you'll bring that stool over here and sit near the

candlelight, I'll brush and braid your hair." The lady visitor seemed oddly disquieted by her presence, and Tess wondered why. Had Lady Alyce heard some small portion of the tales attached to her name? Yet what matter could that be to Lady Alyce? No woman wellborn had care of a serf's wanton behavior. (Of serfs, they expected little more.) Only might a lady be concerned if the man involved was her husband. But that logic provided no explanation for Lady Alyce's strange discomfort as, although Tess had been told the lady was wed, her husband was neither here nor of an age to cause such troubles. Dark lashes fell for an instant's time. Beyond husband, a lady might be distressed by the straying passions of another man beloved. Pale brown eyes opened to curiously study the other woman.

Alyce looked between the brush firmly held by strong hands and the small three-legged stool while irritation began flicking sparks at her temper's dry tinder. Rightfully mistress of this meeting, she could simply turn her back on the woman to don the deep blue veil and barbette worn the day past and still lying neatly aside the wooden chest (despite their failure to complement her dress). But what victory in an action which would leave her feeling woefully ill prepared either for meeting Dare's doubtless continuing disapproval or for dealing with the unpleasant *recent* memory of a Tess fresh from his embrace? Pleased with her ability to use cool logic in suppressing a fiery spirit, she instead submitted again to a servant's, *this* servant's, direction.

Once Lady Alyce was seated, Tess began methodically stroking the brush through masses of gleaming tresses. "Why do you hide such lovely hair 'neath them things?" Tess nodded toward the head-garb Alyce had nearly donned and followed her purposeful compliment with a pointed observation. "I had thought you must be shamed by locks either thinning or drab in color. Clearly 'tain't so."

"My father raised me to modesty." Distracted by a suspected contempt wrapped in flattery, without thought Alyce gave the reasoning which for a lifetime had directed her actions. "He taught me that modesty demands a woman keep her hair as well covered as her form."

"Most men wouldn'a have it so. Has been my experience

that they like to see hair flowing free and pleasure in burying their hands in its thickness. And don't matter whether serf or noble. Even the earl enjoys such pleasures." Tess felt the tiny cringe earned by her talk of the earl's preferences and, standing safely behind, smiled in triumph for having won the proof she sought of the lady's emotions. Seemed plain Lady Alyce had indeed heard of the "relationship" which for years she'd claimed to share with the earl. Were this lady's feelings returned, 'twould provide Tess with the perfect opportunity to see the earl's insult of the night past returned in kind.

"Asides," Tess continued in a tone unchanged, "your stepmother don't cover her hair so completely, and betimes even Lady Elinor merely braids and coils hers."

Alyce had no rebuttal for the last calm words of the woman efficiently plaiting her hair into fat braids that hung well past her waist. In addition to a vision of Dare running his hands through Tess's dark locks, Alyce clearly heard a repetition of his distaste for the restraints she placed upon hers.

Alyce fervently hoped that once done, Tess would depart and leave her in peace. Peace, hah! There was no peace to be had in the whole of this castle. Here in her chamber she'd either to face darkness and walls that closed in or endure another's unwanted company. To go below meant a renewed visual confrontation with Dare, which, with disheartening thoughts of Tess and him together, would be a complication too difficult to be borne.

A small smile lifted the once flat line of her lips. Only if she descended while he was still within castle gates. To circumvent that danger she need merely avoid entering the great hall before he'd departed. Rather, she would slip from the castle and its courtyard to retrace the path of the previous day's walk—alone. Mayhap this time she'd be able to enjoy the orchard's bright display. Pleased with her plan, she immediately set it into motion.

"Pray leave me." Although gently said, Alyce reclaimed the authority to command. "I'll coil my own hair later as I've a fierce throbbing in my head and wish to lie down once more. Take this news to Lady Elinor with my plea to be excused from the morning meal." Glancing into pale eyes with credible distress, Alyce rubbed her forehead convincingly.

Tess frowned but nodded and obeyed. Left in privacy, Alyce sighed in relief for one impediment overcome as she began hastily coiling braids at the back of her neck. Surely a leisurely stroll through the beauty of autumn colors would soothe ragged nerves and in some measure restore an ability to objectively view matters beyond her control.

Another knock sounded just as Alyce lifted a brilliant white barbette. Dropping her hand, she guiltily thrust the garment behind her back. "Enter," she called, hoping her voice sounded appropriately frail.

"Lady Elinor says as you've another headache and sent me to see what I might do to ease its pain." Cleva rolled into the room, radiating concern.

Alyce bit her tongue in frustration. She'd gone witless! How could she have failed to consider that any excuse used so oft, if believed, might rouse anxiety? Alyce worried that by lying now, she risked the friendship she'd hoped to earn from Cleva.

After running from Dare the past day, she'd gone, as intended, to her chamber. But despite her belief that anger would make it elsewise, its walls had soon begun closing in. To escape its tightening hold, she'd slipped out and joined Cleva in the curtained alcove where medicinal herbs were stored. She had spent the remainder of that afternoon helping this open and cheerful woman and learning much of herbs and their uses. It had been the most serene and pleasant time she'd ever spent in Castle Wythe. And now it hurt to think that by her ill-considered action she might disillusion the older woman she'd come to admire. Slowly shaking her uncovered and bright head, Alyce decided to speak honestly to this person she chose to trust.

"I lied—but for an innocent purpose. When last I saw him, the earl and I had a . . ." Alyce paused, struggling to find a word appropriate but not too harsh, and settled for the first she'd thought to use. The truth and yet a choice softening the dispute's intensity. "A disagreement. A simple disagreement."

Cleva's eyes widened and sparkled. She doubted any "disagreement" with Earl Dare could ever be described as "simple." And, all other considerations aside, given the intensity with which the man constantly watched this female, she was certain their conflicts would never be so restrained they could be that easily described.

Alyce saw the amusement her choice of wording lit in Cleva's eyes but doggedly continued. "Merely would I avoid meeting Dare this morn. I thought it would be a relief to us both were I to seek a private time away from the castle, a walk in the orchard, while others are at their morning meal. Once they are done and Dare has departed, I meant to return and lend help wherever needful." Sincerity rang as true in her claim as the bells of a cathedral.

On Wythe, gossip traveled very quickly; talk of their "demon" faster still. Cleva had been told of the confrontation betwixt earl and young damsel even before that same damsel had joined her the previous day. Yet during their time together, she'd sensed the girl's distress and now accepted this explanation without hesitation. "Aye, well, you go on out to the orchard." Cleva smiled in gentle understanding and gave a conspiratorial wink. "I'll tell milady that you'll be up and about afore the morn's gone—so long as you are left in peace for a time."

Though sympathizing with the damsel's hurt, Cleva was more than a wee bit relieved by the pair's conflict. She'd watched them closely and been forced to admit that a tame, "distant" liaison such as the minstrels sang about was highly unlikely to long survive untested between them. Nonetheless, she would do what she could to ease their distress.

Alyce beamed her gratitude while quickly wrapping a narrow strip of white cloth under chin and settling one larger over bright hair. Then, swirling a bark brown cloak about her shoulders, she slipped past her indulgent conspirator and hurried down dark stairs, letting one hand brush the wall's cool, rough stone while peering cautiously ahead to avoid unforeseen encounters. She met no one and soon escaped the castle. A new day's chill gray light engulfed her as she moved down broad wooden steps and into the courtyard. The heavy bars of the two portcullises guarding castle and courtyard were still rising to permit the day's business, and the sound of their clanking chains greeted her with a reminder of the awesome might they represented.

Too aware of the faceless bulk walking the ramparts above, Alyce passed beneath the deadly iron grillwork of the first and on through the short but gloomy tunnel between it and the next. Fearing the sentry might question her going, she hastened across the wooden drawbridge on its far side. But, though from his post on the walkway surmounting the massive stone wall, he'd an excellent view of her progress, no word was spoken.

Having moved past the gateway unchallenged, she felt her courage rise and set free an anticipation for time alone which she'd earlier restrained for fear it might yet be foiled. She paused to take a deep breath of crisp autumn air and, blessed with a clear view unsullied by the normal mists of morn, looked all around. Fairly high on the rise whereon the castle perched, she could see the fertile countryside beyond the outer bailey wall. Despite the early hour, an unharvested field was already busy with distant workers who appeared to be crawling over it like a plague of insects.

Returning her attention to a scene nearer, Alyce visually followed the path skirting the village to where trees, though half-denuded of brilliant leaves, yet offered a welcome haven and much-desired solitude. Its silence beckoned her and she lost no time in physically following the same path to gratefully penetrate its wooded boundaries. The small orchard had long since been both harvested and gleaned of apples, crab apples, pears, and what little else of tree-borne fruit could be coaxed to grow. Here was a retreat where she could not easily be subjected to the interruptions of others and where she could ponder the tangled web of duty and personal desires, of jealousy and love. Aye, love. She had loved Dare for as long as she could remember and doubtless always would no matter the impossibility, the forbidden sin of any relationship between them.

Wandering inattentively through uneven rows, with her toes she absently ruffled the multihued leaves layering the ground. Troubled thoughts rolled over her like storm clouds clashing against each other. Pain for the attentions Dare had given Sybillene, and anguish for the view of Tess fresh from his embrace. Irritation with Wythe's people for unjustified suspicions of their lord, and despair for her failure to secure proof of the man's innocence of true evil.

Too preoccupied even to host an honest appreciation for the beauty surrounding her, Alyce was caught utterly unprepared by the brawny arm reaching out from behind to lock about her waist. Its vise effectively trapped her arms uselessly against her sides while a hand clamped tight over her mouth, forestalling all but the faintest of muffled cries.

Pale blue eyes glittered dangerously. Although Dare believed the news of Alyce's disappearance, the beam of his penetrating glare swept the near-deserted great hall and delved into the shadows of its each corner. He had ever encouraged Alyce's fiery spirit. Yet this time she'd gone too far. Seemed clear the obstinate female had not merely ignored his logical opposition to her plan but had already departed Wythe for Wrexdale. And, more foolishly still, set off alone!

"I . . ." Walter shifted uneasily when the Demon's attention fell heavily upon him. "That is, not one among us have seen Alyce yet this day." Despite a discomfort under the man's unrelenting stare, Walter delighted in the earl's surely frustrated anger and only with difficulty restrained a smile. That the willful damsel had gone to do as he'd urged was a fact Walter did not rue. After all, what could the Demon do to alter a done deed? The urge to grin faded. He'd rather not have an answer to his own silent question and wished the fearsome man hadn't unexpectedly returned at midmorn. Men he'd thought reliable had assured him the earl rarely appeared for the noontide meal, and never earlier. And today it would've been far better if, as expected, the earl had remained busy elsewhere the whole day long, for Walter had set a plan into motion whereby, should Alyce fail to flee of her own accord, those who watched would "aid" her toward success in the deed.

When Sybillene glided to Dare's side, candlelight glowed on golden hair coiled and restrained at her nape by the fine mesh of a nearly invisible snood. Though she'd never defy the rules of propriety so far as to leave it flowing free, she saw no reason to completely hide the gleaming mass she knew to be one of her greatest assets.

"Seems my misguided stepdaughter has flouted your will and set off for her dower lands." More than a small bud of satisfaction bloomed in Sybillene's tone. A bloom so hardy that it wilted only slightly beneath the blue-ice glare briefly turned her way.

Dare purposefully withdrew his attention from the irritating woman and returned it to the bearer of unpleasant news, the creature he could view as no more than a half man. A blue gaze dropped to nervously shifting feet and went hard. Walter wore fine shoes, shoes like those given him by Gilbert, shoes like those which had left a print in ashes. How many pairs did Walter possess? These showed no sign of the punishments assuredly rendered the footwear worn by one who'd stood close to the flames. Giving a brief shake to dark hair, Dare scoffed at suspicion surely gone awry. What possible reason could Walter have for inflicting such senseless harm upon a stranger? Plainly, Dare admitted, he'd focused upon the matter for too many long hours, far too many when it distracted him even momentarily from the missing damsel.

He whirled toward the exit, and a black calf-length cloak swirled about his powerful form. Praise the saints, after completing the depressingly fruitless house-to-house inquiry through the village, he'd had reason to return to the castle. Elsewise this unwelcome report would have been left too late. Even now 'twas questionable whether or not he could achieve success in saving the impetuous woman from her action's likely hazardous consequences. Nowhere in England was it safe for a lone woman to journey abroad, and assuredly not here on a fiefdom that had long suffered under his sire's lax control. Partially through the entrance tunnel's shadows, a quiet voice brought him to a halt.

"Dare . . ."

He turned toward the bottom of ascending stairs where nervously hovered the single woman, asides mother and the two visitors from Keniver, who would risk calling him by name rather than title. Gentle Cleva's round face was puckered with worry.

"Lady Alyce told me she meant only to walk in the orchard while others partook of the day's first meal. Said she'd return to the castle once—" Cleva paused, sending an apologetic grimace to Dare "—once you had gone. She confessed as you two had a falling out. Plainly uncomfortable 'neath your disapproval, she sought only to put off facing you again this morn." After a long moment of telling silence, Cleva hastened to defend her new friend, although not totally convinced of the verity in her own words. "But Lady Alyce promised she would then return and lend aid where needful—as she's done each day since her coming." Beneath her breath and in a tone of disapproval she added, "Unlike that other one."

The grim line of Dare's mouth took on a cynical twist in acknowledgment of Sybillene's self-centered and slothful nature. His mind then closed against matters pertaining to one of negligible interest while the damsel far more important was in a danger her fiery spirit had likely counted for naught.

"My thanks, Cleva." Weak flamelight rippled over black hair as he nodded his gratitude. "I'll begin my search in the orchard and pray Alyce is safely there. If not, still I will find her—in the end."

The morning repast had ended so long ago that the next meal was drawing nigh. A fact which left little hope Alyce's absence could be so innocently explained as the ever optimistic Cleva would have it be. Determination tensed his every muscle as Dare turned to move through the dark tunnel and begin the hunt for a quarry more precious to him than any ever sought before.

Thomas stood waiting with good-natured impatience at the bottom of the castle's outgoing stairway. Expecting a return to the continuing search for clues pointing them to the perpetrator of this ghastly fire at the tanner's home, he held the reins of two massive destriers. As Dare strode past a door thrown wide, only the abrupt raising of bushy brows betrayed the older man's surprise at sight of the icy mask robbing his friend's face of emotion. Thomas knew the man well enough to sense a savage war between fury and fear raging beneath his impassive surface.

"Alyce is missing." The low and ominously gentle words were issued even while Dare swung into the saddle. "I am told she planned a walk in the orchard. We'll start there, but I am near certain her trail will lead beyond outer bailey walls." Dare chose not to summon his whole garrison to join the search as he and Thomas possessed the most experience and could more easily follow the trail unhampered. Asides, 'twould do both Alyce and himself more harm than good were the inevitable rumor-sown seeds of this new wrong to sprout into unsavory whispers before the truth behind it were known.

Mounting just as quickly, Thomas followed the forbidding man's lead while his thoughts moved along similar lines. Wythe's gossip vine was one of the healthiest he'd ever encountered, and along its ever-lengthening tendrils the tale of Lady Alyce's defiance against the earl had quickly spread. He liked the fiery young woman and, as did Dare, recognized the danger in her apparent rebellion.

The two men raced headlong toward a portal which on arrival so short a time past they'd found strangely unguarded. An irritated Dare had intended to investigate the reason for this unmanned gate, but news of Alyce's absence had driven the wrong from his thoughts. Focused now upon deeper concerns, he wasted no time on the matter as they passed beneath the heavy iron grilles of two lifted portcullises and sent huge steeds thundering over the day-lowered drawbridge.

Soon leaving the village behind, Dare motioned Thomas to circle around and pass through the orchard from its far side to meet him in the middle. The day's slight breeze, increased by the speed with which the mighty destriers raced, rippled his black cloak like an ominous flag threatening any man foolish enough to stand against him with approaching danger. Their calls went unanswered by aught but the thudding of their own horses' hooves and the shifting of wind-scattered leaves. In the midst of cheery boughs they met, but the absence of the prize they sought clouded the view with a dismal fog. Dare surrendered to fury, for the peril if not the woman about whom it almost certainly swirled. Directing their horses to turn, they made short work of departing the place of bright leaves and headed straight for the outer bailey gate.

On their rapid approach to Wythe's farthermost defensive gate, they discovered it, too, was not only unguarded but gaping open. Fighting to close his thoughts to bitter images of what might be, Dare hardened his expression beyond thunderous anger to a renewed but more deadly impassivity. Neither man need speak. The awful implications could be seen as clearly as treacherous rocks at the bottom of a shallow stream. Either the two guards had ignored their lord's will and lent their aid to the errant Alyce's flight or . . .

Dare hurled Fiend into a further burst of speed. Once beyond the gate, the two riders raced toward the woodland's dark wall. The forbidding destination presented an image of dense gloom only intermittently relieved by the rare stray beam of dull daylight striking an autumn-bright hue. Once they were within the forest of close-grown trees and riding side by side, their pace eased to facilitate an intent scanning of greenery edging the route marked by heavy use. Of a sudden Dare reined to a halt.

"Either they count me for a fool or expected no pursuit for some lengthy time." A cold blue gaze narrowed on broken bushes and crushed ferns—confirmation of the truth in his words. Dare was disgusted by how little care had been taken to hide the point from which the perpetrators of this latest wrongdoing had departed the path.

Rather than answering the obvious, Thomas dismounted and bent to examine the evidence more closely. When he looked up, his normally genial face had gone harsh. "Two horses. No more."

Dare was as utterly unmoving as the stone monoliths on Salisbury Plain. Had Alyce gone willingly, there would surely be three sets of hoofprints. Yet relief that this was not a case of her fiery spirit turned against him in rebellious flight could not completely douse either the discouragement lent by proof that two of his own purposefully worked against him or the rage roused by the certainty that Alyce had been assaulted. Even the last odious thought caused no flicker of reaction to cross Dare's face, although black lashes dropped to prevent a glimpse of the mingled delight and anger flashing in blue eyes. Only Alyce and all matters having to do with her could so thoroughly disrupt his proudly held emotional control. And only where Alyce was concerned did he deem it necessary to maintain the shield of that control between himself and Thomas.

Fearing for Alyce's safety and anxious to waste no moment more, Dare instantly turned his black stallion to follow the trail foolishly laid between massive trees whose half-bare limbs made strange patterns against a bleak overcast sky. As they pressed deeper into thick foliage beginning to surrender to the icy grip of coming winter, a pungent odor rose from the path's recently trampled undergrowth. While tracking their quarry with all the haste allowed by a virginal trail where stumble holes and half-hidden obstacles waited to catch the unwary, helmeted heads safely ducked low-hanging branches that then caught at shoulders only to slide harmlessly over mail-clad bodies.

Lifting a guantleted hand, Dare again came to an abrupt halt. The path of the two horses unaccountably diverged. One set of hoofprints turned in the direction of Wrexdale. The other veered in nearly the opposite direction. This time it was Dare who dismounted to study the marks.

"You follow that path." Without looking up, Dare motioned his companion toward the south.

Thomas's expressive brows shot up. "You want that I should be the one who reaches her lands?"

Dare glanced up with a wry smile for his friend's apparent confusion, but the curve of his lips did little to lighten a dark expression. "Nay, only track him to the end of Wythe lands; and if you have not overtaken the wretch by then, return to Castle Wythe. I cannot afford to be without your support for as long as it may take to search him out, and will send another to do that deed."

"But what if it is he who carried Lady Alyce?" Observant by nature and training, Thomas had long since recognized the hopeless bond betwixt her and Dare and couldn't believe Dare would willingly put her care into the hands of any other.

"He isn't," Dare flatly stated, simultaneously pointing toward the prints leading off in each direction. Only did Dare wonder who was so foolish as to think he might be misled by a trail so obviously false. Must have been planned by someone possessing neither experience nor training in tracking fleeing foes.

Bushy brows furrowed above narrowed eyes. By closely watching Dare, he'd failed to see the physical evidence supporting his friend's reasoning. Even from atop his steed Thomas could see that the tracks leading away from Alyce's dower lands were far deeper, assuredly left by a horse bearing a heavier burden upon its back. 'Twas barely possible yet most unlikely that the difference was caused by a single, much bulkier rider. He'd no doubt but that this factor had already been weighed by Dare, who, aware of which two men were assigned to guard the gates, knew their relative sizes. Though the gray afternoon's light was limited, it glowed over the intermingled gold and silver on Thomas's head as he nodded a wordless acceptance of his task.

While Thomas urged his steed away and into a relentlessly steady pursuit, feeling close to his goal, Dare remounted and put Fiend to as near a full gallop as conditions allowed.

Each moment seemed the length of an eon before Dare caught his first glimpse of a heavily laden steed carefully picking its way through thick undergrowth. Plainly its rider had no expectation of a possible pursuit.

Exhausted by useless struggles, a discouraged Alyce felt like a trussed stag carcass draped over the rump of its hunter's steed. Or more aptly, as she was hooded and her limbs were bound by thin leather strips, like a captive falcon. To whip her flagging spirits into renewed vigor, Alyce silently vowed that she could be equally as fierce!

I will not be easily taken! Nor will I fall craven before faceless foes! To lend credence to her bold assertion afore weary limbs and gloomy thoughts prevented further efforts, she resumed the lost struggle. Twisting wildly, she fought to roll far enough to the side that with feet tied together, she could kick against the huge beast carrying an unwilling burden. Her attempted escape won from her captor only a heavy, flat-handed blow to her derriere and a derisive bark of laughter. Fuming beneath both muting gag and blinding hood, Alyce silently swore to wreak upon this . . . this worm a retribution of some kind . . . someday . . . somehow. 'Twas a fine goal, yet the list of variables did more to dampen her courage than inspire self-confidence.

In an effort to restrain growing panic and keep her attention from the ever greater discomfort in being draped facedown over the rear of a horse, she methodically reviewed the few facts of which she was certain. From her abductors' whispered conversation at the outset she knew there were two of them. But who were they? And why had they taken her captive? Moreover, why had one veered off in a different direction? The fading sound of thudding hooves had attested to the truth of that fact.

There seemed more questions than answers. And that irritated Alyce, who deemed herself a sharp-witted woman, one who ought be able to find leastways her abduction's underlying purpose. Yet how else but that she should be thwarted in her quest when with her head pointed toward the ground for so long, she'd gone dizzy. Further vexed by the instinct to justify her failure in following right logic, she cautioned herself to the need for clear thinking. Fiercely concentrating, Alyce needlessly clenched hood-shielded eyes and through sheer effort of will sifted through woefully muddled thoughts for a query addressing the initial problem; the single one which, if answered, would expose a clear path through the maze of inexplicable actions and motives.

Surely had it not felt like all the thistledown from an entire field of such weeds had been packed into her head, it would've been conspicuous and easy to frame. No! Alyce's fiery spirit heatedly rejected this further excuse, particularly as the question she sought was plain enough: For what earthly purpose had she been taken? She'd silently asked the same before, but the answer was not so simple to state. Did these men mean to hold her for ransom? Poor choice. Even bound and gagged as she was, a spark of wry humor flared to lessen her feeling of futility. She was of absolutely no political import, and heiress to no great fortune. Indeed, as she was the daughter of a far less than wealthy man, worse a man declared traitor and whose every possession had been held forfeit to the crown, those who had seized her had no remote hope of being paid for her return. Yet what other reason could there be for her abduction? For the abduction of anyone? It made no sense at all.

As effectively blocked as if the grille of an unyielding portcullis had dropped, she turned her thoughts from the frustrating, disheartening endeavor to force senseless deeds to reveal some sensible reasoning. Instead, she refocused her energies on devising a plan for winning free of restraints and captor. If not from both, then leastways from one.

Had her earlier repeated attempts to see the horse rear up and throw both her and the vile toad occupying the saddle in front of her to the ground succeeded, 'twould've provided the slight possibility of injury to her captor and thus increased chances for one hooded, gagged, and bound. Unfortunately, it had failed, leaving her with one last chance.

Slung over the tail end of a powerful steed, it should be possible to simply separate herself from the beast by stealthily wiggling farther and farther back until she fell free. Having been motionless for some little time, surprise would be on her side. Were she to achieve this goal, the wretch in front would know her intent the moment she dropped from the horse. Then it would require nothing less than a true miracle to prevent the man lacking her impediments from regaining custody. Yet she was forced to acknowledge this as her only remote hope.

Despite an erratically pounding heart, without hesitation Alyce put the plan into motion. In a quiet broken only by the relentless thud of hooves crushing a new path through the greenwood, she made slo-o-ow but steady progress while time seemed to pass with the haste of a particularly inert slug.

"God's blood!" The exclamation reverberated through deep woodland shadows like a clap of thunder. A powerful destrier reared up, forelegs kicking, while hindquarters tangled in stout rope and wool skirts were near immobilized.

Startled screams muffled into mere whispers of sound, Alyce belatedly questioned the wisdom of her scheme. Sensing she was dangerously entangled with the steed's mighty legs, she instantly retreated into fervent prayers in the name of every saint she knew and a few which, in desperation, she canonized herself.

Light flashed over the sharp blade which in an instant severed long cords attached to the back of a saddle. Alyce felt herself roughly rolled into safety and thanked divine powers for the miracle she'd earlier acknowledged necessary to see her freed. Blinded by a hood, still she'd no doubt of her savior's identity.

Even as Alyce offered up a prayer of gratitude, that unseen figure, like a dark avenging angel, lashed out to knock a rider from his agitated mount. The freed stallion wildly crashed farther into the forest while, in the eyes of the man lying supine beneath the point of sword, the damsel's furious rescuer was no heavenly being—unless the son of the fallen Archangel Lucifer could be deemed such a one.

Dare wanted answers from this worthless piece of wastement. Had Leonard, a traitor proven, some part in the tanner's fire? Of far greater import, what wicked intent lay behind the attack upon Alyce? Aye, answers Dare wanted, but with the wrongly taken woman lying so near, he'd settle for only one—until later.

"Who sent you to capture Lady Alyce?" Despite Dare's motionless stance, the leashed violence simmering within radiated from him in waves of heat.

When no answer was forthcoming, Dare pressed a sharp tip the wee bit further required to see a single drop of blood sprout in the vulnerable dip at the base of his disloyal guardsman's throat. *"Who?"*

Fear overwhelmed the once proud warrior. He licked dry lips to rasp out a response. "'Twas Darwyn."

Black brows drew into a fierce frown. Darwyn? The lame man as twisted in mind as in form? The man who ever skulked through shadows and constantly sought to manipulate others with the secrets he learned? What purpose could Darwyn have for this attempt? Were his wits so addled that he'd convinced himself it was right to thus repay his earl for the humiliation of being cast from the hall after telling the full nature of Howell's fire and murder? He'd surely no better reason. More perplexing still, what could Darwyn possibly have offered equal to the purchase of two guardsmen's treachery? Certain that more lay behind the deed, though he'd meant to seek answer to only one, Dare spoke the last puzzling question aloud.

"What had Darwyn to give worth the price of your honor?"

Beneath the earl's contempt, Leonard rebelled, defending his action as one carefully considered and done. "He paid a fine price and promised both additional gold and a safe harbor at the successful end to our deed."

Dare wanted to know who had given Darwyn the wherewithal to pay for the service of traitors—he assuredly possessed no gold of his own. A further dangerous mystery lay in what "safe harbor" could await men willing to betray their lord. What noble would risk accepting such unreliable support?

Leonard saw a face carved of granite go harder still. Fearing what the Demon might do in an attempt to force a confession of things he hadn't been told, Leonard made a fervent claim. "That's all I know. I swear it on the holy cross!"

Though Dare believed the terrified man who, plainly fearing imminent death, would not profane a hallowed relic with untruths, he was not done with questions to be asked of both Leonard and the worm who'd employed him. Yet now was not the time to seek further answers, not when concern for the motionless, voiceless figure lying in an awkward heap increased his impatience to be done with this worthless creature, and free to do all to see Alyce restored.

"Leonard, you will answer for this once you've been confined in Castle Wythe's dungeon."

Blue eyes as sharp as the sword point lightly braced against the tight cords of a thick throat deflated what remained of the offender's fleeting bravado and held him immobile. Here, Leonard felt, was proof of the verity in rumors of the Demon's dark powers. He himself had observed the lethal confrontation between father and son, and he'd little doubt but that this earl could see him dead with the same ease. Wouldn't even require the well-honed blade he wielded so skillfully. Afraid to breathe, Leonard lacked the courage to risk a single word, even to plead for his life.

On the badly frightened man Dare squandered no moment more than unavoidably required. After stripping his foe of sword and dagger, he sliced three strips of cloth from the man's cloak to gag and truss him hand and foot. As he hoisted the hefty but trembling guardsman to his feet, the man's alarm-widened eyes and mumbled prayers returned a cynical half smile to Dare's lips. Once he had the bound Leonard leaning against a rough and unyielding trunk, Dare fastened the man tightly to the tree with the stout rope cut from a frightened horse to free Alyce.

Dare turned immediately to the fallen woman, relieved to find her healthy enough to have struggled into a sitting position. Dropping to his knees in the crushed grass, he gently tugged the hood from her head, and with it the veil long since knocked askew. The bruises on her cheek renewed his fury with those who had dared do this to her. Yet at one and the same moment, the crystal tears of relief brimming over thick lashes surrounding deep green eyes softened his infamous cold heart to molten ore. Though formed not of precious gold or even of silver but rather of some worthless alloy, it was hers did she have need of it. The contempt in his crooked smile turned inward with pain for the fact that his heart could never be more than a worthless bauble to this wedded woman, this woman whose virtue he'd sworn to protect—against even its greatest threat, himself.

Alyce watched the change in Dare's expression and thought it a condemnation of her foolishness in walking out alone, thus making herself an easy target. He had rescued her, but seemed plain he blamed her for the need, and once the crumpled barbette used as gag had been removed from her mouth, she instantly defended her action.

"Only did I seek a solitary stroll through the orchard. The fields were full of workers, and never did I expect to be seized from behind and hauled away like a sack of grist for the mill." The remembered ignominy revived her disgust with the dastardly deed.

In the green fire beginning to glow, Dare saw Alyce's spirit revive, and his smile deepened. "'Struth, I'm certain you didn't anticipate the danger. But then, once your impetuous nature has won free of the fetters wrapped endlessly about it, you seldom pause to consider the possible consequences of any action." He'd been angry with the tender beauty for foolishly putting herself in harm's way—one way or another. He should be the same now, but his relief for her safety robbed him of the will to rebuke the one he had far rather embrace.

Alyce nibbled at her bottom lip, unsure whether to be relieved that he was not angry with her or upset that he expected the worst despite all her honest efforts to restrain that "impetuous nature"—efforts he took pains to foil at every opportunity.

At sight of the faint frown generated by her quandary, Dare's amusement increased. "I initially thought you had defied my wishes and rashly set off for Wrexdale alone. But even before I overtook your assailant, I knew you had no part in arranging this wretched wrong." By unwinding the thin strips of leather tightly fastening her wrists, he revealed the bruised and broken flesh beneath, and grimaced. "Although your intended walk was ill considered, I understand the reason you found it necessary—"

The quiet claim brushed over Alyce's ragged nerves like the soothing touch of velvet. And in his expression she found such warmth, it convinced her that he had truly recognized her distress over their argument of the past day and sympathized with her need to seek a quiet solace.

"I understand, and in no way do I blame you for the villainy in which it ended." With the last words, his tone took on a grim edge, but the gentle touch of his fingers was a balm for both the minor sting of physical wounds and the ache of emotional distress.

When green eyes went so dark they threatened to swallow him whole, Dare very nearly bent to sip the wine of a pleasure of which he'd been too long deprived. But, fortunately for her virtue and his honor, he was vividly aware of the audience no more than a few short paces distant— bound and gagged but doubtless watching their every moment. After quickly dispensing with the cords about Alyce's fortunately slipper-protected ankles, he rose, lifting and cradling her safely in his arms.

Alyce lay against Dare's broad chest in complete trust, and within moments they were atop his mighty destrier. Exhausted by the day's muddle of rapidly shifting events, emotions, and responses, she couldn't have prevented herself from leaning into his welcome strength to save her soul from perdition. If the worst fears of others were justified and the nature of her savior what they whispered in secret, 'twas precisely the price she would pay. In that moment it seemed well worth the cost.

The deeper they rode into the forest, the deeper became the awareness stretching between them. From beneath her ear, pressed against the fine wool of a sleeveless surcoat covering his hauberk, Alyce could hear the pounding of Dare's heart. Its cadence was almost as rapid as her own. A green gaze rose to study his tightly clenched jaw. Unable to prevent herself, with trembling fingers she stroked over its rigid tension.

Dare shuddered. Alyce's touch broke his fierce effort to keep from looking down at the forbidden temptation he'd little hope of resisting. Here lay a small and tender wrong. The fiery curls he loved to see, having escaped braids loosened in the struggle with her captors, framed a heart-shaped face while an unblinking fascination filled eyes that studied him so intently, they burned a brand of possession into his soul. 'Twas a mark adding its power to the unspoken and wrongful but ever-strengthening bond of love between them.

The sweep of blue-flame eyes dazed Alyce with their singeing heat. She felt as if she'd waited forever to again be close to him, to feel him enfolding her in his embrace. Purposefully closing her mind to the conscience fair screaming warnings of a shame to come, she reveled in the remembered feel of his hard mouth on hers and ached for its return. A moan rose from her depths. The sound was more than Dare could withstand. He bent his head to take lifted and silently pleading lips in a succession of slow, brief, tormenting kisses.

Clinging to his powerful shoulders, Alyce helplessly shifted to brush lush curves across muscles that, even beneath surcoat and chain mail, she felt rippling in answer to her desperate movements. He dropped the reins, wrapped both arms about his tender prize to crush her even nearer, and for feverish moments gave her the unrestrained ardor of his devouring mouth. But still it was not enough. Urging her head to fall back atop one mighty arm, his lips dropped to follow the line of a throat thus laid bare while with his free hand he struggled to dispense with the gown's front closing laces. Once they were sufficiently loosened, he tugged crimson wool down. He groaned in response to an unexpected reward—breasts high, firm, tip-tilted, and lacking even the minimal protection of the modest camise he'd believed all wellborn damsels wore, and most definitely this demure virgin.

She should cover her nudity, should regret the absence of a camise. Yet, lost in the thrall of an unsuspected but aching pleasure, she could not. In a never before experienced depth of sweet anguish, Alyce's lips parted on an unsteady breath while she instinctively arched upward toward a caress unknown but urgently sought.

The deep sound rising from Dare's throat was muffled by the sudden giving of what she sought, of what he had hungered for too long to now forgo—the taste of her velvety skin. Alyce cried out, shivering under the burning pleasure of his mouth on her breasts, a painful joy that both satisfied an initial need and roused another much deeper. Alyce wound her fingers into black strands, holding him tightly to her aching flesh and trembling with an unfamiliar hunger she feared far too deep to survive.

By her desperate shaking, Dare slowly became aware of her helpless desire's depths. It brought him painfully to his senses. His face went rigid as he tangled his fingers into curls reflecting the fires blazing within them both to hold this yielding woman, this source of every erotic dream he'd ever had, a whisper away. With the intensity of a frustrated conqueror, and azure eyes gleaming with a pain whose source he would never regret, he memorized every pliant line from uplifted breasts to kiss-swollen lips and passion-hazed eyes. This vision of complete submission, he could and would live on for a lifetime.

Even undirected, Fiend had brought them to where the trees were thinning on the forest's outer edge. Wythe lay just beyond. Dare clenched his eyes shut for a brief moment before dropping one more tender kiss on each breast and another on soft lips. He then tugged the crimson gown into place and efficiently fastened its laces modestly at her throat. While Dare wordlessly cradled her near and Alyce cried tears of a frustration he shared, the huge black stallion broke from the forest and began carrying them toward the first unguarded bailey gate.

10

From atop Castle Wythe's main tower the earl's pennant rippled in a moody breeze as Fiend bore a silent couple into the courtyard.

A majority of its garrison's men, having returned with their lord from the questioning of Wythe's people, had resumed the business of a normal day. Thus, save for two boys laboring within, the sizable stable built against bailey wall some small distance from the main tower was deserted. Accompanied by another who was to learn a page's tasks by following his example, James led an inspection of stalls to assure that wastements had been properly mucked out and fresh straw laid. The latter had been only indifferently accomplished in the shadows of stalls farthermost from door, and this was a lack they'd correct. Once done, they'd ensure adequate feed awaited returning horses.

Young shoulders tensed at the sound of thudding hooves. A worrier by nature, James prayed they'd not left their tasks too long undone and stepped into the wide center aisle to glance toward those approaching. Charcoal-rimmed light gray eyes near popped from their sockets. He'd heard a tale whispered by his elders. Among the few positive aspects of being short, wretchedly short even for his age, was the fact that adults seldom noticed his presence. They paid no more attention to him than to a pesky fly on a summer's day—until it moved too close and became a nuisance. James never moved too close, only near enough to hear. And just before he'd set out to fulfill this chore, from serfs toiling over a caldron bubbling above the great hall's fire he'd heard the tale of how the visiting daughter of Keniver's baron had defied their Demon earl and fled to escape him.

Despite how recently Lady Alyce had arrived, from talk in the guardroom on the castle's ground level, James knew the men of the garrison thought well of her. Even castle serfs, in the norm suspicious of strangers, admitted of a liking for her. She'd proven willing to thank a body for a task well done—a courtesy those noble-blooded seldom offered those born to serve. More amazing still, when needful, she had lent her energies to see a task completed. The last person who'd spoken against their earl had died, and the people of Wythe as a whole were concerned for Lady Alyce's safety. Under formless specters of dire danger, James's fertile imagination had supplied ghastly images of what punishment might be exacted from a rebellious woman—specifically the disheveled damsel now lying motionless, limp in the Demon's arms.

The boy in James's care, of an age with him but strangely a novice in knightly training, tore off for the castle. James remained, although he swallowed—hard.

Dare could almost read the lad's terrified thoughts. The bravery of a boy standing firm despite his fears earned from him not anger but a gentle smile few had seen. Riding into the gloomy interior where the scent of fresh hay half-spread overcame more pungent odors, Dare slowly loosened his hold on the soft form cuddling close.

Alyce reluctantly sat up, blinking to focus her eyes on a "startled" boy while Dare swung down.

"You're doing a fine job, James." Knowing that so vivid an imagination too often flourished as shield for low self-confidence, Dare seized this opportunity to give praise. "At the risk of slowing your progress, I'd deem it a favor if you would take my destrier to his stall and see him comfortable."

James nearly glowed beneath his lord's approval, swelling

with pride for being allowed to take responsibility of not merely any knight's steed but the *earl's!* Here was a weapon he could use in defense against the constant ridicule of another. Not even David, an unceasing bully, had yet been allowed to undertake this chore usually reserved for older boys on the brink of graduating to the status of squire. The Demon—nay, the earl—wasn't the wicked being some said. In fact, James decided, those who claimed it so were witless fools.

After laying Fiend's reins in a hand trembling with anticipation, Dare turned to lift his companion from her awkward seat. Alyce had watched the exchange with growing admiration. Having caught a glimpse of the boy's initial fear, she'd worried Dare would be infuriated by this demonstration that his people's continuing fear had spread to a youngster sent to foster within his castle. Instead, he had exerted the charm so oft buried in the depths of icy reserve. The smile she gave Dare as he lowered her to the ground glowed almost bright enough to lighten the stable's dark interior.

His hands still wrapped about her small waist, Dare's response was a look so intense, she felt herself melting into a spineless lump. Fortunately he offered his upheld arm, and by laying her fingers atop its extended strength, she maintained a sense of reality, and with a fair imitation of composure, stepped into the light of day—gloomy but dangerously revealing.

In that same instant double doors atop the castle's wide stairway burst open. Walter led the way but stumbled over a half-size whirlwind dashing around thin legs to be the first to reach the returning two. Hal deemed it only just as 'twas he who'd carried the news inside and fetched the others.

With a fine show of disinterest, Sybillene languidly followed the sedate Elinor from the entrance tunnel's gloom. Elinor's penetrating brown eyes acknowledged the pair but searched beyond for another. It was immediately clear that Thomas had not returned with her son and his lamentably disarrayed guest. She frowned; Lady Alyce had clearly met with the violent actions of another, a fact leaving Elinor all the more concerned for the missing man—always cheerful and always near, too near. Thomas remembered a woman "dead" a lifetime past, and she feared he'd one day learn the truth of young Lady Elinor's demise. Still, she worried about his absence and was determined to do all that a woman could to see him safely back inside Wythe's walls— she would pray. While others approached Dare, she demurely settled joined hands at her waist and closed her eyes to begin silently beseeching divine powers to see Thomas returned, and returned of a piece.

"Did you run away, Alyce? Did you? Did you? Mother says you did. So does Uncle Walter." Hal gave the latter an undisguised look of disgust while his questions tumbled out so fast, there was no hope for an answer to slip between. Though Hal thought his half-sister's action smashingly brave, he'd naught but disdain for his weak uncle.

"But you caught her, didn't you, Dare?" Hal's admiration for Alyce's courage was equaled only by his awe for the never-defeated dark earl. "Father said you were his best knight. Said you could do anything. And you can, too, can't you?"

Dare let his head fall back while unrestrained laughter filled the courtyard. Here was a first glimpse of the good to be won by seeing that Hal join his peers and start knightly training. Freed of his mother's smothering control, the unnaturally quiet child had begun breaking from the shell he'd developed to endure her demands. It reminded Dare of the equally unnatural restraint Alyce had struggled to wrap about her fire—and failed. The last a fact proven full well by the raging heat of their embrace, despite the certainty of its wickedness.

Alyce felt the touch of blue eyes sweeping over her as surely as if 'twere a physical caress and, already standing close to his side, leaned even nearer. Dare's gaze narrowed to a greater potency, but then he shook his dark head to restore the rightful barrier between himself and the forbidden damsel.

Hal scowled up at the distracted man. Demon Dare didn't laugh, leastways hardly ever. Had the earl been laughing at him? The mere suspicion roused Hal's indignation.

Dare pulled his attention from the tempting beauty too

near and again looked toward Hal. Dark brows arched at the sight of the boy standing stiff, clearly in defense against a suspected slight. Ruing an action which had left the youngster feeling insulted, Dare gave the lad a smile of such gentleness, it calmed the sting of his earlier amusement.

In response, a broad grin broke Hal's darkling glare, and he listened cheerfully while Earl Dare gave succinct answers to the questions he'd asked.

"First, Alyce was not running from me." Dare held up a single finger to make his point and then added another. "Second, as you see, I did bring your half-sister safely home." His own last word struck with the power of an unexpected blow. Dare only wished Castle Wythe were truly her home as well as his.

None of the three closely involved gave a moment's notice to either Sybillene's disapproving frown or Walter's disgruntlement. Never had Sybillene seen her stepdaughter's hair, and it was a shock. Alyce had been taught to keep it confined before her father's second wife became a part of Keniver Castle; and as the girl had dark brows and lashes, Sybillene had never suspected this fire. A sapphire gaze glittered with fierce dislike over the mane even brighter than her own golden locks. The inevitable comparison was one which even she could not fail to see was to her disadvantage. It deeply upset Sybillene. Though they were very close in years, she'd never really looked at Alyce or considered the girl a possible threat to her status of preeminent beauty.

"Alyce, I thank the Good Lord in Heaven for your safety. I was worried, so worried." Walter had had enough of the child's interference in matters not of his concern, and stepped between Hal and the returning couple. Taking Alyce's hands in his own, he tugged her a short distance from the overpowering earl. "I shamefully admit I did, as Hal said, think you'd run from Wythe, and greatly feared for you." With suspiciously glistening eyes, he squeezed the small woman's hands. "'Twould've been a foolish, dangerous deed to go alone."

The ice filling a blue gaze should rightfully have frozen joined hands. Dare heard Walter's disapproval—but only of Alyce having gone alone, and not of her going at all. This was no surprise as he'd expected Alyce's apparent flight to win unadulterated pleasure from Walter. The surprise was that Walter had worried in the first instance. Dare's usual impassive mask dropped over the earlier rare open expression. Leonard's forced disclosures had left him wondering if it was Walter who'd conspired with Darwyn, Walter who'd supplied the gold to see Alyce captured. In the next instant he mocked his own query. Walter, dependent always upon others, surely possessed no gold with which to bargain. Furthermore, despite suspicions Dare could not completely quell, Walter's fear for her safety seemed proof that the man had nothing to do with the abduction. Still . . . Dare was far too experienced a warrior to believe things were always as they first appeared.

"How can you be certain that Alyce didn't run from you, Dare?" Sybillene moved forward and smoothly inserted herself between the powerful man and a couple now forced to step further aside. With her new awareness of Alyce's attractions, she sensed a closeness between her stepdaughter and the handsome earl. She was determined to see it shattered. "Only the night past, Alyce told us in unmistakable terms what she meant to do." Deep blue eyes peered up through coyly lowered lashes, searching for any flicker of response from a man purposefully reminded of the other woman's defiance.

A shadow passed over Dare's face, yet it revealed no more emotion than did the cold, deep voice with which he answered. "No one chooses to flee slung over the back of a horse. Moreover, she was tightly bound, bound as tightly as her abductor is now."

"God be praised!" Walter's response was immediate and fervent. "You've caught the wicked varlet who did this wrong. But where is he?" The speaker made a show of looking all about the sparsely populated courtyard. "Or," he asked with feigned horror, "have you already demanded the ultimate price for his misdeed?"

"The swine has been captured." Thick black lashes hid all but a narrow slit of pale eyes. "But I was far more concerned for his victim and left him tied to a tree deep in the forest."

Dare stopped there. Best some details be privately held. He would not state exactly where the man awaited, nor was there a worthy reason to announce that he'd been betrayed by not one but two of his guardsmen. Those who'd conspired in the abduction knew the last fact already. (There was no question but that Darwyn had a confederate.) And beyond the personal humiliation in a failure to hold his men's loyalty, the illusion of being unaware of the wrong's full extent opened a possible strategy for unraveling the knotted scheme's whole. His ruse might allay fears sufficiently that they'd trip over whatever tangled strings he pulled free. Darwyn represented the first dangling end, and when brought to account for his actions, likely he'd provide more.

Dare glanced to the side and his gaze instantly fell upon the beacon-bright head of a man beginning to climb steps ascending to a walkway atop the inner bailey wall.

"Arlen," the earl called in a voice of command that had its subject instantly turning to hurry toward him. "Find Darwyn and bring him to me in the solar." Fiery brows rose in surprise at the choice of destinations, and Dare smiled wryly. In the norm the solar was a place held private for family and wellborn guests. Yet it was also the only place Dare could be certain of privacy to ask questions he'd no wish for others to hear.

Penetrating blue eyes watched the younger man set off to fulfill his ordered deed. At the same time Dare mentally laid out plans for dealing with the wrongdoers whose identities he already knew. Beyond the summoned Darwyn, he would see the one in the forest retrieved to receive just punishment —later, after the man had time to ponder the disgrace in his action. The second erring gate guard would be dealt with once he'd been tracked down, if not by Thomas, then by another dispatched to see it done. No matter the time or toil required, the man would be returned to face justice at Wythe. Yet before either guardsman was required to face judgment, it would become obvious to the ever curious and watchful inhabitants of his demesne that two were missing from the garrison. Doubtless most would deduce the right cause for their absence, but how many would understand why they'd perpetrated the deed? 'Twas more than Dare knew.

Although Walter still held Alyce's hands, he absently frowned at the courtyard's use-packed floor. The plan had failed. No question there. But where was Sir Thomas? And did the earl truly not realize a second guardsman had worked against him? He'd more questions than answers but daren't reveal his curiosity by asking for the explanations his masters would assuredly demand of him.

Sybillene, irritated that the focus had somehow been shifted from both her and her denunciation of Alyce's action, sundered the clouds of the men's dark thoughts with a strident observation. "Seems to me an apparent abduction is a fine ruse to shield my stepdaughter's true intent." She would not have her reasoning be so simply swept aside, nor would she see Alyce permitted to easily escape Dare's disfavor.

Alyce felt as if she were at the center of a whirlwind and being dragged deeper into dangerous waters. What with having been forcibly abducted in the first instance, then rescued and near seduced, next surrendered to a too possessive Walter and now accused of her own ill treatment, she'd had enough and more! She moved to abruptly thrust her delicate wrists a mere breath beneath Sybillene's haughtily lifted nose. They were bruised and marked with red, ragged lines where the flesh had been broken.

"As willful as you may think me, even to win my own way I would not deem it a victory to be so tightly bound that blood is drawn." Hot disgust burned in the words. "Nor could I find satisfaction in being thrown over a horse's rump to be roughly hauled deep into the forest. That witless I am not!"

Though Alyce's fervent rebuttal was addressed to her stepmother, except for a brief glare directed to the overly proud beauty, green eyes never strayed from the stunningly handsome man standing as firm and unmoving as stone. His expression, too, appeared carved of an equally unfeeling substance. 'Twould seem impossible for him to be the same man who not so very long ago had fair melted her with the wicked pleasures he so expertly wielded. Surely Dare wouldn't, couldn't, believe her capable of such duplicity. Not when she'd spoken the truth the moment he loosed her gag. Yet his utter lack of response smothered her temper's fire and threatened to freeze the last ray of hope that he would believe her innocent of Sybillene's accused calumny. Dare was, she feared, far too familiar with a spirit too easily roused to always respect the bounds of good sense.

Beneath his unyielding surface, Dare was warmed by Alyce's flaring temper. Only through years of practice was he able to restrain an urge either to teasingly tweak her nose or to congratulate her on a truly fine display of fire. To do so, he knew, would both embarrass Alyce and push Sybillene to further wild accusations.

"Come; as your stepmother lacks sympathy for the trial you've survived—" Dare ignored his own mother's presence as completely as she had for years ignored his existence "—I'll clean and bandage your wounds." Despite Sybillene's huffy demurral, Dare took Alyce's elbow in a gentle but inflexible grip to urge her past the gaping Hal and furious Walter to begin ascending the broad wooden stairway.

Amazed by the notion of any man undertaking a woman's task—and not merely any man but an earl—Alyce stumbled over the steps and glanced down to keep her footing. Head bent, overwhelmed with relief that he did believe her blameless, she failed to see the visual exchange between Dare and his mother.

Elinor had watched the scene from a pace outside one open door. Now, as the pair approached, she would've stepped forward and offered either to do the deed for him or send for Cleva, the one most qualified to treat injuries, had his icy glare not forbidden her such actions. As they passed her by, Elinor lightly brushed elegant fingers across her lips to hide their slight curve—a response brought by memories filled half with pain and half with joy. She had long since recognized the silken cords entangling the pair, recognized and remembered them far too well. Greatly she feared their knotted destinies could have no better resolution than she'd found lost in the center of her own. Yet watching them over the past few days as they struggled with feelings too powerful to be subdued by rules others decreed, she was no longer certain that she'd surrender her memories for the opportunity to change past wrongs. In the next instant, nothing could restrain the smile welcoming a physical answer to recent prayers.

Focused on the one atop a broad stairway, Thomas rode directly to its bottom step and by his action unintentionally forced those lingering there to hastily move aside. The warmth sent his way by the castle's lady was a reward near equal to mitigating the disappointment in being unable to overtake his prey before reaching Wythe's outer boundary. After dismounting, Thomas tossed his steed's reins toward the shadow of the only man standing near. He was so intent on Elinor that he little cared 'twas a disgusted Walter who caught them. On reaching the highest step, he motioned the woman his ideal for a lifetime to precede him into the tunnel. They arrived at its far end just in time to see Dare starting up the stairway with Alyce.

"Dare," Thomas quietly called as he had not when first entering the courtyard to find his friend escorting a rescued damsel into the castle. 'Twas best no more curious events be offered up in sacrifice to Wythe's voracious gossip vine than could be avoided.

When the dark earl turned his way, Thomas grimaced his failure to finish the hunt and at the same time nodded affirmation that their quarry still traveled the route anticipated. The same flamelight that glowed on Thomas's pale hair slid over a black mane like flashing steel as Dare tilted his head to signal understanding of the unspoken message before turning to resume the upward climb.

As the young couple climbed to the family solar, Lady Elinor led Thomas into the hall. While baths were prepared for her son, his beloved, and Thomas, she meant to see the latter provided with wine and tender morsels from the previous meal.

In the courtyard Sybillene attempted to herd Hal back into the castle, over his protest of work left undone and awaiting him in the stable, while a visibly irritated Walter stomped toward that near-deserted structure, leading the wearied steed left in his care. Leastways the insulting task provided him with a fine excuse for retreating to where he would secure a mount for himself.

Before Sybillene succeeded in forcing a recalcitrant Hal to her will, the earlier departed couple reached the quiet solar on the level above. In that blessedly peaceful room, Dare settled Alyce into the soft comfort of a huge padded chair. 'Twas a seat normally reserved for the earl and drawn close to the hearth over whose coals a young serf labored to stoke new and feeble flickers of flame into roaring heat. As Maudie's "particular friend," Clyde had heard much of Lady Alyce's generous heart. Seeing that lady now in odd disarray and plainly chilled, he put his all into the task meant to return her to warmth, utterly unaware of his earl's frown.

"M-M-My l-l-lord." The call was soft and hesitant but instantly won the notice of the three within the room. As he was uncomfortable being the center of attention, Arlen's face took on a ruddiness to match his hair, a deeply regretted condition that he knew would not be eased by the news he brought and wished he could get said with the effortless ability others possessed. "D-D-Darwyn is n-n-nowhere—" Arlen's lips compressed in frustration while arms outspread gave his unmistakable meaning.

"He's gone?" Dare asked, arms crossed over a broad chest and standing to one side of the serf returned to his task.

Arlen nodded repeatedly before struggling to add, "I s-s-searched for the g-g-gate g-g-guards to s-s-see had he f-f-fled but—"

"You can't find them either." Dare's smile was grim, but Arlen was relieved that the earl had understood with nothing more to be added.

In the next moment Dare's frown returned, and with it Arlen's unease. Arlen felt he'd personally failed his lord and wished he could simply disappear. Hah! Between his flaming hair and constant blushes, he'd glow in the dark. His gaze dropped beneath the power of penetrating blue only to fall upon a fearful sight. He'd seen Lady Alyce's ruffled state when his lord had given him the command to find Darwyn. Moreover, he'd assumed Darwyn had some connection to the wrong perpetrated against her, but not until now had he realized how badly she'd been mistreated.

"Lady Alyce, will you be all right?" Arlen's hazel eyes clouded with concern for the bruises darkening on her face and the red welts on her wrists.

Did every man respond thusly to Alyce? Dare held his face emotionless. In watching Arlen's gaze soften with concern and hearing him miraculously, if briefly, free of a persistent stutter, he found it true of yet another. First Walter, then Clyde, now Arlen—and ever himself. How many others? Of greater import still, what justification had he for being jealous when he had no more rightful claim to a woman wed than they?

Alyce was amazed by the sudden cessation of stuttered words but thought it best to reward the achievement by letting it go unremarked. Instead she sent the plainly worried guardsman a gentle smile and nod of reassurance. "Your lord says I will be, and I think it best we trust him. Don't you?" Green eyes shifted from Arlen to a Dare whose frown had further deepened.

Arlen glanced to the black-visaged earl and nodded. "Y-Y-Yes. I t-t-trust h-h-him."

"For that, Arlen," Dare immediately responded, gifting the man with a level gaze of honest appreciation, "I am more grateful than you can know. And because I believe you a man of honor, I've a further task for you." Dare was sincere in what he'd stated. How could it be else but that the son of a man as honorable as Sir Ulger be equally trustworthy? Who better to send to track down the missing guardsman than one who already knew the wrong done, one who doubtless wanted to see the man punished for harming Alyce as badly as did he himself?

"Wait for me in the guardroom and soon I'll come to provide details of a journey and deed that must be performed by a man I can trust."

Arlen almost visibly swelled with the new confidence lent by his lord's stated value of him. The earl must have a respect for his abilities, a belief in him that Arlen seldom had in himself. That he'd demonstrated it before Lady Alyce lent an even greater pride and pleasure.

As the younger man turned to depart, Dare's eyes narrowed on his retreating back while he questioned his own intents. He truly did trust Arlen to faithfully fulfill any command given. But, Dare wondered, had he settled upon the man for that reason or because he wanted him away from Alyce?

Dare's brooding thoughts were distracted by Cleva's arrival with a bowl of fire-warmed water and . . . He frowned in earnest. Carrying stacked strips of clean cloth, Tess swayed into the room behind the older, much wider woman. Face set into harsh lines, he purposefully turned his back on the pair and sank to his knees beside Alyce's chair. Of itself the action forbade an already compassionately clucking Cleva from supplanting him in caring for wounds needful of attention.

Though audibly sniffing, Cleva carefully handed the brimming water container to the earl before motioning Tess to neatly lay the pile of cloths at his knees. In Dare's insistence upon personally caring for injured wrists Cleva, too, clearly saw the path of his feelings. Her apprehensions grew. At first she'd been pleased to find in Alyce another fervent supporter for Dare. Now, caring far too much for him, for them both, she couldn't blindly look away from the dangers in the bond she feared would tighten into a forbidden relationship. Such a regrettable liaison could bring naught but further pain to the man already emotionally scarred, and disgrace to a woman she'd come to like.

Cleva had specifically brought Tess in hopes that the younger woman's presence would somehow lay a block between the other two. Apparently to no purpose as the "cure" had been ineffective in altering dangerous emotions for the wellborn two. Yet the disappointment in that was leavened by an unexpected success won by the confrontation she'd unwittingly caused between her soon-departing son and the too oft disparaging Tess. During those brief moments Arlen had demonstrated Tess's power over him sundered at last, proved it by enduring her latest insults with a complete lack of interest and by turning from her spurning tongue with utter indifference.

Doing what little more she could to forestall the earl's

forbidden path, Cleva refused to depart in spite of the blue-ice glare Dare sent her way. Moreover, until she went, Tess would remain as well.

While Dare and Cleva fought a wordless battle over her care, Alyce felt Tess's presence like one more blow on a day already subjected to an overabundance. Despite the flames Clyde had urged to raging heat, she shivered.

Sensing the tremor passing through Alyce, Dare imperceptibly shrugged aside Cleva's stubborn presence to return the full force of his attention to the injured fire-vixen gone cold. He was worried for her condition after she'd suffered the abuse of not only her physical attackers but of those within Wythe who'd either verbally assaulted her or added to her strain by striving against each other to treat her wounds. Lashing out at himself as the one responsible for the last, he watched her closely while beginning the simple task of cleansing the abraded flesh of her delicate wrists.

Under the power of Dare's gaze, Alyce's awareness of all others faded. His nearness lent her new strength while each gentle touch warmed her with vivid memories of their fiery embrace on the return ride. He was so close, she could visually trace the dark line encircling the pale blue of his eyes, could identify each tangled lash framing the potency of a gaze abruptly lifting to meet her own and pierce her flimsy self-restraints. Soft peach lips parted.

Alyce tightly shut her lashes, hoping to hide her fascination with the man from those who, of a sudden, seemed closing in as fearfully as ever the shrinking walls of any too small space. No help at all. If truth be known, 'twas more dangerous still. Yet her panic intensified when, eyes open again, she found herself the subject of several too-interested observers—and Dare's dangerously knowing half smile.

"Thank you." She rushed into words the instant he'd finished fastening the last bandage, only to be appalled by how breathless they were. Clearing her throat, as if some minor discomfort were its cause, she stared sightlessly at the neatly wrapped cloth. "My wrists feel much better and by the morrow will be fine."

"Mayhap so . . ." Dare paused.

As silence lengthened, Alyce glanced up to discover his

half smile had intensified into the potent one she'd come to know too well for either peace of mind or hope of happiness in a future without him.

In words like rough velvet, he asked, "But will the same be true of you?"

Alyce silently gasped. Had Dare read her mind? Surely not. She'd always sworn he hadn't that kind of power. Yet, though ever shying away from the fact, she knew he assuredly possessed experience enough to sense a woman's thoughts. Whatever his source, how could he expect a public answer?

Cleva frowned in reaction to the unspoken but clear demonstration of what lay between the two while Tess smiled with secretive satisfaction for the revealing visual bond's further confirmation of what she sought. Here she had proof of emotions equipping her with the weapons to wreak a personal vengeance upon both the earl who had shunned her advances and the fine lady who'd clearly stolen another admirer, previously unappreciated but hers since always.

"Never mind, sweeting." With a gentle finger Dare tapped Alyce's chin until open lips closed. "Assuredly a warm bath awaits in your bedchamber." He acknowledged the folly in seeing bandages applied before this doubtless anticipated soaking was complete. "If you can't manage alone, I'm certain my mother will send someone to aid you."

"Nay, I would much prefer to manage on my own." The desperate look of horror Alyce instantly sent Tess spoke volumes more than the simple words of her denial.

Dare had been unaware of the order his mother had already given for Tess to serve Alyce's personal needs, but read the fact in Alyce's response. Ruing both his mother's poor choice and his own unwise suggestion, he instantly sought to soothe Alyce's inadvertently increased stress by quickly moving the conversation forward.

"Once you've bathed, best you rest. Leastwise until the day's last meal." Her fiery response to Sybillene's accusation, followed by the less than calming attentions of others, seemed to have cost so much of Alyce's spirit that she looked to be continuing now on sheer effort of will alone.

Dare wanted to take her into his arms again, wanted to hold her in comfort, but rather than comfort, such an action would merely lay upon her the heavier burden of whispers certain to follow. Again he reminded himself of facts which he had already once this day put dangerously aside. She was the wife of another, the daughter of his foster father, and a woman he owed naught but respect. Dark whispers of wicked deeds were a thing to which he was well accustomed, but he would not be responsible for seeing their shadow insidiously spread from him to swallow her into their acrid depths as well. Forcefully maintaining an emotionless facade, he turned toward those still hovering near.

After Dare shifted his attention from her, Alyce pulled scattered wits together and, without need of further admonishments, struggled from the depths of the massive chair to hasten to a welcome privacy above.

Having left his steed safely tethered to a barren bush some distance behind, Walter fought to safely traverse a moss-slick stream bank. He pushed aside what low-hanging branches would yield and ducked under those that wouldn't until, at last, he reached his goal. Two formidable men stood amidst dense-grown trees rapidly fading from lush green to falling leaves and bare limbs.

"We have failed." Walter nervously rushed into speech while clasping a wet branch to steady himself. "The Demon's got her back."

"Nay, *we* did not fail. *You* failed." The burly speaker emphasized his charge by tapping against their slender protagonist's chest forcibly enough that he stumbled and almost fell.

Only Walter's desperate grip on a limb of questionable reliability saved him from tumbling backward into slowly flowing waters. Well aware of how near he'd come to landing in an awkward and shaming heap, Walter shook with fear of the one who'd gladly have seen it so.

"Aye . . . aye . . . 'tis as you say, Lord Peter." Voice slipping into a piteous whine, he faltered, finding as much difficulty in articulating the words as in remaining upright. "But how could I know the earl would return midmorn when by the word of his guardsmen he's never done it afore? I'll find another way to discredit him." Walter fervently prayed he could do what he said. "I swear it!"

"Aye, once again, as with the foolish villager, you will." The statement was a sibilant hiss at whose core lay the poison of an unadulterated threat. "Yet, in this instance," the venomous voice continued, "already have we turned your ineptitude to our advantage. Whether or not you 'save' your damsel is of no concern to us. Yet you cannot win your goal by failing my uncle, the bishop. He is a dangerous man to cross. So beware. He is relying upon your aid in this crucial campaign. It would be well for you to ponder the dangerous folly in disappointing him." A lengthening pause built the heat of Walter's tension to feverish heights. "Thus," Walter's openly sneering master continued, "you must turn your thoughts to what more can be done to see discontent swell in a tide deep enough that, when the moment arrives—and it rapidly approaches—the demon will be defeated from the inside out."

Despite the arduous task of maintaining his precarious footing, Walter nodded vigorously until his two "companions" disappeared into the shielding gray of misting rains.

Alyce used a crust of wheaten bread to unobtrusively nudge another morsel of roast venison to the near edge of her trencher. From there she could more easily arrange for its fall to the floor beneath. The castle's numerous dogs would feast upon it—later when released to roam the hall. Thankfully her actions went unseen by the huge room's gathered many, who were, in the main, enthralled by a juggler's antics. Was a time when she'd have been equally entranced by the amazingly thin and agile man skillfully keeping an assortment of colored wooden balls in the air. He was a part of the itinerant troupe of entertainers who'd lingered at Wythe over a period of several days. Such troupes had rarely stopped at Keniver, and when they did, had quickly moved on to larger and more rewarding destinations. Memories of the day's myriad events were far too consuming to allow her any such easy distractions this night.

After awkwardly bathing while trying to keep bandaged

wrists dry, she'd accepted Dare's strong recommendation
and sought peace in quietly lying atop her narrow bed. She'd
found no rest at all. Rather her too long restrained conscience had brutally berated her as a weak-willed, sinful
fool. She, a wedded woman, had at every turn either lost her
infamous temper or readily surrendered to Dare's enticements. Even now, seated several chairs distant, she felt the
likely unintended pull of his presence. Having joined the
meal resolved not to fall again into wrongful ways, throughout the long progression of dishes (seemingly more than was
customary), she'd looked no higher than the table edge.
Frowning at a trencher nearly emptied, though she'd consumed not a single bite, she reaffirmed a determination to
reinforce the rightful wall between them.

Dare, in hopes of tempering gossip likely sown by his
personal treatment of Alyce's injuries, had withheld his
attention. Yet he sensed her mentally pulling away, and his
face went to ice. So intense was his unfocused displeasure
that the juggler faltered beneath the fierce blue glare.
Colorfully painted balls crashed about the shamefaced
performer gone a brighter shade than his instruments'
cheeriest hue.

Hal's childishly unrestrained laughter sundered the bleak
cords of Dare's absorption. Suddenly knowing himself to be
the commotion's cause, he forced a smile.

The unplanned break in the evening's entertainment
permitted the advance of a guardsman waiting one pace
inside the entrance tunnel for just such a propitious moment. Tightly wrapped in a cloak damp from the steady rain
falling beyond thick stone walls, Harley strode into the
space now open below his lord.

Seated at the head of a lower table, Sir Ulger half rose to
halt the unexpected intrusion—leastwise until he, as guard
captain, had in the proper way been given the report firstly.
Ulger fell uncomfortably back as Dare raised his hand in a
gesture of restraint.

"In the forest I found what you sent me to fetch." The
clipped statement provided expected information, but the
grimness in the tone of its delivery narrowed Dare's gaze to
a penetrating force. It sounded more accusation than simple

report of a command fulfilled. Dare had thought the man brought news of a traitor returned to face justice, but now regretted permitting him to speak so publicly.

"You found the renegade where I said he would be?" Dare briskly requested confirmation of the facts behind this strangely emphasized account.

A tight smile and quick nod was Harley's only response, but one which Dare, though more than curious, cautiously chose to let pass—for the moment. "Put him into a cell in the depths below." He restated the command given when dispatching this guardsman to retrieve Leonard. "I'll interrogate him later and then deal with what problems remain."

Harley's expression contorted with an odd mixture of distaste and horror. "If you think to speak with him, then you *are* what your father proclaimed you!" To ward off apparent evil in the flesh, he signed the cross, bolstering his courage to remain steady beneath eyes gone to a strange twinning of piercing ice and searing flame.

"Nay." Dare heard only the audible renewal of his sire's curse, the curse he'd spent months—nay, years—fighting to disprove. Without forethought he let his low voice roll over the hall like a thunderbolt. "A son of Satan I am not."

Alyce silently gasped at his public denial of wicked claims. Dare must deem this situation truly desperate to break a lifelong rule.

"Later—" Dare clamped down on his rarely loosed temper and continued with a softness more dangerous still "—I'll speak with Leonard as one man speaks with another. Or, more rightly, as a lord betrayed demands explanation from a traitor."

"Then you speak with the dead!" Harley would've fled this fearsome confrontation with the Demon had Sir Ulger not held him immobile by clasping his arms from behind in hands unbelievably strong for one of such age.

"He was alive when last I saw him," Dare calmly stated.

Lank clumps of rain-wet, shoulder-length hair moved like tangled ropes over Harley's shoulders as he deliberately shook his head. "You rode alone this afternoon." He trembled with fear, yet, as if forced to erupt by some irresistible inner pressure, heated words spewed forth. "I saw you leave. Now the one you accused of committing a wrong against you is not merely dead, but upon bare flesh the devil's sign has been marked—in the man's own blood!"

The last words were choked out on a gasp. Then, overcome by the strain, their speaker slumped in an awkward heap at startled Ulger's feet. Pandemonium instantly filled a hall reverberating with the terrified cries of those who thought Harley, like the old earl, had fallen dead beneath the Demon's fierce glare.

11

From the outgoing stairway's highest step, Alyce gazed across a nearly deserted courtyard. Having busied herself for the past fortnight either easing Lady Elinor's burden by taking on the more mundane chores of castle management or by accompanying Cleva on her many visits to treat those ailing, she was near exhaustion. Dusk's gentle hues, filtered through the mists of a rain so fine, individual droplets were invisible, failed to fulfill her dubious hope for quiet moments spent in bright, fresh air.

Neither long hours of toil nor this dreary scene provided the escape Alyce sought from the overwhelming tension building within the castle until it seemed a miracle the massive structure had not exploded. Since the fearsome scene wherein news was given of her abductor's murder, serfs spoke in hushed whispers, and even guardsmen skittered nervously from their earl's path. That the message bearer had sustained no worse injury than the bruises unavoidable following an abrupt faint clearly made no difference to the fear of those who had either seen or merely heard of the fall. Their attitude was foolish in the extreme. Moreover, in the days since that awful event, each time she saw yet another person surreptitiously sign the cross as Dare passed, her irritation grew until only weariness prevented her temper from issuing a heated rebuke. Instead she'd made a point of casually raising the subject of Dare's long days in Keniver Castle to all those she treated with herbal cures or guided in household chores. She told them of his gentle patience with the pestering of an impulsive girl-child and how her father had admired, even loved, his "best and bravest knight."

And repeatedly had she sought an explanation of Cleva's oblique reference to Dare's birth which Lady Elinor had interrupted during her first day in the castle. But each time she broached the subject, Cleva adroitly shifted the topic until, the day past, she'd frankly warned Alyce that to press deeper only threatened Dare with a far greater danger. Cleva's opinion on the matter was perhaps the only one Alyce felt she might trust. Still . . .

A small frown marred her smooth brow as Alyce persisted with her intent to win a few quiet, private moments of uninterrupted thought. She began descending broad steps, purposefully lending no attention to any who might linger close enough to forestall her goal. Though by the disaster that had befallen her lone walk through the orchard, she'd learned better than to risk wandering so far afield, she'd be safe circling the well-guarded courtyard itself.

The gloomy view did little to lessen even the tension within herself. 'Twas not that she worried for Dare's guilt of whispered wrongs. He had no more killed his father than he'd killed the message bearer. Neither was he to blame for the fire that had ended the tanner's life or the murder of the dastardly swine who had stolen her away. Her abductor had been alive when Dare carried her from the scene, and she'd never believe the same hands which had held her so gently could brief hours later perform so gruesome a task.

Yet despite an absolute certainty that no grain of truth lay at the root of wicked rumors, fear grew—fear that Dare would fail in the task he'd undertaken to see Wythe thrive again, fear for his safety should the perpetrator of vicious deeds turn directly against him.

"I yield! I yield!" The words in a child's voice, accompanied by a yelp of pain and several soft thuds, earned Alyce's immediate attention. She hastened into the shadows on the tower's far side where young boys practiced their skill to arms. Green eyes widened at the sight of the ever-reserved James standing over a much larger dark-haired boy sprawled on the ground while a half circle of others crowded around.

"Then say you believe it, David. Swear you agree that Earl Rhodare is not a demon."

David cautiously squirmed up to rest on his elbows, contorting his mouth to test for injuries worse than the bruises he felt already. "I yield, James, but 'twould tarnish my honor were I to swear a thing I don't believe."

James growled and would have renewed his attack on the fallen boy had Hal not stepped forward to lay a restraining hand atop his clenched fist.

"Won't do no good, James. Can't make David believe something he don't—though proves he's a fool." Hal glared down at the one he unwillingly protected.

"Not all goals can be won by force." Alyce stepped into the gathered boys' line of vision. "Some must be earned by logic." Her audience, having been caught either participating in or avidly watching a bully get his due, shuffled nervously but courageously remained to face whatever punishment she meant to see meted out.

"Thus, David, I ask you a simple question. Do you believe the Earl of Wythe is a warrior capable of devising worthy strategies?"

Though watching the lady suspiciously, David nodded without hesitation even as he struggled to sit upright.

"Would a fine strategist, withdrawing from the scene of a stealthy attack on enemy positions, be so foolish as to leave an obvious trail for his foes to follow in pursuit?"

David didn't answer, but his eyes widened in acknowledgment of a conspicious truth they should all be ashamed for not seeing instantly. Hal rushed to his half-sister's side, grinning his approval of her tactics, while a sheepish James turned toward her, revealing his own wounds—an eye that would soon be a colorful sight, bruises on both cheeks, and scraped knuckles.

"Cleva has an ointment that will ease the discomfort of

your 'battle injuries.'" Alyce nodded toward both James and David. She'd willingly tend them herself but suspected they'd find submitting to a woman's care humiliating so close on a proudly enacted skirmish. "Best you seek her out before the day's last meal begins." With that gentle suggestion of a soothing salve, she gave the plainly embarrassed boys the greater gift of her unscolding departure.

Intending a return to the castle, Alyce approached the stairs leading inside. She scowled faintly under a hopeless wish that she could as simply convince all Wythe's people of the folly in their apprehensions for their lord's nature, but their fears arose from illogical superstitions decades old and not so easily penetrated with cool reason. Feeling weighted down by the impossibility of the task, she slowly mounted the first two steps.

"Sweeting, what awful thoughts assail you to cause such a frown?" Dare's deep words were a soft purr, but Alyce jumped so strongly, she'd have fallen back had he not just as quickly swept her near.

Alyce's heart thumped wildly at this renewed, exciting closeness, firmly rejected but much missed.

Dare felt her agitation, and though he well knew how susceptible she was to him, he warily wondered if this reaction was not merely proof of what he had feared might be the path of her thoughts. Did she, too, believe the dark whispers of deeds he'd no part in doing? For all the wicked things he was guilty of committing, these gruesome deaths were not his sins. Somehow he must convince her, if no one else, that he was blameless.

Swept with shame for her too obvious response, when Dare loosened his hold to allow a short distance between them, she could feel herself blushing and prayed 'twould go unseen amidst the colorless gray of rapidly dwindling daylight.

"My thoughts, worries, were for the 'brawl' I interrupted moments past. A conflict between James and another boy. James had mastered the second youth before I came upon them, but they both suffered injuries that need to be treated."

Dare was startled by the unexpected diversion; his dark brows rose. "Are their wounds likely to need serious care? Had I best go or leastways send someone to fetch them back to the castle?" He followed these inquiries on possible important needs with the curiosity of another question. "What was the source of their dispute?"

Alyce smoothed the sides of her barbette, grimacing as she unthinkingly brushed against the last traces of her own lingering bruises. "Nay, their wounds are minor, and to ease their discomforts they'll likely follow my suggestion, and from Cleva seek a soothing ointment. I know by experience what relief her salves contain."

Dare nodded acceptance of her reasoning yet demanded answer to the one question she'd not addressed. "But why were they fighting?"

Alyce could've bit her tactless tongue for raising a matter she hadn't wanted to lay before him. No help for it now. "It seems James took exception to another boy's repetition of castle gossip." Her voice was tight and she looked aimlessly to the side as she spoke.

Thick black lashes half hid piercing blue eyes. She'd no need to say more. Dare recognized the precise nature of the conflict. Boys of James's age simply would find an excuse to fight, if only to establish the inevitable chain of command. Yet, though he was pleased the too-reserved James had found the courage and strength to assert himself, he was sorry it need be in defense of the lord all his foster "sons" should be able to honorably admire and emulate. Like an unending circle, that thought returned him to the subject he'd first meant to discuss with Alyce.

"I want to talk with you." When a green gaze returned to him, Dare harshly quelled his discomfort with her possible —nay, likely—reaction and explained his purpose. "We must discuss the events so heavy on everyone's mind." Intending to quiet whispers threatening to suck Alyce into their unpleasant muck, since the day he'd rescued her, Dare had remained not only physically distant but had strained to keep even his eyes from touching her.

Feeling guilty for having inadvertently raised the issue,

Alyce felt her blush deepen. 'Twas an action she'd have sworn impossible were it not for the greatly intensified heat burning cheeks until she almost expected it would turn the cool misting rain into sizzling steam. Despite an anxious need to assure Dare that she believed him innocent of foolish gossip, an embarrassment-tightened throat trapped all sound.

"Someone wishes to see me fail and loose my entitlement to Wythe." With both the tanner and Leonard dead, and Darwyn having disappeared, there was an ominous dearth of clues to light his path to the source of such ills, yet one fact showed clear. "Plainly that someone will balk at nothing to secure his goal—not deadly fire, nor even vicious murders." Alyce met Dare's bitter glance directly with the open gift of an unstinting support backed by the fervency of her spirit's banked fires.

"Thomas, Ulger, and I have spent days investigating the tanner's fire and have uncovered but a single clue. 'Tis small, but one which greatly limits the list of those who could be responsible." Now came the moment to gently mention a possibility, to suggest the person Dare had begun to believe the most likely culprit. "Your friend Walter is among the suspects."

"Walter?" Surprise broke Alyce's voice free. Though she was as convinced as Dare that someone was attempting to bring him down, the thought of weak, ineffectual Walter being that someone would be laughable were Dare not so obviously serious. "What earthly purpose could Walter have for harming a man he'd never before met?" By asking, she meant to obliquely urge him not to concentrate upon Walter and thus overlook more probable foes.

Dare couldn't provide an answer to her question, couldn't offer proof to support his growing certainty. But it would seem to matter little as, in her disbelieving eyes, he saw she was unlikely to accept any rationale he might give or to see what he did in what limited details he possessed—a partial footprint and Walter's mysterious absences during significant periods of time.

"I cannot fault you for loyalty to a friend. Only do I pray

you to extend that same loyalty to me." The hands earlier curled gently about her upper arms to hold her steady now tightened uncomfortably. Yet under the solemnity of his earnest plea she felt no pain, nor did he recognize her wince.

"Trust and believe me when I swear upon every holy relic that has ever been enshrined that I *did not* commit any of the wicked deeds now being credited to me—not one of them." He'd not spell it out but hoped she would eventually realize that by this oath he denied everything from welcoming Sybillene's invasion of his bed at Keniver to Leonard's murder.

Shielded from view by the shadows a mere step within the entrance tunnel, an observer intently watched. When it looked as if Lady Alyce was naught but a heartbeat from melting into the earl's embrace, Tess glided forward with raised brows and a mildly admonishing voice.

"Ah, milady, here you are—in the rain. We'll have to hurry to see you clad in dry clothes afore the meal begins." Tess sailed down the steps and relentlessly tugged Alyce from Dare's relaxed grip. "Come, come."

Alyce cast a single resigned glance back toward Dare. Never had she more regretted her failure to free herself from Tess's unwanted aid. Lady Elinor had accepted Alyce's choice to have no personal servant, but every time Alyce broached the subject with Tess, the erstwhile servant either brushed it aside or looked perilously near to tears. Though she was almost certain she was being manipulated, Alyce's soft heart ever relented.

"We must make haste, they're already gathering in the hall." Tess jerked her prey's arm more harshly than she'd have dared had the other woman not been so preoccupied. Anticipating the opportunity to begin her planned revenge, Tess near pulled Lady Alyce up the steps and into the dark, empty corridor at the top.

Alyce could've argued that it mattered little who was in the hall as the meal would not start before the earl arrived, and they'd left him in the courtyard. But as she was lost in worry for Dare's safety, it didn't seem worth the effort.

"I am sorry for interrupting you. Truly I am sorry for my

rudeness, but when I see you with the Demon, it frightens me so." Tess came to a halt midway through the entrance tunnel, and in the shifting shadow cast betwixt widely spaced sconces, turned to face Alyce. "You must beware of him. You must!"

Alyce was startled by the earnest plea. Certain enough of Tess's involvement with Dare that jealously still stabbed, she silently questioned the woman's motives in warning her away.

Maintaining an expression of deep concern, Tess used to her advantage the suspicion visible in Alyce's knitted brows. "I know how dangerous he is. He worked his unworldly powers to my cost, summoning me into a thrall from which there was no escape. I was loosed only after he'd shifted his spell to another victim—you!"

Alyce was startled by the ridiculous claim; her eyes, so vivid a green that even the tunnel's somber lighting could not mute their color, went wide. Tess suppressed a smile of glee with great difficulty. Not only would she win vengeance upon the earl, but, too, upon the lady with whom Arlen had become so infatuated that, before departing on the earl's errand, he'd stood impervious to her slights.

Unexpectedly came quiet words filled with a fury so deep, they rolled through the gloom with the bass tone of a tolling bell. "I have stood silent while the thunderbolts of all manner of accusations were hurled at my head, but this lie I will not permit." Dare moved forward until his broad form blocked the light from a flame flickering behind, leaving them in greater darkness. "Tess came to me uninvited and I sent her away. 'Tis her injured pride that puts these lies on her lips."

"Oh, mistress, save me!" Tess instantly huddled behind the smaller Alyce as if in fear for her life. "He'll kill me for speaking truth. He will. Every person who rouses his anger dies a horrible death." Tess sank to her knees and clung desperately to the smaller woman's waist. "Save me, save me, I beg of you."

Alyce was appalled by the whole scene. Her heart's unquestioning belief in Dare's protestations of innocence in the wicked deeds of murder and fire never wavered. But . . . she had seen Tess fresh from his arms. Though never would she accept Tess's claim to have been seduced by "unworldly powers," from her own experience Alyce knew how irresistible were Dare's enticements. Had Tess simply assumed such potent pleasures were too powerful to have been roused by a mortal man? Yet, on closer thought, even that excuse for these words seemed unlikely. By Alyce's remembered first sight of the other woman's flaunted charms and jealousy over the attentions Dare had given another, she felt certain Tess was far too experienced to have been his unwilling prey.

As for the source of Tess's fear, in spite of her experience with Tess's adeptness in manipulating people to win her own way, Alyce suspected even this woman's talents unequal to pretending such convincing terror. Eyelids half-closed hid the concentrated effort Alyce expended to identify a plausible reason for Tess's fear. She decided 'twas merely another example of the irrational alarm growing to dangerous heights within the castle, as if fed by some dastardly foe—which, of course, it must be.

"Alyce." Dare saw Alyce's lashes fall, apparently accepting the lie for truth and rejecting him by blocking the visual bond between them. He instantly fought to see it reestablished. "Never have I harmed a woman, and never will I. Moreover, the only men who have suffered by my hand are those fairly met on the field of honorable battle." Even as the words left his mouth, Dare was disgusted by the faint hint of a plea which, for the first time, he recognized in his own voice. In the next instant Dare realized he'd sounded the same several times in the course of his talk with the fire-vixen. The fact was jarring when he'd sworn never to abase himself to another, neither man nor woman —not even to Alyce. Yet more than once within an hour's time he'd clearly revealed a weakness in the hitherto impervious fortress of ice he'd built about himself over a lifetime.

An unspeaking Dare strode past the women. Tess shrank away as if fearing he meant to strike out while Alyce stood firm, watching with eyes gone to mists of aching compassion. Dare moved into the great hall; and as he drew near, the apprehensive people gathered there to partake of the day's last meal fell back from the fierce blue glare fastened upon the dais and a waiting chair.

The attention of those in the crowded room centered in morbid fascination on their lord as Alyce supported a larger woman up the winding staircase and into her own bedchamber. While the evening repast was consumed below, Alyce restrained her growing irritation with Tess's ever wilder complaints. The dark-haired woman's fear had long since abated and she'd clearly begun to enjoy demonstrating her fine repertoire of feigned emotions, from self-pity to innocence defiled. The only new tidbit of information thrown out, doubtless with intent to win either horror or jealously—possibly both—was the tale of a devil's mark upon Dare's body. The imprint of a cloven hoof upon his left buttock.

With the hurt she displayed in response, Alyce proved that she possessed no small measure of ability in the arts of pretense. 'Twas an unexpected talent which she used to its best advantage in slipping away, although she extended a sop of further comfort by assuring Tess she was welcome to remain in the chamber's privacy until she felt equal to a public meeting with others.

A warming blaze crackled in the family solar but did little to alleviate the somber atmosphere lying heavily upon the three women and two men inside. Directly after the meal's close, the first four had come to escape the strained silence which seemed to have an ominous voice of its own, one which echoed in the cavernous hall. Alyce had only recently slipped in to join the morose company.

"What happened to the vivacious young bride I remember so well?" Bushy brows peaked above Thomas's inquiring eyes as he stared into a proud woman's chilly expression. He'd managed to idly shift about until he stood beside the lady of Castle Wythe.

"She grew up," Elinor firmly responded in the same quiet

undertone. Holding tight to the reassuring wall blocking all emotional responses, the wall that had for long years protected her from endless distress, she made a deliberate addition. "A thing which you, despite the weight of our many years, plainly have not." Her best hope was to drive Thomas quickly away. On the day of Alyce's abduction, she should never have permitted her relief for his safe return to show. Now it would require hurtful actions from her to undo the damage.

Elinor's cool gaze drifted dismissively over the bulky man and moved on to the view of Sybillene shamelessly leaning as close as possible toward a plainly uninterested Dare. He was seated in the massive padded chair allotted for his use alone. She was glad to see that her son, frowning and apparently lost in bleak thoughts, wasted no attention on the brazen creature.

"Grew up? Or died?" Thomas's lips took on a sneer unnatural to his usually cheerful disposition. Beneath his false mask of distaste he felt wounded by the blow she'd so easily dealt his tentative appeal for a return to shared friendship.

The harsh response immediately recalled Elinor's attention to its speaker. "Clearly the former, for as you see, I live." No hint of emotion marred the smooth surface of a face seemingly too beautiful for her certain years.

"The body is resilient and betimes don't know when the soul inside is gone." Firelight accented the scowl into which thick brows lowered, a scowl more of disappointment than assault.

Elinor turned a cold shoulder to the man she remembered so well as a young and impetuous squire. Of near the same age, they'd begun to form the first fragile tendrils of a platonic friendship just as he, newly knighted, had moved from Wythe to Marshal lands.

"You can look away, but you cannot prevent my words from reaching your ears—not without creating a scene such as a woman so bound by convention as you would never allow." That's how he saw her—a moving image of perfect manners with no soul at its core. It hurt. He'd kept the memory of a vivacious yet gentle woman alive in his thoughts for too many years to easily relinquish it now. But his disappointment and distress was as nothing compared with the painful weight she'd forced his friend to carry for a lifetime.

"Of more import, I want to know why you've allowed such awful things to be said about your own son."

Elinor went still as stone and by effort of long practice prevented any expression to betray the anguish these words drove deep into her heart. While the rebuke continued, she fastened a bland gaze on the closed door, silently comforting herself over and over with the oft-repeated lesson that all would pass—pain, wrath, even life.

"You could use your influence in the castle to see the whispered gossip hushed." To Thomas, Elinor seemed frozen, so unmoving, her back was as straight and stiff as a sword. That very lack of human response irritated him more.

"God's blood, you could do far more." He would not apologize for the curse never spoken in a woman's presence. She surely deserved to hear some measure of the anger and frustration she roused with her cool facade. "You could tell them all your son is a man of flesh and blood, a man born of mortal parents and no more a demon than they."

Elinor rose to her feet and without looking back to her tormentor, departed the solar, casting a tight smile only toward where Alyce sat, almost hovering a mere pace within the solar's door and clearly as anxious to be gone as she.

While Thomas and Dare had accompanied the ladies of the high table to the family solar, Walter had excused himself on the pretext of a previous restless night and need for rest. In truth he had waited in the alcove on the upper stairwell's landing for a smirking Tess to begin making her way down to join her peers.

"Tess." Walter's call was quiet but unexpected enough to bring his prey to an immediate halt.

Turning to look suspiciously into the shielding gloom in

dark recesses, Tess waited for the speaker to give his reason for waylaying her.

"I heard your 'work' in the entrance tunnel this afternoon and, believing we seek the same goal, have come to make an offer. I'll help you if you'll do the same for me."

Tess took a step back. The glitter in eyes barely visible in the gloom had taken on an aspect more sinister than any whispered tale of the Demon's wicked deeds. In an attempted rejection of his proposal, she cast him a dismissive look and moved to bypass the alcove. He reached out and grabbed her arm with a hand stronger than she'd thought the wiry figure capable of possessing.

"Come, Tess." Walter had waited too long and had no patience left to negotiate with the woman. "You want to punish the earl and see Lady Alyce gone from Wythe. My goal is much the same. Join we our efforts and it will be the sooner done."

Nervous, Tess used the weapon ever her most effective against any man. She sneered at his outstretched hand and spoke with disgust thickly layering her voice. "Whatever needs doing, I'll do myself as 'tis plain you seek my aid only because you can accomplish nothing on your own."

Under her disparagement, Walter's well-hidden but vicious temper burst forth. Previously lost in shadows, his left hand flew up, and in it a long, thin metal rod such as those used in simple door latches. He smashed it across the side of her head and smiled in satisfaction when the limited force he'd put behind the blow sent her reeling back against the far wall, cupping a bloodied cheek.

"By this I have proven how capable I am of 'helping' our cause, for now you've a tangible injury to lay at the earl's door. Tell Alyce her Demon did this to you and see if our goal is not brought a step closer."

Tess cringed against the wall but managed to rise to her feet and begin sidling away even as her unwanted cohort continued with a threat.

"Do as I say or you may find yourself in no better condition than either your village tanner or Leonard. Refuse you to aid my cause in the manner I've 'arranged' or seek to betray my intents, then know that I would deem the gruesome death of another person known to be close to Wythe's Demon near as effective. Fail me and such will be your reward."

Eyes so wide that white glowed all about their pale brown centers, with a nod, Tess wordlessly gave her pledge to do as commanded and made a hasty escape.

12

"James, demonstrate for Hal again how best to toss a dagger dead to point." Dare's request was accompanied by a smile which charmed both boys from a vague sense of ill humor for the deed's necessity. 'Twas a skill that seemed to come easily to James, yet, though Hal had practiced and practiced, he couldn't seem to get the heft quite right. He'd repeatedly sent his weapon far wide of the mark—a target fastened to the wood of the stable built against bailey wall.

James grinned at the earl, a response near as bright as the shining welts sported on both cheeks and the multihued bruise encircling one eye. He was tired of doing the same trick over and over, but the earl's approval made it worthwhile, just as the still-throbbing wounds sustained in his lord's defense felt like badges of courage.

"Take your dagger thusly." James lightly bounced the bone handle of his own against a steady palm. "Let it be as much a part of your hand as your fingers."

Hal earnestly met the other boy's steady gaze while struggling to do as directed, although to him the weapon felt more like another, and awkwardly placed, thumb. The blade, thankfully turned outward, slipped through tension-stiff fingers. A stricken hazel glance flew to Dare.

"I've no talent for being a warrior." Eyes dropping to the

weapon whose tip was buried in rain-softened earth, Hal glumly confessed what too certainly was now an obvious lack. "Guess I should'a followed Uncle Walter's path and sought a career with the church. Seems all I'm good for." The distaste in his voice made it clear he deemed it a pitiful prospect, acceptable only as a very last resort. "But I'd probably fail at that, too, like he did."

"You haven't yet failed at anything, Hal. Not when with each attempt, you learn, if only what not to do." Though Dare was surprised by Hal's reference to Walter as a churchman, the boy's need for encouragement came well before the need to satisfy his own curiosity. "Moreover—" Dare laid a reassuring hand on the boy's drooping shoulder "—as you are heir to the Keniver fiefdom, there is no possibility that you'll be forced into a life of prayer and penance."

The relieved expression on a young face again lifted revealed the depth of tightly inheld fears for the future. Yet despite a concern that Keniver would continue to be held by the crown, even Hal knew the king's fickle ways, and the earl's confidence in its restoration lent a cheering measure of the same to him.

"But you must learn the ways to command," Dare firmly continued. "And no leader can command but that first he prove to his men he is the most skilled warrior amongst them. You can pay a man to fight, but you cannot pay him for the loyalty required to win victory." Dare's expression went bleak. The two pairs of earnest young eyes plainly lacked the experience to realize this was the source of the struggle he waged now. And defeat loomed in every fearfully averted gaze and each whisper that spread like a plague— invisible but deadly.

Recollecting his purpose, Dare forced a brief smile and continued on the nearly forgot subject at hand. "'Tis a certain truth that no one begins as an expert, and that is a fact to which James can testify."

"Earl Dare is right. When I was just a child"—James enjoyed to the hilt his new position atop an order established by victory over an abuser—"I couldn't strike a tree though it be but two paces distant."

Dare was amused that James spoke as if he were not a child now, but his amusement did not blunt the sharp interest roused by Hal's earlier words. "'Struth, I watched as first he tried. Now, Hal, this is your time for learning by error, so try again."

Well able to control his curiosity, Dare waited until Hal had retrieved his weapon and both boys had loosed daggers toward the target fastened to the wooden wall. James's blade hit the center dead to point while Hal's barely nicked the outermost edge. Yet, by the yells of victory and the congratulatory slap James landed on Hal's back, one would have thought their aims reversed.

"Now you've the way of it, Hal, and each time you practice, your skills will improve." Dare offered his arm to the boy. "You must be relieved you've not abandoned the quest for such skills in favor of joining the church."

In proud honor, to the earl's forearm, Hal joined his own. "An escape that! Never would I willingly spend my life in some gloomy room putting marks on paper like Uncle Walter did for my father—afore my father was taken." Against the hurtful memory Hal tightly clenched his lips, restraining an unexpected tremble.

"I didn't know Walter had ever resided anywhere but Keniver." Dare quickly refocused the conversation away from painful thoughts. "When was this?" He'd no desire to hurt the boy but needed the information and hoped in this way he could both win important facts and divert Hal from an upsetting subject.

"Must have been when I was just little. Being as I've no memory of him before he returned to Keniver last year. But he told me he spent considerable time under the Bishop of Winchester's training. He says he near joined the holy brothers there but was so lonely, he decided he'd no true avocation and wasn't meant to be a monk. Thus, he came home. Don't know if it's true, but my father always said he was fortunate to have a family member he could trust do all his writing for him."

Dare's eyes narrowed. The whole picture was coming clearer like morning mist dissipating under the glaring heat of the midday sun. Halbert, like far too many of his peers, was illiterate. A fighting man, he'd never seen a purpose in wasting time on pursuits he deemed best left to weaker men.

'Twas a sentiment his son had clearly learned to emulate. Returning his attention to Hal, Dare heard the boy say, "What need for a lord to waste time on boring things like that when 'tis better spent in practice of more important skills?" As he talked, Hal steadily gazed at the dagger carefully bounced in his palm to further test its mettle.

"Such abilities can be very important, Hal," Dare seriously told the boy. He had wanted to lead him from a painful subject, but first he must correct a misconception. "'Tis important that you learn a warrior's skills, but equally important to avoid other possibly dangerous lacks."

Hal's hand closed tight about the bone hilt as he glanced up in amazement. Surely the Demon but jested with him.

"Pah." He grimaced. "You are no scribe and yet you are an earl, and powerful, too."

Dare smiled at the plainly disbelieving boy. "Ah, but I do know how to read and write." He hadn't learned, in the usual way, from churchmen, and not in expectation of having any real use for the talent. Rather, he'd sought instruction from others in Richard Marshal's service who'd been better-schooled merely to relieve the boredom inherent in endlessly waiting weeks and even months for battles to come.

"If you can't read what is written about you or what you are given to sign, how can you—as the lord you'll one day be—ensure that you do not sign a document by which you commit treason all unknowing?" From the moment he'd learned of letters incriminating Halbert in treason, Dare had been certain this was how it had come about. The news of Walter's talents simply identified the precise method used and confirmed his suspicion of who was responsible for the whole. The discovery of a now certain truth made it all the more important to guarantee Hal would never suffer the same fate.

Hal was a smart boy; his eyes widened at the oblique explanation for a wrong he'd loyally known was not his father's. The distressing fog of confusion darkening the view of his father's honor evaporated as he unquestioningly accepted both the explanation for how the wicked deed had been performed and the earl's assurance that it would come right in the end. Dare was surely too powerful to be denied. Thus, Hal had no doubt that what Dare said would be, would be. Abandoning his new maturity, the child in Hal threw himself into Dare's comforting arms.

An embarrassed James, too, recognized the vindication of Baron Halbert but also the fact that the same danger extended to their earl. Shuffling uneasily, under the influence of deepened worries, he unthinkingly scribed a Latin letter into the damp earth beneath his foot. Realizing what he'd done and fearing it would make him appear a boaster in the presence of one who had not the talent to do the same, he instantly scratched it out, glancing guiltily up. From atop a tousled, dust-hued head, pale blue eyes looked down.

"You are a most talented boy, James." Dare unhesitatingly spoke his honest reaction. "I congratulate you on knowledge so diverse. Who taught you to write?"

"My mother," James squeaked, face suffused with ruby color at the unexpected praise.

Dare's habitual impassive expression prevented the boy from seeing how truly amazed he was by this news. It was unusual for a lad so young to possess such abilities, but even more unique for him to have been instructed by a woman. There were few enough men of Dare's acquaintance who had mastered the ability to write, and he knew not a single female who had either the knowledge or desire to learn these skills.

"My grandmother, Lady Nessa of Castle Tarrant, was first trained to be a nun. She taught my mother, and my mother taught me." James grew bolder under the earl's approval of his abilities.

"Then you can be a greater help to me, a help I know our friend Hal will appreciate even more—leastways someday. You can teach him what your mother taught you."

Hal had pulled back from the broad shoulder where he'd cried unashamed and scrubbed cheeks dry with his tunic's cuff. Now he gazed at the other boy with obvious admiration for one of his own age who already knew all that he must learn.

"Would you teach me?" Unblinking hazel eyes steadily sought a positive response. "Though I'm not so apt as you plainly are, I swear I'll practice and practice until I get it right."

James's blush deepened, but pride lent an ever greater assurance to his stance. "You are as apt as I, Hal. It's only I started years past. If you want to learn, I'll share what I know, though we'll both have to seek instruction of another once you've learned what I can teach."

Dare lowered Hal to the ground, watching while the pair retrieved their daggers for further practice. The two immediately began making plans for locating suitable pieces of charcoal, amongst those that edged banked fires, to use in writing on old planks of wood. Would that all problems were so easily solved.

Mayhap they could be? Leastways one, and it the most important to Dare. Surely that the two youngsters had so easily understood the implication of treasonous letters signed by a man who could not write meant Alyce would understand more.

"Who hurt you?" Delicate brows lowered into a worried frown and Alyce quickly stepped sideways to block the other woman's attempt to slip past on the dark, deserted stairway. "Tess, how did you get that awful welt?"

Tess laid a hand over her cheek, covering the clearly defined red imprint. Tears, this time quite real, escaped between tightly squeezed lashes. It still hurt and was more than enough to convince her that the vicious little man was as capable as he'd claimed of doing far worse were she to fail in fulfilling his scheme.

"Leave me be, mistress. Spare me, I beg you. Spare me." Eyes wide with terror were the most convincing plea Tess could've given Alyce. Yet Alyce would not leave the woman to suffer alone.

"Spare you? You've nothing to fear from me. In truth, only would I help you. Come, let me put a cold compress on the wound. It'll work to bring the swelling down." With the words, Alyce herded Tess into the privacy of the bedchamber she'd just left, the chamber wherein they'd talked the past night. She'd achieved a fair amount of knowledge and experience in the healing arts—leastways in the treatments for simple ills—during the past several weeks, and gladly offered a measure of relief to one ailing.

However, while Alyce drenched a cloth square in cold water, she wondered if providing Tess with comfort was to become a daily habit. Gently moving aside a hand much larger than her own, Alyce mopped away dwindling tears and softly pressed the cool square to reddened flesh.

"Now, tell me what wickedness wrought this?" she calmly asked while locating a small pottery jar of ointment laid near stacked candles ready for use.

"Don't tell him I told you." The honest panic in Tess's words was unmistakable. "Oh, mistress, I beg you will not, else my life is in danger."

Alyce could swear she felt her heart physically drop into a bottomless void. Despite a sincere dread of being forced to deal with their almost certain answers, she couldn't prevent questions from escaping her throat.

"Who?" Green eyes closed as if to block the sound as Tess broke into renewed sobs. "And what danger?"

"I tried to resist the summons, I did." Tess clutched the cloth square in her own hands, spreading it to shield a contorted face. "Truly I did, but his powers are beyond my strength to deny."

Though the words were muffled, Alyce understood their dreadful claim all too clearly. She could and had believed Dare had taken Tess to his bed, but never would she believe he'd struck this woman or any other.

Alyce again moved larger hands away from an inflamed welt to begin applying the soothing ointment Cleva had provided to treat the bruises her abductors had bestowed upon her. For all Tess's feigned emotions and staged woes, this injury was assuredly very real, as real as the quaking fear surely too deeply felt to be faked. Someone *had* hit her; someone *had* frightened. Not Dare, but who? No matter the answer. Alyce's first priority was to prevent this ghastly tale—attributed to Dare—from spreading and further littering the path toward his goal with wild whispers of wickedness. Toward that end, she must appear to accept Tess's every word as truth.

"The Demon is evil through and through." Amazingly piercing fawn-hued eyes peaked over rough cloth at the smaller woman, who cringed back as if she were the one assaulted. Tess accepted her listener's response as unquestioning belief in her claims, yet her initial satisfaction faltered beneath an unexpected shame. That Lady Alyce continued treating her with gentle sympathy despite the anguish she'd doubtless wreaked upon the woman justified Arlen's admiration of the fine lady.

A fresh bout of tears erupted from Tess. How would she explain this mess to him—if ever he returned? More important still, why should he care what she had done or what awful things had happened to the woman who'd ever taunted him? Soon the tears drenching her cheeks had washed away the healing ointment so carefully spread. Lady Alyce patiently reapplied the salve. That action weakened Tess's resolve. In the next moment she realized that a choice must be made: Either she confess the whole and risk Walter's dangerous ire or instantly intensify her attack. Her sense of self-preservation won.

"Earl Dare was angry with me for saying what he heard me tell you. So angry he hit me and said if I did it again, he'd do worse." Whipping herself to further heights with a reminder of the threat she'd no doubt her unwanted "accomplice" would take joy in fulfilling, Tess doggedly continued. "I beg you, don't betray me to him, else I die."

While for the first time Hal proudly joined James and the other pages in serving the evening meal, each occupant of the high table was preoccupied by problems of his or her own.

Alyce was late to arrive but deemed it a matter of little import when, caught in a muddle of growing worries, she had as well not have come for what few bites she could eat. Her troubled thoughts stumbled over the ever-spreading tendrils of dangerous rumors which, like weeds, seemed impossible to see eradicated. 'Twas a fact which further strained her patience with those foolish enough to believe.

Neither Thomas nor Elinor had recovered from their confrontation less than a full day gone past. And rather than risk glancing at each other, both stared pointedly at barely touched food or into vague shadows. They were as distracted as Alyce, and none of the three noticed Sybillene. Irritated by Dare's disinterest, she turned a cold shoulder to the insulting man and flirted outrageously with any of the several guardsmen who looked her way from seats at tables below.

Throughout the tense meal, Dare's steady gaze never wavered in its silent demand for Alyce to look his way. How else could he convey his desire to speak privately with her? He assuredly could not publicly announce it. So intent on his purpose was Dare that he gave no notice to the satisfied expression of a known foe blatantly studying the pretty damsel's resistance to a wordless blue summons.

Under the power of Dare's potent lure, Alyce, too, failed to feel the weight of Walter's gaze. The only real alarm Tess's tales had raised in Alyce was the fear that she might inadvertently strengthen the whisper-sown tares growing wild in Dare's earnestly cultivated fields. Were she, a woman known to be wed, seen falling 'neath his wiles, would it not reinforce the rumors of wicked seductions whose seeds she apprehensively suspected Tess would one day scatter with intent to see them bloom in fertile imaginations? Determined to prevent that further danger from befalling Dare, Alyce tightly closed green eyes against his call. All for naught. Her heart was lost and she knew it. Yet surely that very fact would lend strength sufficient to refuse satisfaction for her hunger, strength to refuse the feast of tempting delights awaiting within Dare's embrace. The power provided by love would wield both the weapon of her honor and the shield of an imperative need to keep the sanctity of her marriage vow pure.

Since the night her abductor's murder had been reported, no itinerant entertainers had appeared at Castle Wythe. Alyce had no doubt but that the juggler then performing had repeated a tale of fearsome wrongs committed by the "demon" earl—and enjoyed the fleeting importance this story provided him. Warned by the juggler's words, other prospective performers would assuredly have fled from the possibility of similar dangers. However, as those on the dais were anxious to escape from the hall's heavy atmosphere of formless, looming trouble, it was doubtful whether any manner of fine entertainments could've restrained them from departing. Although yestereve the company had retreated to the family solar above, this night their separate tensions led each to flee to private bedchambers. All except Dare, who was not easily deflected from any path he chose to pursue.

As good manners dictated, Alyce stood aside for both Elinor and Sybillene to precede her up the stairway. Sensing Dare's approach, she was anxious to ascend and immediately stepped upward only to be halted by a gentle hold on her arm.

"Alyce, I want—" The deep burr of Dare's voice held an irresistible call all its own. Alyce would have followed him anywhere had another not broken the bond.

"Dare, Hal tells me you've arranged for him to learn the ways of the written word." Walter never spoke to his host unless absolutely necessary, marking this intervention as an obvious ploy to separate the pair.

Alyce's conscience piously told her to be thankful, but instead her rebellious spirit flared back with a frustration so deep, it near forced a cry from her tight throat. To prevent the betrayal of either emotion, she pulled free and rushed up appropriately dismal steps to a dark and unwelcoming room. The candle she'd left burning sent flickers of weak light and daunting shadow across the small chamber. Caught between depression and impotent fury, she threw herself on the bed. Its mattress seemed lumpier than ever before, one more irritation in an altogether unpleasant day. Rising up, she pounded the worst of the lumps flat, then again dropped facedown while useless tears sprouted from angrily clenched eyes. Life had gotten far, far too complex with the passing of those simple times when her father had pointed her toward the right path for a woman.

What drivel! Alyce threw herself to her back. If she'd learned anything from the tangled morass her life had become since the day the charge of treason was imposed upon her father, 'twas that nothing was simple and a woman could survive only by thinking for herself. With renewed spirit, Alyce accepted the challenge of restoring order to her thoughts and purposes. Toward that end she would start with her person.

Rising from the bed, she loosed and painstakingly brushed chestnut hair until it seemed to blaze. Only then did she strip off the simple red gown, her favorite always but even more precious for the memories it held of a ride in Dare's arms. Wearing only her camise, she searched out yet another cloth square to cleanse her own tears and flushed cheeks before lifting a ewer from the small trunk beside her bed to pour into the bowl a portion of the fresh water provided for her evening ablutions.

"Alyce, I've come to speak with—" Dare was stunned, his black brows rose so high, they near joined the dark lock fallen on his forehead. The hour was still early, and this visit, for all that no male save husband might rightfully enter a wellborn female's chamber, should've presented few dangers.

Shocked, Alyce whirled toward the unexpectedly opened door, spilling the vessel's contents down the front of herself in the process. In the next instant every rational thought fled and she trembled beneath the blue inferno of a gaze scorching over her, from masses of freed curls to bare toes.

Not since the day he'd rescued his fire-vixen from the heartless hunters who'd captured sweet prey had Dare seen a sight so enticing. Plainly frozen by surprise, she stood motionless, inadvertently providing a pulse-pounding display of delicious curves inadequately shielded by either the white silk of a brief and soaked camise or the abundant flame-bright tresses tumbling past rounded hips. Like an unseen but devastating blaze deep in the forest, Dare's desires raged and incinerated any remote hope for cool reason as he moved toward the source of forbidden dreams waiting just beyond his reach.

Dare's steady approach broke through a haze of impossible fantasies come to life and thrust upon Alyce an awareness of her utter lack of adequate covering. She dove toward the bed and jerked up the gown left draped across it. A mortified blush vastly outshown its crimson hue.

That he'd neither taken nor wanted any other woman in so long intensified Dare's wrongful need of this particular damsel. It required the full force of his will to clamp iron control over an ill-conceived compulsion to strip away her flimsy shield and thus liberate the bounty of pale ivory flesh to his sight, touch, taste . . . Dare halted and shook a midnight-dark head to free it of too-tempting images.

"What did you come to say?" Meaning to restore sanity with sane talk, despite a mindless urge to move toward and not away from the wicked temptation so near, Alyce held the gown's voluminous material tightly to her chin and spoke as naturally as breathless words allowed.

Backing her efforts, Dare strove to put a mask of normality atop his unforgivable intrusion. "I learned from Hal only today that Walter was trained by the Bishop of Winchester." Beneath thick black lashes, pale blue eyes searched Alyce's face as he produced the fact which had made the whole scheme so plain to him. Though this simple fact had exposed the plot to two young boys, Alyce was looking at him as if he'd lost his hold on good wits.

"I know that, Dare. I've always known that." Admittedly hampered by the tangled weight of the day's too many conflicting emotions, Alyce fought to make sense of Dare's puzzling presentation of a never-concealed reality—as if it were some long-sought treasure won with great difficulty. "If I had known you deemed it important, gladly would I have told you earlier."

In truth, she'd do almost anything for Dare. Having been warned away from fulfilling her vow to reveal whatever ominous boulders of unfairly smothered truths or nasty secrets barred his path, Alyce was all the more determined to uproot as much of its dangerous tangle of whisper-sown weeds as she could. She would endure the company of his leastways onetime lover and listen to the wild tales Tess told in hopes of limiting the scope of their plague's contagion. Even would she hold Dare at a distance to prevent others from using her as the focus of further damaging rumors. Hah! Her conscience instantly scoffed. Only see how easily her virtuous instincts were subdued by Dare's mere presence. She should order him to leave. Any pure and moral woman would ... She could not, not when private moments of time spent in close proximity were so rare and so soon to be forever lost.

Beneath the darkening storm of Dare's expression Alyce realized of a sudden how far her thoughts had wandered from the subject of his arrival. Green eyes blinked rapidly while fingertips turned white with their desperate grip on forgotten crimson cloth allowed to dip perilously low.

Black brows impatiently scowled. Dare was upset. Not because Alyce had, of course, known of Walter's training, but with himself for not having made that fact's connection to present dangers more blatantly apparent at the outset. Her disarray was distracting, yet he blamed himself for permitting the never-forgotten feel and taste of her to knock him off stride and make thinking with any measure of calm reason so difficult. He groaned silently. Then, in an attempt to block the power of such impediments to his presentation of the rationale supporting his belief of Walter's complicity, blue eyes closed—only to discover the vivid images engraved in his mind supplied a vision even more potent. One wherein she lifted soft alabaster flesh to his mouth and yearned for more than he could give the chaste wife of another.

"The bishop is the force behind our king." Dare dove into the subject's cool waters to waylay the dangerous heat his memories had ignited. "It is he who arranged your father's downfall—a deed that could only have been performed by help from within. There can be no doubt but that he was aided by the one who studied under his direction, that he was aided by Walter." Despite a conscious effort to restrain the assuredly errant action, an azure gaze stroked the expanse of satin skin foolishly exposed by one too lost in other considerations to note the tempting droop of soft wool.

Dare was less than a single full pace away and far too close to permit Alyce clear thoughts—particularly as his intense scrutiny abruptly reminded her of an immodest state of dishabille. Still, Alyce fought to understand his meaning. A single point rang too true to be mistaken, one she'd earlier recognized of her own. She'd no doubt but that a traitor within had not only endangered her father's hold upon Keniver but now attempted to see Wythe stripped from Dare. Of a certainty someone had arranged two murders and her abduction—but she felt it just as certain that 'twas not Walter. Surely no one unbiased could view him as more than an insignificant pawn in the game of life. She felt disloyal in naming Walter thus, but 'twas better than allowing even Dare to name him a traitor to her father, his own brother-in-law and benefactor. If anything, Walter was too loyal, always underfoot or hovering near with his worries. The simple fact that he had trained at Winchester was no convincing indictment of wrongdoing. Assuredly not to her who knew that the bishop had seldom dwelled within Winchester during the years of Walter's training.

Moreover, Alyce well remembered that 'twas the Bishop of Winchester who'd led Gabriel on the doomed crusade. What part had that fact played in convincing Dare, mayhap subconsciously, that the pontiff was the villain responsible for the troubles at Keniver and Wythe? And further, by taint of Walter's limited association with the bishop, a belief in his guilt?

"Nay." Alyce firmly shook her head, sending loose curls forward to lie atop ruby-toned wool once again clutched to her chin. Light from the room's lone candle caressed it with a fiery glow. "Mayhap someone inside, but not Walter." Even as she spoke, Tess's terror-stricken words and the image of her injured face came back to mind. That was a wrong of which Dare had yet to learn, and one Alyce was certain frail Walter could nowise have committed.

In what she'd been told, Alyce saw no more credible evidence that Walter was traitor and murderer than that which lay in the facts of Dare's own history at Keniver. He'd fostered there and been cast out for a serious wrong. Surely anyone who chose to make the accusation, though a fool, could use the argument of vengeance as a motive to assert that Dare was the culprit. 'Twas an unpleasant rationale, which she did not believe to be true, but one as probable as the reasoning he'd given to support his charge against Walter.

Only to show Dare the illogic of thinking Walter capable of involvement in a plot surely requiring more courage than he possessed, Alyce tilted her bright head and calmly stated, "Might as easily have been you. The letters by which my father was shown guilty seemed to say it was so."

"But I did not write them, Walter did!" Dare vehemently answered, losing patience with Alyce's stubborn defense of the other man. Would that she'd as much loyalty for him. Loyalty, huh! He'd come with proof of Walter's part in the wrong only to have her accuse him! "Why can you not believe me? What have I ever done to harm you?" It was an anguished cry.

Alyce was caught off guard and felt unfairly struck; her green eyes went sad as scenes flashed across their vision. She saw again her seductive stepmother lying in Dare's bed; Tess with tangled hair and open gown plainly fresh from his chamber; and the painful image of the moment wherein he'd sent her from Castle Wythe though she'd near begged to remain.

Dare instantly realized she still thought him guilty of betraying her father with Sybillene. And if Alyce accepted that lie for truth, why should she not believe him capable of betraying Halbert in larger matters as well? How could she be expected to dispute the dark whispers of a demon's powers and evil?

Looking infinitely weary, Dare turned away, but Alyce shot out a hand to catch his arm. "I *do* accept that you seriously believe what you say, and I *would* trust you to lead me anywhere. I only question the possibility of a far weaker man's ability to find the strength to risk your wrath by opposing you."

As he gazed into her winsome, earnest face, a mirthless smile came to Dare's mouth. He could not blame her for shying away from the ever-deepening muck deliberately thrown in his path. Plainly the fair damsel, despite her own qualms, wanted to trust him. That fact lent a bittersweet joy and renewed determination to fight his way through the bog of filth meant to drag him down.

Without forethought Dare reached out to lift and gently pull taut a single flame-bright curl. Alyce watched, heart in her throat, as he let it go. As if possessing a will of its own, it bounced back against the pale flesh of an uncovered shoulder.

"As bright and full of spirit as you." No matter the restraints ever placed upon the fiery mane, once freed, it resumed its unruly ways—a prized reflection of Alyce's irrepressible spirit. Blue eyes rose to delve into green, which instantly went to near black. Never equal to resisting their enticement, Dare felt himself drawn inside. Closing the short distance between them, he towered above while slowly lifting her chin with one finger. Only Alyce could so smoothly penetrate the shield of his emotional control.

Beneath the warm threat of his powerful body, overwhelmed by a renewed awareness of his masculine beauty and strength, Alyce's tension grew. To waylay its flow, she quietly spoke her thoughts aloud. "Is it some unworldly power that calls me to you whether I will it or no? Or is it simply the sinful nature my father has warned me to tame?"

"'Tis neither." Dare mentally pushed aside her oblique reference to his reputation, not wanting to investigate it for fear he'd find her faith in him wavering. Rather he sought to reinforce a deeper truth, one mayhap doomed yet undeniable. "We've a bond near a lifetime in the forming. And, as once I warned you, 'tis one which cannot easily be sundered by either you or me. Since I departed Keniver (with a belief, proven untrue, that 'twould save us both), some force—whether God or another, I do not honestly know—has thrown us thrice into each other's path. Too many times for it to be mere happenstance. Though years apart, our bond has weakened not one whit."

In his black visage and ice-hard eyes, Alyce believed she read Dare's resentment of that fact. Yet her heart acknowledged the truth he spoke. 'Twas a truth she'd recognized too oft herself to deny. She loved him. She always had and always would no matter what others claimed he was or even what he had in truth done. In spite of the insurmountable barriers between them, he was her heart and all she knew or wanted of love.

"We must accept the impossibility of our wrongful relationship," Dare continued, and the chill tone of his words was purposely wielded to reinforce a dangerously weakening resolve. "We must resist its ever-tightening cords. My honor as knight and lord, along with your virtue as wellborn daughter and wife, depend upon our success." He saw both the faint tremor his statement put on peach-soft lips and the small teeth used to still the betraying motion. Fighting down an instinct to pull Alyce close and assure her the prospect was no more welcome to him than to her, he used his considerable skill as a tactician to strike a further blow. Surely the one which would put an end to this scene before he fell victim to his own needs and the enticingly ill-clad fire-vixen's unwitting seduction.

"Toward that end, very soon will I see you delivered either to your husband or, accompanied by an appropriate guard and chaperone, to your own lands." Dare saw the pain of loss clouding green eyes, a weapon well able to match his own and endowed with power by its honest emotion. "Our only hope, I greatly fear, is physical distance."

In Dare's words Alyce heard the death knell to her every dream and desperate wish. She obediently nodded but, lost amidst a remorseless riptide carrying her out into the future's endless sea of despair, could not look away from the incredibly handsome man. 'Twas as if she were drowning and he were the last glimpse of land. Instinctively Alyce fought against the dragging waves of her father's training and the shrieking gale of her conscience to wrap her arms about Dare's strong neck and, oblivious to the loss of a crimson shield released, twine slender fingers into thick black strands.

While striving to subdue the fire in his blood, Dare foolishly glanced down and into the beguiling face of the only woman he desired as, open and trusting, she offered herself to him without reservation. Having fallen that far, he compounded the error. His gaze followed her fiery mane's path from where it curled in glorious disarray about soft cheeks and gently pointed chin to where it framed enticing glimpses of luminous flesh teasingly revealed by the fine silk of her damp camise. Her blatant surrender sorely tested his last tenuous threads of restraint. Dare's hands swept down the curve of Alyce's back and drew her tight against his powerful form.

Alyce exalted in his strength and arched into it as shudders of wild excitement trembled through her. Caught in the dark but welcome whirlpool of sensual pleasures he so easily wrapped about her willingly given body, she burrowed nearer still in mindless fear of spinning away from her anchor amidst the storm. She barely felt the hand sliding beneath thick hair to cup the back of her neck and tilt her face upward. His lips descended to tempt her with a touch so light, it was a torment. Her faint whimper called him to completely fit his mouth to hers. When he deepened the kiss to drink a full measure of her peach-wine, sensation rippled through Alyce's body—proof how weak were even treasured memories when laid aside the firestorm found in his potent embrace's reality.

The savoring of one remembered delight increased Dare's hunger for others. He wanted to touch every texture, taste all of her honeyed sweetness, and swallow her into the endless possession of his arms. While never relinquishing the delights of her mouth, his hands tangled in the insubstantial cloth barring him from his goal.

Having thrown the logical caution urged by her conscience to the ravenous wolves of desire, Alyce sank headlong into the vortex of blazing hunger and failed to notice the action heedlessly rending her lone covering in twain. Unable to think, she recklessly submitted to the hot pleasures of caressing hands laying a slow, searing path up her sides from the gentle swell of her hips to the sensitive flesh beneath arms clinging to broad shoulders.

Only the strength of masculine arms held Alyce upright while the kiss deepened to a hungry ferocity. She melded a body gone boneless into the support of thews so powerful, they must surely be formed of fire-forged iron. Then, while she drifted in helpless surrender, his hands curved over her rounded derriere to lift and fit her to the changed contours of his body. Inside Alyce a tempest of stormy sensations quickly grew to unbearable heights, and unaware of the dangerous hunger thus roused, she innocently writhed against his throbbing need.

This far and no further. Every muscle tensed beneath Dare's unspoken demand for returned control. In truth, already they'd gone too deep into forbidden delights. Only by exercising every shred of his famed iron will did Dare lower the tempting beauty before spearing faintly trembling fingers through the thick mass of her hair. The action bared a vulnerable nape to nuzzling lips anxious to comfort the rejection soon to follow. Then, gently tugging fiery curls, he steadily urged the uncomprehending Alyce a brief whisper away.

One last time before dropping the necessary shield betwixt them, penetrating blue eyes desperately studied the delicious, yielding damsel offering all of heaven. For him 'twas a treasure assuredly worth the guilt and shame which was as certain to follow the seduction of this virgin-wife of another as hell was the price for mortal sin. His lips twisted with self-disdain. What difference the cost to him who was already doomed? The overbalancing consideration was the awful price Alyce would pay. He could nowise justify defiling the only woman he had ever loved or permitting her to pay for a wicked wrong he should have strength enough to forestall.

Alyce sensed Dare's intent to set her aside yet again. Eyes flashing green fire, she tenaciously clung to him, twining the lush temptations of her form tight about his long, hard body. Her father had attempted to push her into the ways he deemed rightful while Dare sought to choose the path of her wrongs past and present. He delighted in rousing her unruly temper and ever ignited the fires of her passions—but only so far as could be controlled. She was done with permitting any other to guide her path and meant not to allow Dare to leave her aching with the same unmet hungers that had assailed her with anguished tears after the abrupt end to their forest embrace.

"'Twill happen whether we will it or no." With each word she laid an untutored but exciting kiss against a portion of sun-bronzed skin exposed by a series of gaps provided by comfort-loosened laces down the front of his tunic. "Long past you told me so and I believed you. I spent years striving to smother the flames and sunder the bond, but as you foretold, I could not then nor now. The invisible bond betwixt us is one I have never, can never, share with another." Knowing it was so for him, Dare abruptly realized she likely spoke true. "More than once you've permitted me a taste of forbidden fruit. If now you mean to hasten my exile to the bleak and distant domain of another, first grant me a portion of passion's feast." Dare had gone utterly still. Her bravado wavered, but she added a desperate plea. "Leastways give me this one night, this one memory to exist on for a lifetime."

With his certainty of the wrong in a single night of paradise shaken by her earnest plea, and badly wanting the same consolation for his own questionable future, Dare's honorable resistance and good intents fell to ashes. He'd be sorry and he knew it. Yet studying the enticing damsel through glittering blue eyes near-hidden by black lashes lowered, he took a step back.

To Alyce he looked forbidding, and she believed his action a demonstration of her failure to win the longed-for goal. Her heart seemed stabbed by a silent cry of defeat. In the next moment, with one smooth motion Dare stripped off the impediment of his tunic, and green eyes widened. Stunned anew by the magnificent and frightening view of his hard male torso, she felt her breath catch painfully in her throat. When Dare reached out to draw her back into his embrace, wanting nothing more of life than to feel its heat, Alyce swayed toward the burning strength of his body, but powerful hands tamed to gentleness held her the briefest distance away—while a tormenting need grew and heightened her senses.

Though anxious to revel in the sweet-silk brush of full curves, only at an agonizingly slow pace did Dare ease soft, fair flesh nearer until she lay completely against his dark skin. Yet Dare chose not to risk frightening Alyce by pulling her too close, but rather waited until she proved it her desire by renewing the earlier tight embrace of clothed bodies.

She was shaking with the wild pleasure of her bare skin brushing the heat of his wide chest, and her heavy lashes drifted down. On a moan, Alyce buried her lips into the curve between broad shoulder and neck. Then, with a curious, honest passion and following the example provided by the incredible caresses with which he'd once lured her, she slowly moved her mouth across the tempting planes of a massive chest rising and falling heavily. Sensing a potent hunger growing in him, she grew bolder in her explorations.

Dare permitted Alyce's curious exploration, still cradling her in powerful arms and restraining the need to crush her to his aching body despite her intensified provocation. But when her lips found a flat, masculine nipple, an unbidden growl rumbled from Dare's throat. He could bear no more. Alyce looked up and fell into blue flames. He lowered his head for a devastating kiss which so enveloped her, she'd no thought to spare as he lifted and laid her across the narrow bed's limited comfort.

Blue flame eyes held Alyce in thrall even when, to divest himself of the last impediment to their joining, Dare pulled away from arms reluctant to permit any small space between them. Neither had she the will to look away from the awesome display of the magnificent bronzed muscles highlighted by candlelight and shadow. Filled with aching hungers for an unknown end, she breathlessly reached out to claim Dare. When he came down, she twined her fingers into cool strands of black and savored the texture of his back's hard planes while he moved his lips to trail sweet torment over breasts that swelled to meet them. Alyce tumbled completely into the welcome darkness of wild, sinful desires so deep, she thought it an endless descent into wicked pleasures and gladly entered its realms.

In the utterly pliant and sensuous body soon writhing against his own painfully taut form, Dare recognized Alyce's wordless plea for surcease. Yet, even in this moment of a desire more powerful than any he'd know, guilt stung. Alyce's initiation into the rites of passion should have been conducted in a bridal chamber bestrewn with sweet-scented flowers where a fine-draped bed and soft feather mattress would ease her passage into womanhood. It should have been in such a place and not here in this tiny, dark room and atop a crude, narrow bed. Feeling the end of what little control he'd retained slipping away, Dare knew he could no more stop than she. Still, for all that he would later pay a price in honor forfeited, Dare meant to see that this woman beloved would remember without cloud of pain their one experience—and it could only ever be one—of piercingly sweet satisfaction.

While restraining his own wildly insistent need, he caressed every curve, teased with stinging pleasure her every sense until she was sobbing in his arms, begging for an end she did not know. Then, sliding one leg between her silken thighs, he shifted to lie full atop her slender length and rise on his forearms to watch a passion-rosed face wreathed in brilliant curls for the first slight hint of discomfort as he gently pressed intimately near.

Alyce moaned but with pleasure as he tilted her hips to make possible a tender joining. Yet she could not bear the gradual, tormenting pace of his movements. Caught in the tumult of a raging tide, desperate to be carried deeper into the fire storm, to be consumed by the blaze at its core, she instinctively clasped his hips nearer and, as if 'twere a sudden bolt of lightning, felt his body merge with hers. The flash of pain seemed naught but a natural part of the fury and pleasure. Entwined by soft limbs, yielding to the power of innocent enticements and the strength of erotic dreams too long unfulfilled, Dare rocked them both deeper into the ever hotter conflagration. When he went still in the eye of the storm, with a cry of feverish yearning Alyce surged upward and pushed the two of them over the precipice of incredible sensations that burst in a shower of searing sparks.

While Alyce drifted through the billowing smoke of a blissful lassitude, Dare tumbled all too quickly through the mists of sweet contentment rapidly dissipating beneath the chill winds of self-mockery. He'd meant to prolong their play, heighten the pleasure which could never be repeated. But as he had waited so long for the passionate virgin, her wanton provocation had brushed aside the steel-sheathed weapon of his control as if 'twere naught but the flimsy wooden sword of a child. He landed hard against a sheet of icy truth: The justification that their one night of shared passion would provide a consoling memory to last them a lifetime was a fool's dream. In reality that one taste would fill every coming day with the torment of knowing too well the full measure of a satisfaction forever denied. It was a purgatory of his own making, and the thought dropped him into an abyss where loneliness awaited. As he rolled to his back, keeping cherished Alyce within the circle of his arms, Dare's anguish found escape in an unbidden, despairing whisper. "Never again. Never again."

Washed over by waves of contentment, clinging to the master of the welcome storm which had carried her to a serene shore, like distant thunder Alyce heard his deep, faint groan of unalterable fact. In her ears it reverberated with condemnation of her for forcing upon him a deed he'd sought to forestall.

Though preoccupied with thoughts reproaching his wrongful actions, Dare became aware of a soft cheek's dampness and then the tiny splash of a single tear falling to his chest. Certain Alyce was regretting their sweet play, he who never admitted to fear found himself unable to meet a green gaze too surely dark with distaste. Instead he gently held her closer, smoothing one big hand over a tangled mass of unruly curls and brushing comforting lips across the top of her bent head.

"I will never forgive myself for the transgression of taking you, and less for the compounding wrong in my failure to see the possibility of a higher price greatly lessened."

The once pliant body went taut, and Dare assumed she had just realized the full depth of the danger. "Aye, I lost all good reason and selfishly permitted the chance that you will breed the 'demon's' child."

Alyce knew how babes were got but hadn't paused to think it related to the storm just past. Yet the image of a black-haired, blue-eyed babe seemed a warm and welcome dream. Dare's next words robbed her of that naive fantasy.

"Never, never again can we risk this dangerous pleasure lest you lose all hope for the good name and respect you were meant to possess." Alyce could feel the low rumble of his voice beneath her ear and instantly knew 'twas an even deeper tension which roughened his next statement. "Our babe would be cursed with a burden even more dreadful than that which I've ever carried. Not only would he be forced to bear the weight of his sire's curse, but be spurned for a wrong not his own—his illegitimate birth."

Alyce was devastated and remained completely motionless while hours passed on leaden feet and the castle settled into unstirring silence. While their own fires had burned bright, the candle had guttered out unnoticed and the chamber now lay in utter darkness. Waiting in a confused mass of pleasures remembered and guilt, she listened patiently until long after Dare's breathing had settled into the slow, steady cadence of deep sleep. Only then did she carefully ease free of sheltering arms to rise from the narrow bed—and nearly tripped over the remnants of her ruined camise. Thankful as never before for the small and uncluttered room familiar enough to be crossed in a darkness rendered unthreatening by Dare's presence, she found where the crumpled crimson gown had fallen. She pulled it over her head before stealthily slipping from the chamber.

The rest of the night she spent within the meager circle of faint light which, it seemed, the stairwell's first sconce only reluctantly provided. She deemed its wavering gleams a proper setting for her own uncertain emotions. Thinking of Dare's justified but crushing rejection of deeds she'd known already could never be again, she shuddered with shame for her selfish action. Once more her fiery spirit had led her into ill-conceived deeds which had hurt not only herself but another far more important to her. For the sake of selfish desires that unruly spirit had smothered the conscience striving to remind her of a loving decision to hold Dare distant and thus not become a further impediment in the path to his people's acceptance. She'd failed him in that and more. It had never occurred to her that an innocent babe might be forced to pay the price of her unmanageable spirit's ill deed. Nor had she suspected he would blame her more for that wrong—though rightly so.

In a vain attempt to quell now useless self-castigations, Alyce sought to focus on the foolish task of smoothing wrinkles from the dress whose wearing for two days running she'd somehow have to explain. Or mayhap not. Her strange choice might pass unnoticed by others distracted by the castle's ever-growing tension—the only positive aspect she could imagine for the fearsome strain wearing everyone's nerves dangerously thin. A more difficult task than the dress's crumpled condition awaited. She must tame tangled hair leastways into the questionable propriety of braids. Yet the prospect of publicly appearing in an embarrassingly wrinkled gown and without her usual modest headcloth was a paltry matter compared to the incredible wrongs committed in recent hours.

While Alyce was fighting to restore order to the rumpled crimson of her skirts, Dare woke alone. He was certain that, once the cool touch of reason had won through the blinding clouds of hot passion, Alyce had been horrified by an awful realization of her ruin's full extent and had fled the man who'd stolen her most precious possession—her virtue. Never before had he felt so thoroughly a wicked wretch. If he was not truly son of the devil, his soul was surely as black. By ruthlessly using his far superior experience, he had robbed a vulnerable woman of what could never be restored. He had taken Alyce's maidenhead, and by the doing had forfeited what honor he could ever have claimed. Yet that sinful mark against his name, though the most sincerely regretted, was but a further extension of the many he'd accumulated in his life, while Alyce's lost virtue might see her dropped into a pit of disdain similar to the one wherein he'd long dwelled. In a black fury he silently cursed himself for opening to his innocent fire-sprite the gates of that pit filled with shame. Feeling weighted down by the harsh judgment of the dark chamber echoing with his sin, Dare rose, threw on a modicum of clothing, and departed.

The faint gray of predawn had lightened the narrow arrow slit on the landing above when the sound of a door thudding closed brought Alyce to her feet. Peering fearfully over the top step, she saw that her chamber door was slightly ajar and in great relief hurried into a room that had never seemed emptier. In an unthinking parody of her entrance the night past, Alyce threw herself on the bed. This time, however, rather than pound intractable lumps, she instinctively found the hollow left behind by Dare's body and cuddled down, drinking in his lingering scent. The unavoidable certainty that their pleasure had been a mortal sin which could never, must never be repeated wrenched forlorn tears from the depths of her soul.

13

L ady Alyce."

The one called turned in surprise toward a young girl hesitating in the opening of a sizable alcove's gently parted curtains. It was here that Cleva kept her medicinal stores in neat order, and here where that worthy woman and Alyce were occupied with sorting through drying herbs for those ready to be crushed into the powder required for healing tisanes and poultices. Plainly the ever shy girl casting apprehensive glances toward Cleva worried that she'd be scolded for interrupting a task under way. And indeed it was Cleva who responded.

"What brings you here, Maudie?" The direct question was softened by a warmth in gray eyes. But the gentle gaze's reassurance went unseen by the one who, lacking courage to meet it, had dropped her attention to the unthreatening floor. Cleva knew it her duty to keep house serfs in line, but she'd yet to rebuke an innocent blunder, and this timid maid could never be guilty of more.

Straightening with relief though unable to lift her eyes, Maudie began again.

"Earl Rhodare sent me to fetch Lady Alyce to the hall. There's news arrived he says she must hear."

"What news?" Alyce's brief question contained an overabundance of curiosity, but a curiosity tightly restrained by the tangled guilt and anticipation in this prospect of seeing Dare for the first time since leaving his side in the shadows of night. She'd not descended for the day's first meal until after he was gone, and he'd not returned from duties elsewhere for the midday meal.

"Don't know." Maudie's uncertain gaze rose in answer to the quiet question of a much-admired lady. "The lord simply said as there was news." She paused. Then, knowing her response inadequate, she hastened to add, "Arlen must'a brought it as he's there, too."

At tidings of her "baby" son's return, with unusual lack of care, Cleva laid aside the bunch of dried rosemary just released from its place amongst the many stem-tied to a rod above. She'd been about to give Alyce a repeated demonstration of crushing techniques best-suited to render them into the minute particles she deemed superior for future use. It would have to wait. She hustled toward the door so quickly, Maudie had perforce to jump aside and make way for the larger woman.

Alyce followed Cleva's lead—but slowly. In the wake of her initial confusion over the call to Dare's presence came a growing dismay for its likely purpose. She smoothed temples and cheeks, unmindful of a tight-fitting barbette's absence. The feel of skin far smoother than finest linen interrupted Alyce's concentration and laid a slight frown on her brow. The garment had been left off for want of one fresh and ready to be worn, a lack caused by the past night's distractions (what a tame description for so profound an experience of pleasure and shame) from the mundane matters involved in preparing for bed. Leastways this light blue gown had been ready to be worn, saving her from the once-feared need to wear a wrinkled crimson gown two days in a row. Alyce shrugged aside thoughts useless when, after the overwhelming wrong of deeds committed in dark hours, the absence of a single narrow strip of cloth was utterly insignificant.

While approaching the stairwell's gloom, she returned her thoughts to the problem at hand and reluctantly acknowledged the almost certain reason for her commanded appearance. Had Dare not warned her of his intent to send her from Wythe? As she knew that Arlen had been dispatched to the lands of her dowry, news on what other subject could he possibly bear? As a mere woman, she'd not be consulted on matters of the fiefdom's administration. Therefore, Arlen's report must concern a more personal subject. The only such topic in that vicinity was her young husband and his claim on her. Alyce's feet fair dragged with dread of the bleak, long-delayed future too surely about to become reality.

A scant three steps below, Alyce paused. *Nay, I have prepared for this a decade and more. I will not falter now.* The courage in the wordless claim rang hollow even to her. Yet the fiery spirit so long restrained came to her rescue. She lifted her chin to boldly confront the depressing prospect so close, it loomed ahead like the heavy iron bars of a dungeon cell waiting to forever lock her away. Soon she would be delivered into the care of her spouse's family.

Alyce resolutely resumed her descent. 'Twas wise that she depart Wythe and leave behind the castle containing memories too evocative. She should welcome the chance to sunder the bonds of her lover's potent lures and thus save them both from a greater, leastways more public, shame. She should welcome this departure. She should but she didn't.

With each downward step on the winding stairway, her pace slowed. Despite her determination to bear the coming news unflinchingly, the burden of dread increased until on reaching the stairway's bottom, Alyce felt as if she were carrying the mighty castle's great weight upon her shoulders. Seeking a brief moment of respite, she purposely tripped and leaned against the archway opening into a gloomy, almost deserted hall. Happily would Alyce have paid near any price for the ability to absorb a portion of the cold stone's strength. Instead she received a deepening chill.

Azure eyes flickered as the damsel stumbled. From where he and Arlen waited on the outer edge of the fireplace's ring of warmth, Dare wanted to rush forward and escort Alyce safely inside. But although few would see—save one group of serfs toiling over a huge ox being roasted in the fireplace, and another carefully setting large tapestries aside before applying a fresh layer of whitewash to smoke-dimmed walls—such attentions from the Demon could only darken her name. He'd not place that small measure more upon the one about to face a drastic change in her status.

Concerned as he was for the damsel's reaction, Dare's worried gaze lingered on the delicate oval of her lowered face, for once uncovered by barbette, while a long blue veil hid bright hair. Though she refused his silent command to look up, Alyce straightened and moved forward unfaltering. 'Twas plain she was distressed. Had the gossip trail, which Dare knew to his cost was the most effective instrument on Wythe, already carried the life-altering news to her? Nay. Couldn't be. Only he and Arlen shared the facts, and Arlen had not left his side since their first telling. Even had they both seen the apprehended fugitive confined to a dungeon cell. While the men of his garrison were busy elsewhere, they'd secretly imprisoned the traitorous gate guard down where no one would willingly go for any reason save a direct order to do so. Thus Dare believed that, unlike the man left tied in the forest, this guardsman could be left to await interrogation—a chore to be performed once had been completed the more important duty of gently apprising Alyce of an unwelcome truth.

When, with eyes lowered, Alyce stood in valiant yet unnatural meekness before him, Dare reluctantly spoke. "Arlen returned with a startling report." The low voice came to an abrupt halt while Dare motioned toward a young man standing proud despite the weight of an affectionate mother firmly clamped to his arm.

For the first time, Dare wished he'd sent another man to Wrexdale. Not because Arlen had in any way failed to see his commanded deed done with all haste and vigor, but because another could've delivered the verbal blow whose telling Dare would far rather have been spared. Dare's dark face went as hard and unyielding as pure granite. He quailed before no man but balked at the need to state what must be told.

"Arlen journeyed to Wrexdale."

Of his listeners, only Alyce knew Dare well enough to

recognize the strain required to force cold words from a tight throat. Did Dare find the prospect of her departure from Wythe as unpleasant as did she?

"From thence he moved on to the small fiefdom beyond." Alyce would know this to be her child-husband's home, but Dare deemed it unnecessary that serfs drawn by curiosity to tarry near be provided every detail. Ice blue eyes turned upon one trespasser after another. Immediately responding to the unspoken order, they turned away to continue assigned tasks with renewed energy.

Certain that the news would be unpleasant, Arlen was ill at ease with his role as the messenger who'd brought it to a gentle lady deserving of better treatment. His discomfort increased when Lady Alyce's gaze flickered over him and then instantly dropped. Further shamed that his lord found it necessary to fill his duty in giving the report, to the others' surprise, it was Arlen who doggedly picked up the telling.

"I-I-I met S-S-Sir B-B-Brian." Arlen paused. His mouth compressed, but only for a moment, and when he continued, the stutter seemed less pronounced. "A-Asked w-when his s-s-son would require his b-bride."

Once again Alyce lifted nervous fingers to temple and cheeks, pressing the edges of an invisible barbette modestly near. Doubtless now would come greetings and the summons she decidedly did not want to hear. Awaiting words which would make the call an irrevocable demand, to prevent revealing both the desolation and resentment they would bring, green eyes glared at an unmoving floor.

Deeply regretting his unavoidable task, Arlen clenched his hands but through stiff lips forced hurtful words. "He s-s-stated that h-his only s-s-son was n-not wed."

A startled emerald gaze flew up. It was impossible. As quickly as it rose, Alyce tamped down a small, weak flicker of hope. The red-haired guardsman must have gone to the wrong destination. Her husband's sire was a Sir Brian, true. But surely Brian was a common enough name to account for this mistake.

Arlen saw green eyes widen, and thought them filled with horror. "I-I-I s-s-specifically a-a-asked 'b-b-bout you—"

Under his concern for the woman, Arlen's stutter had intensified again.

To spare Arlen's ruby-faced embarrassment and expedite the process, Dare smoothly resumed the report's telling. "To Arlen, Sir Brian said that though you'd once been wed to his boy, the marriage was no more."

Alyce blinked at this unequivocal announcement, but met Arlen's guilty glance directly and with a soft smile lent reassurance that she was not so witless as to blame the messenger for the message. Beneath the smile her thoughts whirled until one fact rose to the top like cream. Her onetime family by marriage had wished not only to distance themselves from her long enough for the shame of her father's crime to fade but had chosen to completely sever all ties with the traitor Halbert Bohan. It was reasonable, even forgivable. Moreover, she could not fool herself that it was else than a welcome reprieve. She need not leave Wythe. Leastways not immediately. This time when her attention fell to the floor, it was to hide a tiny but irrepressible smile.

Dare's heart bled for the sense of abandonment he feared Alyce was experiencing. Again he wanted to draw her close and provide an anchor to hold her steady, save her from drowning in the watery arms of life's treacherous sea. He restrained the urge for the sake of preserving her, first, from the assault of whispering tongues, and second, from what he was certain she'd deem a renewed assault by the predator whose arms she'd fled the night past. From their passionate embrace he knew Alyce had drawn as much pleasure as he. But today she'd yet to permit the briefest glance his way. Clearly she thought their shared intimacy a great sin—which in truth it had been whether the surrender were that of a married woman or virginal maid. And, so far as they'd known, she'd been both.

Self-disgust hardened blue eyes to a depth of ice which seemed capable of freezing all in its path. "Sir Brian stated that an emissary from Winchester presented the annulment as an unalterable fact. Furthermore, the deed was done and reported even before your father was charged with treason."

Dare studied Alyce for any sign that she recognized the

import of this fact. She neither shifted her stance nor lifted her gaze. Was she too intent on the struggle to keep her head above the threatening waves of her rapidly changing circumstances to recognize the slant these facts gave the whole?

Shivering beneath the unaccountable fierceness of his earl's countenance, Arlen glanced to the side but courageously went on with the necessary task. "P-P-Priest s-s-said—" Arlen paused again and shuffled his feet before continuing "—b-b-bishop found t-t-too close a f-f-family t-t-tie."

Dare exchanged a knowing glance of disgust with Arlen before explaining the nature of this "discovery" to Alyce. "The 'holy'—" The spoken title held a wealth of scorn "—Bishop of Winchester reported that your great-grandmother was stepsister to your husband's great-great-grandsire. Thus, Sir Brian was informed, the bishop had felt duty-bound to annul the wicked union afore a wrong, though innocently begun, could be consummated and develop into a sin more serious."

Having channeled the whole of her oft too strong will into betraying no hint of unseemly relief, Alyce heard little of what was said beyond the news that she was no longer wed. Carried on the soft, obscuring haze of that truth, she was utterly unprepared when reality parted the gentle mists with the harsh blade of a far different but equally accurate truth.

Since she was an unwed woman, her identity disappeared. Alyce could claim no feeling for the boy-husband she'd never met. Nor could she regret her freedom from the manacles of their marriage. Yet an unexpected and resented sense of loss overwhelmed her while her conscience almost gleefully pointed out that she'd been reduced to mere chattel, a *thing* of questionable value. At an age when all wellborn women were married either to man or church, she'd become naught but the daughter of a baron disgraced, a female with no dowry of worth. Her negligible holdings were inadequate to compensate for the blemish laid upon her heritage by charges blackening her sire's honor. And that blemish was insignificant when considered against the stain of purity surrendered.

Dare had told her he would soon see her either in her young husband's domain or settled on the lands of her dowry. As the former was now impossible, it needs must be the latter. She'd recently told herself that 'twas best a woman think for herself. Now she would have the opportunity to prove it was possible for a woman to direct her own path. That challenge she would accept, although, despite the chaperone and guardsman Dare had promised to provide, the loneliness in the prospect of a future without Dare was disheartening.

As Arlen's voice faded into silence, the unmoving Alyce held the attention of the hall's occupants. Servants once assiduously presenting the image of concentrated toil abandoned the effort. Spits were left unturned, while it was uncertain if those earlier laboring to swab the walls would've noticed had their huge vats of whitewash been overturned. Lady Alyce had not been a part of their castle for long. Yet with her generosity of spirit and willingness to help those in need, she'd earned both their respect and a measure of affection, enough that they were sorry to see her subjected to this humiliation.

A motionless figure, unimposing and, indeed, near fading into the soot-darkened fireplace wall behind, watched the scene playing out before him. With little more substance than a shadow himself, Walter shrewdly weighed the coin of these events and schemed for methods to imperceptibly shave their edges until the scale overbalanced to his advantage. Once again facts he had wanted hidden had been revealed, but he'd wits enough to reshape them for his own uses.

In response to the younger woman's troubled expression, Cleva deserted her healthy "baby son." Fussing over the unjust wrong done Arlen's "lady fair," she settled the unnaturally chilled damsel into a chair by the fire.

Dare stood aside, thankful in this instance that onlookers would not question his lack of action. Few men would pause to soothe a woman's troubles—certainly not in public. Though he'd once bound her injured wrists, he was certain the interference of her seducer would only add to her burdens. Thus, he held back and watched Cleva care for the woman who was wife no more. A further assault added to the blow of false accusations against her father.

While attempting to kindle her spirit to meet the challenge of life on Wrexdale lands and a future devoid of Dare's company, an unheeding Alyce was unaware of the gazes centered upon her. Alyce acquiesced to the other woman's ministrations until, for the first time this day, she looked up to the man who had always been her world. Helpless as she was beneath the power of a blue gaze which instantly went from ice to brilliant flame, the trail of her thoughts took another sharp turn. Others worried about her, yet she was abruptly disgusted by the selfishness in the energy she'd wasted on herself. Her troubles were paltry compared to those Dare had long survived and which still threatened him with dangers looming ever nearer. Before being exiled to Wrexdale, she would redouble her efforts to see Dare accepted by the people of Wythe, his people, and his future bright.

Dare saw distress lay a shadow across green fire and assumed it was his proximity that increased her woe. With this depressing thought, he acknowledged that the granting of the once hopelessly wished-for end to her marriage did nothing to ease his guilt for the past night's action. Rather it was deepened. His expression went cold and grim.

Although he'd not claimed another's wife, he had stolen the one possession wellborn women were taught from birth to guard as their greatest treasure. Moreover, by his seduction of Alyce, he had dishonored her father, the man he most owed respect. This time he had truly committed the crime with which he'd been earlier charged. Innocent of taking Halbert's wife, still he had taken the man's chaste daughter. The only comfort to be found amidst a landscape of brutal truths lay in the knowledge that this time he could and would willingly pay the ultimate penance.

In silence Dare turned to stride from the great hall and thence from the castle. He'd a task to be done before the next dawning. That his "penance" was also the goal he'd most fervently desired for years uncounted surely did not lessen the value. Leastways, during the hours of his long ride, this was the reassurance he repeated in steady cadence with the sound of Fiend's hooves pounding over autumn-dying grasses and through near barren trees.

Walter's eyes narrowed on the departing figure until Dare disappeared into the outgoing tunnel. If only he could make the earl truly vanish as easily. Under the deadline drawing close—very, very close—'twas an impossible wish driving him to desperate measures.

Sensing her friend sidling near, Alyce smiled up at him with strained welcome. It was no surprise that Walter had stayed in the background until after the intimidating earl he clearly feared had gone.

"I fear for you, Alyce, I fear for you." Walter's murmur fair dripped with overindulged anxieties.

Alyce restrained a growing irritation with all those who seemed intent on treating her as an object of pity. Her conscience scolded that such a reaction was unjust. Walter's concern, like Cleva's, was sincere. She couldn't rebuff their attentions without the risk of hurt feelings. Still, she had far rather be left alone to set aside the suddenly shattered arrangements for her future and concentrate on seeking methods to remove or leastways halt the spread of weeds threatening to smother the healthy growth of all Dare had done to return prosperity to Wythe. Distracted by these thoughts, Alyce neither comprehended nor wished to understand Walter's doubtless exaggerated worries, but again forced a smile that she hoped he'd think born of appreciation.

"Seems all too plain." Walter, like a well-trained hunt hound, was not easily diverted from the scent of his quarry, particularly this one too important to lose. "Don't you see? Here is proof that the Demon arranged your father's downfall. Surely you *do* see it?"

She was perplexed by a claim that made no more sense to Alyce than Dare's accusation of Walter's involvement, and her smile faded while she considered one man's charge and the other's countercharge. That the bishop who'd dissolved her marriage was the same man whom Dare claimed responsible for both her father's fall and his own danger was significant. This possibility she could not deny as 'twas the

Bishop of Winchester who controlled the king, and the king who laid charges of treason. And significant, too (though she'd earlier sought to reject its logic), might be the fact that 'twas this bishop under whose training Walter had been for several years. She frowned but did not respond.

"The Demon has long harbored a wicked jealousy of your father, as witness the blatant attempt to steal his wife. Further, I deem it plain that since being banished from Keniver, Dare's hate has grown apace, and wielding his evil powers, the black earl schemed to see Lord Halbert lose all that he most values." Walter smugly congratulated himself on a talent for neatly reversing true facts. "His wife, the Demon first claimed. Now, in collusion with the king Dare fought beside so oft, Keniver has been held forfeit to the crown."

Alyce's frown deepened. 'Twas true. Her father's fall could have been plotted by either the Bishop of Winchester with Walter's aid, or King Henry in conjunction with Dare's desire for vengeance. To weaken the first possibility, again rose the same stumbling block that had earlier convinced her of Walter's innocence. What purpose could Walter have for harming her sire, his brother-in-law and the man who supported him? Alyce's hands smoothed over a blue linen skirt to tightly clasp the edge of her chair. On the argument's opposite side, she would never believe Dare guilty of dishonoring a foster father she was certain he respected. The memory of Sybillene in his arms weakened her confidence, but only briefly. She'd had ample opportunity to observe her self-centered stepmother's determined pursuit of Dare. And for all that the memory of the pair abed hurt Alyce, she could not lay the blame solely on him, and no longer believed he'd purposefully set out to shame her sire.

Seeing that a battle was being waged behind a gentle scowl, Walter fervently seized Alyce's tightly curled fingers, and with them the opportunity to advance his goal. "You must see what prize is intended next to fall into the Demon's hands." He looked earnestly into wide green eyes wherein confusion surely provided fertile ground for the sprouting of suspicions he'd sown.

Focused on this next step toward his long and patiently

executed guest's ultimate goal, Walter failed to see the
mother and son still near and listening with growing disgust
to his disparaging charges against their earl. Nor would he
have considered their reaction of import enough to interrupt his relentless pursuit of the prize in sight.

"Now Lord Halbert will lose even the right to bestow his
daughter where he chooses." Walter produced the statement
with the assumed assurance of irrefutable fact. "Seems too
certain that, as reward for his part in producing the papers
which saw your father named traitor, Demon Dare was
promised the annulment of your vows and will seek to wed
with you."

Alyce blinked rapidly. Dare marry her? 'Twas a witless
suggestion, yet Walter's persistent voice went on.

"Our host doubtless knew your sire would never permit
the union of his beloved daughter to the vile worm who'd
seduced his wife into adultery. 'Twas a tidy scheme: set your
father aside and leave the path clear to attain his goals—
both Halbert's dishonor and you in marriage."

Straightening, Alyce tried to pull her hands free while
slowly shaking her head. Echoes of Walter's charges joined
memories of Dare's accusations and added a further cloud
of confusion to those already whirling through Alyce's mind
so madly that she felt dizzy. Was it true that Dare wished to
wed with her? She shook her head more firmly to disperse
hopeless wishes.

Despite Dare's talk of unending bonds, he'd claimed no
deeper emotion for her than the physical intimacy he'd
earlier shared with Sybillene. Once he'd taken the latter, it
seemed he'd wanted her no more. Was it not most likely that
the same was now true of her? At the end of their intimate
embrace he'd warned her that it must never happen again.
Had her marriage merely been a convenient excuse for this
rejection? An excuse negated by the news of her annulment?
Was it the unpleasant prospect that she might expect more
which had driven him to leave her side so abruptly? She
purposefully roused her temper to defy the man's assumption that she would be so lacking in pride as to attempt
forcing herself upon him.

"As an earl, Dare can arrange a far more advantageous

match. He would not settle for one possessed of a dowry so insignificant." The truth of her argument struck with a pain Alyce hid behind lowered lashes and sought to squelch beneath glowing coals of anger. "And rightly so."

Alyce rose and turned her back on Walter to proudly approach the two plainly irritated observers. "Cleva, I beg you will give me some task to do."

Cleva looked doubtfully at the younger woman. Would it not be better were she to have quiet time alone to review the awful things this strange man had said, think about them and realize how foolish they were? Asides, Lady Alyce had just received a life-changing blow. Surely she should be alone . . .

"Please, Cleva, busy my hands and free my thoughts." Alyce recognized her mentor's hesitation and the reasoning behind it—faulty reasoning. "Better yet, send me to deliver medicants to an ailing villager—anywhere beyond castle walls where there's fresh air to help clear the view of my future."

This rationale made more sense, and though not totally convinced of its wisdom, Cleva nodded a head whose white and black pattern seemed more pronounced amidst the haze of smoke escaped from the massive fireplace.

"Come with me to the alcove where we labored when the summons was sent." The errand she'd begun to plan would leastways free Alyce of curious serfs apparently busy with tasks of their own but assuredly listening to every word that had been spoken since the earl's departure—and before. "There's a woman who ever *thinks* she needs powerful cures and will greet your offer of succor with fervent welcome."

In the oblique description Alyce recognized a type of person she'd known even before her training to treat the ailing had begun. Her nursemaid had been such a one—healthier than most but utterly convinced that death hovered threateningly close. Green eyes met gray with perfect understanding, and the two women exchanged a conspiratorial smile. Alyce then followed Cleva across the hall and up the winding stairway she'd so recently descended with trepidation for a prospect wildly different from the truth awaiting.

The moment Alyce disappeared into the gloomy tunnel, Walter's interest was caught by a motion at the fireplace's far corner. As he watched, Tess stepped from the stairwell, rising from the busy kitchen below. The satisfied venom in his eyes drew her immediate attention, and backing away, she instinctively laid a hand against her cheek. Her reaction pleased him. Though he was not as physically strong as the demon earl, who was to say his powers were any less effective? True, he'd no warriors with blade and arrow at his command, but he believed his weapons would be proven as deadly. Gaze heavy on his target, he steadily crossed the distance between them.

Tess took a further step back and then another, but perilously near the stairway precipice, she had perforce to halt. The slightest further retreat put her in danger of a frightful tumble backwards and down.

"I'm off to the well house." Walter delighted in the woman's terror and the power it lent his blandest statement.

The weight of cruel eyes upon a cheek still throbbing painfully felt like another blow, and Tess could not fail to hear either the unspoken command or the renewed threat behind mild words. She flinched but nodded, eyes closed until her tormentor traversed the hall and passed into the shadowy exit tunnel.

A red-haired man, yet standing where two women had left him, observed the exchange but heard nothing untoward in Walter's single sentence. When a clearly fearful Tess passed him, blindly intent on the outgoing portal, his black scowl rested heavily upon her swaying figure, although he made no move to follow as she departed the hall. The woman had too often shown him how unwelcome was his interest for him to interfere in whatever nasty game she'd begun with the unsavory and much less than grateful visitor from Keniver.

14

To one side of the courtyard, a small wooden structure rested. Although insignificant in appearance, it sheltered an asset of great import—a freshwater well. This single resource improved by a hundredfold Wythe's prospects for outlasting any siege. It was this well which figured prominently in Walter's future plans. But first other schemes must be concluded.

The eyes peering from just inside an unbarred door's shielding shadows glittered with perverse anticipation on the approaching woman constantly casting worried glances over a homespun-clad shoulder.

"Welcome." Walter leaned casually against a waist-high stone ledge laid about the well's perimeter and smiled in foul triumph as Tess stepped within.

"The time has come to begin a serious campaign that will see the fruition of goals we share." He knew better than to plainly speak words which might be overheard and wielded against him. "'Tis a simple matter. Only need you continue on a broader stage the performance earlier begun. Limit your audience not to a single person but reveal your talents to the whole."

Pressing into the small building's farthermost corner,

Tess nodded. Yet beneath the deep resentment of her expression there flickered an underlying guilty regret. She'd been a fool to attempt punishing her lord; a fool who, by that ill-conceived deed, had stepped into a ghastly bog of her own making, one she feared would suck her ever deeper until she drowned in its poisonous muck.

Fear Walter welcomed, but the woman's obvious regret might bode a dangerous weakness in his carefully interwoven plots. He couldn't risk allowing it to continue unchecked, and set his devious mind to spinning a stronger web of rewards and restraints.

"Keep ever in mind what rich prize a fair maiden may win at the end of a game well played, like the fortunate woman who finds the bean in a Christmastide cake and thus becomes queen of the Yule Feast."

The wellborn man's words, coated with sticky honey, put a bitter taste in Tess's mouth, and rather than bringing the earl to mind, they unaccountably raised the image of a disapproving Arlen.

Finding that Tess looked even less convinced, Walter lost his precarious patience. He was confident of his control over her, and willing to waste no more time in foolish conversation. From its sheath at his waist he pulled a fine dagger. Its hilt was of burnished silver and bore at its topmost point a single, sizable ruby.

"Simply do as I have said." As Walter spoke, he turned the blade in his hands until its sharp edge caught a stray shaft of weak daylight falling through the door left ajar. His ominous meaning was clear. "Fail me and the 'reward' I promised will be yours." With the dagger he pointed to the outgoing portal.

Tess lost no time either in departing or setting about the task commanded. By the time the deeper gray of dusk had overtaken gloomy day, the tale of their earl's wicked seduction, seduction by practice of the Black Arts, had begun to spread. Gaining strength from the physical proof of a vicious punishment which Tess's cheek bore, it hissed through kitchens into stable and was carried from castle through the humblest village cottage. The strange thrill lent by fear was a vine inseparably entwined with the gossip trail's rapidly spreading weeds. 'Twas further nurtured by additional morsels of rumor that whispered of Satan's mark upon their Demon, a mark which with her own eyes Tess had seen.

Inevitably the rumors, as weeds are wont to do, outgrew their boundaries. They spread beyond serf, villein, and men of the garrison to reach Walter where he sat in the shadows of a guardroom ever warm for sharing the level below the great hall with the kitchen.

"Oh, 'tis true, I fear." Behind a rueful grimace Walter hid his pleasure in this evidence that Tess had bowed to his demand. "Though I regret the need to speak ill of my sister's foster son, and thus in some degree my kin as well, I can no longer stand mute while the Demon practices his wicked arts upon the inhabitants of Wythe."

Silence fell as every man waited with baited breath for the explanation which surely must follow the disloyal admission spoken with understandable reluctance. They had not welcomed the intrusion of this weakling into the bastion of warriors, but as he was wellborn and their lord's guest, they'd been unable to eject him, and now were glad.

"Aye, Earl Dare was my brother-in-law's foster son, yet neither that honorable bond nor the loyalty he owed Lord Halbert prevented him from attempting to work the same evil spell upon Sybillene."

A gasp rose from listeners who moved closer as if drawn by some invisible lure. Walter shook a downbent head in an apparent despair that prevented others from seeing the glow of satisfaction in his eyes.

"Thank the saints, and it must be they who are responsible for the miracle of a baron awakened and sent to the bedchamber of his favorite knight—the Demon. Lord Halbert saved his wife and preserved the honor of his name." Walter paused to look slowly about strong warriors quietly gathered in a tight circle about him and hanging on his every word. Inwardly he sneered. See now what powerful weapons could be words carefully wielded.

"But doubtless you knew all this before? You knew that 'twas for this grave wrong that the Demon was banished from Keniver?" Walter sent an innocently inquiring gaze from one silent man to the next. "Ah, I'd forgotten. To shield his own from threatened shame, Lord Halbert explained Dare's departure from Keniver as an action taken of his own choice, one made to secure a position of greater prestige and wealth from Richard Marshal, now Earl of Pembroke."

Walter rose, shaking his head again. "Who knows what fiendish deed the Demon ponders next?" He turned to leave, well satisfied with his work.

Certain the guardsmen left behind were too absorbed in talk of what he'd said to notice, Walter went not up the stairs to the hall, but down. After taking out the candle he'd earlier tucked into the folds of his ankle-length robes, he held it against the sconce's flame until it took light and then continued to descend with the intention of undertaking a search for the postern door. The hidden exit most probably lay somewhere in the seldom-visited gloom of the castle's lowest level. Its placement was doubtless known to the fortress defenders whose company he'd just departed, but likely 'twas a secret not shared with those who served within—such as Tess.

The darkness at the stairway's bottom was oppressive, and an unexpected rustling sound from a distant corner sent a shiver of terror down Walter's spine. If the noise's source was merely one of the rats common in such dark surroundings, then it must be one of prodigious size. He moved forward while, with a trembling hand, holding the candle out before him like an amulet against evil. The outer edge of flamelight crept forward. Abruptly he came to a halt, eyes narrowing on an unexpected sight.

"Hmmm, a new addition to the collection of oddments housed here." Head tilted, Walter studied the bulky man who'd moved to tightly grip the bars of his cage and peer out suspiciously.

"The Demon sent *you* to force confessions from *me?*" The words were a sneer as Roger visually measured the slight man before him. Strange greeting aside, not for a moment did he think the powerful earl would choose so weak a man for such a chore.

Temper roused by the insult one reduced to the status of

prisoner had delivered, Walter was instantly determined to see this man, like Tess, quail beneath the power of words. He knew both precisely who the other was and the nature of his crime. Though neither gate guard had been told the identity of their employer in the matter of Lady Alyce's capture, Darwyn had pointed out the pair to Walter. This knowledge lent him not only the opportunity to cow Roger but a further weapon to wield against Dare.

"I wonder at the secrecy of your imprisonment. Unless . . ." Walter's pause echoed with unspoken meaning, and Roger's chin lifted to meet its threat. "Nay, the Demon cannot mean to work upon you the same wicked arts he wrought upon the traitorous gate guard captured."

Roger's face tightened against this oblique but ominous reference, and he had to clamp down hard on a hasty tongue to restrain an urge to beg for details.

"Ah . . ." Walter was pleased to see his prey take the bait so smoothly. "Apparently you've not heard of the price demanded of a guardsman who foolishly sought to cross his Demon earl." Walter hid his enjoyment of the scene while matter-of-factly giving a brief, truthful account of events . . . but with gaps in pertinent areas. "The captured Lady Alyce, your earl rescued, leaving her abductor to be found deep in the forest—with the Devil's sign written in blood on his dead body." Walter could barely contain the glee endangering his solemn mask as a strong shudder passed through the much larger man.

"Aye." Walter nodded with apparent sympathy. "Leastways, you may count yourself fortunate not to have been a part of that deed, elsewise I'd not give you a gnat's chance of surviving against the devil's ire."

Roger let go of the bars and sank down on the matted straw covering the floor of his cell to bury his face between clenched fists. "'Tis truth you speak, and now it'll be me what next pays the devil's price."

"Don't say you, too, were a part of that wrong?" A wonderfully realistic horror seemed to tinge Walter's gasped words.

"Aye, that I were." As if already he'd surrendered hope, Roger's confession was flat and lifeless.

"I'll not let it be. Not again." Seemingly aghast at the prospect, Walter rushed toward the caged man. "Surely one sacrifice is enough to propitiate the Demon's god."

Through a lifetime of suspicion Roger glanced up at the man wringing his hands.

"I'll find a way to set you safely free—if you'll give me the necessary tool." Walter swore the wild oath with appropriate fervor.

Aye, Roger decided, this strange little man looked the fanatical sort willing to offer himself as martyr for some mad cause. Likely the man truly would do what he could to see a demon's will diverted. Yet he gave the fool small chance of success. Nonetheless, this fool represented his only small ray of hope.

Eyes skeptically narrowed, he asked the question certain to snuff out even that tiny light. "What tool have I here in the dungeon and stripped of blades and mace?"

"The knowledge of a secret exit," Walter answered promptly. "A path of escape."

Roger's heavy brows lowered. "What good is that when I am locked behind stout bars of iron?"

"If I could be certain the way would be clear were you free of its confines, I would risk my own life to secure the key to your cage."

The faint glimmer of hope gained in strength, only by a tenuous thread but enough that Roger shrugged and waved toward the vast lower level's opposite corner. "Over there, behind the many baskets of apples stored here in the cool to last until next harvest."

Walter immediately spun to move steadily in the direction indicated and thus prevented Roger from any glimpse of his triumphant grin. It was a triumph not lessened by the fact that the thick and iron-bound door, found at length, was locked.

"Doubtless the key that opens your cell will also open the postern door. If you give me your oath—on the one 'True Cross'—that you'll hold our pact a secret, I swear to offer my all in obtaining that selfsame key to secure your freedom afore the Demon's wrath overtakes you."

Once Roger had given his solemn oath, Walter departed

with an ever-increasing sense of destiny. Seemed even matters unsuspected hours past were turning to his advantage, and the journey toward his quest's goal progressing splendidly.

Alyce pulled the edges of her brown cloak more tightly about a shivering body. Only could she pray Sir Ulger was correct in his claim that they were very near their destination. They'd set off in the chill of midafternoon, but the temperature had rapidly dropped until it felt as if the air itself had gone to ice.

"Berdene lays there, milady." Ulger gestured toward the journey's goal, as relieved as his companion. Though a man well used to the rigors of an outdoor life in all manner of weather and not personally suffering from the cold, he was concerned for Lady Alyce. He'd warned his wife she erred in sending the wellborn damsel on such a task on such a day . . . but betimes there was no reasoning with the woman.

Pushing her discomfort aside, Alyce studied the minor fortress they neared. 'Twas of a very old and simple style. A wide circular ditch had been dug, and the earth removed piled in the center to form an unnaturally high hill. Atop this perched a plain wooden building. On the outer perimeter logs tightly bound together created a wall whose tips had been sharpened into dangerous points.

Alyce smiled to herself. In an earlier time it would've been an admirable defense, but against the siege weapons of the current day, 'twas woefully inadequate. Yet with Dare to protect this vassal and his dependents, the man was safe—so long as his earl was safe. As the bleak thought returned all the dark worries she'd spent the whole long ride alternately pondering and attempting to brighten with the sparks of an undaunted spirit, she failed to notice when both steeds passed through an open gate.

"Sir Ulger, welcome, welcome." The gruff voice seemed unaccustomed to the effort of speech, but a broad smile proved the greeting's sincerity even as its speaker glanced sidelong and with leery curiosity at the second visitor.

"Lady Alyce has brought your good wife a new tisane to

treat her ills." Ulger matter-of-factly answered the unspoken question. "My Cleva says as it has a miraculous effect."

While Wythe's guard captain helped her dismount, Alyce caught a glimpse of their host's skeptical grimace, but she looked demurely down as if she had not seen.

"Milady." Ulger offered his upheld arm, and once small fingers had been placed atop, he turned Alyce to face the other man. "May I present you to Sir Niall."

The man made an awkward bow, and Alyce gave a sweet smile in return. Stunned by the beauty's visit in the first instance and by her unassuming response in the second, Niall quickly led the way into the small keep. There his wife, heavily layered in bed furs, huddled amidst a pile of further furs and coverlets arranged near the central hearth.

"Moira, Lady Alyce has come with a miraculous new potion to cure you." Niall's tone was heavy with sarcasm, but Alyce suspected it was aimed at his wife and not at her.

"Cleva has tested this blending of medicinal herbs and finds 'tis true." Alyce lost no moment in moving forward to face her 'patient' with a bright smile. "I know only that it did wondrous well for my old nurse, who, by what Cleva tells me of your ailment, suffered much the same."

Moira's red-rimmed eyes lifted with a hope that reminded Alyce of another certainty she'd learned from her old nurse: no matter whether the cause was in mind or in body, the illness was real.

"This is a potent tincture." Alyce pulled a small vial from the bag she'd tied to her waist before setting out. "Once each day put a single drop into a cup of water—only one drop, else you risk danger. You should begin to feel much improved after the first usage, and by the end of a sennight, I warrant you'll be cured."

While Moira took the offered vial and held it up against the fire's light, Alyce arranged for a cup of water to be fetched. An amazingly short time after the water with its drop of potion had been drunk, the patient's eyes cleared noticeably and she was sitting straighter to enter into a lively conversation with this female guest, a rarity amongst their many male visitors.

"Keniver? You're from Keniver?" Moira questioned, anxious to prolong the conversation.

Alyce imperceptibly straightened, wondering if rumors of the charges against her father were this question's source. Still her smile did not waver. "Aye, my father is the Baron of Keniver and your earl's foster father."

"'Twas there then that Demon Dare—" The flow of the woman's words came to an abrupt end. She flushed in deep embarrassment for unthinkingly prying into their earl's past. Moira's husband and Ulger frowned while moving nearer.

"Dare came to Keniver Castle when I was a babe." Meaning to merely divert the woman's attention from the accusation against her father, Alyce had not intended to put Moira in the way of the men's ire and hastened to further waylay the attention of all.

"The poor boy patiently put up with me very nearly from thence on . . . and a pest I was, ever trailing behind while he practiced with sword, lance, and dagger. He teased me something awful, but whenever I'd a need for aid, he was always there—for me or for anyone in want of a strong arm to rely upon. 'Tis why, many and many a time, my father proclaimed to all that Dare was his 'best and bravest' knight."

After that rough beginning, the lopsided exchange quietly continued, with Alyce sharing memories of specific instances wherein Dare had protected the weak or proven loyalty to those who had earned it. Her three listeners appeared spellbound by the true stories she shared.

In the last, even did she admit how, when little more than a toddling and with copious but false tears, she'd begged Dare to climb up and rescue her unwilling kitty from a tree. Once her knight errant, scratched as the price for his feat, brought the creature to her, she'd merrily laughed for the success of her prank. He'd paddled her derriere so smartly, she'd found it difficult to sit at the evening meal. It had been, she told her audience, a just punishment, yet Dare had been as upset by her discomfort as she. Nonetheless, by the experience she'd learned never to tease at another's expense.

The day had aged and gone to a gray fading toward its end before the couple in Berdene Keep reluctantly bade Lady Alyce and her knight-escort farewell.

As he returned in the full dark at the end of a long and wearying day spent visiting far-flung farms and restless farmers, Thomas's usual good humor was more than strained. Though expected, Dare had not come to join him, and he'd worried for the why of it. 'Twas an anxiety greatly increased by the growing suspicion amongst the common folk, who constantly made oblique references to wild tales repeated everywhere.

As he entered Wythe's great hall, host to an amazing number of idle serfs and lounging guardsmen, a guilty silence abruptly quashed the heated growls of an instant before. That again Arlen's face glowed brighter than his hair betrayed overwrought emotions. Clearly he'd been arguing with another while onlookers gaped in open curiosity. The dispute's sudden cessation left no doubt in Thomas's mind but that its subject was their earl. Flickering flamelight emphasized the scowl lowering bushy brows over a hard glare.

In the scene Thomas found proof, at the very least, that someone had failed to exert rightful control. He glanced about for that someone who ought prevent the wasting of time better spent. He found neither Elinor nor Cleva. Not even Alyce was about. Though this was not properly Alyce's responsibility, he was certain the overly dutiful damsel would've sought some method to divert the conflict's flow and nudge dawdlers into more worthwhile pursuits. That Sybillene was elsewhere was not surprising. Where there was the possibility of work to be done, she never was.

He descended to the busy kitchen below. Although the work of cleaning away the remnants of the day's last meal did not cease, again a steady murmur came to an immediate halt. Thomas had lived enough years to recognize the situation for what it was—precisely what he'd already discovered too oft this day. Glowering gaze not finding what he'd come seeking, he turned on his heel and purposefully climbed dark steps in a return to the great hall. A goodly number of those earlier within had fled.

"Can anyone here tell me where I may find your countess?" Attempting to speak as politely as possible, Thomas restrained his temper but with a difficulty which lent an unnatural tightness to his normally hearty voice. Meanwhile expressive brows scowled so fiercely, the now sparse audience trembled.

Despite his support of their Demon Dare, Wythe's inhabitants liked this near ever pleasant knight. In truth 'twas partly their earl's solid bond of friendship with Sir Thomas and the unwavering trust given him by Lady Alyce which impeded the growth of the people's suspicions. Though Sir Thomas had on rare occasions been observed to be seriously vexed, never afore had they seen such anger in him.

Irritated the more by the bewilderment of those watching, he lost the reins of his ire and barked out a blunt demand. "If you do not know where your countess is, leastways tell me what happened to your earl and the lady visitors."

Arlen had waited for the knight's return, knowing it his duty to report on matters pertaining to what had been asked. He stepped forward to provide the answers demanded—insofar as he was able.

"With me on my return from Wrexdale, I brought disturbing news for Lady Alyce, and not long after 'twas delivered, our earl departed . . . unaccompanied and without saying where he meant to go. Shortly thereafter Lady Alyce, too, left Castle Wythe, although she went with my father and to a vassal's keep." Arlen did not speak of the captured gate guard. Earl Dare had commanded him to hold the news private, and 'twas the earl's decision who would be told.

"Much later, the moment the evening meal was done, Lady Elinor pleaded the strain of an overlong day and retired to her chamber. Lady Sybillene withdrew as well." On the statement, disdain like sour wine flavored Arlen's voice, but it sweetened when he added, "Lady Alyce returned late from her visit with the vassal's ailing wife and took her meal alone."

Bushy brows arched in surprise. In the first instant

Thomas wondered where Dare had got to and why (but then, he'd been mulling that very question for most of the day). In the next he was perplexed by Alyce's uncharacteristic behavior. She had done much to ease the way for others and never before had been willing to require of busy servants such special treatment as the serving of private meals.

He would have liked to know what news had been brought to send Dare haring off alone and distract Alyce, but as 'twas plainly of a personal nature, he'd no right to demand more. The young guardsman had respectfully given the answers he'd sought, and this information opened the path for him to deal with another matter, likely one of greater consequence.

With a troubled smile of thanks and brief nod, Thomas crossed the hall to climb the upward stairway. He knocked briskly upon the thick oak planks barring the portal to Elinor's chamber and impatiently waited for a response. To his relief, she came to the door before he needs must hammer more loudly still. But when faced by the slender sylph wrapped in naught but a daygown, obviously donned in haste, he blushed like some stripling lad.

Elinor was amazed by this nighttime visitor. Having disrobed and retired, she'd thought the call a portent of some dreadful news and had answered the door with little care for modesty. Though she hid the fact well, she was amused and, yes, pleased by this particular man's heightened color. Proved she was not as unbearably old and unattractive as she'd felt for the majority of her years.

His uncontrollable reaction irritated Thomas all the more, and his frown deepened. Having at last gotten this far, he was confronted by yet another problem. They must speak on a matter of supreme import—alone. That's where the problem lay. It was a conversation which could not be held in a hallway where anyone might hear, nor could an honorable man ask admittance to a noblewoman's bedchamber.

Near gnashing his teeth, Thomas motioned her to join him in the corridor. Although as lady of the castle, it was Elinor's prerogative, he led the way to the family solar. And once she'd followed him inside, 'twas he who firmly shut them into privacy.

Not waiting for Elinor to take a seat or even to question the motive behind such odd behavior, he bluntly spoke his mind. "If you fail to soon stand up for your son, I fear it will be too late to save him."

"Save him from what?" Elinor's fine brows rose in cool query. "What manner of danger would respond better to a woman's weak hand than a man's—most particularly when that man is an earl and acknowledged as an invincible warrior?" Elinor feared she knew the answer but feared even more the truth that she could do nothing to right the wrong.

Thomas heard the surprising note of pride beneath her words but had no time to wonder at it now. "Dare cannot rule the fiefdom without the people's support, and 'tis a support he cannot win while these mad rumors run rampant. They seem to feed upon themselves. This day in distant crofts I heard strange stories of impossible wrongs which the tale-mongers claim he has committed. Then upon returning to Castle Wythe I found it fair bursting with dangerous ill will sprouting from a new crop of vicious gossip."

Pausing, he glared at Elinor, who stood in calm control. As if intent on breaking through that facade, he smashed the mighty fist of one hand into the palm of the other. "You must stand before the people of Wythe and with the words only you can speak convince them of the foolish, dangerous error in what they're coming to believe."

Before Thomas's shocked eyes, Elinor's proud visage seemed to crumple. Yet although trails of silent tears washed her delicate face, she would not speak. He felt like a monster, too awkward and inept to tread lightly enough to safely draw nigh so fragile a creature, but unable to stand helplessly by while she trembled like a leaf about to flutter to the ground, he reached out and carefully drew her near. He would not see her fall because of his blundering words, not when he was more than strong enough to support her slight weight. He only wished he could lighten the load of her emotional burdens as easily.

As descended a cleansing rain of tears long years restrained, Elinor whispered words she meant never to be heard by ears other than those belonging to this man proven a friend to both her son and she.

"I swear by God's Holy Cross and with all my heart that Dare is no son of Lucifer. More I cannot say else I set him at risk of a far greater danger than any you imagine."

15

Rise and greet a glorious day!" The deep call close to Alyce's ear was accompanied by a sudden rough shaking of her bed. Bursting through blinding tendrils of sleep, she struggled to sit up, all-unthinking of her nudity or the identity of her awakener.

Her reminiscences with the couple at Berdene the day past had directed the path of dreams wherein she'd wandered through the past in the company of her childhood's mocking hero only to awaken and meet him in the flesh. She shook mussed curls from eyes struggling to focus on the wickedly grinning man standing aside her bed, hands on hips and radiating satisfaction with his view. Following the path of a blue gaze, Alyce glanced down.

Saint's Tears! She instantly fell back, clutching the counterpane tight above her head—too late. Plainly the pleased toad had seen everything between the top of unbound locks and covers bunched about her bare waist. Lashes squeezed tight together, she lay in a darkness too sensitive to the heat of a vivid blush spreading over every inch of the exposed flesh he'd wrongly glimpsed—never mind that for glowing hours out of time he'd held her against his own nude form. The thought intensified an enveloping wave of heat.

Twice now the wretched man had barged uninvited into her chamber as if he owned her as surely as he owned the castle itself. With a measure of self-disgust she acknowledged that her proudly claimed intent to stand distant and independent was no sturdier than the restraints which for years she'd placed about her unruly spirit. Dare could easily brush them all aside to rouse the fires of a temper she could feel flaring up once more.

"Rise and dress, sweeting." Dare couldn't stop grinning. He had succeeded where he'd feared to fail, and with that first success, the next was certain to follow. "We've a visitor of great import whose goal is your company." Blue eyes scorched over the form modestly veiled, but by a coverlet held so tight, it revealed more than it hid. Asides, he'd a vivid memory of her delicious charms.

As utter silence lengthened, Alyce peeked rebelliously over the edge of her flimsy shield only to find Dare still studying her with the insolence of a master for his slave. Temper flashing higher, she jerked up again, though this time she firmly held a covering close to her shoulders with one arm while reaching for the first solid object that came to hand. In the next instant she flung a pottery jar at his head. He ducked, laughing with pleasure while the fine mist of medicinal herbs she'd crushed for Cleva billowed from its point of impact on the door's oaken planks.

"Ah, sweeting, you'll shock a guest most reserved if you fail to demonstrate a true lady's refined demeanor." With this mocking jibe at her lifelong struggle to show just such restraints, Dare turned and strode to the door.

"Wear the crimson gown. I like it best." Green eyes glared at the overwhelming figure pausing with one hand on an unopened latch. "And leave your hair flowing free."

Alyce neither spoke nor moved until he'd gone and the door was closed. Wear a gown because he liked it? Hah! It made no difference that only hours past she'd have bowed to this or any other request he spoke. After the dampening travails of days and weeks gone by, her temper burst completely free to send its flames to new heights. How dare he tell her one moment to act like a lady and in the next command that she leave her hair unbound as no lady would.

Overwhelmed by impossibly conflicting emotions, she dropped back to the crude mattress, welcoming the pricks of individual straws seeking freedom from the ticking's bonds while struggling to restore a measure of calm sufficient to face those waiting below. Alyce was certain that there was no time to waste, for doubtless were she not to appear within a short time, Dare would boldly reappear and force her to it. Or, if not he, then Tess. The prospect of an arrival by one who claimed to be Dare's unwilling lover was almost as daunting. Flinging back covers recently abused by clutching hands, she slid from the bed and moved toward the pegs driven into a wooden wall from which hung her meager wardrobe.

Wear the red gown? Alyce deemed it as well to obey and justified her submission to Dare's command with the awareness that 'twas near the only one worthy of a guest. After donning a delicate white camise (the single silk garment left to her as he'd rent the other in twain during his first invasion of her chamber), she pulled soft crimson cloth over her head and tightened its front laces. Her thoughts then turned to the next step in her grooming, and she reached for a bone-backed brush.

Alyce had yielded in the matter of the gown, but leave her hair loose? In this Dare had demanded too much. Far, far too much. Still, once she'd begun briskly stroking the brush through her hair, she modified her decision. When chestnut locks gleamed in the light of the candle Dare must have left behind, for she had lit none, she remembered years-hidden but precious scarlet ribbons. They'd been purchased long ago for their beauty from an itinerant peddler passing through Keniver—but worn only once. Her father had chided the child she'd been for her extravagance in trading near all she had of worth for naught but the sake of vanity. Shamed by such disapproval, after one of the three gleaming strands had been lost, those remaining she had tucked carefully away ostensibly as reminders of wrongful pride.

Certain her time was limited, Alyce wildly dug through the wicker chest, turning well-ordered goods to a muddled heap before finding what she sought. After plaiting her hair with bright ribbons entwined, she chose the brazen path of merely coiling the fiery mass at the nape of her neck. So Dare thought to command her to unseemly ways, did he? She would not merely comply but toss modesty aside with a vengeance. She loosened the lacing down the center of her gown to tease with revealing glimpses of the nearly invisible silk which sheathed the curves beneath. She had seen others—Sybillene in particular—wear garments far more indecent, but for her, this array was wildly daring. With a sweet retaliation in mind, she sailed from the chamber intent on paying Dare back by shocking his "most reserved" visitor.

The shock was hers. One step into the great hall, her face went to a hue so vivid, it outrivaled her ribbons.

Dare turned toward the sound of the one he awaited, and blue eyes widened. The vision seeming to glow against the stairwell portal's dark background caught his breath. In the norm he deemed himself impervious to shocks, yet the one person in the world who could do so with ease was this stunning beauty, and he should not be surprised that she'd managed to accomplish that feat again. He'd issued a challenge with his commands, but not for a moment had he expected obedience, if this could be deemed obedience. In truth, she'd plainly chosen to tweak the devil's tail. A knowing half smile tilted his mouth as a blue gaze glittered over the alluring damsel whose cheeks had gone so delicious a hue that they looked like peaches sun-ripened while her eyes snapped with green sparks.

"Lady Alyce." A slender man in priestly robes stepped without qualm into the uneasy silence. Between the lady's rebellious glare and the earl's amused grin he'd seen the truth of the matter and found delight in the discovery that the too oft brooding and ever-intimidating Dare had found so right a match. "I know now why Earl Rhodare was so impatient to see the deed done that he could not wait upon my convenience."

Though she was stunned by the unexpected nature of this visitor moving to meet her, inbred good manners laid a polite smile on Alyce's lips. It shouldn't be that he was left to greet her. She, as castle resident of one sort or another, ought be welcoming him. Her failure to extend proper courtesy increased her embarrassment to such a point that his strange reference to a deed to be done passed uninvestigated.

"Come, Alyce." Dare motioned her to his side. "As the whole of my demesne has been invited, the chapel is too small and all are gathered here to witness our wedding."

This was spoken plainly enough that no amount of confusion could prevent his meaning from blaring through Alyce's mind with the clarity of a hunt horn blown. Yet, what with two days of constant upheavals piling tumultuous emotions atop, against, asides, and beneath every angle of thought, she passed confusion and stumbled into pure bewilderment. Had Walter prophesied true? Or mayhap she'd so lost touch with reality that her dreams had breached the boundaries of illusion to take literal form.

Moving without conscious thought to obey Dare's summons, she glanced surreptitiously about a hall ablaze under such a myriad of candles, 'twas like day brought within, and filled, nay, crowded with curious onlookers. In the forefront of the masses Cleva, looking as proud as if 'twere a deed she'd personally arranged, stood between a more than pleased Arlen and an Ulger host to a rare smile. One pace distant, good humor fair burst from a watching Sir Thomas rocking on his toes with satisfaction yet lingering near a quietly smiling Lady Elinor.

"It is no more lawful for you to claim this maid without her sire's agreement than for you to seize another lord's lands." Walter stepped firmly forward, certainty in his argument's truth lending strength enough to stand in firm opposition to the powerful earl. Still, he restated the case to further emphasize its surely irrefutable logic. "Lady Alyce is Baron Halbert Bohan's chattel and may not be pledged to another without his leave."

Despite a look that could have frozen fire, Dare's voice was calmly reasonable as he replied. "Aye, her marriage needs must be sanctioned by her father—or, in his absence, by her closest male relative."

Walter's eyes narrowed as if to restrain the threat to his attempted block of the union.

Dare motioned toward the boy standing almost within

reach. "Sir Halbert's son and heir has given that approval in his father's stead."

Walter hissed, "He's a child and has not the right to make such decisions."

"When 'tis a decision supported by his mother and guardian, it stands." The unexpected feminine voice sliced through the vicious glare Walter had fastened upon Hal like a death grip.

In his disbelief, Walter's condemning gaze shifted from the boy to Sybillene. He was stunned by his sister's defection. Yet even did both she and her young son approve the alliance, it still was not legal. Of that he was certain, although with the marriage about to be church-blessed, he hadn't the time to apply to King Henry or even to the bishop for support in preventing the wrong which in his view was the most heinous the Demon could ever commit.

Sybillene, accustomed to her brother's tempers, turned from his fury unscathed. Had she to choose between support of the younger or the older "boy," her own son would always win. Of recent days it had come to her that since arriving at Castle Wythe, Hal had begun the inevitable withdrawal from her grasp. Soon he would stand independent, and either she allow him the leeway he sought or be discarded and left forever behind.

Dare was amused. With victory in his hands, confirmed by an unexpected source, he could afford to be. In his opponent's sullen expression, Dare recognized frustration. Walter was right. In the normal way of things, this marriage could never have come to be—not without his royal liege lord's approval and the paying to him of a sizable fee. Dare had chosen to hasten past these obstacles, minor infractions compared with what he, it seemed certain, was soon to be charged. The sardonic smile on his face firmed into grim lines. He was not so lacking in honor that he'd willingly have flouted both her father and his sire. Had he the choice, he'd have followed the accepted path to seek Alyce as bride. Indeed, once he'd won his own fight (and pray God he would), then he would see her father's name cleared and discharge the fines required to lift all clouds from their horizon.

Beneath the Demon's icy stare, Walter whirled toward the one destined to become a bride. "Alyce, remember what I said. I warned you, and now my prediction is coming true." His expression reflected a very real despair. How had this calamity come about when all else had been going so smoothly his way?

Shaking her head, Alyce dropped her attention to the rush-and-herb-covered floor while struggling to think rationally and decide what action she must take in response to this utterly unanticipated scene. Yet what choice had she? With so many watching and most so pleased, how could she do else than what was expected? How could she when it was what she wanted more than ever anything in the whole of her life? At the same time she wondered what Dare's motive was. Guilt for having taken the innocence of a wellborn virgin as he'd once sworn he never would? Did he deem marriage the price for honor restored? It was a distasteful thought despite the never before questioned fact that all such alliances were made for material gains.

A proffered arm clad in pale blue velvet appeared within the periphery of Alyce's vision. As she recognized the importance Dare gave this ceremony by virtue of seldom worn garb reserved for court occasions, guilt smote her. By thinking only of her own concerns regarding the commitment about to be given, she'd again proven herself abominably selfish. She'd vowed to brighten Dare's path and now contemplated deepening its gloom by allowing even a hint of so public a rejection. Alyce glanced up and read the anxiety hidden behind eyes purposefully blank. In spite of her earlier intent to defy Dare for his demanding ways and no matter her own qualms, Alyce couldn't refuse him this or likely any other boon he sought of her.

When small fingers settled lightly on his upraised forearm, Dare gave the thus-consenting damsel a blindingly potent smile. His plan had succeeded. Presented with a nearly accomplished fact, Alyce was too softhearted to publicly reject him. And once wed, surely he could honorably win the trust he'd forfeited by seducing and stealing her virtue.

Gently placing a hand over small fingers, Dare turned

them both to face Father Mordane. The priest stepped atop one of the long, narrow benches lining parallel walls, cleared his throat, and lifted a heavy golden cross. Seeing these final preparations for laying the blessing of faith upon their union, Dare felt more hope in the future than ever before in his life. He gently urged Alyce to kneel with him on the rush-strewn floor and receive words that would hallow their bond with a power which could be put asunder by naught but death itself.

The difficulty of a task at which he'd failed repeatedly, the task of finding a priest willing to so much as enter the "demon's domain," had initially seemed impossible. But then he'd remembered a perceptive and gentle man of God who dwelled on Richard's Pembroke estates. A single member amongst a small army of clergymen there, Dare knew Father Mordane had never believed the ridiculous tales attached to his name. This priest, Dare had been certain would come, leastways to perform the service requested.

The circumstances were strange, with no meeting at church door to ratify a marriage contract whereby the bride surrendered her dowry into a husband's hands, and the groom formally named the dower that would be hers should he precede her in death, but the ceremony itself was reassuringly unchanged. Once the mass laying the blessing of faith upon the union had concluded, Dare turned an amazingly warm smile to the watching crowd.

"Father Mordane, who was so kind as to journey with me through the midst of night to see the ceremony done this morn, has done me—and all of us here on Wythe—the great honor of accepting the position of castle chaplain and, with Earl Pembroke's good wishes, will remain."

Through the crowd passed a soft and gentle murmur of approval near as warm as their earl's smile. This, Thomas observed from his position on its fringes, was a wonderful step forward in winning the people's acceptance of and even loyalty to their earl. At last a fact to weaken their growing but unjustified fears. He'd seen Alyce hesitate and had trembled in fear of an action that could've seen the whole spoiled. Thank the Good Lord she'd clearly understood the price Dare would've been called to pay for her rejection.

The ceremony was followed by a full day of abundant food. First from the kitchens came dishes hastily prepared by servants awakened in the night with the news of a celebration to come, but as the sun made its journey toward the western horizon, the feast was supplemented with a whole roast boar and haunches of venison as well as smaller game and fowl. Moreover, all were accompanied by a river of ale and flood of wine that mightily cheered the wide variety of feasters—serf, freeman, and vassal; guardsman and knight. And once the travel-weary priest withdrew to the long empty village cottage allotted the castle chaplain, the people's revelry grew wilder.

Sheltered within the circle of Dare's warmth, Alyce uncomfortably watched celebrants who seemed to be drowning in fiery spirits and growing ever more riotous. Although leastways a hundred toasts had been proposed to the new-wed couple, she'd taken only small sips. To her surprise, Dare had also limited his drinking and drained little more than one large goblet during the length of the day. She thought that Walter, on the other side, must have quaffed a whole cask by himself and now had sunk into a morose pit from which he steadily glared at her. Sybillene, too, had consumed far more than was wise. But rather than sink into silence as her brother had done, her unceasing voice grew constantly more shrill and her comments so bawdy in their appraisal of Dare's charms that Alyce fervently wished it were possible to sink unobserved beneath the high table's white cloth.

"Do you blush, Dare?" Sybillene's laughter echoed above the crowd's drunken racket. "But you cannot deny it so when I saw you that night I shared your bed. I saw how be-e-autiful you are." The sotted woman leaned heavily against Alyce, as if she were a negligible impediment. Reaching across the smaller woman, a determined Sybillene ran her palms over Dare's strong arms and chest.

Dare saw the rosy shade tinting Alyce's downbent cheeks and, uncertain whether its source was anger or embarrassment, gritted his teeth. Only for the sake of preventing a too public demonstration of his disdain for Sybillene did he restrain an urge to shove the disgusting woman away.

Instead he freed himself of pawing hands as graciously as possible.

Alyce clenched her lashes tightly together while Walter's words of the previous day echoed in her thoughts. Could it be true that Dare had wed her only to claim yet another of her father's females? She'd dismissed the charge as foolishness when first heard, but irrational jealousy, fed by temper, made it more believable.

"Alyce, it's time for you to retire before this further descends into—" A grimacing Elinor stood behind Alyce's chair and waved dismissively at the gathering rapidly getting out of hand.

More than anxious to escape the mayhem, Alyce rose so promptly, her high-backed chair would've fallen but for Dare's quick action.

Although it would've been proper for Sybillene, as the only other wellborn woman present, to accompany Alyce to her groom's chamber for the traditional bedding of the bride, she was lost to propriety. In Alyce's departure she saw only an opportunity to move into the vacated chair and drape herself against the earl.

Approving the support lent Hal before the wedding began, Alyce had come near to liking the woman. But even before Alyce reached the ascending stairway at the hall's far end, Sybillene had nearly climbed into Dare's lap. Alyce was furious with the drunken woman but even more so with the man who laughingly permitted—or was it welcomed?—the action.

"I don't know how many weddings you've attended," Elinor began, "but pray you will not blame the participants for their folly. They'll be punished for all these wrongs and more when they try to rise on the morrow." She'd seen Alyce's growing temper and had wished to mitigate the younger woman's distress, yet found her ability to deal with this matter woefully limited.

Alyce blindly followed the countess into the lord's chamber. It had been decorated with late-blooming flowers and twined with ivy while sweet-scented herbs had been strewn all about. Too shy to object when Elinor began to disrobe her, a practice Alyce suspected was traditional, she stood motionless while the older woman efficiently divested her of slippers, gown, and camise. Once she was settled in the middle of the largest bed she'd ever occupied, with pillows piled behind and rich coverlets draped modestly about her bare form, Elinor unbraided her hair. The countess carefully folded precious scarlet ribbons before brushing thick, fiery tresses until they crackled.

"This is the point at which either the bride's mother or the woman of highest rank present gives counsel to the new bride. But as you've been wed before—albeit to a child— and as I've no experience in the art to draw upon, save the talk my mother gave me—and it of no good use—I will simply wish you well and promise to pray that you'll find happiness with my son."

With that convoluted speech, Elinor smiled and withdrew, leaving Alyce alone in a large, unfamiliar chamber.

Prey to dark thoughts of the scene doubtless continuing below, when a tension-wearied Alyce slipped into restless dreams, she found herself caught in an unpleasant memory gone even more horribly awry. Once again she was an unwilling witness to the vision of Sybillene in Dare's bed, only now, the image embellished by caresses she'd experienced, he held the writhing beauty in a passionate embrace. Alyce tried to pull away, tried to close her eyes against the painful sight, but though desperately struggling to escape, she couldn't win free until at long last Dare thrust the other aside and swept her into his arms.

Dare had entered his chamber to find a quietly sobbing Alyce fighting a welter of tangled cloth and, warmed by the fact that now it was his right to comfort a beloved so clearly distressed, bent to free her from the badly mangled bedclothes. Once she was quiet in his arms, he again laid her down and attempted to move back. She desperately clung to him.

"It's all right, sweeting," he soothed. "Permit me to rid myself of these fine clothes afore they're destroyed, and I swear I will return and hold you the whole night through."

These words drove mists of slumber from Alyce's mind as effectively as a cold winter wind sweeping in off the sea. In one motion she sat up and scooted as far back in the bed as possible. Though she was no longer sleepy, the crushing scenes enacted in her dreams still seemed devastatingly real.

"Stay away from me." He couldn't spend the evening enjoying Sybillene's fawning hands and then expect her to welcome him.

Dare was amazed again by this woman who moments before had clung like a limpet only to now warn him away. "This is my bed and yours as well since we are wed." He tried to reason calmly, though he found her abrupt rejection bewildering.

"Aye, we are wed by virtue of your powers in manipulating us all to do your will. But 'twas not done with my father's consent." Even as she spoke, Alyce was shocked by her words, words she didn't truly mean. Nonetheless, they continued to pour out from some frightened corner of her jealous soul. "He would never have consented to this alliance with the man who shamed him by bedding his wife."

A muscle clenching in Dare's cheek was the only motion in his suddenly frozen face. What had brought on this sudden attack by one who'd repeatedly stood firm at his side, by the only one whose criticism could cut to the core of his soul?

"I have done many ill deeds, but again I swear by Almighty God that I am guilty of neither of the wrongs you've named." Dare reached out to take Alyce's shoulders between his hands. "Please, sweeting, believe me. You are my wife and the last person to whom I would lie." He laid his lips against hers, but she was as unresponsive and stiff as a solid oak plank, and when he pulled back, he realized she was staring blindly at the bed's drapery.

"As you say, I am now your wife." Still caught in the power of the disorienting dream with its painful vision of Sybillene in his arms, Alyce heard the emotionless words as if they'd been spoken by another. "I'm your property, and the law says you may do with me as you wish." Falling back, she lay a limp offering, a martyr to an unsought spouse.

Dare pulled away. Rising to his feet, he looked down upon the motionless figure. With despair he paid for the joy in which the day had begun.

"I have never taken any woman against her will—you least of all. Nor have I ever required the powers of a demon to lure them into my bed—where more than one has appeared uninvited." His smile was bitterly cynical. Such events had been the source of many troubles—Sybillene, Tess. Even the much-sought appearance there of Alyce had won only this greater woe.

"If you'll not have me, so be it. There are many who will. I can bear the burden of your rejection. 'Tis a task much the same as that which I've been called to endure for all my life and to which I am well accustomed." A flash of blue ice froze the cynical mockery of moments before. "But what of the babe we may well have made in our night of pleasure? What of him? Will you name him the son of the devil as my parents did me? Will he in his innocence be called to pay the price of our misdeed?"

Dare's impenetrable mask began to shatter under the fierce emotion vibrating in his words. He first pressed fingertips to eyes aching with the strain of scalding tears withheld and then ran them through thick black strands. A devastated Dare then turned and strode from the chamber without further sound.

Shame swept over Alyce, and the shock of Dare's departure crushed and scattered the remnants of a jealousy-inspired dream. Always had she known that a caldron of deep emotion simmered beneath his cold armor, but had never expected to be the cause of its boiling over. She wanted to run after him, to beg him to forgive her jealous, too hasty tongue and words unmeant. Yet his assuredly true claim of the many who'd welcome him into their beds held her firmly where she was. By her wretched temper and irrational jealousy she'd won a greater punishment for herself than even for him. She was forced into a desperate inaction, unable to do more than remain in his chamber, his bed, and pray he would return once the wild storm of emotion had run its course and he'd mended the armor of his impassive shield.

It was a forlorn reality that brought more guilt than comfort. She'd ever wanted to be with him, to ease his pain, yet she'd accomplished naught but the widening of the breach betwixt them, and at the very moment when her most fervent wishes had nearly been granted. Although wrung out by wild extremes of emotion, still she could not sleep until the image of a tiny being with black hair and pale blue eyes snuggling close in her arms lulled her into slumber's frothy clouds.

16

A new bride so early risen?" Sybillene's brows rose in exaggerated amazement as she approached the dais where Alyce had near finished a morning repast attended by only the few hardy souls who'd shown a measure of restraint during the previous day's festivities.

"I should've known your dutiful nature would send you promptly from your bed. Yet I fear 'twas done for naught." As Sybillene added purposefully casual words, she carefully lifted the chair awaiting her arrival. This she very precisely and with a modicum of noise placed far enough back to accommodate her descent. "Father Mordane will not begin performing daily masses until the morrow—likely he knew few would be capable of attending this morn."

As her stepmother took her seat, close proximity showed Alyce the pallor of face proving that Sybillene suffered from the same ailment. What reward, she wondered, had drawn the self-centered woman from the comforts of bed? She had not long to wait for the answer.

"But how could a priest know that a lonely bride would have nothing to keep her abed?" Alyce had secured the prize Sybillene wanted for herself. Alyce had Dare and more besides. Alyce had the fine home and position she envied.

But Alyce had failed in one matter, and a petulant Sybillene saw no reason to hesitate in using it to somewhat level the score. "As a man who is not truly a man, Father Mordane cannot be expected to recognize the signs pointing to a bride incapable of holding her groom's interest for even the length of a single night has much to keep her abed."

Spiteful words stung Alyce as sharply as the lashes of an earnestly applied whip. Biting back a gasp, she nervously smoothed the sides of her modest barbette against icy cold cheeks. She had risen early in hopes of catching Dare at table, but if he'd appeared for the day's first small repast at all, he was gone before she arrived. As for where he'd spent the night, her stepmother's gloating knowledge that he'd not been with his bride seemed to make the answer abundantly clear—to Alyce and likely to the others waiting near to serve the high table's occupants.

This apparent proof that a rejected Dare had turned to Sybillene for comfort strangely roused in Alyce less jealousy than self-blame for driving him away. She'd allowed irrational jealousy to blind her to unquestionable facts. Dare was a man of honor, and if he swore a thing was true, it was true. Repeatedly and with both indirect and straightforward statements Dare had sworn he was guiltless of seducing his foster father's wife. The past night he'd talked disparagingly of women who'd come to his bed uninvited. Pondering the matter in the cool light of dawn, Alyce had become firmly convinced that, despite the evidence of her own eyes, she should've given Dare the trust for which he'd pleaded. She should have believed his protestations of innocence. Instead she'd plainly sent him into Sybillene's welcoming arms.

Caught in a private conflict, neither woman gave notice to the third wellborn female on the dais. Lady Elinor silently observed the entire scene and felt the clash of emotions behind it. As any gracious hostess must, the countess moved to intervene and ease the strain. That and for the bride she meant to do yet more.

"Alyce, if you've eaten all you intend, I would appreciate your aid in one small matter above."

It would be impossible to refuse Lady Elinor even did she

wish it, and Alyce didn't. She'd have welcomed any excuse to withdraw, and pushed her chair back so hastily, it scraped loudly across the dais's wooden planks. Wincing, Sybillene instantly pressed trembling fingers to throbbing temples. Alyce blushed with embarrassment for her thoughtless action, although she could not have claimed to be honestly repentant for the discomfort given the woman whose condescending smile had not faltered.

While Elinor calmly joined Alyce in departing the awkward scene, her unflinching gaze forced the snickers of a few into uncomfortable coughs. Leading the way partway up the stairs, Lady Elinor paused once they'd ascended high enough to ensure they would be alone and not overheard. Anxious to see the younger woman's discomfort lessened, she turned and quietly spoke.

"As the new Countess of Wythe—" Elinor answered Alyce's startled expression with a wry smile. Clearly this change in status was a consequence of the marriage which had not weighed heavily with the bride. Though she'd already believed it was thus, Elinor was pleased with this demonstration that the damsel had wed her son for reasons else than his possessions. 'Twas an unusual boon.

"Aye," Elinor continued. "You have become Wythe's countess, while I've been relegated to the secondary position of dowager countess. Moreover . . ." Her smile deepened. Here was the point in which Alyce, she was certain, would find pleasure, and leastways a small portion of comfort. "At table it is now your right to take the seat at Dare's right, while I, as the woman of second import in this castle, will be seated on his left."

These were welcome facts Alyce had not paused to earlier consider. Meeting unwavering brown eyes, she found gleams of an amusement they could share. The pretentious Sybillene would receive her just comeuppance when this physical demonstration of their shift in rank was enforced. The prospect earned from Alyce a shy smile, though it could not fully lift away the unhappy shadows in green eyes.

Again Lady Elinor led the way up winding steps, and this time did not pause until they were inside her chamber and the door was closed. 'Twas a large room well lit by a sizable and presently unshuttered window. Such an opening was defensively possible only at this level and on this side of the castle overlooking a broad river which made an archer's successful attack virtually impossible.

"I've a fine view from my window." Elinor motioned toward the subject of her words. "I can see beyond bailey walls and even to the crest of faraway hills."

Certain Dare would resent her interference in personal matters and having no notion of what reasons lay behind strange facts, Elinor deemed it imperative to tread lightly. Still and all, Alyce's distress seemed to demand she offer knowledge which might lend comfort. How to tactfully do so was a difficult puzzle. With the memory of a warning she'd given Alyce against interfering in matters not of her concern, the damsel might well feel Elinor was now guilty of the same. Thus she could not baldly state what she knew. Rather she would point the way toward discovery if 'twere a prize truly sought.

Alyce nodded. 'Struth, from this height in a castle perched atop a summit, the vista of fields, forest lands, and rolling hills was remarkable. Nonetheless, she suspiciously wondered what this trivial fact had to do with the task she'd been summoned to perform.

Moving to lean casually against the deep window's pillowed lower edge, Elinor gazed toward the distant horizon. "Of an evening I often sit here and soak in nature's peace, watching the slow progress of time from spring's first thin, green blanket to winter's barren limbs and bone-chilling snow. And on fine, moonlit nights I see far more than many like to think I know." With these words Elinor cast an unexpectedly penetrating gaze over her shoulder.

Green eyes widened. This was a confirmation as clear as spoken words that there was no task to be done. The countess had brought her here for another purpose. Was it that . . . Fearing disappointment, Alyce tamped down the hope striving to rise like a phoenix from the ashes of despair.

Elinor saw the flash of green fire quickly squelched and blatantly led the damsel to a truth she was now certain she must see known. "My son and his mighty stallion make a very distinctive silhouette. Last night their image streaking across the fields and cresting the hill with the low-risen moon behind them was a magnificent sight."

Alyce hadn't realized how tensely she'd awaited this news she'd been afraid to seek until every rigidly held muscle suddenly relaxed. She near sagged against a fortuitously placed chest.

Elinor was pleased that this fact revealed was so plainly welcome. She had taken the chance for Alyce's sake but also for Dare. Alyce had defended Dare from the first, had stood steady at his side against the fear-filled many the day Cyril died. She wanted to see the young couple in peaceful harmony, for amidst Wythe's ever-increasing tensions, Alyce was among Dare's few reliable sources of support. And by the steady gaze he ever turned her way, it seemed likely Alyce's support was near the most important.

"Thank you, milady, thank you." Alyce's words were eloquent in their simplicity.

Though nodding acceptance of Alyce's gratitude, Elinor asked more. "I pray you will stand firm beside Dare, wield the fire of your spirit to thaw the ice of his pain. He needs you more than he may ever be capable of saying. Proud and so long experienced in standing alone, it may be hard for him to admit the need for another."

Alyce realized at once that Lady Elinor thought Dare had purposefully left her the night past, left her because he could not accept the implications of a binding tie. She felt a fraud and forced herself to confess the error in that assumption.

"He did not choose to leave me. I drove him away." The wretched well of tears Alyce had believed dried up in the night overflowed again. "'Twas a wicked, shameful deed, and I would perform any penance to earn his forgiveness."

Into comforting arms Elinor gathered the damsel plainly embarrassed by her lack of control. "'Tis a feeling I know all too well. I, too, have been guilty of driving Dare away." While patting the younger woman's back, with anguished eyes Elinor blindly studied the heavy door as tightly closed as the invisible one between herself and Dare. "Thankfully there are differences between your wrong and mine. The rift I created can never be bridged—both circumstances and time make that an impossible task."

Moving gentle hands to Alyce's shoulders, Elinor held her a handsbreadth away and met an unflinching green gaze. "You may be surprised to learn that I see much of a younger me in you. 'Tis why I have at times earnestly tried to divert your path from a journey parallel with my own. Now, to further that goal and see both you and Dare happy in your future, I pray you will accept the counsel of one who has made too many mistakes. Never allow a breach between the two of you to widen with time. Mend it before the opportunity is forever lost."

Alyce believed the fervent words, believed the necessity of acting with haste (for the sake of the child she prayed would come to be if naught else). Yet she had little faith in the likelihood of success. Nonetheless, she would try.

"The moment Dare returns I will seek him out to beg his forgiveness and the return of his good favor."

Elinor nodded and offered the younger woman a fresh cloth square to wipe away tearstains. As Alyce dried her cheeks, she silently admitted how wrong she'd been in once believing the countess too cold for honest emotion. Plainly Lady Elinor, like Dare, had built an emotionless wall to shield herself from hurt. Too, Alyce was certain that, like the weak spot she'd found in Dare's wall the night past, there was a vulnerable point in his mother's. The secrets hidden behind the countess's wall were the secrets of Dare's past, the secrets Alyce had once sworn to reveal. Yet with the new maturity and clearer vision lent by recent experiences, she accepted the warnings of too high a price for their exposure, and bridled her impetuous spirit. Rather than seek hazardous truths, she would in the future turn her full attention to the challenge of eliminating whisper-sown weeds, dealing with their human source and standing firm at Dare's side to face impending dangers.

Once Alyce had restored her appearance to its usual state, they descended to take up duties divided betwixt them since near the first day after her arrival. Alyce found pleasure in this further demonstration that she and her mother-in-law would live in peace. Not all brides were so fortunate in new homes where a woman long first in the castle refused to relinquish the slightest portion of control.

Scowling with dark thoughts, Dare gave no notice to a young boy scurrying from his path as he strode with unswerving intent toward the stable. Standing atop the battlement moments past, he'd seen Walter ride across the drawbridge and out toward the far bailey wall. Dare knew Walter was not fond of horseflesh and could hardly believe the man had willingly sought both a saddle's discomfort and the possible dangers lurking beyond the confines of castle and courtyard. The weak man's curious action alone was enough to earn Dare's pointed interest and inspire a determination to trail the man to a suspected destination, but he'd more reason for the deed.

On entering the cool stable, rather than call his squire, Fanhurst, to do the deed, Dare hoisted a saddle atop Fiend's back and cinched it into place himself. Much earlier in the morn he'd performed the long-postponed interrogation of Roger, his imprisoned gate guard. The facts surrounding the actual capture of Alyce had not varied from those provided by the first abductor. However, Roger's disgust over his unknown employer's duplicity had provided the first additional crumb of information. Roger, it seemed, had been late in reaching the designated meeting place whence he'd been promised a journey to safety. Arriving a day behind the proposed rendezvous, he'd discovered that Darwyn had arrived on time. But in reward for his promptness, Darwyn had been murdered and his body stuffed into the limbs of a tree, carrion for scavenging animals.

Dare's expression darkened further. Though with no further hope of capturing Darwyn to confirm the identity of his cohort, from the prisoner Dare had learned enough to devise a first flimsy defense—but one of only theoretical use. Struggling against an invisible foe armed with formless weapons and waging surreptitious but deadly assaults, Dare welcomed this stealthy pursuit of Walter as a rare solid action to be taken. A man of action caught in a strange war of nerves, never before had Dare felt so helpless as he did now—both in his dealings with the people of Wythe and, unexpectedly, in his relationship with Alyce.

Like an unanticipated blow came the devastating image of a fire-vixen gone to ice and lying limp across his bed. No matter the course he chose, Dare feared he'd lose the prize. Nobly thinking to preserve Alyce's good name and provide a home to one dispossessed, Dare had wed the maid he'd wronged. Alyce had responded not with gratitude but with disdain for his honorable action. She had spurned his loving overtures. One corner of Dare's mouth tilted up with self-mockery. Noble? Honorable? Beautiful words and mayhap sincerely meant, yet he'd wed Alyce for far less altruistic reasons. He'd wed her because he wanted to, because she was his and though he'd first claimed her physically, he'd been determined to claim her by every law of God and man.

Though a steed trained to withstand the fierce clashes and brutal contact of battle, Fiend flinched against a too tightly cinched saddle. Dare paused to ease the painful strap and murmur meaningless words of comfort to the beast near the only creature standing with him ever loyal.

Alyce's spurning action of the night past was but a single image, though the most powerful and sharpened by pain, amongst the panorama of rejection surrounding him. For the sake of Wythe's people he'd done his best to restore prosperity and justice. Did they recognize the effort? Did they appreciate the literal cost to him in toil, time, and coin? Nay, they greeted him with suspicion and disapproval at every turning. It was near enough to drive him away, near as effective a banishment as his father's rejection a lifetime past.

As Dare bent to retrieve the heavy gauntlets he'd laid safely atop a pile of straw, he warmly recalled the relative peace of days spent in honest battle both in France and in Wales. 'Twould be a relief to meet a foe face-to-face and with open enmity. The thought brought a niggling temptation to resume that struggle. After all, he could return to fight at Richard's side and find an honest welcome there. Dare grimaced against the foolish thought; aye, he could, but never would, meekly surrender to adversity. 'Twould be better that his hidden antagonist see him dead—a possibility which seemed more likely with every passing day. The only comfort in the prospect was the knowledge that leastwise Alyce's future was well provided for by right of her title as Countess of Wythe. For what he'd taken from her, for what others claimed he'd stolen from her father, that much he had given Alyce.

"Dare, where are you off to?" Thomas laid a hand on his friend's tension-stiff and unyielding back. That he'd been able to approach the famous knight from behind without instantly alerting him was distressing. For any warrior to be so thoroughly distracted was dangerous and greatly heightened Thomas's concern for the younger man.

"Our 'weasel' is abroad and needs flushing out." A weasel, they'd agreed Walter was. Because Dare's back was turned to Thomas while he continued preparing Fiend for the task ahead, his cynical smile went unseen.

"Then allow me to summon a band of guardsmen and we'll soon have him in our hands." Ulger's words were not a boast but rather a flat statement of fact. To him Walter's guilt was as clear as it was to his earl. However, he understood just as clearly the impossibility of simply banishing the man from Wythe. Not only would Lady Alyce be upset, but the common folk would see it as yet another example of their lord's wickedness—never mind that they disliked the too sly man and thought it wrong for him to have been brought to Wythe in the first instance.

Glancing over his shoulder at the loyal two, Dare let his gaze settle on the older knight who stood plainly visible behind the shorter, broader Thomas. Ulger had ever been an unhesitating friend, and Dare's tight smile eased into more natural lines as he responded to the knight's calm offer. "I thank you for your willing support, but capture is not the goal. Instead I mean to track this pest to his burrow and seek a glimpse of his fellows. 'Tis a deed best done alone."

Dare meant to go fast and unseen in hopes of coming upon his quarry in the midst of a meeting. Mayhap then he could find a way to break the increasing pressure of their invisible stranglehold.

"A worthy goal." Thomas knew Dare well enough not to argue when the light of determined battle burned in blue eyes. He'd seen it there at the outset of many a victorious fight. Still, there were things the man ought to know, and there might be no better time to have them said. Considering the open conflict between the new-wedded pair, it seemed the previous day's event and celebration had already prevented the telling too long. Thus, when the boy James had reported his earl preparing the ride alone, he and Ulger had come to seek him out.

"Before you set off, pray let us report to you an exchange between the 'weasel' and Lady Alyce. It took place on the day preceding your marriage, and though 'tis unlikely to have a bearing on the task ahead, it seems to provide answer to the question of motive." Having no doubt but that Walter was the source of nasty tales he'd heard about Dare's supposed wrongs in Keniver Castle, Thomas had been anxious to secure this explanation.

Certain that Thomas's report would concern conversation in which Walter had pleaded with Alyce to remember only moments before Father Mordane had begun the wedding rite, the subject fully claimed Dare's attention. He listened impassively as between them the other two men repeated the charges which both Arlen and Cleva stated had been made by Walter. The accusation that he was responsible for Halbert's downfall, Dare had heard before. Of more interest was the suggestion that the action's motive was jealousy and that, after having first seduced the baron's wife, its end was to be the stealing of another female precious to the man—the taking of Alyce in marriage. 'Twas this which seemed a clear statement of Walter's own intent turned inside out. Even this was not shocking to Dare, who had long suspected that Alyce for wife was Walter's ultimate goal. To Dare the most important aspect lay in knowing these things had been said to Alyce so shortly before their marriage. This fact in some way explained her response the previous night and lent him hope that their problems could be overcome.

"I am grateful both that Arlen and his mother thought to

recount this scene to you and that you've told me. I agree that it lends a glimpse into the weasel's reasoning, but lest we forget, we must remain aware that he is naught but a small part of a much larger and more dangerous whole."

The two listeners solemnly nodded agreement before Thomas spoke aloud the unpleasant thoughts they shared. "We've not forgot the greater threat building somewhere beyond Wythe's borders."

Dare accepted their reassurance with a slight smile, then, knowing the importance to his quest of time well used, reaffirmed his intention even as he swung into the saddle. "I'm off to track our quarry."

Impatience as much a part of Thomas's nature as good humor, he could hardly bear to let the matter rest so indecisively and made a request of Dare only half in jest. "Once you've seen what you seek, promise me you'll bring an end to a worthless life?"

"What?" Dare mockingly asked. "And by such destruction lend further 'proof' of the rightness in my lifelong title? That foolish I am not." With this indisputable comment Dare wheeled Fiend toward the stable door. Though knowledge of the damaging words Walter had spoken to Alyce increased Dare's desire to fulfill Thomas's wish, he would merely follow the man and mayhap be gifted with confirmation of the truth in near certain suspicions.

Dare knew himself a warrior capable of meeting and defeating any foe in physical combat, yet in this far, far more important struggle, he sensed himself on the perilous verge of defeat. The irony of the situation tilted his lips into a mirthless smile. A famous warrior's end would come not by sword or arrow but by barbed weapons formed of dark whispers plumbing ever deeper into the depths of human fear.

After the earl had ridden from sight, Thomas turned toward Ulger with a cheerful smile, a smile which these days took far more work to don than ever before. Beneath the weight of Dare's gloom and Elinor's hopeless tears of two nights past, his normally buoyant spirits were sagging.

"If you need me, I'll be on the tiltyard encouraging the

boys in their practice at the quintain." If anything was able to lift his spirits, 'twould be the sight of youngsters in earnest battle against the straw-filled sack suspended from a bar swinging freely around a central pole. Aside from the obvious humor in the ineptness of most mock attacks, there the very air ever reverberated with the invigorating fervor of youth.

Ulger absently gave an agreeing shrug, thoughts on the irritating task awaiting him, one that should be unnecessary. "I've yet to see any sign of a changing shift. Therefore I must *again* hurry along guardsmen late in relieving those doing duty atop the battlements." The average guardsman's slack pace was his constant bane.

While Thomas moved toward the day-lowered drawbridge and the strip of cleared ground beyond moat and village, Ulger turned to the castle's entry. Beyond annoyance with tardy guardsmen lay a deeper concern about these men under his command. Had they the ability (or even will) to insure the continuing health of their earl and the safe future of all Wythe?

As he climbed to entrance doors and passed through the gloomy tunnel, the thudding of Ulger's booted feet emphasized his dismal worries. Relative quiet reigned in the huge hall where only a few toiled. But as he descended to the level below, quiet was replaced by the steady hum of the kitchen's unending activities. The clatter of ladle against pot, the bubbling of stock boiled to plump preserved meats, the hiss of spitted meat's juices falling into flames, and the constant chatter of laborers all prevented men in the guardroom beyond from being forewarned of Ulger's approach. Stepping into their smoke-shrouded haven, Ulger heard with distressing clarity what was loudly said by guardsmen huddled about a single table on the room's far side.

"I was happy our earl had got hisself a wife, happy the Lady Alyce was she. Thought mayhap her sweet goodness would leaven the bitter evil in him." The speaker was a man who, for all his vast girth, had an earned reputation as a fierce and unyielding fighter.

"Though I thought much the same, plainly 'tisn't to be."

Runnolf, an earnest young man who had only recently joined Wythe's garrison, voiced his opinion. "Lady Alyce is too good to sustain the Demon's wicked presence for a single night."

Ulger's scowl was ferocious. Here lay exposed the root of his fears. Before he could step forward to reprimand their foolish, and worse yet, disloyal words, a third in the group of a score and more spoke.

"Aye, a servant in the hall last eve tells as how the demon come crashing down the stairs like thunder and rode off into the night. Now, what man amongst us could safely ride alone in the dark?"

In the first instance, Ulger was disgusted with this man near of an age with himself; one who, by his years, ought know better. In the second, he'd nothing but disdain for all these men who claimed to be fearless warriors but in truth were so steeped in superstition that they feared the night.

"Not us." The young guardsman confirmed Ulger's view. "'Tis a deed *only* a demon could think to do."

Superstition could not be easily eradicated, but to crush their straw-built logic, Ulger's voice came forth sharp and cold. "Were Earl Rhodare truly the demon you fear, how could his bride have rejected him? As the gossip you so readily believe would have it, a demon would exert unworldly powers to bind her to his will."

The men shuffled in discomfort, unable to meet Ulger's gaze directly. He clicked his tongue in vexation and finished with what he'd come to do. "'Tis time and past for the shifting of duty on the battlements. Waste no more time repeating gossip like old women. And before falling to such temptations again, use what right wits our Blessed Lord gave you. Ponder what foolishness you speak, question the sense of what you're told before you accept it as truth."

"Uncle, what's that nasty potion? It smells putrid!" Hal stepped past a door left slightly ajar, freckled nose wrinkled and curious eyes studying the small, unstoppered vial which Walter held. 'Twas filled with a strange liquid, ghastly green and just the sort to intrigue a boy of his age.

Walter's back went as stiff as if arrow-pierced by unseen assailants. First recorking the vial and then pausing to take deep, calming breaths, brows scowling above eyes overbrimming with cold fury, he slowly turned toward his unwelcome intruder.

"Training which allows a child to enter another's chamber uninvited is woefully lacking." He bent to an open trunk and with feigned casualness placed the precious green liquid inside before continuing his rebuke. "I'll speak with your mother on your wrongful actions."

Hal flushed beneath criticism he firmly believed unwarranted but remained steady as he staunchly defended himself. "It was my mother who sent me to beg you will come and write for her a message to my father. Your door was open and I called out before I entered, though I couldn't help but notice that awful odor." Hal couldn't stifle his curiosity and asked again, "What is it?"

Walter glowered at his nephew. In his haste for privacy to more closely examine this additional tool of destruction provided by his cohorts, it was possible that he'd failed to give adequate attention to assuring that the stubborn latch was firmly shut. That dangerous mistake greatly deepened his ill humor and he turned it on the wretched child who had caused him such trouble in the matter of Alyce's marriage.

"'Tis a horrible poison able to eat holes through flesh or bring instant death to any who swallow any drink tainted with so much as a single green drop." Though Walter spoke only the truth, his exaggerated expression and falsely lowered voice were meant to stir in Hal the same childish terrors as the myriad tales of wicked elves who steal the young, and goblins who eat human flesh.

Hal suspiciously watched the man's antics. He decided that his unpleasant uncle did look a weasel. James had told him that Dare and his two most loyal supporters had given Walter this name. And he'd bet the earl would want to know about Uncle Walter's dreadful green potion. Leastways, he'd tell James and see what his friend thought they ought do.

Witless child! Walter shrugged in disgust with the boy

staring at him, apparently lacking the sense to be frightened. Roughly brushing past Hal, he went to answer his sister's summons. He deemed it best to encourage her preoccupation with selfish demands. They would hold her oblivious to the forest of ominous threats and the bog of perils surrounding her tiny patch of firm ground.

OLIVIA WELLIVER

It seemed the whole pack was determined to disparage Dare's bond... the start... her... in the keep... closest to her... to her own...

17

Oblivious to her two companions' concerned attention, Alyce stared disconsolately into flames once leaping against soot-blackened stone but now burning as low as her spirits. Yestermorn's emotional stew of anger, defiance, and embarrassment had by evening been hotly spiced with a jealousy which spoiled the whole to leave naught but an unsavory batch of forlorn regret. Having soured further in the hours since, it threatened now to curdle hesitant hopes for reconciliation.

Dare had ridden out alone early in the day and not returned even for its last repast. After that tense meal's conclusion, though it had become a habit for the high table's company to retire to the solar, a Sybillene disgusted by her change in position at the high table had instead huffily retreated to her own chamber. Walter, too, had shown a continuing disapproval of the marriage by refusing to join Alyce, her mother-in-law, and Thomas in their retreat to this small chamber's warmth and privacy.

After settling near the hearth's welcome heat, Alyce had sensed a concern for Dare's long absence in an unnaturally subdued Thomas and unusually nervous Elinor. 'Twas a concern she'd shared. Not until they'd heard booted feet moving down the corridor and a door loudly closing at its end had the tension pressing down like low-hanging storm clouds begun to dissipate. During the silence following this apparent proof of Dare's return, as clearly as if audibly spoken, Alyce had heard Lady Elinor wordlessly urging her to fulfill her morning promise by going to seek peace with him. Heart pounding at the suddenness of an opportunity anticipated yet—no matter the planning or hours spent waiting—unexpectedly come, she'd found herself incapable of immediately doing more than sending a weak smile to the countess, a silent promise that she would. Soon, but not then.

Remembering her cowardly inaction and ashamed of her unruly spirit's defection in a moment when 'twas most needful, Alyce frowned with self-disgust. She'd justified her craven procrastination with the necessity of first working out exactly what to say in a plea whose success was so very important. Yet as she'd spent the entire day pondering that very subject, shying back when the chance to make her appeal for forgiveness arrived proved just what a complete pigeonheart she was.

At length Elinor retreated to her bed, and Thomas to his not long after. Both were disappointed that the young countess had not already gone to join her husband in the chamber they were now to share. So worried was Alyce that Dare's justified anger would see her tentative approach rebuffed, she barely noted their departures. With each passing moment, growing anxiety for the outcome of her intended appeal further sapped Alyce's ability to seek Dare out and speak it.

Alone in the solar, Alyce continued gazing into the hearth. In a fire not merely falling to glowing coals but threatening to soon be reduced to ashes, Alyce saw the demonstration of an unpleasant future. During the years they'd spent apart, though memories smoldered, her life had been a succession of tepid days lacking either the chill of the present or the heat of happiness. Now, possessing the experience of recent events, Alyce recognized an irrefutable truth. Though they would dwell in the same castle, without Dare's love, the years ahead would be as lifeless as cold ashes. By her own action in rejecting their source, the flames Dare had ever encouraged were being steadily smothered. If she wanted to revive the blaze (and more than ever anything before, she did), then she must lay the kindling and stoke dangerously weakened flames.

Suddenly pursuing an endeavor of irrational importance, Alyce lifted a long, thin stick charred on one end, and fiercely jabbed at the hearth's remains, little more than smoking remnants, until a few weak flames struggled to renewed life. Determination sparked in green eyes while, to feed their hunger, with care she arranged about them small chunks of firewood. Having thus succeeded in this literal task, Alyce rose from the three-legged stool where she'd settled hours past and turned her full attention to another such challenge. One far more important.

Alyce removed her barbette and veil before releasing unruly locks from the restraints of tight plaits. Dare had both told her and proven by his deeds how he disliked seeing her hair bound and hidden. Only the day past he'd asked her to leave it loose; and if he'd told her 'twas for their wedding, she would have complied with the bride's customary wearing of hair freed for the ceremony. 'Twas too late to grant him that boon, but hopefully he would recognize her loosing of it now as a sign of her contrition and desire for reconciliation.

Leaving the solar door ajar, she resolutely approached Dare's chamber. Just as she put her hand on the latch, a sound struck her to a stone far colder than any dead fire's ashes.

Tess's laughter was unmistakable, and though her words were indistinguishable, their intimate tone spoke with irrefutable clarity. Alyce whirled and madly dashed down the corridor to the small, dark chamber Lady Elinor had long ago allotted for her use. At thought of the countess, through Alyce's mind echoed the words of her good counsel to seek Dare out and work to mend the breach between them with all possible haste—before it was too late. She'd waited too long. The sound of Dare's first footstep should've sent her immediately to his presence. She had rejected the man guiltless of an alliance with Sybillene, and he'd warned of the cost. He'd warned her of the ease with which he could find solace elsewhere. Unjustified jealousy had driven Dare away the night past, but her cowardice was to blame for tonight's pain. Had she promptly sought his forgiveness, it might've been her in his bed and in his arms.

That acknowledgment did nothing to lessen Alyce's pain in the vision of his powerful limbs wrapped about Tess's bountiful form. Having driven Dare into the other woman's arms, she struggled not to compound her initial wrong by again blaming him. At the same time, beneath the hurtful sting of Dare's action stretched a burning ache of anger at Tess. Anger first for bedding her mistress's husband, but second, and just as strongly, for her duplicity. Tess sought Dare's passionate embrace in the night, but during the day spread wicked tales which could do naught but increase her lover's danger.

Sinking to a narrow, lumpy mattress so unlike the feather-filled one which graced the lord's vast bed, Alyce felt herself sinking just as surely into depression. Yet never so deep that it could prevent her from continuing the fight to win Dare back to her.

At the sound of rapidly retreating footsteps, the deadly threat of sharp blade against throat eased.

"You did well."

The cryptic words hissed into Tess's ear did nothing to relieve her fears, although they were lessened in small measure by being allowed to pull a brief distance from the cruel hold on her arm. Yet lying supine atop the lord's high bed within striking distance of the tormentor at her side half reclining against piled pillows, she was trapped. When he released her with a flourish of his once-restraining hand, she edged farther away without taking apprehensive eyes from the glittering dagger in his other hand.

Walter watched the voluptuous maid slowly moving to the very edge of the bed. Gratified by this display of terror wrought by his power over her, he tossed the focus of her fear lightly from one hand to the other in silent demonstration of his skill.

"You've proven to a bride the wickedness of her groom, and I am pleased." Walter's smile gleamed near as wickedly as his weapon. "Now I've another task for you. 'Tis more difficult, but one I'm sure you'll accomplish with equal success. Elsewise . . ." His calculated pause filled the air with foreboding.

Dread of what unthinkable demand his strange words might portend overwhelmed Tess's fear. She rose from the bed and backed away.

"Stay." The flat command brooked no rejection. "Stay and hear what you must do, elsewise you'll lie dead before you reach the door."

Tess went motionless. Only her pale brown eyes flickered at sight of the blade dexterously flipped tip over end.

"Might well be the best course." Walter pondered the matter, delighting in her growing distress. "'Twould be another fine testament to the blackness of the Demon's soul were his lover (and his wife would attest to that) found dead in his own bedchamber."

The scenario promised the thrill of an impromptu danger. Though Walter had always preferred actions carefully planned and executed, he was proud of his new adeptness at taking risks and suspected the danger ever at their core could be addicting. The deceiving of Alyce, his most recent impulsive chance, had provided a strong dose. Knowing Dare had yet to return but could at any moment, while Alyce and the others retreated to the solar, he'd "borrowed" heavy boots and stomped down the corridor with Tess tiptoeing at his side. Once the chamber door had slammed shut and they were safe inside, he'd been filled with an exhilaration never before experienced. Convinced by that preliminary triumph that Alyce would eventually seek the lord's chamber, hers by marriage, he'd waited. It had taken longer than expected, but in the end his trick had succeeded and he was well pleased with this new strand in his web.

Long, dark hair whipped in wild disarray about narrow shoulders as Tess vehemently resisted the ghastly vision of her own end.

"Aye, you are right, 'twould be better still were it the Demon himself whose lifeless body was found." Tess gasped, and Walter's brows arched in mock surprise.

Again and again Dare had interrupted the flow of a

carefully executed plan, an annoyance forcing Walter into making constant repairs. But by wedding Alyce, the Demon had thrown entirely out of kilter arrangements made with precision and at a not insubstantial cost. In order to restore balance, Dare must die.

"The choice is yours. If you fail to see the earl dead either tonight or before this hour on the next, I will see your gruesome murder laid to his door." Walter shrugged, eyes narrowing on the minion he meant to force into performing this all-important task. "Either way, I win."

Tess cringed beneath Walter's piercing gaze. Her sinful greed for more than was her lot had led to this awful choice. Greed and pride in her ability to manipulate men with ease. For most of her life she'd succeeded in the latter, so mayhap 'twas God's judgment that she should come to her end at the hands of a man far more skilled at such deeds than she.

Nay, she would not surrender so willingly. There must be some action she could take to survive. Accept the proffered knife and then flee from them all? 'Twould be the move of an addlepated fool! Tess's desperation had not that thoroughly fogged her wits. She'd be offering herself up to a fate likely as dire as that threatened by Walter. A serf running from her owner was sure to be caught and returned to face her lord's retribution. Moreover, a lone woman traveler would be subject to all manner of predators—animal and human. Yet the alternative was to remain here and kill Earl Dare—an awful thought both in the unwanted doing and certain punishment to follow. To restate Walter's claim in reverse, one way or the other, it seemed she would lose.

Seeing pale brown eyes go cloudy with fear of a retribution hers no matter the choice, Walter quickly countered the danger to his scheme. "Once you've fulfilled your part of this bargain, a safe haven awaits."

Tess's gaze held steady on Walter. 'Twas difficult to believe such a miracle could exist.

"You surely agree that the deed would best be performed in darkness and solitude. 'Tis why I encourage you to have done with it this night." Impervious to the doubts behind her emotionless expression, Walter went on with his enticements. "Whatever propitious moment you find, once the

Demon is dead, come to me and I will help you safely escape through the postern door and see you off to the camp of my confederates. They'll provide you with food and lodging until the end comes."

The skepticism roused by such wild claims smothered any curiosity for his foolish talk of an approaching end. Tess could no longer restrain either a jeering smile or statement of facts proving the ridiculousness of his assurances. "The postern door, wherever it be, is assuredly locked. Moreover, no strangers can be lurking on Wythe lands but that it would be known and they harshly dealt with." Asides, Tess had wits enough to realize that her protection was of no true interest to Walter. In reality, once the crime had been committed, a man so cunning would surely see himself permanently rid of his only link to the crime.

Walter shook his head as if frustrated by a child's stubborn refusal to learn. "'Struth, secret doors would be of no value if left open to all . . . but I have the key." From a bag tied to a wide leather belt and dangling hidden in the folds of his ankle-length robes, with his left hand he pulled a heavy key longer than the dagger still in his right. Dare plainly hadn't expected his chamber to be searched, elsewise he'd surely have found a better place to keep this prize than at the bottom of the carved trunk aside his bed.

"As for the location of my confederates"—Walter shrugged while gifting Tess with a sly smile—"They are not so foolish as to be seen, nor am I so foolish as to share that knowledge with you before my command has been fulfilled. But whether or no Earl Dare survives, soon—very, very soon—a new order will be established here on Wythe. How you fare after depends upon the report I make of your actions—for good or for ill." That his confederates still refused to share with him the exact timing of the coming conflict was a continuing irritation. But of its imminent arrival, he was certain, and why he'd laid special plans for the rest of this night.

Tess shuddered. She needed time to consider the matter and all its hazardous angles. A thing not possible while threats so knotted her thoughts, 'twas impossible to untangle the thread of right reasoning. Intending to stave off the decision, leastways until she'd escaped her master's hold, Tess moved slowly forward to gingerly accept the evilly glittering dagger. She then turned to scurry from the chamber.

Walter watched the retreating maid with such vicious intent and deadly determination as to force her—if necessary, by the strength of his will alone—into ending the Demon's life. Yet even were Tess to fail him, he'd the means to assure that all-important deed's accomplishment.

Years past he'd won his first battle against Dare by convincing his selfish sister to set aside her incapable husband and seek pleasure from the man she desired. Thus Walter had successfully forced Dare from Keniver and placed what he'd believed to be a permanent block between the man and Alyce. Walter had then set out to cultivate a useful relationship with men possessing power enough to give him what he desired.

Shortly after he'd arrived to begin training at Winchester years past, Walter had offered to supply Peter Rievaux with information in exchange for Alyce's annulment. He'd known that the information he provided was destined to aid the bishop—the father Peter called uncle to shield his illegitimate birth—in plotting against nobles he deemed too powerful and a danger to his ambitions. However, the bishop, a man whose cunning Walter grudgingly admired, had purposefully chosen to secure the dissolution of that marriage by means of a too close family tie, by a step-bond more than two generations in the past.

Blind to the growing gloom lent by dying candlelight, Walter grinned in acknowledgment of a trap he deemed worthy of his admiration although one built at his expense. Toward preventing the same argument being used to block his goal, Walter had willingly become more deeply involved in schemes the bishop and his "nephew" had devised to see not only Pembroke but Keniver *and* Wythe fall forfeit to the crown. All three were destined to end in Peter's greedy hold while the bishop's opponents would be lessened in number. Walter sneered in disdainful memory of foolish, trusting

Halbert putting his seal on traitorous letters a brother-in-law had written to secure the dispensation allowing him as stepuncle to wed Alyce, his niece.

As for Dare's absence from Alyce's life . . . Walter's frown was as fierce as any gargoyle's. Just as Halbert's dependents were about to be taken where Walter desired they go—the royal court and the bishop's seat of power—the Demon had made an unwelcome "rescue." Still, even that unfortunate diversion, Walter had turned to his advantage. He'd earned yet a greater measure of the bishop's appreciation by seeing dissension spread across Wythe. Surely he'd thus smoothed the way for its defeat.

Although Walter had initially welcomed the disgrace of the interfering Dare as an additional reward for all he'd done, the man's mere disgrace was no longer adequate. Walter had long since realized the need to go beyond the bishop's plan. Dare's mere fall would leave Alyce still unattainable, thus the Demon must die!

The room abruptly went dark as the candle's flame guttered out. Walter shook his head in self-disgust. The thrill of danger had its limits, and by remaining here so long, he'd doubtless come dangerously near to overreaching them. Best he be off on his night's final adventure. Holding the postern door's key tight to his chest, he crept to the door and peered out. His exit was welcomed by a corridor filled only with shadows cast by flickering torch flames.

Candleflame picked up the fiery highlights amidst lush tresses flowing free. A vivid blue gaze caressed the tender face in their midst while Dare's faint smile reflected a love tinged with desperation. What he'd learned during his prolonged absence made it all the more important that they settle their troubles and claim what happiness they could during the night's few remaining hours.

Finding his chamber empty, Dare had come in search of the woman for whom he'd brushed aside all wise and just restraints to claim as wife. By the mussed covers on his bed, it seemed certain that Alyce had begun the night there, and he feared he knew what had sent her fleeing to this inadequate resting place. Too likely his late return had convinced her that he'd truly done what his angry and deeply regretted words of the past night had threatened, that he'd sought some other woman's bed. Before the next day forced itself upon them, he meant for Alyce to be as certain as he that never with another could either of them ever share the wild passion or attain the exquisite satisfaction found in each other's arms.

Dare dropped to his knees beside the humble bed, intending to gently awaken the sweetly sleeping damsel. Yet as he settled a candle atop her wicker chest, its glow caught the traces of dried tears. They smote him with guilt. What good had he ever done for this fire-sprite? Only had he drawn her with him down a trouble-pitted path into dark dangers. Only had he caused her unhappiness. In valiantly facing that cheerless truth he admitted an unwelcome fact. He could not take the chance of increasing her distress—the very thing he least wanted to do—by waking her to face the unpleasant view of a man she too certainly saw as an adulterer ever seizing what was not his, a traitor to honorable foster bonds . . . and the despoiler of her own innocence.

Lips curling down in icy self-contempt, Dare permitted only his eyes to caress sweet temptation. She shifted in her sleep, dislodging the cover across her tender breasts, and his chin jerked back as abruptly as if he'd been landed a direct blow. Then he, a famed warrior renowned for his emotionless control, found himself unable to prevent his gaze from drinking in the view of soft curves or to halt burning memories of their fiery brand crushed against him, flesh to flesh.

Having chosen to put aside his selfish need for the reassuring feel of Alyce willingly curled in his embrace and instead give her the boon of peaceful slumbers, a shield against the tensions of rapidly approaching danger, *now* was the time to depart, *now* before he lost all hope of seeing it so. Though earnest in his intent to retreat to his cold bed alone, he permitted himself the small consolation of a whisper-soft kiss against a flushed cheek, and carefully leaned down.

As if a warming ray of bright hope had suddenly pierced the chill gloom of dismal dreams, Alyce instinctively shifted her mouth to meet Dare's. She'd fallen asleep praying for another chance to set things aright between them. Thus, when heavy lashes rose, allowing misty green eyes to greet the miraculous appearance of the longed-for man, 'twas a gift whose source she would not question. Alyce lifted up to twine her arms tightly about his strong neck, urging him to lie down beside her and accept her wordless plea for forgiveness and reconciliation.

Dare was surprised by Alyce's unexpected action—though why that should be when she made a habit of doing what he least expected, he did not know. Unwilling to waste precious time on useless ponderings, he surrendered to her silent entreaty and sat beside her on the bed that creaked ominously beneath his formidable weight. As he lifted her body full into his embrace, his hungry mouth gently brushed against hers, gradually increasing the pressure, enticing her lips open to the heat of joining.

At the exquisite pleasure of being in his arms, a breathless whimper forced its way out from her throat. Although sinking fast into the smoky haze of desire, she was determined to prove that she harbored no faint wish to reject him, and moved her sweet bounty against him. The kiss Dare deepened with devastating slowness whirled her into smoldering flames while each slight rasp of Dare's hand over tender flesh kindled sparks and reignited fires only he could light. Drowning in her own longings, she barely felt the fingers of his other hand sliding through a mass of chestnut hair to tug her head back and lay bare the elegant line of her throat.

Dare held Alyce a handsbreadth away while the blue flames of heavy-lidded eyes burned over the pale cream and soft peach of her slender body. His lips next began following the path of his gaze. Slowly, so slowly it was torment, they brushed over the velvet softness of generous curves, trailing delicious fire. Tantalizing caresses brought an urgent and ever-increasing need until Alyce twined her fingers into thick, black strands, arching up in an attempt to bring his teasing mouth to the center of the ache he had caused. But still he held back until again she moaned. The hand in her hair unintentionally tightened as at last his warm lips on the tip of one taut breast provided the sweet suction that was both achieved goal and kindling to hotter flames.

While passion blazed in his blood, rushing it through his veins like wildfire through the forest, Dare gloried in the feel of Alyce sweetly trembling beneath his desperate hunger. When he lifted his head, Alyce tumbled wildly into the mesmerizing depths of a simmering blue gaze. She wanted more; she wanted the freedom to touch Dare as she had the last night they'd shared this small bed. Slender fingers took advantage of the space between loosely fastened laces to caress bronze skin and wiry curls. Yet it was not enough and she tugged impatiently at the coarse tunic barring her from the goal.

Readily yielding to her unspoken demand, thankful that he'd taken the time to earlier rid himself of chain mail, Dare suddenly withdrew his arms and pulled back long enough to rid himself of both homespun shirt and chausses. He came down to her sweet beauty bristling with pride for the fact that now he could truly claim her his. He intently watched his dark, sword-callused fingers reach out to trace across the incredibly soft and nearly luminescent white skin of lush curves.

Face tense with desire and green eyes gone near to black, in silent praise Alyce let her hands wander in fascination over the erotic combination of hard muscle and abrasive hair of her husband's superbly masculine form. Feeling every line and curve burn beneath her touch, under a longing that robbed her of strength she melted against Dare, clung to him unashamed of her need of a man beloved. Twisting against him, she reveled in the heavy beat of his heart and the harsh groan earned by her bold actions.

Dare immediately took command of their tender battle. As he had too long gone hungry for her, during their previous encounter she had driven him over the precipice too quickly. This time he meant to demonstrate to his fire-vixen, innocent for all her fiery spirit, how truly deep was the sea of desire, how intense was the blaze of desire. Moreover, as he'd meant to do in seeking her out this eve, he would teach her that they could find the wild passion and exquisite satisfaction of these delights only in each other's arms.

Dare urged Alyce back and overwhelmed her with the enticing, exciting fires in a myriad of slow, steady caresses. With hands and mouth he guided her descent into delicious torment and shocking pleasures until she writhed beneath him, trembling wildly. He then slid his palms down the long, slender curve of her back to cup her derriere, lift her hips tightly against his, and join them in the most intimate of bonds. Bodies merged, in a rhythmic motion as old as time, Dare rocked them both beyond sanity and into the desperate abandon where storm and fire meet and crash together in an explosion of unfathomable ecstasy.

An uncounted time later, basking amidst the smoldering coals of passion replete, Dare rested his chin atop the head Alyce laid against his shoulder, a satisfied smile curving hard lips while he slowly stroked her passion-tangled hair.

"That was the physical demonstration of the bond of love we've shared near a lifetime." Dare's voice was still deep and darkly textured. "The bond that can never be sundered and that now is our right by the laws of God and man."

Alyce pressed a tender kiss into the flesh beneath her cheek in pleased contentment that what he said was undeniably true. Floating in the euphoric lassitude that had slowed the pounding of her pulse until it felt as if thick honey flowed in her veins, it took time for rational thought to return. When it did, she pondered a subject whose importance had nearly faded into nothingness. The incredible experience just past provided all the answers she would ever need, yet to challenge a liar, she must have Dare's spoken denial.

"You've been out?" Alyce diffidently inquired, rising on an elbow to lift the homespun shirt which in its hasty discarding had become caught on the bed's corner. Although she uselessly strove for some small semblance of normality, slumbrous green eyes stroked over a broad, bronzed chest with its thatch of dark curls spreading down over Dare's flat stomach.

Thick black lashes dropped to level upon Alyce a startled

look of hurt surprise. Surely she couldn't have failed to even notice his long absence any more than he could fail to be concerned about possible dangers to her? "Aye." There was a curt harshness in his voice. "Near the whole long day and most of the night."

Pleased by this confirmation of the right in trust given, as proven by a hurt too honest for him to have feigned, Alyce could not suppress a sweet smile of relief. Still, she continued her quest for a specifically stated denial of a sham event. "Then you were not in your chamber this eve?"

"I've not been there since I rose with the last dawning." Dare's suspicions were fully roused by Alyce's strange interest in his bedchamber. Had it to do with the mussed bed? Suddenly uncomfortable with her persistence, to avoid any possibility of a later misunderstanding, he flatly stated an additional fact. "Nay, 'tis not quite the truth."

Alyce's breath caught in her throat, all the satisfaction in a prize won suspended awaiting his explanation.

"I peeked inside when I first returned, expecting to find you curled up in my bed. Alas, you were not there, so I had perforce to seek you out and do my poor best to convince you that 'tis where you rightly belong." The mock humbleness in his words was belied by both the gleam of blue eyes and the boldness with which he pulled her down into his arms.

"Someone was, and I thought she was with you." Alyce murmured against his throat, perfectly content now that she'd the denial she needed to pluck a weed from this strong man's path afore it could take root and flourish.

"What?" Now it was Dare who rose up on his elbow to demand explanation, but Alyce once more tangled her fingers into black strands and tugged in an effort to bring him back to her.

"It doesn't matter." Alyce's response was brief and sincerely meant. That she'd been purposely misled by Tess was plain, a deed she meant to investigate—later. In this moment she'd matters of much greater import to care for, a husband who she meant to see would never again believe her less than his loyal, loving wife.

Dare would've argued the point except for the distraction

of the little, teasing kisses Alyce had begun pressing to his face and bared throat.

"I was wrong to even question it of you, just as it was shamefully foolish of me to allow my jealousy to lead me into rejecting you yestereve." When she paused in her intent to cover him with kisses, green-crystal eyes directly met pale blue. "'Twas the witless act of a fool when our union, church-blessed or no, has been my deepest desire for near all my life." The hands Alyce had tangled in Dare's mane to draw him to her relaxed, enabaling her to slowly stroke through its cool thickness while she spoke, her heart throbbing in every word. "You are the embodiment of my every dream. And I swear only wicked jealousy put the poison of an adder on my tongue and the chill of ice in my veins. Forgive me, Dare, I beg you."

With dainty, tempting kisses again crossing his cheeks and down his throat, she added power to a plea Dare would've granted her instantly from the far side of the world. As he'd earlier acknowledged when deciding to leave Alyce peacefully sleeping, he was guilty of all too many wrongs in bumbled attempts to deal wisely with her to fail in understanding, and absolving her of any wrong.

"I will forgive you of every wrong you've ever done if you'll forgive me of mine—not the ones of which I've been accused so oft and will swear to my grave I am innocent of committing, but for causing you unhappiness and bringing you into the midst of the many dangerous suspicions and dark threats abounding in Castle Wythe."

Alyce demonstrated her immediate acceptance of the pact with a kiss so heated, it incinerated all lingering traces of fear and doubt. Recognizing this invitation to a renewal of sweet play and more than anxious to accept its physical reaffirmation of their love's unshakable bond, still Dare pulled from a tender embrace and rose from the bed.

Green eyes already glazing with passion stared up at him with such a depth of aching regret that he near tumbled again into enticingly extended arms. Yet he held back. Though he had every intention of seeing them both again consumed by the flames of desire, he was determined to first see them ensconced in his bed's far greater comfort.

"I mean only to do as I intended when coming to this chamber. I will return you to where you belong at this time of night—my bed." Alyce smiled her welcome of the prospect even as he continued. "'Tis more suited to my size than this pitiful structure from which either my head or my feet uncomfortably hung unsupported."

Alyce made to get up, but Dare forestalled her willing compliance by lifting her full into his arms with a strength that would have it seem she weighed no more than a feather pillow. He then allowed her to slide down the hardening contours of his body—proof of his exciting true intentions —and stand yielding before him. Pleasurably aware of his great height and breadth, she remained motionless while he wrapped the coverlet around her tempting body. First to preserve her modesty against even the remote possibility of peeping eyes this deep into the night, and second to forestall the danger of an enraged punishment certain to be wreaked on the head of anyone even inadvertently trespassing on a sight that was his alone.

Only after his task was done and he'd moved momentarily away to gather up his discarded clothing and drape them neatly over the end of the bed did Alyce catch a glimpse of him from behind. Though never had she believed Tess's wild tales, still—as with the spoken denial of an eve spent in his chamber with Tess—'twas no bad thing to have this visual proof adding implacable certainty in support of rebuttals Alyce meant to speak.

No mark of Satan marred Dare's form, although in the dying candle's fading light she saw the faint scars crisscrossing his otherwise perfect body. She frowned. These marks reinforced a fact she knew to well—Dare was all too human and subject to the same dangers as any other man. Despite his renown as a famed warrior well able to meet any physical danger, she feared for him.

Feeling the weight of green eyes on his back, with the confidence of love returned, Dare glanced behind at his curious wife. "Searching for the infamous 'Mark of Satan'?"

The mocking grin he'd been casting her way for as long as she could remember seemed to hold no hint of rebuke, but Alyce bit at a tender and slightly swollen lip. She had believed, leastwise hoped, that by her action in feigning belief in its dastardly lie, Tess's tale had been confined to her ears alone.

Black hair brushed over the smooth skin of bare shoulders as Dare slowly shook his head. "Surely you've heard Tess's most recent invention. Seems the mere tale of my seduction of her by unworldly powers grew too tame to hold the attention of an audience ever hungry for new fodder. Thus, she now claims my posterior bears the print of the devil's cloven hoof."

Alyce grimaced with disgust for the woman's continuing deceptions, but Dare laughed with remarkably lighthearted amusement.

"Of course, I forgot you didn't believe me when I first assured you that her spite was born the moment I refused her 'generous' offer to share my bed." He bowed his dark head in false despair over her lack of trust, yet the gleam in eyes not quickly enough shielded reassured her that he gladly accepted her innocent of this. "But by the bond proven in hours past, you've surely learned 'tis true when on my honor I swear—" a steady blue gaze met green eyes with a sincerity at the core of their flame that could never be doubted "—that as the woman I love, and love to the very depths of my soul, you are the only woman I desire."

While Dare again swept Alyce up into his arms, the smile on his dark face singed her with its potency. Alyce cuddled nearer as he strode toward the door. Reveling in the warmth and power he exuded, she buried her face against his throat and whispered.

"My demon you are, and I'll love you for all eternity. But even more"—she tilted a fiery head back to gaze up at him with such open emotion that it shook him with reverent appreciation for this gift so precious, it humbled him —"I would have that you believe any babe born of our fire will be a treasure to me. Against any adversity will I stand with our children, just as I will stand by you. Though born to 'Demon Dare,' they will be treasures heaven-given."

In a soul-binding kiss Dare claimed sensuous lips turned cherry-bright by their earlier play even as he carried Alyce to the bedchamber now rightfully theirs to share tonight and every night for a lifetime to come . . .

He refused to sacrifice precious moments of happiness to the depressingly insistent dark and silently whispered warning that their lifetime together could be so fearfully short as the span of a single day more.

18

And last night we let fall just the tiniest droplet into a puddle outside the stable. This morn 'twas surrounded by more dead rats than I ever thought to see!"

The honest amazement in Hal's voice was tinged with a disgust that put a wry smile on Dare's mouth. Light from the fire a servant had only just finished stoking to renewed life glowed white on black hair as Dare tilted his head to more closely examine the curious green liquid filling the vial in his hand.

A distressed Hal and equally agitated James had been waiting for him when he descended from his bedchamber, unusually late for the company of a too sweet temptation to linger abed. The boys had pleaded for a conversation with him alone and without delay. He'd brought them here as the solar, at this hour of morn, was near the only location promising the privacy they clearly deemed all-important.

Dare had never nor would ever easily believe the myriad of wild tales which came to his ears. Only see what troubles lack of cool consideration in such matters had brought down upon him. Moreover, Dare was well aware that youthful imaginations could find fanciful dangers in even the most innocuous facts and deeds—and James, he knew, was particularly talented in this realm.

On the other side, it was Walter who'd smuggled the potion into the castle, and anything having to do with Walter was worthy of careful investigation. The previous day's discoveries, made by tracking the weasel, were enough alone to earn Walter that distinction. Add then the man's strange absence at the morning meal and . . .

"You did well to bring it to me, Hal." Dare's smile warmed with fondness. "And I promise to take good care in seeing its deadly danger eliminated."

The boy beamed at the dark man offering praise, but he was quick to lend credit where due. "James it is who ought be thanked. He's the one who convinced me we'd best remove the awful potion from my uncle's possession."

Knowing that Walter's guilty hand had participated in the many vile deeds done on Wythe, Dare narrowed his blue eyes in concern. By taking from the man, the boys had put themselves in jeopardy. "Your action was brave, James. Yet I worry for the reprisal it may bring."

Beneath the earl's approval for the action he'd suggested, James displayed a rightful modesty, but his humble expression was soon overtaken by a proud grin for yet another accomplishment. "We were not such dullards as to take and not put back. Though couldn't find anything so bright a green, we filled a vial from Cleva's store with water and fine-ground parsley. This we placed where we found the first."

"Ah." Dare smiled. "I admire your inventiveness and—"

"My lord." A diffident voice intruded.

Dare instantly shifted his attention to the young guardsman who had quietly opened the solar's door.

"I bear grave news." Runnolf was not happy to be the messenger chosen for this task. After the scolding they'd received from Sir Ulger on the loyalty rightly owed their lord, he was embarrassed to be in the earl's presence at all. To be sent bearing such awful tidings left him wondering if he hadn't rather be dispatched to carry water to the denizens of hell.

In the long pause following the ominous announcement, Dare waited with strained patience for the plainly uncomfortable man to speak further.

"Strangers approach." The brief statement was ragged, having been forced through a disconcertingly tight throat.

"Strangers?" Black brows lifted in dubious question. "No pennant to announce their identity?"

Heart pounding with vicious force, Runnolf gulped audibly. Now he'd no option but to tell what was certain to infuriate the Demon while in the back of his thoughts lingered the vision of an earlier messenger seemingly struck down for his unwelcome words. "They bear the three lions of our king."

Dare gave the speaker a grim smile even as a cold mask descended to wipe further honest emotion from his face. During his ride through the dark forest on his return only hours past, he had foreseen this unalterable confrontation. Spirit strengthened by Alyce's unconditional love, with steady deliberation he rose to his feet and motioned the other man to accompany him to meet the challenge awaiting. Despite the likelihood that dark whispers had already succeeded in robbing him of the desperately important support of Wythe's own, for the sake of the name he would leave behind for his beautiful wife and the babe he'd done his best to see conceived, he would never concede defeat but fight on against all odds.

Hal looked meaningfully at James. Though they'd not had the advance warning of its swift approach that Dare had won by following a "weasel," between them unspoken they knew exactly what event was under way. The king had sent his representative to declare their earl a traitor and call his lands forfeit to the crown.

In this instance James's natural penchant for worry was more justified than usual. Would Earl Dare surrender? Pray God not! Or would a full-scale battle ensure? He was young and inexperienced; to him the latter prospect offered leastwise a chance to prevail. Asides, though he was somewhat ashamed to admit it so, the notion of seeing his first battle fought in earnest was thrilling.

Meanwhile Hal was terrified. He'd been through this same moment before when a like force had descended upon Keniver. Aye, he was terrified. Not so much by the cruelty and pain which was the certain result of even an honorable battle as by the fear that yet another man much admired might, by easy surrender, confess a guilt Hal desperately didn't want to believe.

As Dare moved toward the door, he caught a glimpse of the boys' faces and rightly read their emotions. Undersized James, in his earl's defense, had fought against overwhelming odds. And Alyce's half-brother, Hal, had already been forced to watch his father submit and be wrongly stained with dishonor. Though there had never been any possibility of Dare bowing to the awful charges certain to be laid at his door, his resolve to resist was further reinforced by the need to prevent these youngsters from being disillusioned by someone they clearly admired. Unconditional approval was a rare commodity and a prize never to be lightly cast aside.

As he quickly descended to the great hall and on through the exit tunnel, booted feet beat a firm cadence of determination. Fanhurst waited at the bottom of castle steps, with Fiend saddled and waiting. Dare gave him a broad smile of congratulation. When 'twas most important, the youngster had been more than prompt and completely prepared. Dare chose to take this as a sign of how well the day would fare. Clad in full chain mail, as near every day, he swung up into the saddle, yet while wheeling Fiend about, bade his squire to see that both Ulger and Thomas join him with all possible haste. Not pausing to ensure that Fanhurst would instantly set off to do as commanded, he spurred his mighty destrier through an open gate.

Breath caught in Alyce's throat as from the stairwell's thin arrow-slit she stood watching an impressive sight far below. A dark and powerful man hurtled his black steed across the lowered drawbridge to race toward the outer bailey wall. She'd no attention to spare for the second man taking the same actions. He was naught but a shadow of the stunningly handsome man she would, with glad contentment, claim hers for all eternity. Only as the riders approached the distant gate was her haze of admiration and warm memories harshly broken by the realization that iron-bound doors, normally opened to welcome the day's business, were closed and stoutly barred. Heart pounding an ominous beat in her ears, Alyce instantly turned to descend with as much haste as possible on steep, winding steps.

When Dare reined in at the foot of the outer wall, he found the guardsmen atop its walkway standing with bows drawn and arrows pointed threateningly downward. Quickly, purposefully, he climbed the sturdy wooden ladder to join those confronting unwanted visitors, heartened by leastwise this initial support. Air heavy with unfallen rain laid overall a chilling pall matched by the ice in penetrating blue eyes as Dare calmly spoke.

"As you welcomed me to Keniver, Sir Lester, I would welcome you to Wythe—did I think you had come with peaceable intents." Seemed this man was the deputy Henry ever dispatched to see his unpleasant deeds done. And Dare had no doubt but that Sir Lester's allegiance was to the king rather than the bishop, although 'twas assuredly the latter behind the whole.

"I do not seek the welcome of the devil's spawn . . . Demon Dare." Lester used the term with a grim pleasure that made it plain he'd been looking forward to this man's certain disgrace. "I come to deliver the writ of *our* liege lord, King Henry. In this document validated by royal seal . . ." He waved the parchment triumphantly as if 'twere a sorcerer's magical weapon certain to slay any opponent foolish enough to resist. "In this document you are revealed for the traitor you are, and for your crimes Wythe is held forfeit to the crown." The last he announced triumphantly, fair bristling with enjoyment in the soon-coming fall of a man who'd earlier bested him.

'Twas as Dare had expected. Indeed, the only fact unforeseen was that his monarch had sent this sorry man to attempt his defeat. Blue eyes narrowed on an overconfident foe. After Dare had so oft stood at the king's side in battle, by what daft notion had Henry thought Lester equal to the deed? Not that their king was any fine tactician or warrior either, for he was neither. A cold and sardonic smile curled Dare's mouth. Must be that Henry saw proof of abilities not readily visible in the knight's successful return from Keniver carrying its baron in chains. Even while hope's weak flame burned higher, Dare's mouth firmed into a harsh line. He perceived an honest chance to defeat this knight ill equipped to stand against one far more experienced and better trained—by Keniver's wrongly accused lord. Thus would the king learn his folly in assumptions so unworthy.

"What wrong have I done to be named traitor by the king to whose cause I've rallied and lent my strength so many times?" Dare shoved back his mail coif and shook long black strands as if in physical demonstration of his undaunted courage.

"How can you ask when even those guiltless of any crime see it plain?" The question reverberated with a cultivated disdain. "How when your foster father was charged with the same by virtue of letters answering your plea for him to join you in plotting treason?"

"Lord Halbert cannot read and knows no more of composing script than how to inscribe his name or affix his seal. Moreover, he *did not* instigate those letters. Neither did I nor any known to me request his aid in such a heinous deed." The implacable statement baldly dared the other to prove it wrong. "I proclaim both myself and my foster father guiltless of any wrongdoing."

While unmoving men on both sides watched, the words fell between the two opponents like heavy rocks falling from the parapet to lie as inert, rejected lumps upon the ground.

"Do you come down and submit to your liege lord's command?" Lester's harsh tone demanded an answer of the foolishly defiant earl.

"Nay, I will not." The mocking smile accompanying this immediate refusal was boldly meant as a further irritant.

Sir Lester gritted his teeth. He hadn't expected open resistance from this man whom he'd been assured possessed few resources to call upon. A reaction which laid a sardonic smile on the glare at the earl's dark face.

"You leave me no choice but to force you onto that path." The glare sent to the dark earl flashed with promised retribution.

"With that small force?" Azure eyes narrowed on the men gathered below—a sizable army but far from overwhelming, and smaller than many Dare had faced and defeated while backed by fewer troops than those presently at his command. Closing his thoughts against the weakening possibility that some number of his garrison's men might refuse to answer his call to arms, he examined his opponents and found more interest in who was not there than who was.

"By sheer numbers yours may be the greater, but 'tis naught but an illusion as I have it from a reliable authority that a goodly number of your 'supporters' will submit to their king rather than fight a demon's cause."

Gone to unflinching stone, Dare reacted by neither sound nor blink of a steady gaze. He gave the knight points for striking straight to a foe's most vulnerable area. It felt like a physical blow, this audible statement of a fact whose probable truth he'd known since returning to Wythe years past, and silently Dare chided himself for its pain. As these troubles had been purposefully increased by minions of enemies he now faced, there'd never been any doubt but that they would be wielded against him. Dare forced a grim smile to his mouth yet would not waste breath on denials no one would believe—himself least of all.

"Believe as you choose, yet still I'll resist until untrue charges are admitted to be false—or you've killed me."

"Even though you'll have no one to guard your back or stand at your side?" Sir Lester's words were a verbal sneer, but behind them lay a distinct uneasiness at the prospect of meeting this famed warrior in direct combat.

"If you stake your success upon a strategy so flimsy, then you will loose."

The speaker stood beside an earl as surprised by this unanticipated defense as the man below. But Dare's surprise was for more than the fact that another had joined the verbal sparring. The words themselves were amazing. Steady and clear, they'd come from a flame-haired guardsman standing bold against an aggressor.

"Show Sir Lester what we think of his slur upon the loyalty we give our lord." It was the earl's right to command an assault, yet Arlen's cool order was instantly obeyed by archers lining the wall's summit.

A hail of arrows filled the air while, as if in heavenly

support, the clouds abruptly loosed the long-threatened downpour. Pandemonium broke out amongst once orderly ranks. Huddling beneath judiciously raised shields and dragging along several of their fallen companions, the unwelcome "visitors" beat a hasty retreat to a point just beyond the reach of even the most expertly fired arrow.

Warmed by his guardsmen's unexpected display of support where so short a time past he'd been filled with a chill sense of overshadowing defeat, Dare lingered atop the parapet and watched Sir Lester's contingent settle to prepare for the struggle to come. Amidst a field covered by the stubble of scythe-shaven wheat and rapidly deepening mud they pitched camp. Sir Lester and a few of his men soon withdrew into a hastily erected pavilion, plainly to plot their next move in the deadly game of war.

Every person in both castle and village knew their earl had gone to face a fearful threat dangerous to them all, and tension rolled a deep hush over the whole.

While Sybillene hid in her chamber feeling sorry for herself in having been caught a second time between a traitor and his king, Alyce had taken the ominous news to Dare's mother. They'd shared brief words of mutual encouragement before each set out to earn what little comfort could be had of hands busied with mundane tasks. Thus it was that Alyce descended to the hall, intent on searching out chores to be done.

In a great hall normally humming with activity, the only sounds were the crackle of flames fed by young hands, the sizzle of juices dripping from roasting meats—and the subtle murmur of lies. A group of idle serfs huddled over a table drawn near the huge fireplace's welcome heat. Approaching from behind, Alyce caught enough of what was said that her cheeks instantly burned as bright as her determination. While Dare met the enemy without, she would wage as fierce a battle within.

The steady green flame of her gaze never wavered from the back of a woman bent near full across the table's breadth to emphasize whispered words. The subject plainly held listeners engrossed. Eyes widened, some clicked tongues in disgust while others were caught in silence by the thrill of fears stoked ever higher.

"Spreading more lies, Tess?" Alyce's clear voice filled the hushed chamber and immediately won the attention of all. "Methinks you ought be stripped and examined for this cloven hoofprint you claim to know so intimately. I can swear before Almighty God that my worthy husband bears no such devilish mark."

"*You* lie!" Ropes of tangled hair flew about Tess's angry face as she whirled to meet her accuser's steady gaze. "I saw the mark myself, saw it last eve."

"In the lord's chamber you were, but with whom? Not my lord husband, I vow. Expecting some such treachery, he was with me in the room which was mine before our marriage."

While Tess's face went a clear, bright red, her eyes clouded with fury for the one who'd shamed her before so many. She'd honestly intended to stop spreading the lies, but everyone who'd heard them from another sought her out to hear details firsthand. Never before had her company been in such demand. Unable to resist the telling one more time, she'd assuredly not expected this awful confrontation. This was the end to her new popularity. This was death to any happiness she'd ever thought to win in her future. No one was so shunned as a spiteful liar revealed.

"As I've sworn for certain true that Earl Dare is unblemished, we can but assume you lied. With what other untruths have you sought to blacken his fair name?" Alyce knew the answer. Now these proven gossips would also. Hopefully they'd as quickly spread the tale of Tess's dishonesty and thus begin to undo the wrong. "Did you falsely claim to have been forced to your lord's bed when in truth he was called to banish you from its realm after you spread yourself atop it uninvited." Alyce was jubilant over having uprooted from Dare's path a whole bushel of weeds in one wide sweep.

Alyce's pleased smile intensified Tess's mindless rage. Lost in its haze, she clenched her hand tight about the silver hilt of a dagger concealed in the folds of her skirt. Leaping forward, raised blade gleaming with deadly intent, she near landed a fatal stab to the other woman's heart when a solid wall thrust itself between to absorb the blow and knock her aside in one smooth motion.

Alyce, momentarily transfixed by the vision of death descending, quickly recovered her wits. Sparing no thought to the woman lying limp on the floor and quickly surrounded by the drawn swords of many guardsmen, she instantly reached out for the man who'd plainly saved her life at the cost of his own safety.

The dagger, having struck between hauberk and thrust-back coif, had been driven to the hilt in Dare's right shoulder. Seeing green eyes agonized by the sight, he gritted his teeth against certain pain and pulled the blade free. He'd heard her emphatic defense of him and felt this discomfort a small burden to bear in return for the gift of her unstinting support. Jerking off the cloak still falling from broad shoulders, he wadded it tightly against the wound to staunch the flow while giving Alyce a reassuring smile. Leastwise the cloak's black hue would conceal from her worried gaze the all too likely profuse stream of blood.

"Come upstairs, so your wound may be treated in good time to achieve the greatest benefit." Alyce had learned from Cleva the need for haste in such matters and carefully wrapped an arm around his uninjured left side to urge him toward the stairway. It was like attempting to move a mountain. "Please, Dare, humor me in this."

"Aye, Dare, please do." Cleva's words were less plea than demand of one who'd known him as babe and child. A fast-thinking boy once turning the spitted venison over low-burning flame had dashed to call her from work with medicinal supplies in the alcove above.

Though he'd survived far worse and under infinitely more dangerous circumstances, Dare turned toward the steps both to appease Alyce's fears and yield to the older woman who'd been his loyal advocate for so long. Despite strength in no way lessened by the injury, Dare gladly kept an arm wrapped about his wife's tiny waist. He'd not been so robbed of his wits as to forfeit the excellent excuse to hold her near. Moreover, while peril loomed on every side, he was not so foolish as to ignore the need to treat an injury which, if allowed to go putrid, would threaten his sword arm. At the same time 'twas important he be seen to possess undiminished strength as, under the present menacing circumstances, any hint of weakness might undermine his position and encourage the defection of those he already feared wavering in their defense of Wythe.

Hearing noise at the door of the chamber facing the one wherein he stood, Thomas peeked out and frowned. Quickly shutting the door, he leaned back against it, striving, unsuccessfully, to appear unperturbed.

Lady Elinor was not easily fooled, and never by this open man whose normally ruddy face had gone a ghastly white. What further wickedness could have occurred to make Thomas so abruptly lose the blustery cheer in which he'd begun gently telling her of the charges laid against Dare and her son's response?

Thomas had arrived at the site of the confrontation in time to see arrows loosed and foes retreat and had returned to the castle with Dare. Determined to give Elinor the event's details before she heard a likely inaccurate version from thoughtlessly cruel lips, he'd immediately come to her. To soften the report, he'd begun with the reassurance that the only blows delivered were by Wythe's archers, and none amongst Wythe's own had yet been injured.

Elinor knew as well as any other the dangers of the path ahead—the blood, the deaths, the illnesses without which no siege could pass. She'd begun to steel herself to face the coming conflict only to now see in Thomas's open face that a more immediate threat had already arrived. Glaring at the impediment to her path, willing it to move aside, she steadfastly moved forward.

If possible, Thomas blanched a paler white. "I swear I rode to the castle with Dare, and he was in perfect health."

It was Dare; Dare had been hurt! Elinor threw the infinitesimal weight of her body against the bulk barring her way, and only the surprise of her action caused Thomas to lose his footing and stumble to the side. She pulled the door open wide enough for her slender form to slip out and across the negligible width of the corridor.

* * *

Though a fine sheen of sweat glittered on Dare's brow, no sound escaped his throat as a hastily summoned Fanhurst worked to ease the hauberk's great weight from his lord's body. The chore's accomplishment could only be attained were arms held uplifted, an action which sent searing pain through the punctured flesh of Dare's wide shoulder.

When Dare fell back against the bared white sheets of his bed, Alyce bit her lips to restrain the cry clawing at her throat as if her body suffered the same hurt. Leaning nearer, despite trembling hands, she laid a cool, damp cloth against the wound again profusely flowing with blood until Cleva gently brushed her fingers aside to peer at the area needful of attention. Alyce then exchanged the stained cloth for a fresh one to hold at the ready in one hand while threading the fingers of the other through thick black strands and smiling bravely into the pale blue gaze lifted to her.

It was the sight of a dark and copiously bleeding Dare spread atop a white background that met Elinor's eyes as she silently stepped into the room. "Will he be all right?"

Dare's eyes instantly turned to the woman hovering near the door as if fearful of an imminent need for its solid support. The husky whisper revealed far more emotion than anything his mother had ever said in his presence.

Without glancing up from her work, Cleva nodded, setting the watery daylight falling through the chamber's large window at play on the chessboard pattern of her coiled plaits.

"Aye, 'twas a clean cut and in an area where little damage was done. Course, much depends on how quickly we halt the flow of blood and if we can stave off festering in the flesh about the wound." She leaned to the side, plucked up a hastily prepared poultice from the wooden tray on a bedside chest. "This, with God's good will, should do what is needed, and by morn he'll be greatly improved."

Dare let thick lashes fall to shut out the troubling images raised by Cleva's talk of a demon's recovery resting on "God's good will." Two days, even one day past, feeling surrounded by other's fear and distrust, he'd have felt doomed by the words. Now, with Alyce's unconditional love and this day's unexpected support of leastways a portion of his men, he'd a bright nugget of hope more precious than gold. Hope for more than his recovery, hope for a shining future. He meant to polish that nugget to gleaming brilliance and guard it against the sly thieves of mistrust and suspicion.

"What do you intend for this evil potion?" Cleva's question echoed with unspoken disapproval. Above Dare's startled face she held an item found in the folds of the homespun shirt worn beneath mail and which, attention full on seeing the earl's wound treated, had earlier been set aside without closer examination.

Blue eyes narrowed on the vial of green liquid Hal had given him that morn. He answered Cleva's question with another. "Is it poisonous?"

Cleva grimly nodded. "The most deadly that I know."

"Then"—Dare responded to her initial question—"I intend to see it destroyed."

"The danger is such that 'tis best no time be lost." Cleva was not a one to be easily frightened, and by that fact her obvious apprehension bore greater weight. "As you must not rise again for at least the length of this day, pray give me leave to dispose of it now."

Once Dare had agreed, Cleva tucked the vial into the basket of unneeded supplies she meant to return to the alcove and attempted to see even the subject forgotten.

"This poultice, Alyce, will need to be changed and reapplied regularly throughout the night. You've learned how 'tis prepared, so to you I leave the task of rendering this service to your 'worthy husband.'" Cleva's mouth twitched with amusement.

Though neither Dare nor his mother noticed Cleva's wording, Alyce recognized the reference to the title she'd given Dare in her defense of him. Since Cleva had not been present to hear the words spoken, clearly the tale of Tess's dishonesty had begun spreading with all the haste Alyce had hoped it would. It could only have reached Cleva's ears during the brief span of time she'd been absent from this chamber to gather needed medicants. Worried spirit somewhat lightened, Alyce accepted Cleva's gentle teasing for what it was and with green eyes innocently widened, nodded a silent response.

Having done her best for the reluctant patient and sensing Lady Elinor's desire for private time with the couple, Cleva rose to her feet.

"I'll return—later—with a tisane which will ease the earl's pain and entice sleep's healing embrace."

That said, Cleva moved a stack of fresh cloths and jars filled with the poultice's ingredients into proper position before slipping quietly away. Meeting Thomas just outside the door, she adamantly shook her head. He was obviously intent on entering the chamber, but she took his arm in a remarkably inflexible grip and led the startled knight firmly away.

Inside the chamber Elinor hesitated under her son's understandably distrustful eyes while calling upon seemingly endless years of practice in performing whatever task was required of her—no matter how unpleasant or painful.

"I've waited a long time, too long no doubt, to speak with you of matters of such import that I can no longer hide them from the one whom they most concern."

Blue eyes seemed to instantly freeze into chips of ice. He was that one. Of that there could be no doubt. Only could he wonder if this was the moment for his mother to confess a liaison with Lucifer. The cynical jest did nothing to lighten his anxiety for the unknown.

Studying the dark and handsome man before her, Elinor thought it must be by the blood bond that she was able to read his thoughts, for she'd never really known this son. "In truth you *are* the son of a demon, but *not* the devil's spawn!" She choked on the words and halted, striving to regain some measure of composure.

Dare's expression gave nothing away, but blue eyes narrowed against the foreboding roused by this cryptic announcement. Alyce ached for the hidden pain in a frozen gaze but continued her ministrations without pause. For all the unswerving attention focused upon the older woman, Dare recognized in Alyce's actions further proof of a loyalty too strong to be shaken even by these fearsome words.

Under the force of a strong will, Elinor regained control of her voice, faint and raspy as it might be. "You are not Cyril's son, nor are you the first Rhodare's grandson."

Not by the slightest movement or faintest flicker of his gaze did Dare betray a reaction to words whose speaking had plainly required great courage. He could almost deem it a relief that he was not the child of the first, a man filled with hatred despite his cloak of piety. As for his link to the second, it could not be seriously denied. For as long as Dare could remember, he'd been proclaimed the man's mirror. A faint smile slowly warmed firm lips while blue eyes met deep brown directly.

Elinor again read her son's thoughts and spoke them aloud. "You are Rhodare's son." The confession came out on a sigh so heavily laden with guilt, it seemed impossible that the speaker had not been crushed by having carried the weight of such guilt alone for so many years. "'Twas my sin and I did all that I did to ensure you would not suffer more than I could prevent."

Dare's only response was a deepening smile while Alyce's tender heart wept for the woman's long-borne pain. Yet she thought, too, of the burden which Dare had carried the same length of time, and without foreintent softly spoke her thoughts aloud. "But he did suffer—suffer the hurt of your unremitting rejection even as he bore the awful cross of Earl Cyril's curse."

"'Twas a dreadful, horrible price we both paid, yet not so costly as that which would've been demanded had I done else." Brown eyes luminous with unshed tears begged acceptance as Elinor explained what surely they must see. "Had I intervened on Dare's behalf, Cyril would've seen him named far worse—bastard."

The moment his mother had confirmed the truth of his parentage, Dare had recognized the inherent dangers. Now in these plaintive words Alyce saw the meaning behind repeated warnings not to pry into Dare's past lest worse befall him. Had Cyril denied parentage, not only would Elinor have been abased, but Dare could've been reduced to mere peasant status left to labor in the fields, with neither position nor hope for the future.

"Why didn't he?" Knowing how deeply his "father" had hated him, Dare found it difficult to comprehend such restraint on the man's part. "Plainly he despised me enough to have taken delight in the doing."

"He took more delight in seeing me suffer for my wickedness. Day after day, year after year passed by while I was required to sit in the background and watch, unable to comfort you for his cruel slights, unable to deny awful tales and untrue rumors."

Alyce sensed that the depth of hurt Elinor had so long survived was threatening to overwhelm the slight woman's strength. She moved forward and urged the trembling woman onto a stool close to hand. Taking up the mug and pitcher of water provided for the wounded Dare, Alyce insisted Elinor take a cool, soothing drink to ease an aching throat. Yet once Elinor had complied with these considerate and welcome actions, determined to finish the task begun, she waved Alyce back to her husband's side.

"I would not have you believe ill of your true sire, Dare. Already you've spent a lifetime forced to accept the ill treatment of the other." Elinor directed a level gaze at her son. "Thus I mean to give you an accurate account of the actions which ended in our twisted paths." Revived by the caring actions of a fondly regarded daughter-in-law, and hands carefully folded in her lap, she was ready to continue.

"One spring day Earl Rhodare visited my family's castle, and my sire was honored by his presence. Throughout that summer he repeatedly returned and sought me out. My father was thrilled. I was flattered by the attentions of a noble so important and soon infatuated with the stunningly handsome, charming man who'd been widowed and saddened further by the loss of two sons. I wanted to comfort him." Elinor's gaze fell and she blushed like a naive maiden. "In truth, I wanted a great deal more.

"And when at the end of the summer the earl came for yet another visit, castle gossip had it that arrangements were being settled for me to be wed with Wythe. I was ecstatic!" Elinor's listeners got a glimpse of what she must then have been, for as she spoke, her features relaxed into the warmth of a girlish delight that made their abrupt hardening into a mask of ice the more painful to see. "Not until I, garbed in a fine new gown and highest hopes, entered the chapel to be betrothed did I learn that my spouse would not be the present earl but his sole heir—a bloodless monk taken unwillingly from the cloister to sire an heir."

Elinor's words were shards of ice, and as the last fell from her lips, she pressed them so tightly together they turned white. Releasing hands clenched together, she lifted the abandoned mug and took another sip of cool liquid before forcing herself to complete her confession. "And sire an heir Cyril did. But once Gabriel's conception was certain, he retreated entirely from my company. I cannot say I missed his stern gaze and constant censure of my 'wild ways,' his rebukes for laughing and enjoying the entertainments provided by minstrels and mummers and other such gaieties. Nay, I did not sorrow when my husband spent all day and most nights on his knees." A bittersweet smile fleetingly crossed Elinor's face. "I had, you see, the company of the one I loved."

Although blue eyes remained steady on the speaker, Dare's hand curled warmly about Alyce's trembling fingers. They were so very, very fortunate to have one another in a love no longer barred to them.

"The sin was mine and *not* my Demon Dare's." This was the point Elinor most emphatically wanted her son to fully believe. "'Tis important you understand. He did not seduce me. I went to him, crying out my heart's regret that I was wed not to him but to his son. My Dare held me in his arms and comforted me, though I sensed in him a despair as deep as my own. It was a sweet pain when he confessed that he'd fallen in love with me during that first spring visit and had unnecessarily returned to my home so many times solely for the sake of seeing me. He could've completed negotiations on the marriage contract much sooner had he not put off sealing the pact that would end with me bound to another."

Blinking the haze of memory from her eyes, Elinor straightened and continued in a tone devoid of emotion. "But in the end he knew it was Cyril's wife and Cyril's son who must be his first consideration—for the sake of Wythe and the continuation of his line. I found it difficult to accept, but he patiently explained that had we wed, any son I bore him could not inherit. Everything would go to Cyril, his eldest, and Cyril would've taken Wythe into the church's hold. And once more he repeated that it was to ensure the continuation of his line that he had been forced to see Cyril wed and the father of a son."

The tears of that moment fell again from desolate brown eyes. "Still, I could not let him go so easily, and though we neither of us intended to fall so far from grace . . ."

The smile Dare gave his mother was sad but utterly devoid of bitterness. "We've both paid penance enough for any wrong. 'Tis time now to find peace in the knowledge that my father has what he desired. His line will continue, and Wythe will pass down through his descendants." Dare's mouth went hard with determination. To see it so, he would defeat the threat beyond bailey walls and by right of force prove his innocence of the wrong to his king. Then he and Alyce would raise a family justly proud of their heritage.

"Mother, I pray you will forgive me of wrongly accusing you of so many ill deeds—leastways in my mind."

At the sound of this title falling from Dare's lips for the first time, the sun of Elinor's radiant smile defeated the falling rain of tears. She unhesitatingly arose and hastened toward the man sitting up with arms held out to her.

"Is Earl Dare all right?" The words rasped from a raw throat. "Tell me he is, please." Tess had passed hysteria to lie shaking with dry sobs atop the matted straw in a stoutly barred cell. "I did an awful wrong to attack Lady Alyce, but never, never did I mean to harm the earl."

Arlen's hands went white with the strength of their grip on iron bars. In her words he heard an unceasing obsession with the earl. It did nothing to lessen his growing anger with the dangerously foolish maid. Yet her ailment must be contagious, for how else could it be that someone so plainly unworthy, so clearly disloyal and—atop it all—easy with her virtue should have so long consumed such a large portion of his thoughts? Must be a serious ailment, for despite an aching hurt, he'd yet to be cured.

Light cast by the single torch Arlen had placed in a ring

driven into the stone wall was utterly inadequate to do battle with the dungeon's unrelieved blackness. Only a small, weak ring of illumination survived to struggle on against the darkness closing in all around, too weak to reveal the silent observer in a cage beyond its outer edge to the pair caught in their own troubles.

Tess rose from deep gray shadows to move toward the man whose hair seemed to burn in a bright reflection of his fierce condemnation. "I didn't set out to harm anyone. Truly I didn't." She wrapped her fingers imploringly about the strong hands of this unexpected visitor, desperately anxious not to lose her only opportunity to convince him of the honesty in her earnest claim. "I was forced to act, elsewise my own life would've been held forfeit."

Tess was speaking of the whole long list of misdeeds committed over the past fortnight and more, but Arlen heard her words only as a worthless excuse for the physical attack. His lips instantly curled down in disdain. Her tales had been full of blame placed upon others. Had lying become such a habit that now she thought it possible to invent a tale believable enough to explain away her crime? Worse yet, would this false story seek to further defile the earl's good name?

By Arlen's expression Tess realized her assertion had been misunderstood. "Nay, I do not seek to justify my wrong—the spite with which my downward path began. I accept the wrongs of my life for what they are. I must. I admit even that had I not first committed a spiteful deed, the man from Keniver would've been unable to trap me into his service. But, though Walter gave me the dagger to attack the earl, never would I'a done the wicked deed. I swear it upon the Holy Cross."

Surely not even Tess would risk damnation by placing such an oath atop a lie. In a plaintive silence which opened the potential for softening Arlen's heart, her tears fell again. Moreover, as he'd no good opinion of the man from Keniver and could well believe him capable of forcing a woman to his will, it was possible Walter shared a measure of the blame. He'd seen the burnished silver dagger recovered from the hall's floor rushes and knew it to be too rich a prize

304

for Tess to possess of her own. Still . . . Arlen's face tightened. No matter the source of the weapon, it had been wielded by Tess's hand. Here she swore herself innocent of the intent to attack their earl. That she hadn't purposefully done so in no way mitigated the wrong she had undeniably committed.

"Nay." His voice was rough, but not half so hard as it had earlier been. "You didn't mean to harm the earl, but you cannot claim you'd no intent to harm his lady. Not when all in the hall watched your assault."

Tess looked straight into Arlen's eyes and saw the end to her hope for his understanding. In an utterly flat tone she spoke what was certain to seal its doom. "In unreasoning anger I did the deed which no depth of regret can undo."

Arlen shook his head in rejection and made to pull away, but Tess clung desperately to his hands and with words wrenched from the depths of her soul, revived broken pleas.

"You've got to believe me, please. If won't no one else, I don't care. But you must! Please, Arlen, please!" Tess hadn't realized how important his opinion of her was until this moment when she'd glimpsed the certainty that the young guardsman, now suddenly a man in her eyes, would never think better of her than the worst. Her hands fell away and she sank into the straw again, shamefully burying her head into the dank mass while Arlen took the torch and strode relentlessly away.

19

Floating in the pleasant haze of early morn's fading dreams, Alyce snuggled closer to a source of warmth treasured even in sleep. As she became aware of lips brushing across the top of chestnut curls, a tiny smile curved soft lips which were promptly pressed against the firm flesh below.

"I'm pleased you've at last demonstrated a willingness to share your husband's bed."

Low words rumbling from the chest beneath Alyce's cheek brought wakefulness, memory—and anxiety. Seeking a reassuring view of this patient, remarkably alert for one who'd been dosed with Cleva's powerful sleeping tisane, a drowsy Alyce rose up on one elbow. Her effort was rewarded with the discovery that even at this hour of a day, Dare's white smile possessed the potency to make her feel weak.

"Apparently the secret to winning your favor was to be injured in your defense." Dare tugged a single bright lock to bring her mouth to his for a brief and unsatisfying kiss.

Despite their married state and shared hours of loveplay, Alyce blushed. 'Twas true, her previous night's action of slipping into bed with the wounded man sleeping too heavily to notice had been the first time she'd come to join him . . . but it would not be the last.

"I regret only that I was unable to provide the welcome you deserved for your good deed." Dare kissed her again and more thoroughly before restating his grievance with the potion which had held him so deep in its toils, he'd failed to be aware of her before waking this morn. "Must've been that foul stuff Cleva insisted I drink despite its nasty taste. I only agreed because she reminded me of my duty to regain my strength and defend my own."

To Alyce these words brought the intrusion of remembered danger hovering near to steal Dare from her arms, and they began to chill the warmth lent by his earlier gentle banter.

"Nay, sweeting." Recognizing in Alyce's small frown the path of her thoughts, with one finger Dare smoothed the furrow between delicate brows. "Don't permit our foes a victory in robbing us of the precious joy in our moments alone." Moving his hand to thread fingers through her hair, he urged her mouth to his.

Their passion, never far from the surface, quickly warmed to a sweet fire demanding more, and only with great reluctance did Alyce pull away. "We cannot endanger your wound's mending. Not even honeyed pleasures are worth that price."

"I've survived far worse," Dare whispered into the ear he nuzzled. "A fact you know is true by the scars you examined so closely during your intimate survey of my flesh."

Alyce's blush returned.

"There are ways and there are ways," Dare murmured, and unfazed by her attempted retreat, urged silken curves to conform to the hard angles of his body. "Our passion is certain to be the best healing potion ever brewed."

Alyce surrendered logical arguments unspoken to sink willingly into the flames of her fire-master's design, and together they built a pyre of consuming desire.

When burning coals had been again banked and Alyce lay replete in the circle of her lover's arms, from the corner of her eye she caught a glimpse of gleaming scarlet. Not moving from her welcome pillow of hard muscle and smooth skin, she reached out, just barely able to grasp what seemed a tiny flag caught between the edges of a bedside chest. Her continuous tugs were rewarded with a long, bright ribbon.

"Though this chamber is where your mother helped to remove my hair ribbons on the night of our wedding, I thought them stowed safe away in my wicker trunk the next morn." Alyce's puzzlement deepened to irritation with herself for being less than careful with an item of value, leastways of value to her.

"No doubt you did see your ribbons tucked into the wicker trunk." The low words rumbled from beneath her cheek. "That one is mine."

When Alyce lifted up to give Dare a quizzical look, the wealth of her hair fell like a cascade of fire to pool against his cool skin. "Yours?"

"Aye," Dare promptly agreed, blue eyes widened with an innocence unreal. "If only because I've had it so long."

"But where did you get it? Of more import, who gave it to you?" Alyce bit off the flow of questions she ought not to have asked and pushed back the wicked nibbles of a jealousy she'd sworn would never again be allowed to grow within her.

"A beautiful creature and one of such import that I've carried this, her favor, into battle with me since the day it became mine." Behind closed eyes and dreamy expression, Dare struggled to suppress a grin.

Alyce decided this keeping of oaths was far more difficult than she'd expected and firmly bit her lip to prevent the demand for a name and explanation—needlessly. He repented his jest and gave answers to questions unasked.

"That pretty trifle belonged to a small spitfire, rebellious enough to purchase what her father thought a foolish extravagance and careless enough to misplace it the very first day." Blue eyes glittered with teasing lights.

"Oh-h-h." Alyce sighed with deflating jealousy. She should've known by its match to the ones she'd thought left behind and by the remembered disappearance of a third so long past.

"You've had it all these years? And like the minstrels' sing, worn it as your ladylove's favor?" This confession was near as affecting as his first declaration of love. She held the scarlet cloth tenderly to her cheek and in quiet happiness nestled closer against his side.

An unwelcome knock shattered the glowing aura of their contentment, forcing upon them the unpleasant realities of a new day begun, one fraught with far more difficulties than its warm beginning could've foretold.

"Come." Dare barked the command once Alyce was buried beneath bedclothes she'd modestly drawn about herself.

The terse invitation was immediately accepted. Bushy brows flew up as Thomas stepped into the chamber to discover an embarrassed damsel. Plainly passion-disheveled, the alluring Lady Alyce lay beside her wounded husband with covers clutched tight to gently rounded chin.

"My apologies for interrupting," a blustering Thomas hastily began. "I would not intrude on your . . ." Flustered by his own ill-chosen words, he awkwardly rephrased the explanation. "I mean, injured and all, for any lesser reason I'd not have come."

Thick black lashes were half-lowered over eyes gone to blue ice against the almost certain news about to be given. "Then waste no more time in telling that reason."

Irritated with himself, the circumstances, and— illogically—his friend, Thomas abruptly did as commanded. "The trebuchets and battering ram you warned us were concealed but waiting are rolling from the eastern forest toward bailey walls."

This confirmation of predictions proven true summoned from Dare a slight and bitter smile. Abruptly sitting up, oblivious to his own wince, he threw covers from himself to pile in deeper concealment upon his bride.

"I'll join you in the courtyard as soon as I am dressed." Dare thrust open the lid of the bedside chest, pulled out the first garment that came to hand, and jerked on the black chausses. "I assume the worthy Ulger already has ordered all guardsmen to their posts?" The words were muffled by folds of homespun as Dare thrust his dark head through the tunic's neck-slit. Wasting no motion, Dare pulled lacing tight and then, teeth gritted against the discomfort to his shoulder, instantly began forcing the close-fitting mail shirt over the top.

Though Dare's statement that they'd meet in the courtyard had been an obvious request that he leave, Thomas remained. While the hauberk was tugged into place, he gave another piece of information, information that at the outset of the previous day Dare had commanded be earnestly sought. "Of our weasel there's been no sight, though many have searched."

The gazes of the two men met in a perfect understanding that Alyce, buried in layers of cloth, wished she shared.

Dare retrieved the belt and empty scabbard neatly laid to one side. "Pray God Fanhurst has—"

Thomas responded to the words he'd interrupted. "Your squire awaits your coming with polished sword and saddled steed." Though the stirring castle was promptly moving into frenzied action, he had lingered this long, intent upon winning Dare's agreement that their plan should immediately be put into motion.

"Under the pressure of honest need the boy is proving himself more capable than ever he did during days of simple training." This earned praise Dare intended to later give the one who deserved it, but he now paused in his swift preparations to send his friend a steady look.

Knowing the unspoken purpose behind his impatient friend's persistence in remaining here, Dare offered him the consolation of an action he could take, though only a limited portion of the whole Thomas was clearly anxious to begin. "Go to the point we agreed upon, but wait until you hear the pounding of the battering rams. 'Tis a sound we both know can be heard from great distances."

Thick brows scowling under the effort required to restrain his impatience, Thomas nodded, but an indistinct grumble trailed behind his departing figure.

Dare's fond gaze followed the retreating man. "Go with care." The call won from Thomas a quick glance over his shoulder and an exasperated grimace that passed for an answering smile.

By their almost wordless exchange, Alyce realized that between the two men lay a plan to meet approaching danger, and the mere fact that one existed was a measure of comfort in itself. She knew little of battle or its strategies but trusted Dare implicitly. Yet with Thomas gone and Dare's back turned to her as he bent to lift a folded surcoat, Alyce assumed she'd been forgot in the heat of his preparations for an immediate departure. And rightly so—except it seemed he'd also forgotten one additional item of defense. Anxious to see it given him, she rose from the bed without thought of her nudity.

"Dare, pray accept my favor to guard you in battle." She formally offered the token he claimed to have always carried in the past with hope that it would have greater power for having been purposefully given.

Startled by the sound of her voice so close behind his back, Dare spun about. Black brows arched while blue eyes went instantly to flame. Here was a view able to inspire him to incredible deeds for the sake of seeing it would always be safely his, a view amazing for the unexpected boldness of one ever overly modest.

Suddenly aware of her lack, Alyce could feel the heat of a blush rising but restrained her immediate urge to dive back into the bed's mounded covers. They belonged to each other now, and she'd no reason to retreat from the giving of her token. With Dare standing motionless before her, this was the time to see the deed complete. Around his mighty arm Alyce slipped the ribbon that had been in her hand since she pulled it from the trunk, and firmly tied it there in a brave bow.

"Return safely to me," she whispered, rising on her toes to offer a kiss of good fortune. He accepted the kiss most willingly, but when the too-tempting body leaned into him, stepped back.

"You would tempt me to stay when my duty firmly lies elsewhere." After first allowing eyes of blue flame to sweep over her one more time, he snatched his second cloak from a peg on the wall nearby and swirled it about her shoulders to cover her from throat to toes. "Now that there's hope for a moment of rational speech, I thank you for a favor knowingly given at last." He lifted the scarlet-tied arm (he had indeed carried this ribbon with him to every battle fought—

but tucked secretly inside his tunic) and smiled from the ribbon's neat bow into green eyes.

"Don't worry for me. Even should my skill as a warrior fail, this is certain to bring me back to you all of a piece." Though he'd the experience of many battles, this would be the first he'd ever fought wherein something, *someone,* he cared for was at stake. He'd never had reason to feel his own life was of enough value to take care in preserving it. But for Alyce's safety, for her happiness now, he would. He ran a finger tenderly over a cheek gone pale with the worry he'd meant to lessen. To distract in some small degree, he began to speak of an order to be given and the management its fulfillment would require. "You'll be too busy to think of me once the order I intend to issue is heard."

"Nothing could achieve that," Alyce earnestly denied, meeting blue eyes steadily although she then waited patiently for the explanation he was certain to give.

"Against the unlikely possibility of our foes breaching the outer wall, as I leave for the battlements, I mean to send out a message summoning villagers to retreat into our castle's safety, carrying with them all the supplies they can gather with haste."

Alyce slowly nodded. It was a wise precaution against a danger she refused to weaken her courage by pondering at length.

Dare's first concern was ever and always Alyce. And he felt easier in leaving her surrounded by the many, as she soon would be. But, too, Thomas's report that Walter had not been inside the castle since the conflict broke into the open had been welcome. Believing the man likely too craven to return to a site of battle, he foresaw no danger to Alyce on Walter's account. Yet . . . one more precaution Dare would take.

"It is my wish that no one descend to the dungeons, not even to use its cool emptiness for the storing of all that the villagers will bring with them to the castle."

Lest he should be weakened by concern for her, Alyce nodded bravely and sought to hide her own anxieties as with one more quick kiss he left her alone in the chamber whose size seemed to double once drained of his overwhelming presence. Intent on following a proven path for waylaying fear, she would seek tasks to busy hands and mind. Toward this end she gathered up her garments and hastened to don them. Her efforts, as well as those of both Elinor and Cleva, would be needed to direct the surely massive task of preparing their castle to meet the reality of a siege.

Just beyond the rim of a light ascending the stairway between dungeon and the level above, Walter patiently waited. Once total darkness reigned again, he spoke.

"Now you've your meal, such as it is. And doubtless the ever conscientious Cleva has done well by you despite the demesne's pandemonium." Neither of the two he'd come to free responded, but he hadn't expected that they would. "Mayhap your captors have failed to make you aware that the attack upon Wythe has begun in earnest and all who do not fight have retreated to the castle's questionable safety. But worry not, friends, I've come to rescue you." Walter took twisted delight in naming these two doomed minions "friends."

"Tess, I learned from our wonderfully effective gossip vine that you leastways attempted to do as I commanded, and for that I will free and lead you to the safety I promised for a completed deed." In truth, Walter knew very little about what had happened—only what had been repeated by a peddler passing through the forest and erring in stumbling upon the hidden camp. He'd been stopped by Lord Peter—in the end permanently. The poor man, trembling with fear, had known naught but the bare facts of a failed attack on Wythe's earl made by a crazed female servant.

"Do we leave now?" Roger's brusque voice showed no hint of anticipation, a fact which made Walter uneasy. But, Walter comforted himself, 'twas most likely that the prisoner merely found his good fortune difficult to believe.

"As soon as you've done the task for which I paid you." The soft words had the texture of an eminently reasonable bargain. "And, too, by that deed you'll earn the safe haven you were promised."

Unseen in the darkness, Roger frowned. This slimy little toad, then, was the provider of gold to see Lady Alyce abducted. Roger was not surprised—but Walter would've been had he known that his "friend" was aware of precisely what "safe haven" awaited, the same that had been provided Darwyn. Had Walter the ability to see in the dark, he might have been frightened into leaving where he was this man whose frown had become a ferocious glare.

Walter was satisfied with plans that had thus far gone smoothly—save for Tess's failure, and he'd a contingent plan to correct that error. Unaware of the other man's thoughts, he continued, "I'll free you before finding some method to lead our prey into your trap." The sound of a key being fitted into a lock was unnaturally loud in the vast chamber; before the final click, he added a warning. "Lest temptation should strike and you think to take my key and escape alone, I've people waiting on the postern's far side. If you appear without me, you'll die immediately." The door clanged open.

After hours of work, Alyce at last took a brief moment to lean against the guardroom wall. Knowing to do so would sink her into a useless gloom, she tried not to think of the perils presently being faced by the chamber's usual inhabitants, all manning the battlements in fierce defense. Rather she sought to draw strength from the relative peace of the chamber, which, though emptied of men, was crowded with an odd assortment of inanimate objects deserted by the many who on her command had carried them here. She drew what seemed her first calm breath since leaving the bedchamber that morn. The courtyard, hall, and kitchen were crowded either with frightened villagers huddled in tense clumps or with scores of castle-serfs working in remarkable concert with one another to meet a true emergency.

Deeming it the wisest course to ensure that Dare's command was obeyed, Alyce had taken on the responsibility for overseeing the stowing of bushels, boxes, and baskets of foodstuffs brought from beyond inner bailey walls. These were to be hoarded against the possibility of a lengthy siege of the castle proper, one wherein foes unable to take it by force simply waited for hunger to drive its inhabitants out.

Though a difficult challenge, she'd found storage sites for all that was brought. There were now stacks in every available space, from lord's chamber to scullery basin—but not in the dungeons despite the many despairing glances cast her way in silent concern that she'd gone witless.

All this mad activity had leastways the good result of keeping her worried mind from the battle raging not so far distant that any could fail to hear the intermittent crash of battering rams impacting against wooden gate, iron portcullis, and stone walls.

"Alyce."

The quiet, familiar call won her immediate attention. Turning toward the gloomy stairwell, Alyce realized she'd not seen Walter since the evening after her wedding. Nor, truth be known, had she missed him. Likely he'd been off sulking with displeasure over her choice to wed Dare.

"We must talk of private matters." Walter's eyes darted from the shadows behind one stack of baskets into the narrowing between two others, seeking both a reassurance that they were alone and an excuse to draw her into the stairwell.

"Aye," Alyce promptly agreed. Though Walter's voice held an unusual strained excitement, still she was certain he meant only to tell her how wrong she'd been to wed Dare. He'd surely no other private matter to discuss with her. What with all the infinitely more important responsibilities waiting on every side, she would've avoided this demand for her time had it not been for an issue she wanted settled with him.

"What possessed you to lend Tess your dagger?" The query was a censure of itself. "Do you realize what wickedness she used it to perform? She stabbed Dare! That it was me she meant to harm is no excuse for her dreadful deed."

Excuse? Walter blinked in amazement at the foolish statement. Of course it was no excuse. And if Tess had succeeded in what she'd first intended, it would've been a tragedy! This news that, rather than Dare, Tess had attempted to kill Alyce insured that he'd suffer no regret for the end awaiting Tess in the forest.

Walter's eyes glittered with strange lights that made Alyce

uncomfortable and brought to mind Dare's several attempts to convince her of the danger in this friend. Had she been wrong in defending Walter?

"Lend it to Tess?" Walter saw the flicker of suspicion pass over Alyce's face, the opposite of the trust he needed to establish to see his goal won. He deliberately softened his voice into the tones of one wrongly affronted. "Why would I lend it to her?" He had not "lent" it to her, he'd forced her to accept both it and his command—which she had more than failed to carry out. No matter, he'd never relied upon a single method to see so important a task done.

As Alyce started to seek an explanation for how the dagger had come to be in Tess's hand, approaching voices threatened to end this conversation best held private. She frowned in vexation while Walter restrained a pleased smile.

"Come, I'll tell you how it happened that Tess had what was mine." Walter motioned Alyce to follow him into the shadowed stairwell.

The darkness beyond Walter was in itself enough to halt Alyce. Except—the notion of allowing foolish fears to keep her from any deed while not so far away, others courageously fought very real dangers was unpalatable. Therefore, despite Dare's command that no one enter the dungeon (which she'd spent a good portion of the day upholding), Alyce moved toward the beckoning Walter. She justified her action by telling herself they would not actually descend to the dungeon but merely a few steps down to where they'd not be heard. Yet no sooner had she gritted her teeth against illogical dread and taken those few steps into a fearsome darkness even her worst nightmares could not match than an unseen trap closed relentlessly about her. Her short scream was useless, muffled by the depth and width of stone walls. Moreover, 'twas certain to be lost amidst the dull roar of so many people and so many activities. Fine and accurate reasons to keep her silence, but of little power against the terrors of childhood increased a hundredfold. While unseen hands replaced the tight bonds of human arms with the equally tight restraints of stout ropes, Alyce clenched her teeth against irrational cries clawing at her throat.

"Quiet, Alyce, even your loudest screams would be useless. Doubtless everyone on Wythe knows Tess is caged here, and were some faint echo of your cries heard, they'd think it her."

Seeking a weapon to wield against the overwhelming, unreasoning horror of the darkness pressing down on her like a living monster, Alyce tightly closed her eyes and forced herself to concentrate on anything but the source of her fears. She would learn the truth of Walter's nature and the purpose behind his action. "Dare was right in saying you've been behind all these gruesome deeds. It was you, Walter, but why?"

"You give me too much credit, my lady." Speakers unseen, the shading of a voice said as much as the words. Walter's self-satisfaction fair glowed. "I couldn't have done it on my own, but yes, I am pleased to say I've laid the path which will lead to my cohorts' success."

"In my father's false charges?" Bitterness burned in Alyce's words. "In the same charges laid against Dare?" Fear for the insubstantial was rapidly fading into nothing beneath a rising anger with the one who had brought very real peril down upon those she loved.

"I regret Halbert's difficulties, but these deeds were the price for what I sought, and worth the reward." Walter's verbal shrug could be heard as clearly as the pleasure behind his lack of regret for Dare's woe.

"What reward could possibly justify such awful deeds?" Alyce hotly demanded of the man safe somewhere in the black void while both her father and Dare were in grave danger.

"Why, you, of course."

Stunned silence greeted his frighteningly calm statement. He was mad. Unexpectedly aided by the darkness that hides deceitful faces, Alyce suddenly knew it was true. Obsessed and able to commit any heinous act to claim its focus, Walter was completely and utterly mad.

Glad, for a change, of his small size, James huddled behind an apparently discarded but in truth strategically placed crate in one corner of the well house. Long and patient waiting was at last rewarded as the door creaked open and a hooded figure slipped inside. Amidst the many rushing to and fro and in the courtyard, it was unlikely that the man had been noticed at all—the reason James had been posted to watch from within.

Gratified by this further success, Walter pulled a small vial out from behind his belt. He'd been pleased to find it just where he'd left it. Though he hadn't been seriously concerned that Hal would have the temerity to again enter where he'd been earlier rebuked for going, let alone to take something not his, Walter hadn't completely discounted the possibility that his curious nephew might have disturbed it. And had the boy done so, the deadly price to be paid would've been only just.

Walter's vivid memory wrinkled his nose even before he'd pulled the stopper out—for no reason. The noxious odor was gone. Frowning, he held it up against the brightest area of the gloomy structure. He saw no difference, except mayhap . . . Nay, it was the same. The potency of the odor, it would seem, lessened with time. Hopefully the deadly properties of the poison did not. Couldn't be when Lord Peter had said only that it must be done and disposed of before the siege was done and Sir Lester entered.

Holding his hand over the center of the well, he tilted the vial and watched the poison slowly pour out. Motionless, he waited for it to fall down, down, down until at last rose the tiniest sound of a ripple as that small amount of liquid joined the vaster quantities at the bottom. He smiled. So little to foul so much. Dare would die and he would be free to claim Alyce for himself. That everyone else would also die mattered little, although Walter did host a flicker of regret that Sybillene would be among the dead.

He pulled the bottle back and started to replace the stopper, then thought better of it. Best it all go to the same end. Tossing both vial and cork into the well, with twisted smile he turned to depart but froze.

"Parsley water!" A laughing James stood with door latch in hand. "You put parsley water in the well!" Nearly hysterical with glee for the fine jest in which he'd had a part, the boy threw open the door and dashed into the crowded courtyard. James hadn't meant to give himself away, but hadn't been able to resist the joy of gloating. By the time a frowning Hal caught up with him, James felt sheepish. And with a sense of their serious duty, they resolved to do as directed at the first opportunity. As soon as any member of the guard returned from the battlements, they'd report the "weasel's" presence immediately.

Pressing back into the shadows on the door's far side after the boy disappeared, Walter was furious! Plainly his wretched nephew had enlisted this boy in what they must have thought a fine trick. Certain that the boy would spread the tale far and wide and with all possible haste, Walter recognized the necessity for retreating immediately. Head down to shield his face in the hood's shadows, he moved through the crowd of idle villagers and toiling house-serfs to enter an equally crowded castle.

His earlier satisfaction with the smooth progress of his plans had soured with the acid of failure in his most important goal. Two attempts to see Dare dead. Two failures. There would not be a third, because, in the time it took to walk from well house to here, he'd decided he would see it done by his own hand. Though Walter took pride in being a man able to win by might of mind rather than by physical strength, he would take pleasure in killing Dare himself. The murders that had been done before, even those he'd planned, had been performed by others. And as his cohort was ever insistent on destroying evidence, even human traces of involvement, Walter would gladly leave to him the eradicating of Roger and Tess.

Intent on his goal, Walter had passed through the kitchen and entered the guardroom before the unexpected happened.

"Walter, stop and talk to me. Where have you been? Everyone's been looking for you." Golden coils of hair slightly askew were proof that she'd actually been urged into doing something useful. "They asked at least six times yesterday didn't I know where you were. Made me look a fool, and I don't like it."

Walter turned toward his petulant sister with a dangerous fire in his eyes. He'd no reason to hide it as he knew how unlikely it was that she would recognize anything less than admiration or indulgence. "Tell them you don't know or tell them I've gone." He turned and disappeared into the descending stairway's black shadows.

"Gone?" An incredulous Sybillene simply plucked the nearest torch from its ring and followed. "You can't go anywhere, fool. We're under siege!"

Walter stopped on the bottom step and waited until Sybillene joined him there. "You, my good sister, are under siege." With this pithy announcement he turned, crossed to Tess's cage, and put the key inside its lock. "I am not."

A stunned Sybillene hovered, unsure what she ought do.

"He and the prisoners he's released are taking me out the postern door to the camp of those who've laid siege to the castle." Green eyes grown accustomed to complete darkness blinked against the hurtful light in her stepmother's hand.

"You can't do that, Walter," Sybillene announced. "I won't permit it!"

Walter laughed. How like his sister to think that whatever she demanded would instantly be granted—particularly by her younger brother. He turned back to the task, and as the door swung wide, Tess hurried out.

"Roger, I think an empty cell is a dangerous thing." Walter's glittering eyes met Roger's carefully blanked expression. "Don't you?" The last two words were heavy with a meaning Roger could not fail to understand. Walter couldn't have his sister wandering about babbling her irritation with him, betraying his presence.

Sybillene squeaked as Roger started toward her. "Stay away from me, you . . . you . . ." She ineffectually swung the flaming brand at the advancing danger. With what she deemed a disgustingly slight effort, he snatched the torch from her hold with one hand and swept her off the ground with his other arm.

"Walter! You can't do this, Walter! I'm your sister!" Her alternately pleading and scolding words did nothing to waylay her brother's intent. She was rudely deposited on a smelly pile of straw and locked, actually locked, inside a barred cell. "I don't know you anymore, Walter!"

"Sybillene"—Walter met her gaze directly—"you never did. You're so caught in yourself, you've never known anyone else." The statement had leastways the praiseworthy effect of halting her voice.

"So you are the one 'our' Walter would lie, cheat, and likely even kill for?"

Alyce restrained an urge to cringe back from this man of an age with Dare but mountainous and with strange yellow eyes that peered too closely. He'd been waiting for their small party on the outside of the postern door and its long, narrow passage through the depth of the stone wall at Castle Wythe's lowest level. She'd an instinctive distrust of him and knew even if she'd met him in pleasant surroundings, she wouldn't be comfortable in his presence.

"For me the price is higher." He unsheathed his sword and held it idly in one hand. "Walter whetted my appetite with Keniver, but Wythe is the plum. I wouldn't have come near for less." Even through the gloom of yet another dreary day heavy with threatened rain, a green gaze glowed with the anger lit by his stated intent to seize lands belonging to father and husband. In them he glimpsed what Walter so prized.

"Lord Peter." Roger called out to the man Walter had claimed would be waiting to conduct them to the promised safe harbor. He was irritated that the original plan had been driven further awry by both Walter's subtle evasion of oblique and then direct requests for their guide's name, and his unexpected decision to delay his own departure. "We three are guests Walter prays you will accept until he can join us." But for the need to secure confirmation of a suspected identity, the statement had no reason for being.

"Walter told you who would be meeting you?" Displeasure honed the question to a sharpness equal to the blade in its speaker's hand. Throughout the scheme to take Wythe, he had remained always in the background—a defense, one of many, against the dangerous possibility of future charges being laid. Though these "guests" would soon be incapable of providing hazardous evidence, he was disgusted with Walter. Not because the fool had betrayed an oath given (what else could be expected of a man paid for such services in other matters?), but that the man who prided himself on his sharp wits had proven so dull-minded after all. Walter should've known what retribution he courted. Moreover, Walter should be here now. That the man was not increased an already perilous ire.

Yellow eyes flickered over the young countess. Walter would pay for his wrong. 'Twas a price already added to Walter's ledger, yet the prospect of taking it had grown sweeter and would render more satisfaction for the pain it would cause the other man.

Beneath the piercing gaze, Alyce lifted her chin and stood as bravely as one whose arms were tightly bound could do. Her courage won from the man an even more frighteningly intense smile.

"Lead the way, Countess." A gleaming sword was waved toward a seldom-used and barely visible track through grasses gone brown but dense-grown and wind-tangled. "Then, young woman"—he nodded at Tess—"you follow her while your male friend comes next. I with my sword will guard the back of our small troop."

Without hesitation Alyce began carefully moving down the uneven path, vividly aware as each of the others fell in behind. Soon, pray God very soon . . .

Pleased that his command had been complied with so readily, the journey's director did as he'd said he would and took the last position in the line, naked blade in hand. Though Walter delighted in his tongue's power, in the fear which it wielded, he was far too fastidious to actually perform dastardly deeds threatened. Thus the chore of following along behind and clearing his evidence-strewn path was left to another. A soundless snarl accompanied the vision of a disturbing analogy: a king mucking out the stable left filthy by his own serf.

Once the three in front had settled into a monotonous pace, with two hands, the last raised a sword high above his head in preparation for a single, deadly blow.

Roger whirled, joined fists smashing solidly against the swordsman's stomach. The impact's force doubled the groaning man over, facilitating the crashing blow brought down atop his head.

When attacker turned victim at last regained his breath

and rolled to his back, he found himself lying supine beneath the point of his own sword.

"I see Walter and you had plans for me." Roger grinned in the euphoria of success achieved. Yet he knew the danger in overconfidence and wouldn't make that mistake. "Alas, the earl and I have more important plans for you." Never shifting his steady gaze from the captive, he spoke to the two women. "Fair ladies, meet here the illustrious Lord Peter Rievaux, 'nephew' to the famed Bishop of Winchester." The disdain at the core of this introduction bespoke an opinion of the man more ill than good.

Alyce had watched the scene playing out before her with satisfaction and now sent the man a look as long and considering as the one to which he'd subjected her. This, then, was the greedy man at the root of all the wickedness that had befallen those she loved, the man responsible for encouraging Walter's demented schemes. Lying like a fallen, decaying tree trunk, he was as pitiful as he was frightening. As he was captured by the trap Dare had laid and soon to be caged, Alyce could now but pray that Dare would also be able to muzzle the ravenous beast.

"Tess," Roger called, never shifting his attention from the wily foe, "come and take the dagger provided me against a thankfully unmet danger and cut our captive's stout cloak into sturdy strips even before you free Lady Alyce. Leastways, I doubt she'll mind the delay while we see us all safe." He cast an inquiring look to the countess, a flicker of misdoubt in his gaze. She immediately put his unease to rest by nod of bright head and smile of agreement with the wiser course.

As Tess crouched at his side to slip free the small blade hidden in his boot since the day of the earl's interrogation, Roger mentally reviewed the plan then made . . . and the changes he'd been forced by unfolding circumstances to make. Once Roger had warned the earl of Walter's intent to secure the postern key and the offer to set him free (with the purpose, they'd agreed, of seeing another partner in the failed scheme dead), the earl had recognized a barely possible opportunity. He'd offered Roger the chance to redeem his honor by allowing Walter to free and lead him to a forest camp almost certainly somewhere on the river's far side. Believing that the bishop's nephew would be hiding there, Earl Dare had bargained with Roger to see the man taken captive and brought to him. Lord Peter as captive would be the most powerful weapon the earl could hope to possess.

Roger's narrow smile was filled with triumph. With the wanted man in his hands, he had now the opportunity not only to restore his honor but to win back the position he'd lost in his incredibly foolish abduction of Lady Alyce. In the next instant the smile went brittle under the uncomfortable acknowledgment of changes for which his lord might blame him.

During the hour of planning, neither Roger nor his earl had foreseen either the imprisoning of Tess or Walter's scheme to see Lady Alyce taken again. As a prisoner unable to seek counsel from Earl Dare, Roger had been forced to make his own alterations to the plan. First, by including Tess, whose claims of abuse at Walter's hands he had overheard spoken to the red-haired guardsman. And second, by complying with Walter's command and again seizing Lady Alyce. But in doing the latter, leastwise he'd lessened the wrong insofar as he was able. Once Walter had departed on some unknown errand, leaving the three of them alone in the dungeon, he'd told Lady Alyce of the earl's plan to see a villain captured, and followed that news with assurances of loyalty and intent to set her free from both him and Tess.

Alyce stood motionless between unyielding stone wall and swift-flowing river while Tess again approached her with a dagger in her hands. The other woman had assured her of regret and sorrow for the assault she'd made, and piteously had she begged forgiveness—but Alyce remembered too many pretty lies to easily believe these words more sincerely meant. Particularly as they, too, would win a prize Tess sought, if only a way back into the castle's company.

Beneath the well-honed blade, ropes snapped apart and fell from Alyce's freed wrists. Rubbing them, Alyce turned to watch as Roger efficiently finished trussing their captive both wrists and ankles.

That done and not knowing what further duty awaited, Tess spoke. "What next do we do?"

"We wait safe here between outside wall and river." Roger lifted the huge man's feet and with great effort dragged him over ground still soft from the previous day's drenching rains to lie with face brushing cold stone blocks. "While the garrison is fully occupied in meeting the threat in front, 'tis unlikely this rear position, safely guarded by a deep and swift-flowing river, will be closely watched."

Settling down near and yet a safe distance from his captive, Roger laid the flat of the sword blade across updrawn knees. "Aye, we wait until Walter has come out and the postern path is clear. Only then will I reenter the castle to await the ending of day, and with it the battle's pause. Then comes the right moment to gift Earl Dare with our prize."

Alyce silently studied the guardsman plainly prepared to patiently await a moment he deemed right. That patient she was not, nor were her goals the same. Shifting her attention to the path ahead, she narrowed emerald eyes on a barely visible sight some distance farther down the path. She turned with sudden decision to face Roger.

"I see the boat that brought your prize across the river and have no doubt but that his steed will be waiting in shadows on the far side. As I've a mission to see done, I'll take my leave of you now."

Roger scowled. "You must not! The river is not so easily crossed." Asides, all about were foes—never mind that he'd just claimed them surely occupied by deeds of war. She might encounter men who would not know, or even care, that a countess was she and above their reach. She might be assaulted! "You must not go!" This rejection of the deed was even more vehement. Were anything to happen to her, the success of his atonement would be in serious jeopardy!

"I am your countess and you've no right to gainsay me." Despite face dirt-streaked and hair mussed during her capture and then her escape, Alyce's proud and courageous bearing underscored the verity of her claim. Yet she softened it with words half explanation and half plea for understanding. "My husband is in danger, and though, while trapped inside a castle under siege, there was little I could do, now I am free and will do what I can."

Roger's admiration was unbounded, but he offered one last argument. "It is too dangerous for you to go alone."

"She need not." Tess spoke directly to Roger, although her pale brown gaze was steady upon Alyce. "I've experience in crossing the river alone and will aid her in going wherever it is that help for the earl awaits."

The statement was made with a firmness daring anyone to deny her the right. As Tess moved to her side, Alyce nodded acceptance of the offer. Alyce would risk any danger to win the goal of Dare's success and safety.

Faced with two determined women, Roger shrugged in defeat. What choice had he?

20

It was awful, Dare, awful!"

Blue frost eyes rested heavily on hands clutching a mail-covered arm to hold him here in the entrance tunnel's shadows while Sybillene's complaints went on and on like the ceaseless squawking of an enraged hen.

After nightfall brought its temporary cessation of hostilities, Dare had remained at the site of the day's hard-fought battle to inspect the damage by torchlight. He was thankful for the few injuries sustained by the men of his garrison and, too, that the bailey wall had held firm against the battering ram's relentless pounding. However, what was visible from inside was not a reliable indicator of how it truly had fared.

What Dare had seen with unpleasant clarity was the destruction wrought by the fearsome trebuchet's assault. Though the war machine's potential range was long and normally reserved for attacks upon the castle proper, in the evacuated village Dare had found the wreckage of cottages crushed by huge stones launched over the outer wall. 'Twas a bleak demonstration of what would follow were that barrier breached and Sir Lester able to advance close enough to hurl missiles directly upon the castle and into a courtyard filled with many. During his years of experience both in attack and defense Dare had seen the ravages of such constant barrages: shattered walls and people horribly maimed or killed.

Returning alone from this day of fierce fighting—in a dark mood, grimy, tired, and previously injured shoulder throbbing—Dare had no shred of patience to spare for Sybillene's petty woes. He clenched his lips together to restrain a barbed order for her to desist and depart from him, not because he thought her deserving of tact but because such an action would doubtless double her complaints.

Dare shifted his gaze to peer into the crowded, well-lit great hall beyond this gloomy tunnel where he'd been trapped by a waiting Sybillene. Where was Alyce? Alyce was a longed-for comfort, a strength-restoring gift—and Alyce was nowhere to be seen. Black brows frowned. Anxious to go in search of Alyce, a warm bath, and food, he made to shake Sybillene's hold from him.

"'Twas awful!" It was Sybillene who shook Dare's arm in her demand for the return of his attention. "Walter is no longer a brother to me. I swear it. No true brother would lock his own sister in a dungeon!"

Sybillene's mention of the missing Walter succeeded in catching Dare's attention where piteous words had not.

"And he did what I told him he could not do!" Honest indignation burned through the woeful veneer of one grievously wronged.

Dare's mild disgust with Sybillene's absurd expectation of obedience from her brother, her son, or any other male who came too near was near lost in an intense desire to know more of Walter's whereabouts.

"He captured Alyce, Dare. Walter captured and sent her away even though I told him he must not!"

Dare went to pure stone save for the glitter of narrowed eyes compelling enough to force more from Sybillene.

"Walter released your two prisoners from dungeon cells, and they took Alyce with them through the postern door."

The awful fact that Alyce had been taken from him struck Dare with more pain than any slashing sword could ever do. Through a postern door and out from a castle under siege, she'd been taken where he could not follow. He couldn't depart by the same route when his foes surely watched from beyond to welcome those fool enough to risk a force waiting and prepared to defeat opponents able only to exit the low-roofed, narrow postern hunched over and one by one. Dare wanted to scream with frustrated rage and crush the castle's walls himself to retrieve Alyce.

Truly frightened by the embodiment of fury which Dare had become, Sybillene hastened to give what she thought would be a reassurance. "Alyce is in no danger. Walter said someone was waiting for them, someone who would take them to a safe haven."

Was Walter so demented as to wish Alyce dead rather than wed to another man? He felt as if a vise had been wrapped so tightly about his heart that it would soon disintegrate, and a roar of anguish forced itself up from Dare's depths. He knew too well what hidden meaning had lain behind the term "safe haven" for Darwyn, the same end intended for Roger. Roger . . . A small hope flickered in the darkness of despair. If Roger succeeded in the plan they'd agreed upon, surely the man would see to Alyce's safe return, surely he would. But what were the chances for Roger's success? Slim at best.

"What is it, my lord? What dreadful thing made you cry out?" Sir Ulger had rushed to the tunnel's opening while in the hall behind a crowd pressed close.

An impassive Dare, again tightly armored in ice, turned to respond. "Walter has captured Alyce and taken her out through the postern door."

"What— How do we know Walter did the deed? Or for certain that 'twas done?" Ulger asked. His voice, though purposefully calming, had to be lifted above murmured horror at the wrong done their countess which passed through the many listeners. Knowing that as Dare had just returned, the answer must come from Sybillene, Ulger looked to the woman whose sapphire eyes were beginning to darken in mutinous indignation.

Resenting the implication that she might have followed the wretched Tess's example and created wild stories to win unwarranted attention, Sybillene negated that possibility with distinctly spoken words. "I caught sight of my brother passing through kitchens to guardroom and followed. In the dungeon below I discovered two prisoners released and Alyce tightly bound. I attempted to reason with Walter—to no avail." Anyone having the briefest acquaintance with the woman knew how unlikely it was that she would reason with another. They assumed, as was far more likely and as Dare knew to be the truth, that she'd ordered Walter to do as she wished. Yet none rebutted her statement.

"He locked *me* into an emptied cage." This statement picked up a shade of her more usual imperious attitude. "Then after handing the torch to Tess, he led both her and the released guardsman, who carried Alyce, to the postern door and opened it. The torch disappeared into the opened tunnel. Once its light was gone, I was left in the darkness. It seemed a lifetime afore Cleva came down with a meal for the escaped prisoners. It was she who released me—only a very short time past. She and I agree that the news should be given Earl Dare firstly. Thus, I have patiently waited here for his return."

Dare was appreciative of Sybillene's timing in now wielding a seldom-exercised ability to deal in cool reason, although 'twas a choice pointing out his failure to do the same. Irritated with himself for even momentarily surrendering the experience-honed ability to meet any adversity with stoic composure and calm logic, Dare resumed control of the situation.

"Did Walter accompany the released prisoners and their captive through the postern?" This was the single fact of which it was most important they be certain.

"The torch was the first to disappear." Bravado lent by her initial resentment faltered beneath the weight of so many accusing eyes, and Sybillene shrank back. 'Twas not she who had done the wretched deed, but her brother. "Whether Walter departed as well, I truthfully do not know." Responding to the crowd's accusing silence, she defensively added, "In the darkness there was no way to be certain. I called out and received no answer. Yet there were noises, so . . ."

Dare chose not to mention the possibility, nay, likelihood that rats had made the noises she'd heard. No need to risk driving Sybillene over the precipice of hysteria, where plainly she already tottered. He'd enough trouble to manage without that added difficulty.

The mass of people pressing tight to tunnel opening began falling back to permit Lady Elinor's approach. Dare welcomed his mother with a grim smile of relief. She would, he felt certain, lead Sybillene away and see her ragged nerves soothed while he and his guard captain met in the solar above to seek some method to be free of this coil.

Although the night was more than half-complete, Berdene's small wooden keep was ablaze with light spreading wide from both the central hearth's leaping flames and close-spaced torches. It had been thus arranged to greet the steady stream of men pouring into a hall of inadequate size to easily house them all.

"You will have our gratitude forever, Sir Niall." In accompaniment to these heartfelt words, Alyce lent the knight a smile of such sweetness 'twas humbling, more so than he deemed it likely the lady knew. Niall feared the action for which his lady praised him was no more than the harbinger of disappointment. He shifted uncomfortably.

"I realize, kind sir, that the mere speaking of my plea to those gathering may not be sufficient to see it granted." Alyce saw and acknowledged the source of her host's distress and in quiet words sought to reassure him despite similar apprehensions doing battle on the strained strands of her own nerves. "But no matter the end, simply for the success of your call in bringing them here, I owe you great thanks. These I'd not retract for my failure to win what I seek."

Though heartened on one side by the lady's reassurance of continuing gratitude, on the reverse Niall's distress was deepened. He glanced about the crowded hall where a low murmur of voices was an audible reflection of sidelong glances cast at a woman they did not know.

"I'd no notion how to reach the full number of my lord's vassals. Nor even the names of more than a few. Yet there could never be a time when Earl Dare will need his vassals' support more." Alyce continued speaking to the earnest man who'd given his support without hesitation. "Thus, as you are the only one among them whom I've personally met, to you I came with my desperate plea. And you've done all I asked."

Niall returned his unflinching gaze to Lady Alyce. 'Struth, their lord and his lady were in great need of their people's support, but he was less sure of his fellow vassals' willingness to give it. For himself, there'd never been a doubt. Once fealty was given, a knight's honor depended upon its upholding. Asides, if for naught else, he would do it for Lady Alyce, whose magic elixir had truly cured his Moira of her near lifelong complaint.

"Milady, come, take the seat at our table's center." As if summoned by her husband's thoughts, Moira gently touched Alyce's arm to draw her attention. "These men will then know you as a guest of great importance. It may prepare the ground for the crop you wish to harvest." Thickset shoulders shrugged. "At the least, they will listen with good care."

Alyce smiled her appreciation of Moira's wise counsel, and offering up a brief prayer that her plea be granted—elsewise Wythe's ruin was near assured—she moved to do as suggested. Though uncomfortable sitting in the midst of a room crowded with men who had perforce to stand as there were not seats sufficient to do differently, she demurely folded hands anxiety-trembling and began.

"Kind sirs—" At the first sound of her gentle voice, the hall went so quiet that the silence was in itself a goad for Alyce's tension to move into deeper spheres of distress. Taking a calming breath to halt its descent, she continued the appeal that must not fail.

"I am Lady Alyce, Countess of Wythe. A little time after this day's nooning hour I was taken prisoner and hauled from a Castle Wythe under siege." Alyce assumed that leastwise some few of these men were aware of the confrontation in progress but had chosen not to move in support of their lord. This was a wrong she'd come to beg would be righted.

"When rescued by a loyal guardsman, I chose to approach

you with my lord's just call to arms. 'Tis your duty as men of honor to uphold his cause. And, too, 'tis your duty to do what will best serve the peoples of your lands. Those two duties are tightly entwined and lead to the same end. Earl Dare has toiled long and expended much to see prosperity returned to the whole of Wythe. A condition, I am told, has been absent since the days of the first Earl Dare."

Alyce slowly surveyed the surrounding wall of unyielding faces, closed against her appeal, and felt the pit of defeat opening beneath her feet, waiting to swallow her into its gloom. To forestall its hunger, she fought defeat's dragging hold. Green-fire eyes burning as bright as the ripple of fire over chestnut waves, she made a heated demand. "You *must* come to your liege lord's defense. You *must* or it will ever be known that Wythe is the land of such traitors as you."

No member of the shamefaced audience could meet her brilliant gaze, yet from an unidentifiable source at its center rose a voice arguing against her desperate plea. "Better we be known for that than to be known as the land of a devil-marked Demon, and we as his hell-bound minions."

Alyce leaped to her feet. "Dare is no demon! And I as his wife will swear upon God's own life that Dare bears no devilish mark—only the scars of battles honorably fought on behalf of the Earl of Pembroke and of my father, his lord." Alyce saw them begin to shift uncomfortably, unsure of the justice supporting their disloyalty. Immediately she struck again, striving to break through their wrongful decision's weakening fibers.

"Would a demon risk his life for another? Can a demon bleed? Your earl took a blade aimed at me and near died for loss of life's crimson fluid."

"Your countess speaks only the truth." An unknown woman, gone earlier unnoticed in the crush of too many in too small a space, came boldly forward to stand beside Lady Alyce. "Earl Dare was stabbed, and his blood was as quick to flow and red as yours. I know because it welled up over my hand as I drove the blade deep into his shoulder."

A gasp met Tess's shocking confession. But she did not stop with that single wrong confessed, though 'twas assuredly the worst. Beyond her witness to the truth in the countess's words, she would add an all-encompassing proof of the earl's innocence which only she could provide.

"'Twas I who claimed to have seen the devil's mark upon your lord. 'Twas I who lied not only in that but in false tales of an unworldly summons to his bed. That I did these things to save my own worthless life from the worm responsible for the deaths rousing darker suspicions means nothing if the cost is not merely the earl's life but the peace and right future of all Wythe." Pale brown eyes glowing with sincerity slowly moved from one sober face to another. "Don't let my lies cost you that treasure, don't let it be the deceit of a foolish woman which robs you of your honor and causes you to fall disloyal to your lord."

These words, given at Tess's cost and to benefit others, Alyce believed without reservation. While the hall filled with a rumble of voices discussing revelations and pleas, Alyce brushed Tess's hand. When the other woman turned, they exchanged a look of perfect understanding. Whatever the result, they'd the limited comfort of knowing they had both used every available weapon to beg, shame, or coerce intractable men to lend loyal service to their lord.

Dare stared into the solar's fading firelight, resisting the weakening power of unhappy ponderings. In their cheerless discussion before began the belated meal served to weary fighters returned, Ulger had told him of the boys' report of Walter's visit to the well house. Dare blamed himself for failing to arrange some method for seeing their news be given to someone able to act upon it before the garrison returned, before it was too late. Such might have forestalled Walter's capture of Alyce. Alyce. Thick black lashes clenched tight against the wrenching fury and despair in the thought of her in another's hands. She belonged to him, and he desperately wanted her return. Toward the attainment of that goal he and Ulger had explored every remote possibility. But in the end, they had found no better hope for Alyce's rescue than prayers beseeching God to lend success to Roger's quest, prayers begging divine aid to see them alive, free, and safely returned.

Following the meal, Ulger had withdrawn to seek a night's rest, needful in order to face the morrow's continuing battle. Hours had passed while below the gathered many besought open spaces to bed down and the castle settled into an uneasy quiet. Mother retired, and Sybillene having never reappeared after the announcement of Alyce's taking, Dare alone remained in the solar, hoping against hope that Roger still would come. Yet as flames burned ever lower, Dare's hope weakened as well.

"I would've stopped Walter if I could. I would have sooner seen him dead than that he should take Alyce." Sybillene's quiet words were undeniably sincere.

Slowly turning a dark head to glance over his shoulder, Dare sent the woman hovering in the open door a brooding smile. "I, too, wish for the opportunity to step backward in time where I would see an end to Walter's life, and Alyce safe by my side."

The deep harshness in Dare's words was directed more at himself than at Walter. He was the fool who had purposefully allowed the man to find a postern key. That the key had been intended to facilitate his scheme for the seizing of a hostage to trade for the clearing of himself and Halbert of wrongful charges meant nothing aside the loss of Alyce. Why had she gone to the dungeons when he'd ordered that no one do so? Why? He grimaced in self-disgust. What matter why when the deed was done and made dangerous by the key he'd "given."

Moving into the room, Sybillene perched atop a small stool a proper distance from Dare's chair to gaze into fading flames with equal gloom. Her life had gone from one awful event to another even worse since the night all those years ago when Walter had convinced her it would be justified for her to seek Dare's bed. She wished she could go back and undo every misdeed.

"My good husband will never forgive me for what my brother has done. His imprisonment was sin enough, but this wickedness done his beloved daughter . . ." Though untidy and slipping free of neat coils, golden hair glowed in fading flames.

"You knew that Walter was behind the false charges

against Halbert?" Dare was both startled and disgusted by the prospect of this woman permitting such villainy to befall her spouse, the father of her son. But then—he paused and a downward curl came to his lips—had she not committed the same wrong, to a lesser degree, in coming to his bed uninvited?

Sybillene's return smile was bitterness itself. Locked in the dungeon's unrelieved blackness, she'd been unable to avoid Walter's taunting denunciation of her motives. It had repeated over and over in her mind until she'd been forced to accept the truth at its core, although not until after she'd retreated to her bedchamber had she come to realize she must confess what she knew to Dare.

"Not then, not in time. Rather, I closed my eyes to that which would make my life uncomfortable. I didn't allow myself to admit what I'd done until today when Walter derided me for it as he locked me in the cage."

Dare merely nodded a dark head in respect for a new honesty of spirit uncluttered by self-centered goals.

"Nay, I admit I've long known of Walter's obsession with Alyce." Sybillene was intent on ridding herself of the false comforts of half-truths. "Surely the same may be said of you and near anyone else who watched for more than the length of a single day. What I failed to recognize was the hidden corruption of his soul, like a ripe fruit appetizing without but rotten at the center. Accepting that for the fact it is, I realize Walter is guilty not only of Alyce's abduction but of much of the vileness that has befallen Wythe since we arrived." Sapphire eyes lifted to squarely meet pale blue. "You must deeply regret your noble rescue of your foster father's kin—particularly as Walter and I have been the cause of the greater portion of your woe."

"Never." Dare rejected the thought immediately. "Had I not taken the four of you from the king's hold, I could never have claimed Alyce for wife. And having her as my own, no matter the length of time, is well worth any price in future pain."

The silver tracks of silent tears marked Sybillene's quickly averted face. Such a loving bond was a treasure, one like the bond unconditionally extended to her by Halbert but which she'd too surely thrown away by her selfish actions and foolish demands.

Dare did not see Sybillene's reaction to his statement as the thought of all he'd have lost by failure to take in Keniver's dispossessed consumed his attention. Without foreintent, he added, "Walter would have claimed Alyce, and with the bishop's support, the king would've given her into his hands. Nay, I could never wish my action in fetching you to Wythe undone."

Though she'd not say it aloud to an already hurting Dare, Sybillene did fervently wish it undone. She longed for a return to peaceful days in Keniver with her doting husband.

While both inside the solar were lost in their separate thoughts and sweet memories turned sour by reality, neither noticed another easing through the door Sybillene had left ajar. With fingers turned white by the strength of their grip on a burnished silver hilt, Walter took two silent paces forward and aimed his hand with mortal intent.

Thwap! The impact of a sharply honed dagger hitting dead to point was followed a frozen moment later by a body slumping to the floor.

In the next instant a red-haired storm stood over the fallen form lying midway between chair and stool. Bending to retrieve his weapon from the gushing wound in Walter's neck, Arlen spoke with calm and steady words unmarred by stutter. "Once for my earl and twice for the shame you brought upon Tess."

Walter clenched his eyes shut but opened his mouth to speak, only to find the fluency of words ever his pride, his weapon and power, was no longer his to command. It, like his life, had been called forfeit for his wrongs.

Despite the honesty behind a declaration that she would've preferred his death to the wrongs he had done, a shocked Sybillene sank to her knees beside the brother whose life was rapidly draining away. "To see your soul freed of the weight of the many wicked sins you've committed, Walter, I'll pay for an eternity of masses to be said." Her voice broke on a sob while slow tears dropped into the growing sea of red, a mingled rain of regrets for his wrongs and her inability to foresee and forestall their dreadful end.

Walter gave his sister a weak smile as his last breath of life sighed into nothingness.

Having risen and stepped back to allow the brother and sister one last moment together on the earth, Dare offered his arm to the man who had saved his life. "For this, Arlen, I will grant you whatever you seek."

A blushing Arlen was embarrassed by this praise of an action any loyal guardsman owed his lord. And besides, his motives had not been completely unselfish, not when he'd wanted to punish the nasty little toad since the day Tess had talked of threats made against her. Arlen diverted the subject by explaining how it came to be that he was waiting across the hall in Walter's own chamber.

"I heard the Lady of Keniver say as she didn't know whether her brother was inside the castle or out. I thought we ought not take chances and chose to watch for him where I deemed it most likely he would go."

"Walter's chamber?" Dare questioned, dark brows lifted in mock amazement.

Arlen shrugged. "'Tis on the level with your chamber and across the hall from this room."

Slowly Dare nodded. It was tactically a good position from which to launch his intended assault, but surely difficult to reach through the many, and dangerous to remain.

"Moreover—" Arlen added a further rationale for the choice "—after we'd searched his chamber once with no result, 'twas unlikely any would enter again this night." It was unnecessary to state the fact that, despite crowded conditions, no one was willing to sleep in the dangerous traitor's chamber. Having used the people's superstitions to his advantage so oft before, Walter could hardly have failed to recognize this boon.

"I was hidden amongst a stack of baskets brought from Keniver and stored in one corner before my prey arrived. When he upended his bedside trunk and pulled the silver-hilted dagger from its false bottom, I was so amazed I nearly betrayed my presence."

Dare bent to free the instrument whose sharp point had been driven into the wooden floor below by the force of

Walter's falling body. As he studied it closely, his brows furrowed in puzzlement. He knew of a certainty that the one earlier driven into his shoulder had been locked safely away. He knew it because he had done the deed himself. So how had it come back into Walter's hand? The question roused new and unpleasant visions of treachery.

"We each had one of a matched pair, Walter and I. 'Twas mine that Walter took and gave to Tess," Sybillene explained as she rose from the mortal remains of her brother with unashamed tears still damp on her cheeks. "I wrongly thought the girl, Tess, had stolen it from my chest to see her misdeed done. Had I realized Walter was behind the attack, I would've spoken afore and mayhap the weapon would've been removed and the whole scene prevented." Silent tears began to drip again.

Uncomfortable beneath the lady's regret and grief, Arlen cleared his throat and doggedly continued. "No matter, I knew his mind when he crossed to the solar's door, dagger in hand. I followed. Yet almost was I too late and had perforce to throw my own dagger rather than deliver the blow by hand."

Dare glanced down at the danger expired, an action the other two instinctively followed.

"So . . ." A new voice spoke. "This is why Walter failed to join us beyond the postern door." Roger shook his head, gazing with cold pity upon the poor fool. Knowing, as he did, what a dangerous obsession the man had harbored for the earl's wife, it was clear precisely what had transpired.

Dare turned toward the newcomer with a surge of relief. Roger had come, and with him a bound Lord Peter looking weary and more untidy than he'd likely ever been in his life.

Looking up at Earl Dare, Roger shoved the mountainous man forward. "Our scheme was a success and done within a few paces of the postern door. But fearing our 'friend' might be lingering somewhere just inside and able to reverse the deed, I waited and waited for him to come out and thus make our entrance safe. At last I had to take the risk or tempt the greater danger of arriving too late—so here we are."

"Praise the saints!" Dare's response was heartily meant,

yet blue eyes passed quickly over the prize to search beyond—to no avail. Striding past the two large men, Dare moved to peer into the corridor. Alyce was not there.

"Lady Alyce *is* free." Roger found it even more difficult than expected to present the earl with this doubtless unsatisfactory news—and he thought he'd expected the worst. "She chose not to remain with the hostage and me until the time was right to reenter the castle."

Dare's black frown and ice blue eyes came near to freezing Roger for all time. But after taking a deep breath, he resolutely continued. "Lady Alyce reminded me that she was my countess and that I'd no right to gainsay her."

To the observers' amazement, the warmth of a loving smile answered this statement and wiped every trace of cold from the earl's face. Alyce, it seemed, was truly healthy and in fine spirit. "Where, then, did she go?"

"She didn't speak of a destination but took the boat across the river, certain as she was Lord Peter would've left a horse there."

"So." The earl's expression had begun darkening again. "You allowed a gentle-born woman to take a small boat across a swift-flowing river and then ride off into a countryside direct set for war—alone?"

"Aye— Nay—" Flustered and irritated with himself for it, Roger gritted his teeth before beginning again. "Lady Alyce did cross the river and did ride off across the countryside. I saw her do it. But she was not alone." He said the last triumphantly. "Tess went with her, and Tess it was who manned the boat."

Dare found no comfort in the prospect of the two women traveling together. First, the countryside was dangerous for strong men in the best of times, but for women in days of dangerous conflict . . . Second, Tess had already tried once to kill his wife. Would this escapade not provide the perfect stage for another and possibly successful attempt?

Never in all the days of his difficult and complicated life had Dare felt so utterly helpless and distressed. He could only continue desperate prayers and plan to see every weapon employed to its fullest advantage on the morrow.

Feeling an uncomfortable foreign weight, Dare glanced

behind to meet a pair of yellow eyes narrowed consideringly and glowing with unpleasant lights.

The glaring brightness of a cold, clear dawn after days of cloudy skies was painful to eyes squinting directly into its light, striving to more clearly see the two figures atop the battlements they'd so earnestly worked to see fall for the whole of one day—to no good purpose. They stood near undamaged.

Drawn by curiosity, a foot soldier moved several paces nearer, and nearer still, until well within range of even a poorly skilled archer. Surprised disbelief kept him moving forward to confirm what he thought he saw—two men. The Earl of Wythe, aye. He'd met the man at a time when both fought for the king, and his face and form were unmistakable. But Lord Peter Rievaux? The man adamant in his refusal to approach any site of action? It seemed so but could not be.

"You surely recognize my prize, a leader in your endeavors, I believe. Go, report my new weapon to Sir Lester. Tell him to come and hear my terms."

Losing little time in doing as directed, the listener turned and speedily fled across muddied, heavily trampled fields to the ranks he'd so recently left. Others, a growing number of others, had roused from a hard night's sleep and also stood watching distant figures.

"'Tis Lord Peter, I swear it to be true." He called this to his companions in arms as he raced past on his way to their leader's tent. "Earl Dare calls for Sir Lester to come and speak with him."

It took little time for the king's loyal knight to hastily don his accoutrements. Accompanied by a fair number of volunteer guardsmen more curious than fearful, he moved to stand at the wall's foot.

"Do you, Lord Earl, wish to talk terms for your surrender?" As ever when under difficult circumstances, Sir Lester was at his most pompous.

"If you wish to term it so." Dare's mocking smile did nothing to bolster Lester's confidence. "As you've doubtless been told and now can see—" Dare bodily moved the huge, reluctant Lord Peter to the nearest dip in the crenellated wall "—I have someone whose life you may have an interest in preserving. If not you, then consider his 'uncle,' who I am sure would." Frost blue eyes pierced Lester with ice. "This man, I swear upon my honor, will die before any killing blow falls upon me. Consider well if 'tis a price worth the goal you seek."

It was plain that Lester was both uncomfortable and worried. Nonetheless, he stoutly responded, "I am the king's man and here to do the king's command—not the bishop's nor his nephew's." He spoke only the truth. It was loyalty to his king alone which had made him accept the company and counsel of the bishop and his nephew. "I had rather not have had Lord Peter's company. 'Twas a risk he took, and if death is the price, so be it."

Dare's brows rose and his smile was truly amused. Acknowledging the courage (perhaps foolhardiness) of words spoken in Lord Peter's presence, Dare responded more tactfully to his foe than he would elsewise have considered.

"I believe you to be a loyal and honorable man, Sir Lester. But I know also of your years in the king's court. By that experience and your own astuteness, you have doubtless recognized that loyalty and honor are not always adequate or even desired in matters of politics and power. Take time and ponder well the cost of your choice."

While two men, one above and one below, faced each other in wordless, unyielding conflict, a third approached from the side and startled the others.

"Think you to continue the assault upon Castle Wythe, Sir Lester, and you will have a harder fight than even that which you encountered yesterday." As Clyde, proud to have been chosen spokesman, boldly proclaimed this message, the people of the castle and village, male and female, poured forth in a stream armed with pitchforks, metal ladles, meat hooks, cleavers, pans, and any oddment that could conceivably be wielded with force. The sight might have been amusing but for the fierce determination on their massed faces. "We are not warriors, but we'll fight with all the strength and persistence of people who've spent a lifetime in heavy toil. And we won't be hobbled by noble thoughts of honor.

"If you think to take the land from our lord or our lord from the land, you'll have to kill us all." It was a flat statement backed by the wild cheers of the many behind waving strange weapons. "'Twould be difficult to make the land useful without us to toil and see it so." No need to point out the difficulties inherent in attempting to separate serfs from the land on which they were born and hauling them off to this new and unfamiliar property.

Blue eyes, widened with amazement for this utterly unexpected development, stared down from the ramparts above. Soon recovering from the shock, Dare felt the rare warmth of approval sweeping over him in waves of a loyalty he'd strived to attain but had thought lost.

"I thank you for your deeply appreciated support, but I pray the sacrifice of a single life will prove unnecessary. Despite his laudable honor—or mayhap because of it—I am certain Sir Lester knows the wisdom of choosing when to fight and when to leave the battle for another day and better purpose."

"If not before"—Ulger surprisingly stepped to his earl's side and interrupted—"he will now, I'll warrant." The knight motioned ahead and slightly to the north.

Expecting a welcome sight, Dare glanced toward the northern horizon. He found instead a further shock, yet an even more welcome sight. As the band of riders approached, backed by men afoot, he recognized the banners of one vassal after another. Their support was most unexpected, but that was not the source of his greatest surprise. Unbound hair glowing in bright daylight and dancing on the breeze was the unmistakable banner of Alyce, Countess of Wythe and his much-beloved wife. Dare smiled. So this had been her goal, the calling to arms of his reluctant vassals, and plainly, by her will and charm, she'd succeeded where he had failed.

With the mighty fortress standing strong against the bright, colorless sky of early morn, Alyce easily picked out the powerful silhouette of her husband amongst those lining the battlements. Wanting Dare to know her present at the first opportunity, she hoped the thick swath of her chestnut mane, hidden carefully from sight for so many years but now released and proudly left to be carried on the breeze, would be to him an unmistakable herald. The sun glinted down the cutting edges of the massive broadsword he lifted high to salute her coming. Suddenly positive they would prevail against all odds, Alyce waved back wildly while her unrestrained laughter rolled freely across fields bedded down for winter's rest between them.

Dare's vassals, without exception, had chosen to accompany her return to Wythe and, if necessary, to do battle with the besieging force. A difficult fight it might be, but she knew who would triumph. Even as that certainty warmed her, a movement from the far side caught her attention. Eyes narrowed, she peered at what looked to be a vast, dark swarm on distant hills. Her heart stopped for one long moment in terror of this unforeseen danger—a steadily approaching army of formidable size. The next moment it beat with erratic joy. The Pembroke pennant rippled like a dangerous threat on the wind. Richard Marshal had come to support his friend and former knight. Richard Marshal and . . . Alyce grinned. She should've known. 'Twas Thomas at his side. Thomas, who'd been so anxious to depart but whom Dare had insisted remain until the actual pounding of the battering ram began.

Alyce and the men who had accompanied her reached one outer edge of the besiegers' camp, within hearing range of Dare, at almost the same time as Richard Marshal and his considerably larger army arrived at another. Reined to a halt, their combined forces waited and listened.

"Sir Lester, again I counsel you to consider carefully what action you take. I need not point out that you are surrounded on *all* sides: front, back, sides, and even from above. It might be deemed honorable to fight against such overwhelming odds. It might also be thought the action of a weak-wit. The wiser course would surely be to take my demands to the bishop—not king. Tell Peter de Roches, Bishop of Winchester, that his 'nephew' is my guest and that if he wishes to coax him from the hospitality of my dungeon, the price will undoubtedly be high. Lord Peter Rievaux is a greedy man. I will exchange him for three separate writs absolving myself, Halbert Bohan, and Richard Marshal of treason. For these, each sealed by the king himself, to the bishop I will send Lord Peter—alive and well, although I am not certain we've enough food on all Wythe to sustain his girth."

A most diverse crowd, from scullery maid to earl, laughed heartily at Dare's jest. While Sir Lester and his small army withdrew in such great haste, they abandoned their siege weapons where they rested, barred gates were opened and portcullises raised to welcome the vast and varied force amassed in willing support of Demon Dare, Earl of Wythe.

That evening, as so often on clear October nights, the air was brisk. Yet 'twas also bright with merrymaking and camaraderie. While a plentiful meal was being laid out in both great hall and courtyard to serve the multitude a feast of celebration, Dare stood before them all and lifted his hands for silence.

"Pray heed—I promise I'll not delay you long from your well-deserved merriment." A brief roll of bantering appreciation quickly faded. "Though I greatly appreciate you all for the amazing display of support you demonstrated, there are several people who performed such feats as deserve to be known.

"First, my life was saved yestereve when my 'ungrateful guest' attempted to strike me down from behind as I sat at my ease in the solar. Arlen was too quick for Walter, who instead paid for the attempt with his life. For this deed and his valor in battle, I will soon see Arlen knighted."

While pleasure turned Arlen's face as bright as his hair, a cheer went up from his fellow guardsmen.

"Then, also," Dare continued, "two young boys there are who have done even more. They saved not only my life but a good many of yours as well." Dare wanted to be certain that the boys would be given the credit they deserved for a deed of such importance. "Discovering a vial of virulent poison, which Cleva assures me would've fouled the well and likely killed all who drank from it, Hal and James had the good sense not only to remove the vial but to supplant it with another, innocent bottle of like shape and color. Thus, they prevented Walter from knowing the original was gone and giving him the opportunity to secure more."

This announcement earned first a gasp of horror at a near escape and then calls of gratitude and much slapping of young backs until the boys looked to have doubled in height.

"Others there are who performed great feats—Thomas, who, knowing the postern door unsafe, scaled down the castle wall and on a horse previously secreted away against the need rode to request the Earl of Pembroke's aid.

"But most of all"—Dare turned intense blue eyes upon Alyce, and her cheeks warmed under the heat—"my wife, who risked all manner of hazards, traveling unescorted, to call my vassals to my aid."

Unable to let it rest there and take more credit than she was due, Alyce promptly added, "I was not alone. Tess traveled with me and did much to advance my plea." Alyce chose to go no further into precisely what Tess had done as 'twas possible Tess would prefer not to have the full measure of her confessions so widely spread.

"Drink with me to these people." Dare lifted a silver chalice high, and the crowd immediately responded by raising theirs as well. Dare held Alyce's soft form close to his side while the toast was drunk.

Once the meal had begun, Alyce sat proudly at her husband's side, certain that for the release of their hostage, the manipulative bishop would see both him and her father exonerated of wrong and free to live on lands unthreatened. In truth, all their past and present battles had been won, and around them now flowed clear, refreshing air untainted by dark whispers or greedy dissatisfactions. It boded well for the future. The parade of savory dishes continued, and in a haze of contentment, she listened as soft laughter punctuated the strains of lute, pipe, and trimble being played somewhat inexpertly by serfs in the music gallery above one corner of the hall.

After the end of the formal meal—although food, wine, and ale would be plentiful throughout the night—the tunes changed to airs meant to inspire dancing, and couples began filling the space opened with great difficulty below the high table. Only then did Alyce, wrapped in a glow of happiness and peace, catch sight of another less so.

Rising to her feet, Alyce assured Dare she would soon return and dodged through the boisterous crowd to approach Arlen. He was sitting quietly near his parents with barely a smile to relieve the stern, surreptitious glances he cast toward Tess.

"Arlen, pray may I speak with you alone?" Alyce's question shocked not only Arlen, but his parents, too. Yet Arlen immediately stood to accompany her on the search for a relatively quiet corner—no easy task. When at last they'd succeeded, Alyce wasted no moment to say what she wanted him to know. She was certain this news would be, upon reflection at least, a gift—one she owed Arlen for saving Dare's life if for naught else.

"Tess risked her life to go with me, nay, to ferry me safely across the river. (I'd no notion how to manage on my own.) And when it seemed my plea to the many gathered vassals would fail, 'twas Tess who sacrificed her pride to win the goal. Without her aid I would've failed my lord, lord to us all. Both Dare and I have forgiven her the wrongs she did under the threat of mortal danger. She is deserving of your understanding, too."

Nodding a head whose bright hair was still unrestrained, Alyce turned away to find her husband again somewhere in the crowd. Before she'd the chance, Sir Niall asked her to dance with him, and she could no more refuse than she could refuse any of the many other vassals who had answered the call she'd issued on Dare's behalf.

With music, dancing, and continued feasting, they celebrated with an abandon which proved Wythe prosperous enough to sustain even the now-imprisoned Lord Peter's gluttony—if any wished it so, and none did.

Laughing but wearied by rounds and rounds of dancing, Alyce at last won her way back to near where Dare stood with two friends before the fireplace wall. At near the same moment, Thomas caught sight of an Elinor alone at last and excused himself to join the dowager countess. Richard Marshal accompanied him, anxious to meet this lady of whom he'd heard so much over so many years from both

Dare and Thomas—two very different views. When Alyce reached the powerful figure emphasized by flamelight behind, she happily nestled beneath the strong arm he immediately wrapped about her shoulders.

"Ah, you *do* remember to whom you belong," Dare whispered into the ear at which he paused to nibble. "I had begun to wonder if more tangible evidence were needful, a renewed physical demonstration." As he spoke his hand slid beneath the curtain of bright curls to stroke her back and pull her nearer.

His words and touch kindled intimate memories of fiery scenes that warmed Alyce's blood until she melted against this master of the fires he'd not allowed her to smother but rather had stoked into a raging blaze burning for him alone. From the corners of green eyes gone sultry she gazed up at him and whispered, "I've known the answer to that for many years—yet a further 'demonstration' would never go amiss."

"'Struth?" Light gleamed on black hair as Dare tilted his head back to gaze down at the prize he'd thought could never be his. "Then let us waste no moment further but permit me to provide you with such proof as you will never have question again."

"We can't go now." Alyce mournfully rejected the offer of bliss and against his broad chest hid a face that would surely betray her desires.

"Why can't we?" His soft growl stroked over her sensitive nerves in a further enticement to surrender to delicious temptations.

"We are the host and hostess." She desperately argued with the good sense of a conscience distinctly unwelcome.

"So we are. A fact which merely makes leaving when we choose the easier—who will challenge our right to do as we desire? And I do desire it." The potency of his sensual smile and smoldering heat of blue-flame eyes left no doubt but that he spoke the literal truth. "The others can remain and drink themselves into a stupor—" he cast a glance about the roisterous room which looked well on its way to fulfilling that aim "—but we have better uses for our time."

Feeling the depth of his hunger, one she shared, a happily

surrendering Alyce turned to lean more fully into his big, powerful body. Yet in that moment, oblivious to the wild festivities of the crowd, still he added the one more statement able to instantly clear away all other considerations.

"Forced by the circumstances of my life, I have long survived without love. Over many years I yearned for you but thought never could I claim you. Then no sooner is your love unbarred and mine than another steals my treasure away. Nay, I've waited long enough for love, and I will wait no more to reaffirm our endless bond."

Refusing even to postpone a small foretaste of heaven, Dare paused to claim a soul-binding kiss before sweeping Alyce off her feet and, without care for the teasing comments of their audience, carried her swiftly up the stairs and into his bed's sweet comfort and searing pleasures.

In its shadows the fire storm rose to whirl them beyond the darkness of the past and into the future's bright loving light.

Epilogue

Childish laughter rang out in unrestrained glee, and the earl paused in the castle entry to watch a small, ebony-haired streak cross its rush-strewn surface to disappear into the descending stairway.

"Dare, halt you little demon, else you'll wake your sister." An exasperated Cleva rolled after the five-year-old in slow but relentless pursuit.

Pale blue eyes glowing with amusement turned their warmth upon a woman seated near the fire and cradling a napping toddler in her arms.

To greet the approach of this magnificent man, her husband, Alyce lifted a head wreathed by bright ringlets escaped from coiled braids and gave him an equally bright smile. "Every day I am more firmly convinced of our wisdom in choosing Ulger and Cleva as godparents to our firstborn."

A mocking smile accompanied the nodding of a dark head. "Aye, Cleva leastways has the experience earned by keeping a rein on me at the same age." They'd chosen his guard captain and onetime nursemaid for appreciation of endless loyalty and friendship. Yet it had been no bad thing that by the same action, they'd eased this couple's loneliness

350

after their "baby son" and his wife, Tess, had moved on to Wrexdale. There Sir Arlen was serving as castellan over Alyce's dower lands—and taking from Wythe a woman who, though she'd atoned for her many wrongs by seeing Alyce freed from a madman's hold and cause won, would never again be fully trusted by her peers on Wythe.

Green eyes narrowed in consideration of his reasoning. Alyce slowly shook her head. In the first instance, she knew her husband's childhood had never included the joyous freedoms and abundant love of their son's, and asides . . .

"I doubt even you could have been as wild as our offspring. Nay, that is a fault which can be traced to his mother's rebellious spirit."

"'Tis so that our son has your eyes, but in all other ways he is truly the third in a series of 'Demon Dares.'" The term no longer held even the faintest tinge of the ominous meanings years since disproved. "Asides, I love your rebellious spirit." Voice dropping into seductive depths, impervious to the knowing gazes of the many laboring to see the daily chores of a castle done, the formidable earl crouched down beside his slender fire-vixen grown more precious with every passing day. "I always did."

"I know." Alyce fell willingly into the ever welcome intensity of an azure gaze. "You reignited the flame oft enough while I was so earnestly striving to smother it. Indeed, you've yet to end that wicked habit."

"I hope you don't cherish the worthless notion that I might repent of a habit that's brought such pleasure." Black brows arched above eyes now gleaming with gentle mirth.

"Nay." Alyce's own gaze dropped in feigned modesty only to peek coyly up. "I would not be so foolish as to forgo my own pleasures."

For this confession, Alyce was rewarded with a quick but fervent kiss. Despite the kiss's haste, the weight of a powerful body leaning above awoke the sleeping child. Elinor Gladys sat up. Blinking pale blue eyes, she instantly lifted arms to her father, gifting him with a smile of loving trust.

Alyce, too, smiled in contentment as Dare took his daughter into a gentle hold. "Leastways in her recognition of a worthy man, Elinor is like me, although, despite her bright hair, she seems to have utterly escaped the trials of an unruly spirit." It was true that Elinor's nature was as sweet and placid as young Dare's was mischievous and wild.

"There was a time," Dare pointed out sotto voice, "when your father thought the same of you."

"Only because I tried so hard to hide it; the same cannot be claimed of a babe barely two years old."

With a wide smile Dare shrugged, reminded by his own words of the reason for returning to the castle in the midst of a busy afternoon. "We may plan the knighting ceremony for Whitsuntide. 'Tis only a sennight hence, and I am sorry for the inadequate notice. I've only just had a message from your father—written, it proudly states, by his own hand. He and Sybillene will come then to witness Hal's knighting. That is, of course, if Sybillene's condition permits such a ride."

Alyce and Dare exchanged a glance fraught with wry humor. After Sybillene had miscarried a babe year before last, Halbert had as well have wrapped her in goose down and silk. 'Twas, Dare privately thought, a wonder there was any possibility of a child at all.

"As James's family have said they will come whenever we summon them, the timing of the ceremony presents no great difficulty. The arrangements have been in place for a month and more, awaiting only this news from Keniver." Alyce smiled reassuringly at the strong man she found as stunningly handsome and devastatingly exciting as the day he'd first kissed her in the herb garden behind Keniver Castle.

Since Elinor and her new husband, Thomas—as giddy as newlyweds half their age—had retreated to the privacy of her dower lands, the responsibility for seeing Dare's home smoothly run and such festive gatherings well planned and rightly conducted had become her duty alone. These tasks were only a small measure of the endless gifts of love Alyce wanted to give the beloved man who held her, their family, and all of Wythe safe and happy.

Surrendering to a sinful temptation toward sloth, Dare settled on the floor beside Alyce's chair and gave himself over to the joy of a few stolen moments in the daylight company of his wife and child.

More than a half decade had passed since his confrontation with the king's knight had ended. Peace and prosperity had come to Wythe, a reflection of the contentment of its earl and his countess. But England continued to suffer under inconstant King Henry, although the Bishop of Winchester and his "nephew" had fallen from power. The latter was a welcome fact, but at what Dare and many others believed to be too high a price: the death of Richard Marshal, Earl of Pembroke. The bishop had been foolish, or arrogant, enough to put the order for Richard's murder in written words, and by proof of those letters given to the king, he'd been stripped of temporal power. Unfortunately their weak king had soon fallen under the control of other strong wills—his French bride and her family. Dare could only stand back and pray that, to see his son's world a better place, a wiser king would follow. Until that time, Dare was prepared to continue guarding his own.

Young Dare raced back into the hall and launched himself into his mother's waiting arms, a sight that brought such an infectious giggle from the young maid in Dare's hold that the laughter of all joined to fill the hall with bright joy.

MARYLYLE ROGERS

Marylyle Rogers delights readers with her thrilling, richly woven medieval romances…

- ☐ **HIDDEN HEARTS** .... 65880-8/$3.95

- ☐ **PROUD HEARTS** .... 70235-1/$4.95

- ☐ **CHANTING THE DAWN** .... 70951-8/$5.99

- ☐ **DARK WHISPERS** .... 70952-6/$4.99

Available in Paperback from Pocket Books

POCKET
BOOKS

Simon & Schuster Mail Order Dept.
200 Old Tappan Rd., Old Tappan, N.J. 07675

Please send me the books I have checked above. I am enclosing $_____ (please add 75¢ to cover postage and handling for each order. Please add appropriate local sales tax). Send check or money order—no cash or C.O.D.'s please. Allow up to six weeks for delivery. For purchases over $10.00 you may use VISA: card number, expiration date and customer signature must be included.

Name _____

Address _____

City _____ State/Zip _____

VISA Card No. _____ Exp. Date _____

Signature _____ 417-01

A Captivating New Novel of Passion and Pride in the Bestselling Tradition of *A Knight In Shining Armor*

JUDE DEVERAUX

ETERNITY

The saga of the Montgomery family continues in the stunning new novel from the *New York Times* bestselling author Jude Deveraux.

Carrie Montgomery had never had to fight for anything—until she met the most wonderful, most exasperating man. Savor the romance and adventure as they discover if their love can last for all ETERNITY.

Available in Paperback from Pocket Star Books

POCKET
STAR
BOOKS

470-01

Better With Every Book!
From The Author of The *New York Times* Bestseller
The Prize

THE SECRET

JULIE GARWOOD

Set in the beautiful Scottish highlands, THE
SECRET tells the story of Judith Hampton, a
woman who journeys from her bleak English
home to meet the father she has never known,
only to discover a love she never could have
imagined…and a secret that could change her
life forever.

Coming in May 1992

POCKET
BOOKS

Pocket Books
Proudly Announces

THE EAGLE'S SONG

Marylyle Rogers

Coming in October

The following is a preview of
The Eagle's Song . . .

Late Spring 1092

Capricious clouds drifted restlessly across the pale face of a moon, turned half to the dark. Thus the cool orb shed an ever-changing pattern of light and shadow over Castle Radwell's soaring tower as if conspiring to disguise the extraordinary sight of a figure steadily scaling the fortress's sheer stone walls.

With tenacious care, Rhys sought firm holds in crevices between thick blocks, sporadically dislodging pebbles. He was impervious to dangers forewarned by the pebbles falling for a distance in silence before skittering down a steep, rocky hill to end with a faint splash in the deep waters of the moat at its base. His objective's importance blocked thoughts of the deadly consequences of failure in this initial feat.

Permitting his concentration to be diverted would be to threaten the whole, for attaining the ultimate goal depended upon first securing the prize of this night's hazardous but carefully planned action.

At last the summit was reached. Cautious to make no sound, Rhys swung over the ledge and dropped to the far side's parapet walkway. He crouched in sheltering gloom for a long moment, waiting until easy breathing was restored and full strength revived. Then, as an unseen shadow, he rose and moved toward the lone nightguard standing squarely in a firebrand's ring of light.

Atop an invulnerable tower and gazing out over the motionless countryside at its front, the guard had no earthly reason to be wary of approaching danger and even less to fear the immediate presence of a foe. A single blow from behind proved the folly of these complacent assumptions.

Tapers clustered atop a silver platter cast flickering lights across Linnet's bath as she finished wringing water from a wealth of hair and shifted to lean back against one side of the wooden tub resembling an overlarge barrel's bottom half. All day she'd dutifully met expectations placed upon the sole lady of Castle Radwell, the daughter of its lord. She was anxious to be done with the task at hand and for a brief time released to enjoy the comforts of heated waters, the peace of private moments . . . free to delight in impossible dreams.

While steaming water lapped at the creamy skin below her shoulders, Linnet allowed the weight of freshly washed hair to tumble over the tub's edge to the floor behind. She then lifted the bone-backed brush that was waiting beside a rapidly drying ball of sweet-scented soap on the stool drawn near. After first bringing order to tangled locks, she continued stroking through them with slow and soothing regularity. Her tresses, though neither the glorious gold of the Saxons native to these lands nor the raven black of the Welsh who bordered them, leastways were thick and as they began to dry, their soft umber hue gleamed with warm highlights.

Abundant hair, however, was a small comfort when secretly she wished for the peacock beauty that could never belong to a humble linnet bird. Her name, she'd always known, was singularly, depressingly appropriate. A linnet she was—plain and drab colored—worthy only of an indulgent father's admiration. Oh, 'struth, one day a husband might deem her a prize. Yet, she'd no illusion but that 'twould be for the assets of her sizeable dowry and the valuable alliance with a powerful family which such a match would ensure.

A faint shudder passed over Linnet. Unbidden her mind filled with the features of the most recent applicant for her hand. One of the few Saxon lords who still held lands in Norman England, Baron Osric was an aging, gruff man notorious for his impatience and violent temper. Why her father had sent his all-important young heir to the man for fostering, Linnet had never understood. Yet by the fact that he had, she'd known her most heartfelt pleas would fail in convincing even her indulgent sire to refuse the baron's suit. So great was her silent relief that negotiations for their union seemed to have come to a halt that it dulled the pain of a blow to her already humble self-image. As talks had ended shortly after Baron Osric first met her, it seemed clear the disgusting man had found her appearance wanting. Linnet had deflected his unspoken insult with the armor of a certainty that she found him infinitely less appealing —not that a woman's opinion of a prospective spouse would be sought or considered of any worth.

Linnet determinedly averted her thoughts from the unpleasant subject of arranged marriages and the far more unpleasant baron. Back turned toward the chamber door and with tangles smoothed from hair almost dry, she was free to slide down and rest her head atop the tub's nearly shoulder-high rim. Pale brown eyes gazed through the thin opening of an arrow slit on the facing wall and dreamily searched for brief glimpses of the mysterious half moon alternately peeking flirtatiously around and then hiding behind the dark silhouettes of aimlessly drifting clouds. Soon Meara would return from the hall below with a towel heated by the fire in its central hearth. But until then . . .

Linnet relaxed and welcomed the anticipated delights of warm waters and equally warm fantasies. Predictably the latter were drawn from the oft repeated and well-known mythical deeds recounted of an evening in her father's great hall. But, quite to the reverse, the hero of these exciting adventures was a mysterious, devastatingly handsome stranger of whom, with the exception of one recent humiliating experience, Linnet had caught only rare glimpses.

He looked like a man born to lead, standing out amidst many others, if not by height alone, then by virtue of the hair falling below impressively broad shoulders and so bright it seemed to glow with inner lights. And his eyes! His eyes were as dark as the midnight sky, piercing but perversely lit with humor as if he were laughing at the world and everything in it.

Linnet was a well-born maiden and naturally reserved, yet on the few occasions he'd unexpectedly appeared, she'd found herself helplessly staring at him while the sharp mind on which she prided herself went as soft and about as clear as mud. She'd sought, albeit surreptitiously, to learn the elusive man's name —and more. Her quest had met with no success. Either she was too reticent in her attempts or honestly nothing was known of him. Likely both possibilities were true. Yet, that his identity remained hidden only made the golden-haired, dark-eyed stranger the more enthralling.

Linnet would never have had courage enough to boldly approach the man. Her cheeks burned, even a fortnight later, under vivid memories of the day when she'd glanced over her shoulder to find *him* a mere two paces behind. Although, to compensate for her plain appearance, she ever strived to maintain a modicum of grace, at his sudden nearness she'd gone clumsy. Tripping on her own gown, she'd fallen into an inelegant heap at his feet.

Sir Basil, the guard captain, had clearly been aghast at the prospect of ill befalling the earl's cherished daughter in his presence. Fearing the blame would be laid upon him, the knight had instantly lifted her from the ground—but not before she'd caught a glimpse of the stranger's lips curling with faint disdain. Rather than come to her aid, her hero had stepped quickly back and disappeared into the concerned crowd gathering about their fallen lady—an action of questionable gallantry.

Despite this apparent fault (which she bleakly accepted as a justifiable response to her disgusting awkwardness), he had remained at the center of her daydreams and had invaded her night dreams as well. More shocking still, her fantasy hero's actions could no longer be confined to brave deeds done. No. Now, fresh from victory over evil, the golden warrior inevitably returned to his ladylove—a linnet magically transformed into a peacock beauty by the amazing power only shining dreams could provide. 'Twas a shameful secret. But, Linnet consoled herself, no one need ever know. Thus she excused adding his ardent vows of endless devotion to the growing list of embellishments for the second portion of her every fantasy, the scene rapidly becoming the most important.

Willingly Linnet drifted into the mists of her whimsical imagination while before a background of fickle moonlight her champion did honorable battle against a wicked foe. Time advanced unnoticed by the one lazing in mystical realms wherein a golden hero, in the guise of St. George, boldly met a ravenous dragon.

Under an unaccountable but growing uneasiness, the vision began to fade. No sound bestirred the chamber's silence yet a prickling sensation assaulted the back of Linnet's neck. She shifted nervously and water, which of a sudden seemed to have gone cold, sloshed in gentle waves against the tub's thick, tightbound planks.

"Meara—" Frightened and lacking the courage to glance behind, Linnet's call was precious little more than a whisper. No answer.

She was alone in the solar. Linnet sharply rebuked irrational fears. Of a certainty she was. Nonetheless an erratic thumping shook her heart. The drawbridge was upraised leaving no way across the wide, deep moat. Moreover, the iron portcullis at the castle entrance was lowered. 'Twould be impossible for any foe to gain access to the fortress of Radwell. That sane, rational reassurance lent a comfort remarkable for its small and feeble proportions.

Enough of this nonsense! Linnet scolded a pigeon-hearted nature long admitted but depressing all the same. *You've spent too much time in witless dreams of daring deeds. You've lost reality somewhere in the midst of exciting events which, given substance, would melt you into a craven pool of terror. Turn about and see how witless are your fancies.* Knowing a moment's hesitation would smother every last glimmer of courage, she suited action to silent command.

Linnet's lips opened but, under the collision of shock and fear, sound perished unborn in her throat. It seemed certain that either she had truly lost right wits or a fearsome otherworldly force had given life to her dreams. Before disbelieving eyes, her breath-stealing fantasy hero stood in the flesh yet so tall, so devastating in his masculine beauty and with so potent an aura of power that the image was surely too perfect to be real. Linnet shook her head in a vain attempt to disperse this apparition proving the truth behind priestly warnings that such dreams as hers were a sinful wrong which good women must disallow. Overwhelmed by belated guilt, Linnet inwardly confessed her fall to a tempting lure she should've resisted.

Still—despite a negatively shaken head, thick lashes repeatedly blinked, and fervent silent prayers beseeching forgiveness—the image would not fade. Linnet was left to absorb the staggering fact that his presence was no illusion bred of a too fertile imagination but real, very real. Far worse than that, his broad shoulders rested against the closed door of the room where she sat covered by clear liquid alone!

"Milady—" Apparently at his ease, the intruder grinned with wicked sensuality while mocking eyes visually caressed the creamy shoulders half-turned toward him and exposed above the tub's rim. During the decade Rhys had spent as an unwilling "guest" at the Conqueror's court in Normandy, he'd become accustomed to women, well-born and commoner alike, figuratively throwing themselves at him. But only this coy, pampered daughter of Radwell's earl had gone so far as to actually fall at his feet in a ploy to gain attention. Now that she'd won his interest's full force Rhys wondered how sincerely she'd rue his giving of the gift besought. The wry thought widened a white smile which lost none of its potent charm for the cynicism in its depths.

Barely able to breathe and despite thoughts in total disarray, Linnet knew the impossibility of producing more than an embarrassingly inadequate squeak of protest. She abruptly turned about and sank down until her chin was below the waterline. Through the narrow opening on the far wall she glared at the betraying moon, irrationally blaming it for her predicament while a blush bloomed with such heat that by rights her bath water should've boiled. She wished it would. A froth of bubbles could provide a flimsy cover of sorts between her nude form and a pair of night-dark and far too penetrating eyes. Failing that, she wrapped arms about uplifted knees and pressed tightly back against the wooden wall between the intruder and a forbidden view.

"Who are you?" The question Linnet had long sought answer for popped into being without foreintent. She could've bitten her tongue. Leastwise, Linnet comforted herself, she'd recovered her voice although its usual calm tone had turned husky and came out little better than a whisper. "How did you get in?" This hastily added question was more to the point.

The uninvited visitor ignored her first query to cryptically address the last. "Eagles fly."

"Eagle?" No-o-o. This man, this hero of her dreams, couldn't be he. Linnet's heart pounded so hard it threatened to suffocate her while the implications of such a possibility curled like poisonous vines around her sweet fantasies. Only hours past, her father had taken the castle's entire garrison, save one guardsman, to rush forth and meet his arch-foe in battle. Her golden champion could not, simply could not possibly be the man her father hated more than the devil himself. Asides . . .

"The Eagle is Welsh." Water invaded Linnet's mouth turning the last word into a sputter as in desperation she seized upon this frail argument to wield against an awful truth. By the circumstances of his arrival he'd proven himself an enemy yet her mind fought against accepting a fact which would make her dreams the act of a traitor.

"Aye, that I am." Rhys grinned. He could nearly see the damsel's confusion although her face was turned from him and, by the sound of it, buried so deep she was in danger of drowning. Coming upon the earl's spoiled daughter at her bath had not been envisioned as a part of the plan but he saw no reason to regret the fact. During the few advance forays he'd made into his enemy's home, this tender creature had sent him an abundance of smoldering looks. Surely any female bold enough to repeatedly issue such melting gazes knew full well the precise nature of their dangerous invitation. Throughout the goodly number of years he'd spent in the company of Norman damsels more than anxious to "know him better," similar enticements had been turned upon him too oft for him to have any question as to the reward expected. He had proven himself loathe to disappoint them. Nor would he be averse to indulging in the same meaningless but pleasurable games with this small linnet clearly willing to become the eagle's prey.

Linnet's hair, near the same golden-brown as her eyes, pooled on the floor as she tilted her chin upward to safely draw deep breaths in an urgent attempt to tame a thundering pulse and regain some semblance of normality. How could what he claimed be true? The Welsh were a dark-haired race. This man's mane was as bright as sun-ripened wheat and as fair as any Saxon's. More importantly, *much* more importantly, how could any of this be happening to her—quiet, sensible, dutiful Linnet?

That Lady Linnet had yet to scream for help, as surely any timid virgin caught unclothed by a man would do, reinforced Rhys's belief that her reticence was an act calculated to draw him nearer. So be it. He moved forward with the soundless stealth of a hunter.

"Lady Linnet is Norman, as is her sire. Thus, rightly she should be as dark as he. But you are not. Now you are eight and ten, you must have learned that all things are not as might be expected." He learned that same lesson anew by discovering, despite tightly wrapped arms that did more to emphasize than hide lush curves, she had physical attractions more than sufficient to compensate for a misleading initial impression of pale charms. And not slender limbs of alabaster and generous curves alone. Standing near for the first time Rhys saw what he'd failed to look close enough to acknowledge before—a complexion of pure cream and thick sable lashes certain to emphasize the gold of her eyes. Candlelight caressed a fair mane as he shook it in mild irritation with his own limited perceptions. Pursued too oft, he'd stopped bothering to return enticing examinations in detail.

Linnet gasped. The rough velvet voice came from directly above. What should she do? What could she do? She hadn't and mustn't scream. Whatever else was unclear, his reason for coming was obvious—to take her captive—and to cry out would be to summon the one whose presence must remain hidden. Mentally flailing about for an alternative answer, she stumbled over the meaning of words barely heard above the ever more frantic pounding of her heart.

How did he know she'd recently passed that mark of age? How? Linnet grimaced with self-disgust. With her own eyes she'd seen him come and go in Radwell Castle at will. Plainly he was far more successful in learning what he sought than she'd been in learning more of him. It was irritating, frustrating to know that the Eagle had discovered so much about her while she knew so little of him. Even now she knew only that she'd spent far too many hours in treacherous, wicked fantasies about a man proven to be the deadly enemy who had led his people in repeated raids across Radwell's border.

"I am not Lady Linnet." Linnet recognized the ridiculousness of the claim the moment it was spoken. Nonetheless, she resented the dark velvet laughter with which it was greeted.

"Oh, but you are." Rhys's deep voice went lower to purr a scant distance from her ear. "We both know I've visited here often enough to be aware of you—your soulful stares and well timed tumble guaranteed that I would."

A new wave of embarrassment swept Linnet from

the tip of her toes to the top of her head, and she buried a rosy-hued face into cupped hands resting atop knees just breaching chill bath water. He knew how she'd watched him! Linnet wished she could simply dissolve into the transparent liquid which left no place to hide. She could hardly justify her action by confessing an inability to prevent her gaze from following him as if it were some inferior metal and he the lodestone. More appalling still was his taunt that she'd purposefully fallen at his feet in a wordless demand for his attention. His accusation forced her into greater depths of humiliation.

Rhys frowned. Her reaction was unexpected. After those many sidelong, come-hither looks her retreat from his answer to their call was annoying. Cynicism lent a cold glitter to his eyes. Lady Linnet's response, it would seem, proved her to be a too oft indulged female who teased but never fulfilled. Mentally shrugging, he acknowledged that no matter his initial thoughts, an impenetrable wall had already been placed betwixt them—first by their respective positions in life and second by the parameters of the task underway. Still . . . he meant to warn the pampered maid just how dangerous it was for tender prey to bait an eagle.

One long forefinger slid across Linnet's shoulder blade, leaving a wake of tingling fire on its journey to the dip at the base of her throat. Stroking out to the tip of her chin, with gentle insistence Rhys urged a heart-shaped face up until the back of her head again rested atop the tub's rim. Robbed of sanity by eyes burning with the hypnotic power of a predator for its quarry, Linnet's softly bowed lips parted on a silent gasp. Dark flames flared beneath half-lowered lashes as the hard curve of a very real mouth descended. Rhys took possession in a succession of exciting, tormenting kisses which demonstrated to Linnet just how feeble had been her inexperienced dreams. The heavy pounding of her heart seemed to fill her throat until a faint, strange sound whispered out.

Knocked off kilter by a sweetness he could nearly swear tasted of innocence, Rhys was irritated by this weakening to a woman's surely practiced lures. To punish her he deepened the kiss with blatant expertise, building it to a fever of hungry passion he believed no inexperienced maiden could match. Another helpless sound welled up from Linnet's depths, in part a cry of fear for the unknown but more a supplication for him to ease needs whose existence she'd never suspected. The oddly vulnerable sound broke Rhys free of a rapidly escalating desire sending blood coursing through his veins with the speed of windswept flames. He forced himself to break their bond.

As the invading mouth abruptly lifted, to Linnet's shame, hers followed in silent plea for its return. Feeling bereft, lost in the unfamiliar mists of passion, Linnet's eyes opened to the daunting view of a mocking smile curving masculine lips. It brought from her a whimper of distress and yet she could not look away.

Gone still as stone, Rhys frowned. His open hand absently caressed the cream silk of Linnet's throat while he studied the wild blush on her dazed face and the hurt in eyes gone to molten honey. Wordlessly he reminded himself that it mattered not at all whether she was experienced, a manipulating tease, or truly a virginal woman. She could *never* be his! It was a fact which made the suspicion sweeping over him all the more disturbing, the suspicion that he was going to regret permitting himself even this small taste of a sweetness he'd never forget. Angrily he rejected the mere possibility that any single female, let alone the coddled daughter of a despised enemy, could affect him that deeply.

The sound of a door latch lifting sliced between them as cleanly as any sharp-honed blade. With incredible speed, Rhys swept Linnet's discarded gown from the floor where it had been allowed to fall as she stepped into the tub. Cloth caught in the strong arm wrapped just below her shoulders, he pulled the maid to her feet. With the same arm holding an improvised cloth shield across the damsel's front, allowing her a modicum of modesty, he urged her back to lean helplessly full against his broad and overwhelmingly powerful form. Simultaneously the dagger which had suddenly appeared in his free hand moved to hover a tiny fraction above the graceful arch of her exposed throat. Together they faced a slowly opening door.

Stunned by the Eagle's rapid reactions, Linnet was barely aware that she still stood within the tub. Her haphazardly draped gown's bottom edge floated atop wild waves breaking against her knees and sloshing over the rim to flood the floor about her captor's feet. She knew who and what to expect. Yet, for all that, Linnet would've forestalled the inevitable were it possible, she watched helplessly as . . .

Look for
The Eagle's Song
Available in Bookstores
Mid-September
Wherever Paperback Books Are Sold